P9-EFJ-436

The Hot Kid

ELMORE LEONARD

The Hot Kid

WILLIAM MORROW
An Imprint of HarperCollinsPublishers

HarperCollins books may be purchased for educational, business, or sales promotional use. For information please write: Special Markets Department, HarperCollins Publishers Inc., 10 East 53rd Street, New York, NY 10022.

FIRST EDITION

Designed by Chris Welch

Printed on acid-free paper

Library of Congress Cataloging-in-Publication Data
Leonard, Elmore, 1925–
   The hot kid: a novel / Elmore Leonard.— 1st ed.
     p. cm.
     ISBN 0-06-072422-6 (acid-free paper)
     1. Police—Oklahoma—Fiction. 2. Oklahoma—Fiction. I. Title.

PS3562.E55H66 2005
13'.54—dc28

                      2004063578

05 06 07 08 09 WBC/RRD 10 9 8 7 6 5 4 3 2 1

For my two girls, Jane and Katy

1

Carlos Webster was fifteen the day he witnessed the robbery and killing at Deering's drugstore. This was in the fall of 1921 in Okmulgee, Oklahoma.

He told Bud Maddox, the Okmulgee chief of police, he had driven a load of cows up to the yard at Tulsa and by the time he got back it was dark. He said he left the truck and stock trailer across the street from Deering's and went inside to get an ice cream cone. When he identified one of the robbers as Emmett Long, Bud Maddox said, "Son, Emmett Long robs banks, he don't bother with drugstores no more."

Carlos had been raised on hard work and respect for his elders. He said, "I could be wrong," knowing he wasn't.

They brought him over to police headquarters in the courthouse to look at photos. He pointed to Emmett Long staring at him from a $500 wanted bulletin and picked the other one, Jim Ray Monks, from mug shots. Bud Maddox said, "You're positive, huh?" and asked Carlos which one was it shot the Indian. Meaning Junior Harjo with the tribal police, who'd walked in not knowing the store was being robbed.

"Was Emmett Long shot him," Carlos said, "with a forty-five Colt."

"You sure it was a Colt?"

"Navy issue, like my dad's."

"I'm teasing," Bud Maddox said. He and Carlos' dad, Virgil Webster, were buddies, both having fought in the Spanish-American War and for a number of years were the local heroes. But now doughboys were back from France telling about the Great War over there.

"If you like to know what I think happened," Carlos said, "Emmett Long only came in for a pack of smokes."

Bud Maddox stopped him. "Tell it from the time you got there."

Okay, well, the reason was to get an ice cream cone. "Mr. Deering was in back doing prescriptions—he looked out of that little window and told me to help myself. So I went over to the soda fountain and scooped up a double dip of peach on a sugar cone and went to the cigar counter and left a nickel by the cash register. That's where I was when I see these two men come in wearing suits and hats I thought at first were salesmen. Mr. Deering calls to me to wait on them as I know the store pretty well. Emmett Long comes up to the counter—"

"You knew right away who he was?"

"Once he was close, yes sir, from pictures of him in the paper. He said to give him a deck of Luckies. I did and he picks up the nickel I'd left by the register. Hands it to me and says, 'This ought to cover it.'"

"You tell him it was yours?"

"No sir."

"Or a pack of Luckies cost fifteen cents?"

"I didn't say a word to him. But see, I think that's when he got the idea of robbing the store, the cash register sitting there, nobody around but me holding my ice cream cone. Mr. Deering never came out from the back. The other one, Jim Ray Monks, wanted a tube of Unguentine, he said for a heat rash was bothering him, under his arms. I got it for him and he didn't pay either. Then Emmett Long says, 'Let's see what you have in the register.' I told him I didn't know how to open it as I didn't work there. He leans over the counter and points to a key— the man knows his cash registers—and says, 'That one right there. Hit it and she'll open for you.' I press the key—Mr. Deering must've heard it ring open, he calls from the back of the store, 'Carlos, you able to help them out?' Emmett Long raised his voice saying, 'Carlos is doing fine,' using my name. He told me then to take out the scrip but leave the change."

"How much did he get?"

"No more'n thirty dollars," Carlos said. He took his time thinking about what happened right after, starting with Emmett Long looking at his ice cream cone. Carlos saw it as personal, something between him and the famous bank robber, so he skipped over it, telling Bud Maddox:

"I put the money on the counter for him, mostly singles. I look up—"

"Junior Harjo walks in," Bud Maddox said, "a robbery in progress."

"Yes sir, but Junior doesn't know it. Emmett Long's at the counter with his back to him. Jim Ray Monks is over at the soda fountain getting into the ice cream. Neither of them had their guns out, so I doubt Junior saw it as a robbery. But Mr. Deering sees Junior and calls out he's got his mother's medicine. Then says for all of us to hear, 'She tells me they got you raiding Indian stills, looking for moonshine.' He said something about Junior setting a jar aside for him and that's all I heard. Now the guns are coming out, Emmett Long's Colt from inside his suit . . . I guess all he had to see was Junior's badge and his sidearm, that was enough, Emmett Long shot him. He'd know with that Colt one round would do the job, but he stepped up and shot Junior again, lying on the floor."

There was a silence.

"I'm trying to recall," Bud Maddox said, "how many Emmett Long's killed. I believe six, half of 'em police officers."

"Seven," Carlos said, "you count the bank hostage had to stand on his running board. Fell off and broke her neck?"

"I just read the report on that one," Bud Maddox said. "Was a Dodge Touring, same as Black Jack Pershing's staff car over in France."

"They drove away from the drugstore in a Packard," Carlos said, and gave Bud Maddox the number on the license plate.

Here was the part Carlos saw as personal and had skipped over, beginning with Emmett Long looking at his ice cream cone.

Then asking, "What is that, peach?" Carlos said it was and Emmett Long reached out his hand saying, "Lemme have a bite there," and took the cone to hold it away from him as it was starting to drip. He bent over to lick it a couple of times before putting his mouth around a big bite he took from the top dip. He said, "Mmmmm, that's good," with a trace of peach ice cream along the edge of his mustache. Emmett Long stared at Carlos then like he was studying his features and began licking the cone again. He said, "Carlos, huh?" cocking his head to one side. "You got the dark hair, but you don't look like any Carlos I ever seen. What's your other name?"

"Carlos Huntington Webster, that's all of 'em."

"It's a lot of name for a boy," Emmett Long said. "So you're part greaser on your mama's side, huh? What's she, Mex?"

Carlos hesitated before saying, "Cuban. I was named for her dad."

"Cuban's the same as Mex," Emmett Long said. "You got greaser blood in you, boy, even if it don't show much. You come off lucky there." He licked the cone again, holding it with the tips of his fingers, the little finger sticking out in a dainty kind of way.

Carlos, fifteen years old but as tall as this man with the ice cream on his mustache, wanted to call him a dirty name and hit him in the face as hard as he could, then go over the counter and bulldog him to the floor the way he'd put a bull calf down to brand and cut off its balls.

Fifteen years old but he wasn't stupid. He held on while his heart beat against his chest. He felt the need to stand up to this man, saying finally, "My dad was a marine on the battleship *Maine* when she was blown up in Havana Harbor, February fifteenth, 1898. He survived, was picked up in the water and thrown in a Spanish prison as a spy. Then when he escaped he fought the dons on the side of the insurrectionists, the rebels. He fought them again and was wounded at Guantánamo, with Huntington's Marines in that war in Cuba where he met my mother, Graciaplena Santos."

"Sounds like you daddy was a hero," Emmett Long said.

"I'm not done," Carlos said. "After the war my dad came back home and brought my mother with him when Oklahoma was still Indian Territory. She died having me, so I never knew her. I never met my dad's mother, either. She's Northern Cheyenne, lives on a reservation out at Lame Deer, Montana," saying it in a voice that was slow and calm compared to what he felt inside. Saying, "What I want to ask you—if having Indian blood, too, makes me something else besides a greaser." Saying it in Emmett Long's face, causing this man with ice cream on his mustache to squint at him.

"For one thing," Emmett Long said, "the Indin blood makes you and your daddy breeds, him more'n you." He kept staring at Carlos as he raised the cone, his little finger sticking out, Carlos thinking to lick it again, but what he did was toss the cone over his shoulder, not looking or caring where it would land.

It hit the floor in front of Junior Harjo just then walking in, badge on his tan shirt, revolver on his hip, and Carlos saw the situation turning around. He felt the excitement of these moments but with some relief, too. It picked him up and gave him the nerve to say to Emmett Long, "Now you're gonna have to clean up your mess." Except Junior wasn't pulling his .38, he was looking at the ice cream on the linoleum and Mr. Deering was calling to him about his mother's medicine and about raiding stills and Emmett Long was turning from the counter with the Colt in his hand, firing, shooting Junior Harjo and stepping closer to shoot him again.

There was no sign of Mr. Deering. Jim Ray Monks came over to have a look at Junior. Emmett Long laid his Colt on the glass counter, picked up the cash in both hands and shoved the bills into his coat pockets before looking at Carlos again.

"You said something to me. Geronimo come in and you said something sounded smart aleck."

Carlos said, "What'd you kill him for?" still looking at Junior on the floor.

"I want to know what you said to me."

The outlaw waited.

Carlos looked up rubbing the back of his hand across his mouth. "I said now you'll have to clean up your mess. The ice cream on the floor."

"That's all?"

"It's what I said."

Emmett Long kept looking at him. "You had a gun you'd of shot me, huh? Calling you a greaser. Hell, it's a law of nature, you got any of that blood in you you're a greaser. I can't help it, it's how it is. Being a breed on top of it—I don't know if that's called anything or not. But you could pass if you want, you look enough white. Hell, call yourself Carl, I won't tell on you."

Carlos and his dad lived in a big new house Virgil said was a California bungalow, off the road and into the pecan trees, a house that was all porch across the front and windows in the steep slant of the roof, a house built a few years before with oil money—those wells pumping away on a half-section of the property. The rest of it was graze and over a thousand acres of pecan trees, Virgil's pride, land gathered over the years since coming home from Cuba. He could let the trees go and live high off his oil checks, never work again as long as he lived. Nothing doing—harvesttime Virgil was out with his crew gathering pecans, swiping at the branches with cane fishing poles. He had Carlos tending the cows, fifty, sixty head of cross-Brahmas at a time grazing till they filled out good and Carlos would drive a bunch at a time to market in the stock trailer.

He told his dad every time he went to Tulsa some wildcatter would offer to buy his truck and trailer, or want to hire him to haul pipe out to the field. Carlos said, "You know I could make more money in the oil business than feeding cows?"

Virgil said, "Go out to a rig and come back covered in that black muck? That sound good to you? Son, we can't spend the money we have."

Oklahoma became a state in 1907—Carlos was one year old—and they started calling Tulsa "The Oil Capital of the World." A man from Texas Oil came down from the Glenn Pool fields near Tulsa and asked Virgil if he wanted to be rich. "You notice that rainbow in your creek water? You know that's a sign of oil on your property?"

Virgil said, "I know when the Deep Fork overflows it irrigates my pe-can groves and keeps out the weevils."

Still, he wouldn't mind some extra money and leased Texas Oil the half section they wanted for a one-eighth share and a hundred dollars a year per working well. The discovery hole hit a gusher a quarter mile into the earth, and Virgil found himself making nine to twelve hundred dollars a day for most of the next few years. Texas Oil offered to lease his entire spread, 1,800 acres, and Virgil turned them down. Seeing gushers spewing crude over his pecan trees didn't give him the thrill it did Texas Oil.

When Carlos got back from a haul Virgil would be sitting on that big porch with a bottle of Mexican beer. Prohibition was no bother, Virgil had a steady supply of the Mexican beer and American bourbon brought here by the oil people. Part of the deal.

The night Carlos witnessed the robbery and killing he sat with his old dad and told him the whole story, including what he'd left out of his account to Bud Maddox, even telling about the ice cream on Emmett Long's mustache. Carlos was anxious to know if his dad thought he might've caused Junior Harjo to get shot. "I don't see how," Virgil said, "from what you told me. I don't know why you'd even think of it, other than you were right there and what you're wondering is if you could've prevented him from getting shot."

Virgil Webster was forty-seven years old, a widower since Graciaplena died in ought-six giving him Carlos and requiring Virgil to look for a woman to nurse the child. He found Narcissa Raincrow, sixteen, a pretty little Creek girl related to Johnson Raincrow, deceased, an outlaw so threatening that peace officers shot him while he was sleeping. Narcissa had lost her own child giving birth, wasn't married, and Virgil hired her on as a wet nurse. By the time little Carlos had lost interest in her breasts, Virgil had acquired an appreciation. Narcissa became their housekeeper now and began sleeping in Virgil's bed. She cooked good, put on some weight but was still pretty, listened to Virgil's stories and loved and appreciated him. Carlos loved her, had fun talking to her about Indian ways and her murderous kin, Johnson Raincrow, but never called her anything but Narcissa. Carlos liked the idea of being part Cuban; he saw himself wearing a panama hat when he was older, get one side of it to curve up a little.

He said to his dad that night on the dark porch, "Are you thinking I should've done something?"

"Like what?"

"Yell at Junior it's a robbery? No, I had to say something smart to Emmett Long. I was mad and wanted to get back at him somehow."

"For taking your ice cream cone?"

"For what he said."

"What part was it provoked you?"

"What *part*? What he said about being a greaser."

"You or your mama?"

"Both. And calling me and you breeds."

Virgil said, "You let that bozo irk you? Probably can't read nor write, the reason he has to rob banks. Jesus Christ, get some sense." He swigged his Mexican beer and said, "I know what you mean though, how you felt."

"What would you have done?"

"Same as you, nothing," Virgil said. "But if you're talking about in my time, when I was still a U.S. Marine? I'd of shoved the ice cream cone up his goddamn nose."

Three days later sheriff's deputies spotted the Packard in the backyard of a farmhouse near Checotah, the house belonging to a woman by the name of Crystal Lee Davidson. Her former husband, Byron "Skeet" Davidson, deceased, shot dead in a gun battle with U.S. marshals, had at one time been a member of the Emmett Long gang. The deputies waited for marshals to arrive, as apprehending armed fugitives was their specialty. The marshals slipped onto the property at first light, fed the dog a wiener, tiptoed into Crystal's bedroom and got the drop on Emmett Long before he could dig his Colt from under the pillow. Jim Ray Monks went out a window, started across the barn lot and caught a load of double-ought in his legs that put him down. The two were brought to Okmulgee and locked up to await trial.

Carlos said to his dad, "Boy, those marshals know their stuff, don't they? Armed killer—they shove a gun in his ear and yank him out of bed."

He was certain he'd be called to testify and was anxious, couldn't wait. He told his dad he intended to look directly at Emmett Long as he described the cold-blooded killing. Virgil advised him not to say any more than he had to. Carlos said he wondered if he should mention the ice cream on Emmett Long's mustache.

"Why would you want to?" Virgil said.

"Show I didn't miss anything."

"You know how many times the other night," Virgil said, "you told me about the ice cream on his mustache? I'm thinking three or four times."

"You had to see it," Carlos said. "Here's this bank robber everybody's scared of, doesn't know enough to wipe his mouth."

"I'd forget that part," Virgil said. "He shot a lawman in cold blood. That's all you need to remember about him."

A month passed and then another, Carlos becoming fidgety. Virgil found out why it was taking so long, came home to Narcissa putting supper on the table, Carlos sitting there, and told them the delay was caused by other counties wanting to get their hands on Emmett Long. So the matter was given to the Eastern District Court judge to rule on, each county laying out its case, sounding like they'd make a show out of trying him. "His Honor got our prosecutor to offer Emmett Long a deal. Plead guilty to murder in the second degree, the motive self-defense as the victim was armed, and give him ten to fifty years. That would be the end of it, no trial needed. In other words," Virgil said, "your Emmett Long will get sent to McAlester and be out in six years or so."

"There was nothing self-defense about it," Carlos said. "Junior wasn't even looking at him when he got shot." Carlos sounding like he was in pain.

"You don't know the system," Virgil said. "The deal worked 'cause Junior's Creek. He was a white man Emmett Long'd get life or a seat in the electric chair."

Another event of note took place when Carlos was fifteen, toward the end of October and late in the afternoon, dusk settling in the orchards. He shot and killed a cattle thief by the name of Wally Tarwater.

Virgil's first thought: it was on account of Emmett Long. The boy was ready this time and from now on would always be ready.

He phoned the undertaker, who came with sheriff's people and pretty soon two deputy U.S. marshals arrived, Virgil knowing them as serious lawmen in their dark suits and the way they wore their felt hats down on their eyes. The marshals took over, the one who turned out to be the talker saying this Wally Tarwater—now lying in the hearse— was wanted on federal warrants for running off livestock and crossing state lines to sell to meat packers. He said to Carlos to go on and tell in his own words what happened.

Virgil saw Carlos start to grin just a little, about to make some re- mark like "You want it in my own words?" and cut him off quick with "Don't tell no more'n you have to. These people want to get home to their families."

Well, it began with Narcissa saying she felt like a rabbit stew, or squirrel if that's all was out there. "I thought it was too late in the day," Carlos said, "but took a twenty-gauge and went out in the orchard. The pecans had been harvested, most of 'em, so you could see through the trees good."

"Get to it," Virgil said. "You see this fella out in the pasture driving off your cows."

"On a cutting horse," Carlos said. "You could tell this cowboy knew how to work beef. I got closer and watched him, admiring the way he bunched the animals without wearing himself out. I went back to the house and exchanged the twenty-gauge for a Winchester, then went to the barn and saddled up. She's right over there, the claybank. The sorrel's the one he was riding."

The marshal, the one who talked, said, "You went back to get a rifle without knowing who he was?"

"I knew it wasn't a friend stealing my cows. He's driving them down toward the Deep Fork bottom where a road comes in there. I nudge Suzie out among the cows still grazing, got close enough to call to him, 'Can I help you?'" Carlos started to smile. "He says, 'Thanks for offering but I'm done here.' I told him he sure was and to get down from his horse. He started to ride away and I fired one past his head to bring him around. I moved closer but kept my distance not knowing what he had under his slicker. By now he sees I'm young, he says, 'I'm picking up cows I bought off your daddy.' I tell him I'm the cow outfit here, my dad grows pecans. All he says is, 'Jesus, quit chasing me, boy, and go on home.' Now he opens his slicker to let me see the six-shooter on his leg. And now way off past him a good two hundred yards, I notice the stock trailer, a man standing there by the load ramp."

"You can make him out," the marshal who did the talking said, "from that distance?"

"If he says it," Virgil told the marshal, "then he did."

Carlos waited for the marshals to look at him before saying, "The cowboy starts to ride off and I call to him to wait a second. He reins and looks at me. I told him I'd quit chasing him if he brought my cows back. I said, 'But you try to ride off with my stock I'll shoot you.'"

"You spoke to him like that?" the talker said. "How old are you?"

"Going on sixteen. The same age as my dad when he joined the U.S. Marines."

The quiet marshal spoke for the first time. He said, "So this Wally Tarwater rode off on you."

"Yes sir. Once I see he isn't gonna turn my cows, and he's approaching the stock trailer by now, I shot him." Carlos dropped his tone saying, "I meant to wing him, put one in the edge of that yellow slicker . . . I should've stepped down 'stead of firing from the saddle. I sure didn't mean to hit him square. I see the other fella jump in the truck, doesn't care his partner's on the ground. He goes to drive off and tears the ramp from the trailer. It was empty, no cows aboard. What I did was fire at the hood of the truck to stop it and the fella jumped out and ran for the trees."

The talkative marshal spoke up. "You're doing all this shooting from what, two hundred yards?" He glanced toward the Winchester leaning against a pecan tree. "No scope on your rifle?"

"You seem to have trouble with the range," Virgil said to him. "Step out there a good piece and hold up a snake by its tail, a live one. My boy'll shoot its head off for you."

"I believe it," the quiet marshal said.

He brought a card from his vest pocket and handed it between the tips of his fingers to Virgil. He said, "Mr. Webster, I'd be interested to know what your boy sees himself doing in five or six years."

Virgil looked at the card and then handed it to Carlos, meeting his eyes for a second. "You want you can ask him," Virgil said, watching

Carlos reading the card that bore the deputy's name, R. A. "Bob" McMahon, and a marshal's star in gold you could feel. "I tell him join the marines and see foreign lands, or get to love pe-cans if you want to stay home." He could see Carlos moving his thumb over the embossed star on the card. "The only thing he's mentioned is maybe getting a job in the oil fields once he finishes high school," Virgil said, looking at his boy.

"Isn't that right?"

Virgil and the marshals waited the few moments before Carlos raised his head to look at his dad.

"I'm sorry—were you speaking to me?"

Later on Virgil was in the living room reading the paper. He heard Carlos come down from upstairs and said, "Will Rogers is appearing at the Hippodrome next week. He talks about current events while he's showing off with his rope. You care to see him? He's funny."

"I guess," Carlos said, then told his dad he didn't feel so good.

Virgil lowered the newspaper to look at his boy. He said, "You took a man's life today." And thought of a time in Cuba behind an over-turned oxcart looking down the barrel of a Krag rifle pressed to his cheek, wanting the first one coming toward him riding hard—his friend being chased by the three behind him—to get out of the way, get the hell out of his line of fire, and he did, swerved his mount, and Virgil put his sights on the first one coming behind him and fired, felt the Krag kick against his shoulder and saw the horse tumble headfirst on top of the rider, threw the bolt and put his sights on the second one, *bam*, took the rider out of his saddle, threw the bolt and aimed at the third one coming like a racehorse, the rider firing a revolver as fast as he could thumb the hammer, a brave man set on riding him down, twenty yards between them when Virgil blew him out of his saddle and the horse ran past the overturned oxcart. He'd killed three men in less than ten seconds.

He said to Carlos, "You didn't tell me, did you look at him lying there?"

"I got down to close his eyes."

Virgil had taken the boots off the third one he killed, exchanged them for the sandals he'd worn in the Spanish prison, the Morro.

He said, "Looking at him made you think, huh?"

"It did. I wondered why he didn't believe I'd shoot."

"He saw you as a kid on a horse."

"He knew stealing cows could get him shot or sent to prison, but it's what he chose to do."

"You didn't feel any sympathy for the man?"

"Yeah, I felt if he'd listened he wouldn't be lying there dead."

The room was silent. Now Virgil asked, "How come you didn't shoot the other one?"

"There weren't any cows on the trailer," Carlos said, "else I might've."

It was his son's quiet tone that made Virgil realize, My Lord, but this boy's got a hard bark on him.

2

Jack Belmont was eighteen years old in 1925, the time he got the idea of blackmailing his dad.

This was the year the Mayo Hotel opened in Tulsa, six hundred rooms with bath, circulating ice water that came out of the faucet. They knew Jack at the Mayo and never said anything about his stopping by to get a bottle of booze off the bellboy. It cost him more this way, but was easier than dealing with bootleggers. Drive up in his Ford Coupé and honk the horn, tell the doorman to go get Cyrus. That was the old colored bellboy's name. Sometimes Jack went inside to hang around the lobby or the Terrace Room, see what was going on. It was how he found out this was where his dad, Oris Belmont, kept his girlfriend when she came to visit, at the Mayo. The girlfriend being what the blackmail was about.

Her name was Nancy Polis from Sapulpa, a boomtown in the Glenn Pool grid, barely ten miles from Tulsa.

Jack believed his dad must visit her when he went out to the oil field and stayed the night. He figured his dad was worth ten million or so by now, except it wasn't all sitting in the bank; it was invested in different things like a refinery, a car lot, a tank farm, and a trucking line. It was boom or bust in the oil business, the reason Oris Belmont spread his money around, and why Jack wasn't sure how much to ask for black-mailing him.

He chose a number that sounded good and entered the dad's private study at home, fixed the way Oris wanted it: steer horns over the fireplace, photos of men posing by oil derricks, also miniature rigs, little metal derricks on the mantel, on bookshelves, one used as a doorstop. Jack walked up to the big teakwood desk and sat down in soft leather across from Oris, the dad.

"I don't want to take up your time," Jack said. "What I'd like you to do is put me on your payroll. I'm thinking ten thousand a month and I won't bother you no more."

Eighteen years old and talking like that.

Oris set his desk pen in its holder and gave this good-looking, useless boy who favored his mother his full attention.

"You aren't saying you're going to work, are you?"

"I'll come by once a month," Jack said, "on payday."

Oris said, "Oh, I see," easing back in his chair, "this is a shakedown. All right, I pay you more'n the president of the Exchange National Bank makes . . . or what?"

"I know about your girlfriend," Jack said.

The dad said, "Is that right?"

"Nancy Polis. I know all about your putting her up at the Mayo when she comes to visit. I know you always come in through that outside entrance to the barbershop in the basement and have a drink before you go up to her room, always the same one. I know you and your oil friends have blocks of ice in the urinals, and you bet on who can make the deepest hole pissing on 'em, and you never win."

"Who told you all this?"

"One of the bellboys."

"The one gets whiskey for you?"

Jack hesitated. "A different one. I told him to keep an eye out and call me when she comes in the hotel. I've seen her in the lobby and recognized her right away."

"What's all this information cost you?"

"Couple of bucks. Dollar for her name and address, how she registers. A girl in the office told the bellboy you pay the bill whenever she stays, usually every other Friday through the weekend. I know you met her when you were living in Sapulpa those years we never saw you."

The dad said, "You're sure of that, huh?"

"I know you bought her a house, set her up."

The dad's droopy mustache gave him a tired look staring across the desk, the way Jack saw the dad whenever he thought of him. The big mustache, the suit and tie, and that tired look, rich as he was.

"Let's see," the dad said, "you were five when I came out here to work."

"You left us I was four years old."

"Well, I know you were ten when I bought this house. Fifteen in 1921, the time you took my pistol and shot that colored boy."

Jack looked at him surprised. "Everybody was shooting niggers, the race riot was going on. I didn't kill him, did I?"

"That whole neighborhood of Greenwood burned down—"

"Niggerville," Jack said. "Was the Knights of Liberty started the fires. I know I told you back then I never struck a match."

"What I'm trying to recall," the dad said, "the first time you were arrested."

"For shooting out streetlights."

"And assault. You got picked up for getting that little girl drunk and raping her. Carmel Rossi?"

Jack started shaking his head saying she wasn't any little girl. "You'd seen the titties on her you'd of known she was grown up. She dropped the charge, didn't she?"

"I paid her daddy what he makes in a month."

"She had her panties hanging over a bush before I ever touched her. Was my word against hers."

"Her daddy still works for me," Oris said. "Builds storage tanks, the big ones, hold fifty-five and eighty thousand barrels of crude. How'd you like to work for him, clean out tanks? Get in there in the fumes and shovel out that bottom sludge. Start there and we work you up to your ten thousand a month."

"Everything I got into," Jack said, sitting low in the leather chair, comfortable, "either I didn't start it or it was a misunderstanding."

"How about getting caught with the Mexican reefer? What didn't the police understand about it?"

Jack grinned at the dad.

"You ever try it?"

See what the dad had to say to that.

Nothing. He said, "I don't know what's wrong with you. You're a nice-looking boy, wear a clean shirt every day, keep your hair combed . . . Where'd you get your ugly disposition? Your mama blames me for not being around, so then I feel guilty and give you things, a car, whatever you want. You get in trouble, I get you out. Well, now you've moved on to extortion in your life of crime. What're we talking about here? I pay what you want or you're telling everybody I have a girl-friend? Jesus Christ, you know how many girlfriends there are in Tulsa? Set up with their own place? Hell, I keep mine in Sapulpa. Is that the deal, you're threatening to tell on me?"

"I tell Mama," Jack said, "see how you like her knowing."

Now he was getting the cold stare again, Jack ready to pick up the metal derrick from the corner of the desk if Oris came at him. Be self-defense.

But the dad didn't move. He said, "You think your mama doesn't know about her?"

Shit. Jack hadn't thought of that.

Still, Oris could be bluffing.

"All right," Jack said, "I'll tell her I know about it, too. And I'll see if I can get Emma to understand you're screwing this oil camp whore."

He thought it would set Oris off, get him yelling—the idea of his little Emma hearing such a thing, even though she had no sense of things. The dad stayed calm across the desk and it surprised Jack, the bugger staring, but holding on like that.

When Oris did speak the dad's voice seemed different, delivering a judgment now with no more to say about it.

"You tell your mother she'll hate you for knowing it and never be able to look at your face again. She'll tell me you have to leave and I won't hesitate. I'll throw you out of the house." He didn't refer to Emma. But then gave him a choice, still his dad saying, "Is that what you want?"

Oris Belmont was another wildcatter story.

Glenn Pool had twelve hundred wells piped and flowing to refineries by the time Oris came to Oklahoma to join his wife's Uncle Alex in Sapulpa. Alex Roney, known in the field as Stub, held mineral leases on Creek Indian land, a scattering of half-sections he'd bought for three dollars an acre before the area came into its boom. By the time it did, Stub was broke, had no means of drilling a discovery well. He was drunk the day he highjacked a tank truck of crude, was caught stuck hub-deep in mud and spent the next four years doing his time at McAlester. Stub got his release and called Oris Belmont. Oris arrived from Indiana with a load of salvaged drilling tools, pipe, casing, a pair of steam boilers, sixteen hundred dollars he'd scraped together and twenty years of oil stain under his fingernails.

They drilled two dry holes, Stub No. 1 and No. 2, and the old uncle's luck ran out on him. They were looking to take the No. 2 derrick apart, Stub up on the runaround, the catwalk that circled the derrick sixty or so feet up. He hadn't yet hooked his safety belt to the structure, and when he lost his hold he fell sixty feet to the drilling floor, his final breath smelling of corn whiskey. Oris had been afraid the old uncle might fall or have something fall on his head.

What puzzled Oris were the dry holes. There weren't more than twenty in the entire eight thousand acres of wells and two of them were his. What Oris did, he got mad, changed the name of the company from Busy Bee Oil & Gas—a cartoon bumblebee in the trademark they'd of had one day—to NMD Oil & Gas, standing for No More Dusters, and worked a year as a driller to restore his capital. Now he sank Emma No. 1, named for his baby girl he'd seen twice in the past four years, and sweet crude came up and came up like there'd never be an end to it.

Oris's wife was from Eaton, Indiana, where they'd met while he was working for wages in the Trenton Field. Oris and Doris—he told her they were meant to be joined in marriage. The time came to hook up with her uncle in Oklahoma, Doris was ready to have their third child—three counting Oris Jr., who'd died in infancy of diphtheria. So Doris and their little boy Jack stayed in Eaton with her widowed mother and delivered Emma while Oris was drilling the dusters.

When Emma No. 1 came in, bless her heart, Oris left the boardinghouse where he'd been staying and moved to the St. James Hotel in Sapulpa. He waited until he'd drilled Emma No. 2 and she was flowing before he phoned Doris.

Oris said, "Honey? Guess what?"

Doris said, "If your holes are still dry I'm leaving you. I'm walking out of here and Mama can have the kids. She's raising 'em anyway, spoiling 'em rotten. Says Emma's gonna be a nervous stability 'cause I don't know how to nurse her, I'm not patient enough. How can I be, her hanging over my shoulder. She talks to Emma, tells her, 'Suck on the titty, Little Bitty,' what she calls her. 'That's it, suck on it hard, get all that mookey.'"

Oris said, "Honey? Listen to me a minute, will you? We're becoming rich as I speak."

Doris wasn't finished but paused to hear that much. She was a farm girl, skin and bones all her life, but was strong from working; she had a cute face, good teeth, read magazines and was always respectful of her husband. Saturdays she used to shave him and trim his hair and his big droopy mustache. Then she'd strop the razor and shave her legs and under her arms, the driller twisting his mouth to one side and then the other watching every stroke and getting a boner. Doris was thirty-four by now, the driller ten years older. Saturday was their time to get cleaned up before doing the dirty. She still had a wrathful mood on her and told him, "You know you haven't seen Jack in going on five years?"

"I spent Christmases with you."

"Twice in that time, two days each. He's a harum-scarum, hell in short pants," Doris said. "I'm through trying to manage him. Emma— you haven't hardly ever seen except in pictures, and Mama's driving me crazy. You don't send me train fare right now I'm leaving you. You can come and get your kids you don't even know."

There, she'd told him.

Doris said now, "For true? We're rich?"

"Nine hundred barrels a day out of two wells," Oris said, "and we're about to drill other leases. We had to shoot Emma Number Two with nitro to bust up the rock and she came in angry, almost tore the god-damn rig down. I hired a man's building storage tanks for me." He said to Doris, "You all right? You feel better now?"

She did, but there was some wrath left and Doris said, "Jack needs his daddy to make him behave. He won't do a thing I tell him."

"Honey," Oris said, "you're gonna have to hang on there a while longer. I bought us a house on Tulsa's south side, where all the Princes of Petroleum live. Be just another month or so, I'm having the place fixed up."

She asked him what was wrong with it.

"The oilman owned it went bust. His wife left him, his second one, and he shot himself in the head, in their bedroom. I'm having it re-painted. The house—they had wild parties and broke things." He said, "Honey, the house was put up for auction, the man owing taxes on it. I bought it off the county for twenty-five thousand dollars, cash."

She had never seen a house that cost twenty-five thousand dollars and asked him what it looked like. He said, "It's Greek Revival, eight years old."

She said, "I don't know Greek Revival from a teepee."

He told her it had those Doric columns in front holding up the por-tico, and she still didn't know what it looked like.

He told her there was a dining room could seat twenty people easy. She imagined harvest hands sitting there having noon dinner. He told her it had five bedrooms and four baths, a sleeping porch, a maid's room, three-car garage, a big kitchen that had an icebox with seven doors in it, a swimming pool in the backyard . . . "I almost forgot," Oris said, "and a roller-skating rink on the third floor."

There was a silence on the phone.

Oris said, "Honey . . . ?"

Doris said, "You know I never roller-skated in my life?"

By the summer of 1916 the Belmonts were in their Tulsa mansion, Oris trying to decide what to do about his girlfriend Nancy Polis, a waitress at the Harvey House restaurant in Sapulpa. He felt they should stop seeing each other now that he was living in Tulsa; but each time he brought it up Nancy would cry and carry on, not acting at all like what she was, a Harvey Girl. It hurt him so much he bought her the home she opened as a boardinghouse for income.

On a Sunday morning in September Oris sat with his wife on the patio having breakfast while the children played in the swimming pool. Doris was reading the Society section of the paper looking for names she recognized. Oris watched Jack, ten years old, talking to his little sis, Emma, four years younger. He watched Emma jump in the deep end of the swimming pool and now Jack jumped in and Emma was hanging on to him screaming, her tiny voice shrill but nothing new, Emma was always screaming at Jack, telling him to stop it and then yelling for her mama. Doris looked up and said, as she always did, "What's he doing to her now, the poor child." Oris said it looked like they were playing. Doris said, "She wearing her water wings?" Oris said he couldn't tell but imagined so, Emma never going in the water without her life preserver. Doris went back to reading about neighbors and Oris picked up the Sports section. He saw the St. Louis Cardinals were still in last place in the National League, the Brooklyn Robins, goddamn it, in first, two and a half games ahead of Philly. Oris looked toward the pool again. Jack was sitting in a canvas chair wearing a pair of smoked glasses too big for his young face. Emma was nowhere in sight. Oris called out, "Jack, where's your sister?" Doris put down her paper.

Oris would see the next part clearly anytime he thought about it: Jack on his feet now looking at the pool, then seeing her under water and diving in to save her life.

She wasn't breathing when they pulled her out. Oris didn't know what to do. Doris did, she went crazy screaming and crying, asking God why He took their little girl. Sunday their doctor, who lived nearby in Maple Ridge, was home. He came right away and said, "How long has it been?" And, "Why aren't you giving her artificial respiration?"

Oris remembered Jack talking to her, Emma nodding and then jumping in the pool, not wearing her water wings, and screaming trying to hold on to Jack. Oris believed his little girl was unconscious for almost fifteen minutes before the doctor forced her to breathe again and they took her, stretched out on the backseat of the La Salle, to the hospital.

The lack of oxygen to her brain for that long meant it no longer worked the way it should. She couldn't walk. She sat in her wheelchair and stared, or crawled around the roller-skating rink upstairs scrubbing the floor with her dolls, or throwing them or beating the floor with her babies until they came apart and there were pieces of dolls all over the roller rink the Belmonts never used.

Jack talked his mother out of having the swimming pool broken up and planted over. He would catch his dad staring at him and the ten-year-old would say, "I tried to save her, didn't I?"

Eight years later the smart-aleck, useless kid was trying to blackmail him. It was time to hand Jack over to Joe Rossi at the tank farm, the daddy of Carmel, the girl Jack swore up and down he hadn't raped.

Joe Rossi had dug coal in the mines near Krebs, south of here. He served a few years at McAlester as a prison guard before the Glenn Pool boom came on and moved his family to Tulsa to find work in oil that paid a living wage. Mr. Belmont first had him digging earthen pits, big holes in the ground, someplace quick to store crude gushing out of the wells. Next thing he was setting wood tanks over the field before going to steel plates, setting tanks as high as three-story buildings, some holding eighty thousand barrels of crude before pumping it off to a refinery. Joe Rossi was making a hundred dollars a week now running the tank farm and bossing the hard cases working for him. Tankies all drank their wages, saw themselves as the toughest boys on the lease and looked for excuses to start fights. Joe Rossi had fists the size of mallets and used them on payday to stay in charge, hammer anybody told him to go fuck himself, or some such thing. He didn't mind their getting drunk, but would not take their lip.

Mr. Belmont said put the boy on the worst job there. Rossi said that was tank cleaning. He said, "You think it's what you want him to do? The only thing liable to kill a man quicker is shooting nitro."

"I want him cleaning tanks," Mr. Belmont said, and hung up the phone.

Rossi told Norm Dilworth, a boy he'd brought here from McAlester after he'd done his time, told him to show Jack Belmont the work and stay close to him. Joe Rossi didn't trust himself to go near Mr. Belmont's son—not after what he did to his little girl Carmel, the youngest of his seven kids, fifteen years old this past July 16, the feast day of Our Lady of Mount Carmel. Rossi was afraid if the boy got smart with him he'd crack his head open with a maul and shove him in the muck.

Rossi said to Norm Dilworth, not much older than Jack Belmont, "He's the boss's son. His daddy wants him to learn the oil business."

Norm said, "Cleaning out tanks? Christ Almighty, he could die in there."

"I don't think his daddy'd mind," Rossi said. "He's a bad kid. You knew plenty like him at McAlester, only they weren't the sons of millionaires."

The two boys were lanky and looked like they could run. Jack and Norm stood smoking cigarets waiting for the setter crew to unbolt a steel plate from the bottom part of the tank that rose a good thirty feet above them, pried it free and used a truck with a chain to drag the plate out of the way. Now a thick black muck was oozing out of the opening to spread in the weeds. They could smell gas fumes coming from inside the tank.

Norm Dilworth said, "Put out your cigaret," stubbing his on the sole of a shoe and slipping the butt in his shirt pocket. Jack took another puff before he flicked his cigaret away. Jack was wearing a new pair of Pioneer bib overalls bought yesterday, complaining to the dad at the store with him they were too full in the legs. The dad bought him four pair, a buck ten each, and a pair of work shoes for three eighty-five. Norm Dilworth had on work clothes that would never look clean again but were worn out from washing, suspenders holding up his pants. He wore a hat so old and dirty you couldn't tell the shade of felt, set on the back of his head. Jack wouldn't wear a hat less he had on a suit. His brown hair was combed back and plastered down, taking on a shine in the sunlight.

"That bottom sediment's what we clean out," Norm said. "Wade inside with shovels and rakes made of wood—no metal that could cause a spark—and slosh it out the opening. You last all day you can make seven-fifty. Only if they's gas fumes like in this'n? You can't stay in there more'n ten minutes at a time. You have to come out to breathe. They's some companies tell you, 'Well, you only worked half your time,' and take out for it. You say, 'Yeah, well, the other time I was using to breathe.' It don't matter, they take breathing time out of your wage. Except Mr. Rossi, he pays a straight six bits an hour. You have to come out, he lets you come out. See, you don't want to get weak in there from the fumes. I mean it, you fall in the sludge, you're done. You keep slipping and sliding, you're choking on the gas and can't help but fall in the muck. It's like knee-deep in there, the sediment, and nobody's suppose to help you, try and pull you out, 'cause you could pull them in and you're both gone."

Jack stared at the black ooze edging toward them while Norm was staring at Jack. Norm said, "I never seen bibs that narrow in the legs. Where you buy a pair like that?"

Jack was watching the sediment coming closer and closer. "I thought the pants were too roomy. I had one of the maids take 'em in." He said, "So this Joe Rossi is fair, huh? I haven't seen him."

"He's over in the shack," Norm said. "He wrote to me at McAlester saying he'd have a job waiting for me when I got my release. So I come here and the next thing I know I got married."

Jack was looking at him now, this hick in his worn-out work clothes. "You were in prison, huh?"

"Year and a day for stealing cars, the first time."

"Now you clean tanks for six bits an hour? But you don't have to?"

"Shit, I can make forty dollars a week."

"What'd you do with the cars you swiped?"

"Sold 'em. I kept a Dodge to run bootleg till I almost got caught."

Jack was getting a better feeling about this hick who knew how to steal cars and run whiskey. "You ever think about getting back into crime?"

"I kinda miss running wild and free," Norm said, "but I've known Mr. Rossi from when he was a screw over at the prison. He's always been fair with me. Another thing about working for him, he won't use 'lectric lights when you're in the tank. The vents on the roof don't give enough light, he'll put batt'rey-powered spots up there. See, 'lectric lights, you got to worry about a current leak. Over at Seminole one time, they go in, switch on the light and she sparked. Seven men in there, the whole tank went up afire and you heard the seven of 'em scream like one person, this awful, bloodcurdling scream and like that"—Norm snapped his fingers—"they're dead. They's any kind of spark in there you're fried. Pull you out looking like a strip of bacon."

Jack said, "We the only ones working here?"

"A crew'll be coming," Norm said, and looked over at the shack where Rossi had his office, no one there yet.

Jack moved along the edge of the sediment to the opening and ducked his head to look in at a dim cavern, spooky in there, poles holding up the roof, the floor thick with sediment. He began to cough and walked back clearing his throat and blinking his eyes from the fumes.

Norm said, "See what I mean?"

"I'm not going in there," Jack said. "I got an idea I like better than getting burned alive. I'm thinking of how me and you can make a hundred thousand dollars and not even get our shoes dirty." He had the hick squinting at him now with sort of a grin on his face. "You're the guy I been looking for," Jack said, "somebody's not afraid to break a law now and then."

Norm quit grinning. "What kind of crime you have in mind?"

"Kidnap my old man's girlfriend. Tell him a hundred thousand or he'll never see her again."

Norm said, "Jesus Christ, you mean it, don't you?"

Jack nodded toward his Ford Coupé parked off the dirt road by some trucks loaded with used sheets of metal. He said, "Go on get in my car over there. You won't ever have to clean another tank long as you live."

Norm Dilworth looked toward the car and Jack pulled a pack of cigarets and his silver lighter from the overalls that felt stiff on him. Norm looked back to see him lighting the cigaret and yelled out, "No!" and said Jesus Christ, no a few more times, looking toward Rossi's office, looking at Jack puffing on the butt before he flicked it to arch into the stream of sludge.

Fire flashed and spread over the ooze out on the ground—they were both running now—the fire wooshing into the tank to ignite the gas and there was a boom inside, an explosion that buckled steel plates, blew the roof off the tank and rolled black oil smoke into the sky.

Oris Belmont saw it from his office window high up in the Exchange National Bank Building, his NMD Oil & Gas Company occupying the whole floor. The explosion from eight miles away turned Oris in his swivel chair to see that ugly black stain in the sky, rising where his tank farm would be. He thought of his son walking out of the house this morning in his new overalls; Oris remembering the legs looked funny. In nine years there had never been an accident at the farm, not even by the hand of God like a tank struck by lightning, not until the day Jack showed up for work. Oris wasn't sure what to feel about the situation. He waited for the phone to ring.

Rossi came on to ask him, "Can you see it?"

"A full tank," Oris said, "there'd be way more smoke."

"It's one your boy was to work in."

Oris waited.

"He set fire to the sediment," Rossi said, "and drove off in his car with another tankie, I guess through for the day. If it's okay with you, I'd as soon you didn't send him back here."

Oris felt relief. He did, his boy off to work for the first time in his life was alive. It calmed him till he began to wonder, But now what?

Jack had no trouble getting Nancy Polis out of her boardinghouse and in the car, the woman not even bothering to put on a hat but did grab her purse. She had seen the smoke and believed Jack telling her Mr. Belmont had been hurt in the explosion and sent him to get her. Mr. Belmont wanting her to see he was alive before going to the hospital in Tulsa, as his wife was likely to show up there. No, he wasn't hurt too bad, just some cuts that'd have to be sewed up, maybe a broken leg set, if it was broke. Jack told her he worked for Mr. Belmont in the office; he'd put on overalls today as they were going out to the lease, explaining this to Nancy Polis squeezed between him and Norm Dilworth in the car on the way to Norm's house.

It was toward Kiefer in a stand of pines back of the rail yard. Nancy didn't ask why Oris would be waiting in this workingman's house of upright weathered boards, a porch roof in front, a privy in back where a girl was hanging wash. Jack asked Norm who she was. Norm said his wife, and Jack said to bring her in the house.

She was watching them now, fingering her blonde hair the wind was blowing in her eyes.

As soon as they were inside Nancy said, "Where's Oris?"

Jack told her he'd be along. Mr. Belmont had waited for the doctor they called to have a look at the tankies that got hurt. He had a feeling Nancy was suspicious now, nervous, looking around the house. There wasn't much to it, a pump on the sink, an old icebox and stove, a table covered with oilcloth and magazines sitting on it, three straight chairs, a double bed they could see in the back room.

Jack was ten when they moved to Tulsa and his dad would take him out to the lease every once in a while and explain boring things about oil wells, how the first joint of pipe had a bit on it they called a fishtail that bored the hole and those big pumps they called mud hogs would clean it out. They always stopped by the Harvey House in Sapulpa for chicken à la king, Jack's favorite, and always had the same Harvey Girl in her big white apron, her hair swept up and fixed. Jack would listen to them talk in a low voice like they were passing secret messages to each other. It wasn't until he saw Nancy Polis at the Mayo Hotel he realized she was the Harvey House waitress. She'd be in her thirties now.

Norm came in, the girl behind him with her empty clothes basket. He said to Jack, "This here's my wife, Heidi."

It took Jack by surprise, 'cause up close this girl was a looker, even with her hair mussed, no makeup on, man, a natural beauty about twenty years old. He had to wonder why she'd settled for a hayseed like Norm Dilworth. There was a presence about her, reminding him of rich girls in Tulsa, till she said, "Y'all want some ice tea?" and she was off a farm or an oil patch. Man, but she was a looker.

Nancy Polis, sitting at the table now smoking a cigaret, said, "I want to know where Oris is."

Jack was still looking at Heidi. "You got anything else?"

"I got a jar," Norm said.

Jack turned to the table and the magazines sitting there, *Good House-keeping, Turkey World, Ladies' Home Journal* and a new issue of *Outdoor Life.* He said to Nancy, "Keep your pants on," picked up the *Outdoor Life* and started looking through it.

Norm went to the cupboard over the sink and brought out a mason jar, a third of clean whiskey in it. He said to Heidi, "Honey, will you get the glasses?"

She said, "We only got two," looking at Jack. "Somebody'll have to tip the jar."

Jack smiled at her staring at him. He held up the *Outdoor Life* and said to Norm, "You hunt?"

"Any chance I get."

"Leave this little girl here by herself?"

He winked at her and she winked back.

"She likes it here," Norm said, "after where she's lived."

Nancy said, "None for me, thanks," watching Norm pour the liquor into a couple of jelly glasses.

"It ain't for you, it's for me and Jack," Norm said, handing Jack a glass.

Nancy sat sideways to the table, her legs crossed, showing her knees and some thigh in a dark shade of hose. She looked at Jack and held out the cigaret to tap ashes on the linoleum floor.

"Are you old enough?"

"If Prohibition means nobody's suppose to drink," Jack said, "then anybody can break the law and drink if they want, can't they?"

"You work for Oris Belmont directly?"

"I'm his first assistant."

"What kind of a man is he to work for?"

Jack raised the glass Norm handed him and took a big swallow of the liquor, feeling a nice burn, Nancy staring at him. Jack said, "I won't say anything nasty about Mr. Belmont. I've heard some things but I don't know if they're true or not."

"Like what?"

"He's hard on certain employees in the office, cute girls they say he's especially hard . . . on." He winked at Nancy. Shit, he couldn't help it. He heard Norm laugh and looked over at Heidi grinning at him. He could see her nipples poking against the thin cotton dress. She knew it, too, grinning at him like a cat if a cat had tits. He turned to Nancy drawing on her cigaret, her eyes holding on him, but no smile from this one. He took another sip of the whiskey, smooth going down. He was starting to feel good already. She wasn't going anywhere—he may as well tell her.

"Honey, you're gonna be staying here a while."

She held the cigaret with his elbow on the table.

"Nothing happened to Oris?"

"I told you he was hurt to get you out of the house."

"What're you, holding me for ransom?"

"We'll see how much Mr. Belmont likes you."

"He doesn't pay, then what, you kill me?"

"He'll pay."

"Then you *will* have to kill me."

"What for? We're gone. Nobody knows where we're at."

"But I know who you are."

It stopped him and he said, "I don't work for Oris Belmont. I only told you that."

"I know you don't," Nancy said, "you're his rotten kid. As soon as this goober called you Jack I knew it. You're Jack Belmont. I remember you from eight or nine years ago when I worked at the Harvey House. You'd want to go home and you'd whine and keep tugging at your daddy's sleeve. You were a brat then, now you're what, a kidnapper? I heard the blackmail didn't work."

Shit. He did think of shooting her. It passed through his mind knowing Norm'd have a gun if he hunted.

Nancy said, "You give me the creeps, you know it? You can ask your dad for money anytime you want and he'll give it to you. No, you'd rather steal it from him. Lord have mercy, you want to be a real crook, go rob a bank."

Later on that day Joe Rossi phoned his boss again. He said, "Mr. Belmont, you want to get your boy to straighten himself out? What I'd do is have him arrested for destroying company property."

Oris Belmont didn't say a word. He sat looking out the window at the smudge still in the sky.

"You want," Joe Rossi said, "I'd be glad to call the police on him. Keep you out of it."

Oris took a few moments before saying, "No, I'll call them." It was time he took charge.

3

June 13, 1927, Carlos Huntington Webster, now close to six feet tall, was in Oklahoma City wearing a dark blue suit of clothes, no vest and a panama with the brim curved on his eyes just right, staying at a hotel, riding streetcars every day, and being sworn in as a deputy United States marshal. This was while Charles Lindbergh was being honored in New York City, tons of ticker tape dumped on the Lone Eagle for flying across the Atlantic Ocean by himself.

And Emmett Long, released from McAlester, was back in Checotah with Crystal Davidson, his suit hanging in the closet these six years since the marshals hauled him off in his drawers. The first thing the outlaw did, once he got off Crystal, was make phone calls to get his gang back together.

Carlos was given a leave to go home after his training and spent it with his old dad, telling him things:

What the room was like at the Huckins Hotel.

What he had to eat at the Plaza Grill.

How he saw a band called Walter Page's Blue Devils that was all colored guys.

How when firing a pistol you put your weight forward, one foot ahead of the other, so if you get hit you can keep firing as you fall.

And one other thing.

Everybody called him Carl instead of Carlos. At first he wouldn't answer to it and got in arguments, a couple of times almost fistfights.

"You remember Bob McMahon?"

"R. A. 'Bob' McMahon," Virgil said, "the quiet one."

"My boss when I report to Tulsa. He says, 'I know you're named for your granddaddy to honor him, but you're using it like a chip on your shoulder instead of a name.'"

Virgil was nodding his head. "Ever since that moron Emmett Long called you a greaser. I know what Bob means. Like, 'I'm Carlos Webster, what're you gonna do about it?' You were little I'd call you Carl sometimes. You liked it okay."

"Bob McMahon says, 'What's wrong with Carl? All it is, it's a nickname for Carlos.'"

"There you are," Virgil said. "Try it on."

"I've been wearing it the past month or so. 'Hi, I'm Deputy U.S. Marshal Carl Webster.'"

"You feel any different?"

"I do, but I can't explain it."

A call from McMahon cut short Carl's leave. The Emmett Long gang was back robbing banks.

What the marshals tried to do over the next six months was anticipate the gang's moves. They robbed banks in Shawnee, Seminole and Bowlegs on a line south. Maybe Ada would be next. No, it turned out to be Coalgate.

An eyewitness said he was in the barbershop as Emmett Long was getting a shave—except the witness didn't know who it was till later, after the bank was robbed. "Him and the barber are talking, this one who's Emmett Long mentions he's planning on getting married pretty soon. The barber happens to be a minister of the Church of Christ and offers to perform the ceremony. Emmett Long says he might take him up on it and gives the reverend a five-dollar bill for the shave. Then him and his boys robbed the bank."

Coalgate was on that line south, but then they turned around and headed north again. They took six thousand from the First National in Okmulgee but lost a man. Jim Ray Monks, slow coming out of the bank on his bum legs, was shot down in the street. Before Monks knew he was dying he told them, "Emmett's sore you never put more'n five hundred on his head. He's out to show he's worth a whole lot more."

The stop after Okmulgee was Sapulpa, the gang appearing to like banks in oil towns: hit three or four in a row and disappear for a time. There were reports of gang members spotted during these periods of lying low, but Emmett Long was never one of them.

"I bet anything," Carl said, standing before the wall map in Bob McMahon's office, "he hides out in Checotah, at Crystal Davidson's house."

"Where we caught him seven years ago," McMahon said, nodding. "Crystal was just a girl then, wasn't she?"

"I heard Emmett was already fooling with her," Carl said, "while she's married to Skeet, only Skeet didn't have the nerve to call him on it."

"You heard, huh."

"Sir, I drove down to McAlester on my day off, see what I could find out about Emmett."

"The convicts talk to you?"

"One did, a Creek use to be in his gang, doing thirty years for killing his wife and the guy she was seeing. The Creek said it wasn't a marshal shot Skeet Davidson in the gun battle that time, it was Emmett himself. He wanted Skeeter out of the way so he could have Crystal for his own."

"What made you think of her?"

"Was after that barber in Coalgate said Emmett spoke about getting married. I thought it must be Crystal he's talking about. I mean if he's so sweet on her he killed her husband? That's what tells me he hides out there."

Bob McMahon said, "Well, we been talking to people, watching every place he's ever been seen. Look it up, I know Crystal Davidson's on the list."

"I did," Carl said. "She's been questioned and Checotah police are keeping an eye on her place. But I doubt they do more than drive past, see if Emmett's drawers are hanging on the line."

"You're a marshal six months," Bob McMahon said, "and you know everything."

Carl didn't speak, his boss staring at him.

McMahon saying after a few moments, "I recall the time you shot that cattle thief off his horse." McMahon saying after another silence but still holding Carl with his stare, "You have some kind of scheme you want to try?"

"I've poked around and learned a few things about Crystal Davidson," Carl said, "where she used to live and all. I believe I can get her to talk to me."

Bob McMahon said, "How'd you become so sure of yourself?"

The Marshals Service occupied offices on the second floor of the United States Courthouse on South Boulder Avenue in Tulsa. This meeting in Bob McMahon's office was the first time Jack Belmont's name came up in conversation: Bob McMahon and Carl Webster deciding it was between the bank robberies in Coalgate and Sapulpa that Jack must've got out of prison and joined the Emmett Long gang.

——————

What was different about the Sapulpa bank robbery, Emmett Long walked in and first tried to cash a check made out to him for ten thousand dollars, a NMD Gas & Oil check bearing the signature of Oris Belmont, the company president. Jack Belmont, standing at the teller's window with Emmett, said, "That's my daddy signed it. I give you my word the check's good." The teller reported that he recognized Jack Belmont from his dad bringing him in since he was a kid, but the signature didn't look anything like Oris Belmont's on file. It didn't matter, by then Emmett and Jack Belmont had their revolvers out, as did another one of the gang later identified as Norm Dilworth, and the tellers cleaned out what was in their drawers, something over twelve thousand dollars.

Bob McMahon asked Carl if he knew about Jack Belmont, how he'd set fire to one of his dad's storage tanks, Jack and this tankie named Dilworth, a former convict. The dad didn't hesitate to point Jack out in court. Joe Rossi identified Norm, and the two boys were convicted of malicious destruction of property, each drawing two years hard time.

Carl said he'd read it in the paper and spoke to the Tulsa police about Jack's previous arrests. "And I saw him at McAlester," Carl said, "to find out what I could learn about Emmett Long."

He told how they sat in the captain's office off the rotunda that must be four stories high, where the east and west cell houses met. "You hear wings beating," Carl said, "and look up to see a pigeon flying around inside."

He told how Jack sat across the desk from him in a lazy kind of way like he wasn't interested, his legs crossed like a girl's. "He smoked the cigaret I gave him and stared at me, wouldn't say he even knew Emmett, but this had to be where they first met. Emmett was already out when Jack got his release, right after I spoke to him. So they must've already decided to hook up and do some banks. I can hear Jack telling Emmett he had a new way to rob them, hand 'em a check to cash."

McMahon said, "And I bet Emmett kicked his tail."

"But tried the check first," Carl said. "I'm talking to him, Jack sat there with one arm folded across his chest to the other arm tight against his body, holding the cigaret straight up between the tips of his fingers. He'd turn his head to take a drag, his face raised to it like he's showing me his profile."

"You mentioned his legs crossed like a girl's," McMahon said. "You think he's a nancy-boy?"

"At first I did. I said, 'There fellas here gonna have fun with you.' But he did have girlfriends and was accused of raping one, though he was never brought up. He said he didn't give the other inmates a second thought. He had his buddy with him, Norm Dilworth doing his second stretch and Norm, Jack said, had showed him how to jail. I'm told this Dilworth is stringy but tough as nails. No," Carl said, "Jack Belmont was putting on a show, letting me know he was cool as a fifty-pound block of ice. He asked me what I was, even though I'd showed him my star. I said I was a deputy United States marshal. He called me a poor sap and wanted to know if I'd ever shot anybody."

"You tell him?"

"I said just one. He shrugged like it wasn't anything special. I told him the next time I saw Emmett Long he'd be my second one."

Bob McMahon didn't care for that. He said, "I reminded you once before, my deputies don't brag or speculate. The hell got into you to say that?"

"The way he looked at me," Carl said. "The way he smoked the cigaret. Different things about his manner toward me."

Carl watched Bob McMahon shake his head, McMahon saying, "My deputies do not brag on themselves. Have you got that?"

Carl said he did.

But thinking that Jack Belmont, with what he was up to now, could be number three.

Marshals dropped Carl off a quarter mile from the house, turned the car around and drove back to Checotah; they'd be at the Shady Grove Café. Carl was wearing work clothes and curl-toed boots, his .38 Colt Special holstered beneath a limp old suitcoat of Virgil's, a black one, his star in a pocket.

Walking the quarter mile his gaze held on this worn-out homestead, the whole dismal 160 acres looking deserted, the dusty Ford Coupé in the backyard abandoned, its wheels missing. Carl expected Crystal Davidson to be in no better shape than her property, living here like an outcast. The house did take on life as he mounted the porch, the voice of Uncle Dave Macon coming from a radio somewhere inside; and now Crystal Lee Davidson was facing him through the screen, a girl in a silky nightgown that barely came to her knees, barefoot, but with rouge giving her face color, her blonde hair marcelled like a movie star's . . .

You dumbbell, of *course* she hadn't let herself go, she was waiting for a man to come marry her. Carl smiled, meaning it.

"Miz Davidson? I'm Carl Webster." He kept looking at her face so she wouldn't think he was trying to see through her nightgown, which he could, easy. "I believe your mom's name is Atha Trudell? She worked at the Georgian Hotel in Henryetta doing rooms at one time and belonged to Eastern Star?"

It nudged her enough to say, "Yeah . . . ?"

"So'd my mom, Narcissa Webster?"

Crystal shook her head.

"Your daddy was a coal miner up at Spelter, pit boss on the Little Gem. He lost his life that time she blew in '16. My dad was down in the hole laying track." Carl paused. "I was ten years old."

Crystal said, "I just turned fifteen," her hand on the screen door to open it, but then hesitated. "Why you looking for me?"

"Lemme tell you what happened," Carl said. "I'm at the Shady Grove having a cup of coffee? The lady next to me at the counter says she works at a café serves way better coffee'n here. Purity, up at Henryetta."

Crystal said, "What's her name?"

"She never told me."

"I use to work at Purity."

"I know, but wait," Carl said. "The way you came up in the conversation, the lady says her husband's a miner up at Spelter. I tell her my dad was killed there in '16. She says a girl at Purity lost her daddy in that same accident. She mentions knowing the girl's mom from Eastern Star, I tell her mine belonged, too. The waitress behind the counter's pretending not to listen, but now she turns to us and says, 'The girl you're talking about lives right up the road there.'"

"I bet I know which one it was," Crystal said. "She have spit curls like that boop-oop-a-doop girl?"

"I believe so."

"What else she say?"

"You're a widow, lost your husband."

"She tell you marshals gunned him down?"

"Nothing about that."

"It's what everybody thinks. She mention any other names?"

What everybody thinks. Carl put that away and said, "No, she got busy serving customers."

"You live in Checotah?"

He told her Henryetta, he was visiting his old grandma about to pass. She asked him, "What's your name again?" He told her and she said, "Well, come on in, Carl, and have a glass of ice tea." Sounding now like she wouldn't mind company.

There wasn't much to the living room besides a rag rug on the floor and stiff black furniture, chairs and a sofa, their cane seats giving way from years of being sat on. The radio was playing in the kitchen. Crystal went out there and pretty soon Carl could hear her chipping ice. He stepped over to a table laid out with magazines, *True Confession, Photoplay, Liberty, Western Story,* and one called *Spicy.*

Her voice reached him asking, "You like Gid Tanner?"

Carl recognized the radio music. He said, "Yeah, I do," as he looked at pictures in *Spicy* of girls doing housework in their underwear, one girl wearing a teddy up on a ladder with a feather duster.

"Gid Tanner and his Skillet Lickers," Crystal's voice said. "You know who I kinda like? That Al Jolsen, he sure sounds like a nigger on that mammy song. But you want to know who my very favorite is?"

Carl said, "Jimmie Rodgers?" looking at pictures of Joan Crawford and Elissa Landi now in *Photoplay.*

"I like Jimmy o-*kay* . . . How many sugars?"

"Three'll do'er. How about Uncle Dave Macon? He was on just a minute ago."

" 'Take Me Back to My Old Carolina Home.' I don't care for the way he half-sings and half-talks a song. If you're a singer you oughta sing. No, my favorite's Maybelle Carter and the Carter Family. The pure loneliness they get in their voices just tears me up."

"Must be how you feel," Carl said, "living out here."

She came out to hand him his cold drink saying, "Don't give it another thought."

"Sit here by yourself reading magazines . . ."

"Honey," Crystal said, "you're not as cute as you think you are. Drink your ice tea and beat it."

"I'm sympathizing with you," Carl said. "The only reason I came, I wondered if you and I might even've known each other from funerals, and our moms being in the same club. That's all." He smiled just a little saying, "I wanted to see what you look like."

Crystal said, "All right, you *are* cute, but don't get nosy."

She left him with his iced tea and went in the bedroom.

Carl took *Photoplay* across the room to sit in a chair facing the table of magazines and the bedroom door, left open. He turned pages in the magazine. It wasn't a minute later she stuck her head out.

"You've been to Purity, haven't you?"

"Lot of times."

She stepped into plain sight now wearing a sheer, peach-colored teddy, the crotch sagging between her white thighs. Crystal said, "You hear about the time Pretty Boy Floyd came in?"

"While you were working there?"

"Since then, not too long ago. The word got around Pretty Boy Floyd was at Purity and it practically shut down the whole town. Nobody'd come out of their house." She stood with hands on her hips in kind of a slouch. "I did meet him one time. Was at a speak in Oklahoma City."

"You talk to him?"

"Yeah, we talked about . . . you know, different things." She looked like she might be trying to think of what they did talk about, but said then, "Who's the most famous person you ever met?"

He wasn't expecting the question. Still, he thought about it for no more than a few seconds before telling her, "I guess it would have to be Emmett Long."

Crystal said, "Oh . . . ?" like the name didn't mean much to her. Carl could tell, though, she was being careful, on her guard.

"Was in a drugstore when I was a kid," Carl said, "and he came in for a pack of Luckies. I'd stopped there for a peach ice cream cone, my favorite. You know what Emmett Long did? Asked could he have a bite—this famous bank robber."

"You give him one?"

"I did, and you know what? He kept it, wouldn't give me back my cone."

"He ate it?"

"Licked it a few times and threw it away." Carl didn't mention the trace of ice cream on the bank robber's mustache; he kept that for himself. "Yeah, he took my ice cream cone, robbed the store and shot a policeman. You believe it?"

She seemed to nod, thoughtful now, and Carl decided it was time to come out in the open.

"You said people think it was marshals gunned down your husband, Skeet. But you know better, don't you?"

He had her full attention, staring at him now like she was hypnotized.

"And I'll bet it was Emmett himself told you. Who else'd have the nerve? I'll bet he said you ever leave him he'll hunt you down and kill you. On account of he's so crazy about you. I can't think of another reason you'd stay here these years. You have anything to say to that?"

Crystal began to show herself, saying, "You're not from a newspaper . . ."

"Is that what you thought?"

"They come around. Once they're in the house they can't wait to leave. No, you're not at all like them."

Carl said, "Honey, I'm a deputy United States marshal. I'm here to put Emmett Long under arrest or in the ground, one."

He worried she might've acquired an affection for the man, but it wasn't so. Once Carl showed her his star Crystal sat down and breathed with relief. Pretty soon her nerves did take hold and she became talkative. Emmett had phoned this morning and was coming. Now what was she supposed to do? Carl asked what time she expected him. She said going on dark. A car would drive past and honk twice; if the front door was open when it drove past again Emmett would jump out and the car would keep going.

Carl said he'd be sitting here reading about Joan Crawford. He said to introduce him as a friend of the family happened to stop by, but try not to talk too much. He asked if Emmett brought the magazines. She said they were supposed to be her treat. He asked out of curiosity if Emmett could read. Crystal said she wasn't sure, but believed he only looked at the pictures. What was it Virgil called him that time, years ago? A bozo.

He said to Crystal, "What you want to do is pay close attention. Then later on you can tell what happened here as the star witness and get your name in the paper. I bet even your picture."

"I hadn't thought of that," Crystal said. "You really think so?"

They heard the car beep twice as it passed the house.

Ready?

Carl was, in the chair facing the magazine table where the only lamp in the room was lit. Crystal stood smoking a cigaret, smoking three or four since drinking the orange juice glass of gin to settle her down. Light from the kitchen, behind her, showed her figure in the kimono she was wearing. Crystal looked fine to Carl.

But not to Emmett Long. Not the way he came in with magazines under his arm and barely paused before saying to her, "What's wrong?"

"Nothing," Crystal said. "Em, I want you to meet Carl, from home." Emmett staring at him now as Crystal said he was a busboy at Purity the same time she was working there. "And our moms are both Eastern Star."

"You're Emmett," Carl said, sounding like a salesman. "Glad to know you." Carl looking at a face from seven years ago, the same dead-eyed stare beneath the hat brim. He watched Emmett Long carry his magazines to the table, drop them on top of the ones there and glance over at Crystal. Carl watched him plant both hands on the table now, hunched over, taking time to what, rest? Uh-unh, decide how to get rid of this busboy so he could take Crystal to bed, Carl imagining Emmett doing it to her with his hat still on . . . And remembered his dad saying, "You know why I caught the Mauser round that time, the Spanish sniper picking me off? I was thinking instead of paying attention, doing my job."

Carl asked himself what he was waiting for. He said, "Emmett, bring out your pistol and lay it there on the table."

Crystal Lee Davidson knew how to tell it. She had recited her story enough times to marshals and various law enforcement people. This afternoon she was describing the scene to newspaper reporters—and the one from the *Oklahoman,* the Oklahoma City paper, kept interrupting, asking questions that were a lot different than ones the marshals asked.

She referred to Deputy Marshal Webster as "Carl" and the one from the *Oklahoman* said, "Oh, you two are on intimate terms now? You don't mind he's just a kid? Has he visited you here at the hotel?" Crystal staying a few days at the Georgian in Henryetta. The other reporters in the room would tell the *Oklahoman* to keep quiet for Christ sake, anxious for Crystal to get to the gunplay.

"As I told you," Crystal said, "I was in the doorway to the kitchen. Emmett's over here to my left, and Carl's opposite him but sitting down, his legs stretched out in his cowboy boots. I couldn't believe how calm he was."

"What'd you have on, dear?"

The *Oklahoman* interrupting again, some of the other reporters groaning.

"I had on a pink and red kimona Em got me at Kerr's in Oklahoma City. I had to wear it whenever he came."

"You have anything on under it?"

Crystal said, "None of your beeswax."

The *Oklahoman* said his readers had a right to know such details of how a gun moll dressed. This time the other reporters were quiet, like they wouldn't mind hearing such details themselves, until Crystal said, "If this big mouth opens his trap one more time I'm through and y'all can leave." She said, "Now where was I?"

"Emmett was leaning on the table."

"Sort of hunched over it," Crystal said. "He looked over at me like he was gonna say something, and right then Carl said, 'Emmett?' He said, 'Draw your pistol and lay it there on the table.'"

The reporters wrote it down in their notebooks and then waited as Crystal took a sip of iced tea.

"I told you Em had his back to Carl? Now I see him turn his face to his shoulder and say to him, 'Do I know you from someplace?' Maybe thinking of McAlester, Carl an ex-convict looking to earn the reward money. Em asks him, 'Have we met or not?' And Carl says, 'If I told you, I doubt you'd remember.' Then—this is where Carl says, 'Mr. Long, I'm a deputy United States marshal. I'll tell you one more time to lay your pistol on the table.'"

A reporter said, "Crystal, I know they did meet. I'm Tony Antonelli from the Okmulgee *Daily Times* and I wrote the story about it."

"What you're doing," Crystal said, "is holding up my getting to the good part." Messing up her train of thought, too.

"But the circumstances of how they met," Tony Antonelli said, "could have everything to do with this story."

"Would you *please*," Crystal said, "wait till I'm done?"

It gave her time to tell the next part: how Emmett had no choice but to draw his gun, this big pearl-handle automatic, from inside his coat and lay it on the edge of the table, right next to him. "Now as he turns around," Crystal said, starting to grin, "this surprised look came over his face. He sees Carl sitting there, not with a gun in his hand but *Photoplay* magazine. Emmett can't believe his eyes. He says, 'Jesus Christ, you don't have a gun?' Carl pats the side of his chest where his gun's holstered under his coat and says, 'Right here.' Then he says, 'Mr. Long, I want to be clear about this so you understand. If I have to pull my weapon I'll shoot to kill.'" Crystal said to the reporters, "In other words, the only time Carl Webster draws his gun it's to shoot somebody dead."

It had the reporters scribbling in their notebooks and making remarks to one another. Tony Antonelli, the one from the Okmulgee paper saying now, "Listen, will you? Seven years ago Emmett Long held up Deering's drugstore in town and Carl Webster was there. Only he was known as Carlos then, he was still a kid. He stood by and watched Emmett Long shoot and kill an Indian from the tribal police happened to come in the store, a man Carl Webster must've known." Tony Antonelli, a good-looking young man, said to Crystal, "I'm sorry to interrupt, but I think the drugstore shooting could've been on Carl Webster's mind."

Crystal said, "I can tell you something else about that."

But now voices were chiming in, commenting and asking questions about the Okmulgee reporter's views:

"Carl carried it with him all these years?"

"Did he remind Emmett Long of it?"

"You're saying the tribal cop was a friend of his?"

"Both from Okmulgee, Carl thinking of becoming a lawman?"

"Carl ever say he was out to get Emmett?"

"This story's bigger'n it looks."

Crystal said, "You want to hear something else happened? How Carl was eating an ice cream cone that time and what Em did?"

They sat on the porch sipping bourbon at the end of the day, insects out there singing in the dark. A lantern hung above Virgil's head so he could see to read the newspapers on his lap.

"Most of it seems to be what this little girl told."

"They made up some of it."

"Jesus, I hope so. You haven't been going out with her, have you?"

"I drove down, took Crystal to Purity a couple of times."

"She's a pretty little thing. Has a saucy look about her in the pictures, wearing that kimona."

"She smelled nice, too," Carl said.

Virgil turned his head to him. "I wouldn't tell Bob McMahon that. One of his marshals sniffing around a gun moll." He waited, but Carl let that one go. Virgil looked at the newspaper he was holding. "I don't recall you were ever a buddy of Junior Harjo's."

"I'd see him and say hi, that's all."

"This Tony Antonelli has you two practically blood brothers. What you did was avenge his death. They wonder if it might even be the reason you joined the marshals."

"Yeah, I read that," Carl said.

Virgil put the *Daily Times* down and slipped the *Oklahoman* out from under it. "But now the Oklahoma City paper says you shot Emmett Long 'cause he took your ice cream cone that time. They trying to be funny?"

"I guess," Carl said.

"They could make up a name for you, as smart-aleck newspapers do, start calling you Carl Webster, the Ice Cream Kid?"

"You think so?"

"I'm getting the idea you like the attention."

Virgil saying it with some concern and Carl giving him a shrug. Virgil picked up another paper from the pile. "Here they quote the little girl saying Emmett Long went for his gun and you shot him through the heart."

"I thought they have her saying, 'straight through the heart,'" Carl said. "I told her, they want to know what I pack, tell 'em you think it's a Colt thirty-eight with the front sight filed down . . ." He turned to see his old dad staring at him with a solemn expression. "I'm kidding with you. What Emmett did, he tried to bluff me. He looked toward Crystal and called her name thinking I'd look over. But I kept my eyes on him, knowing he'd pick up his gun. He came around with it and I shot him."

"As you told him you would," Virgil said. "Every one of the newspapers played it up, your saying, 'If I have to pull my weapon I shoot to kill.' You tell 'em that?"

"The only one I told was Emmett," Carl said. "It had to of been Crystal told the papers."

"Well, that little girl sure tooted your horn for you."

"She only told what happened."

"All she had to. It's the telling that did it, made you a famous lawman overnight. You think you can carry a load like that?"

"Why not?" Carl said, grinning at his dad, but starting to show himself.

It didn't surprise his old dad. Virgil picked up his glass of bourbon and raised it to his boy, saying, "God help us show-offs."

4

The first piece Tony Antonelli wrote for the Okmulgee *Daily Times,* about Italian immigrants working in Oklahoma coal mines, he used "Death in the Dark" as a title and "Anthony Marcel Antonelli" as his byline. The editor of the paper said, "Who do you think you are, Richard Harding Davis? Get rid of the Marcel and call yourself Tony."

Tony Antonelli loved the literary style of Harding Davis, the greatest journalist in the world. But every time he tried to dress up his stories with color, with interesting observations—the way Harding Davis did in "The Death of Rodriguez," about a Cuban insurgent standing before a Spanish firing squad with a cigaret in the corner of his mouth, "not arrogantly nor with bravado"—the editor would cross out entire passages, saying, "Our readers don't give a rat's ass about what you think. They want facts."

About his interview with Crystal Davidson the editor said, "Did Carl Webster ever tell you he was avenging the death of that tribal cop?"

"I only said they knew each other."

"You mean alleged to have known each other."

"And maybe," Tony said, "it gave Carl a motive, made it easier for him to shoot the bank robber."

"You're saying he needed a personal reason to gun down a wanted criminal?"

"What I meant, his knowing Junior might've enkindled a determination to do it."

"Did Carl Webster tell you directly that if he pulled his gun he'd shoot to kill?"

"It was something he told Crystal."

"And you accepted the word of a gun moll?"

Tony started looking for another writing job.

He was born in Krebs in 1903, the heart of Oklahoma coal mine country, the son of a coal miner, the reason he wrote about the hazards of working underground, the high incidence of deaths, the mine operators' reluctance to accept safety standards. And the editor chopped the drama out of his stories, telling Tony to get rid of "gasping for breath in a grotto of coal." He wrote about the Black Hand extorting money from Italian businesses, and the editor asked if he knew for a fact the Black Hand was related to the Mafia. He wrote about Italians in general not trusting banks and hiding their savings. "As much as fifty thousand dollars in small amounts buried in the backyards and vegetable gardens of Krebs, McAlester, Wilburton and other communities." He wrote that John Tua, the most influential Italian in Oklahoma, the *padrone* of the Antonellis and all the Italians working in the mines, often sat at night in his restaurant with twenty thousand dollars or more in the drawer of his desk, as much as a quarter of a million in his bank.

The editor said, "Where'd you get your figures? Some other Italian tell you?"

"Everyone knows it," Tony said. "Mr. Tua is a great man, dedicated to the welfare of immigrants. He gives people advice, finds them work, exchanges foreign currency. Why he keeps all that money."

The editor said, "I don't care for the one about the Klan, either. Who says they're out to get you people?"

"They hate Catholics," Tony said. "They believe we're no better than Negroes. And almost all Italians are Catholic. Even the fallen-away ones get married in the Church and have their babies baptized."

Tony wrote a story about the happy Fassino family's popular macaroni factory. Another one about a social club, the Christopher Columbus Society and its twenty-five-piece band that played at festivals and on the Fourth of July.

The editor said, "I think you're getting the hang of it. Now write one about the tendency of your people to overindulge in Choctaw beer and homemade wine."

That did it. Tony Antonelli quit the Okmulgee *Daily Times*. Within a few months he was living in Tulsa and writing for *True Detective Mystery* magazine. Finally, where he belonged.

They'd pay him two cents a word to start. He leafed through one of the latest issues to read a story that opened with "Light beams, sweeping the sky like flowing yellow ribbons against a backdrop of black, shone from the walls of the Colorado State Penitentiary one winter night in 1932."

He couldn't wait to start writing.

Two cents a word even for an "As Told To" story, a hundred bucks for five thousand words, nineteen and a half to twenty pages, and the opportunity of working up to a nickel a word. He'd found out they counted the pages, not the words. He believed he was meant to write for *True Detective*, be able to use more dialogue, the way people actually spoke. Here, the girl saying, " 'I thought you were being hurt. Those screams,' she stammered." The response, " 'I made them good,

eh?' asked the imperturbable diver." Tony turned pages in the magazine and stopped at a photograph with the caption, "The laundry of
Lee Hoey, wither the diver started on a peaceful errand, became the
center of a strange conflict." The writer making even a caption work.

The editor of the Okmulgee paper, his problem, he wouldn't know
good writing if John Barrymore read it to him.

Tony had written to *True Detective*'s editorial offices on Broadway in
New York City, gave them samples of his original, unedited work and
they called him. This editor said he liked the Black Hand piece and
might run it if Tony could expand on the Mafia connection, their
scheme to preside over all organized crime in America. Tony said he
didn't see why not.

And then suggested, how about a close study of a deputy U.S. marshal, a good-looking young guy who was on his way to becoming the
most famous lawman in America. The hot kid of the Marshals Service
who said if he had to draw his gun, he would shoot to kill the wanted
felon he was apprehending. "And Carl Webster has drawn his Colt .38
four times so far in his career. You can tell he's sharp just by the way he
wears his panama, his suit's always pressed. You look at him and wonder where he keeps his gun."

"He's good-looking, uh?"

"Could be a movie star. You may remember him shooting Emmett
Long four years ago? That was only his second. I'm getting details of the
times he shot to kill. They were both in the papers. I might mention Carl
is something of a ladies' man. He's been seen now and then with Emmett
Long's gun moll, Crystal Davidson. He's younger than Crystal, still only
twenty-five or six. His dad was on the *Maine* when she blew up in Havana harbor, and survived. The dad adds color, a touch of patriotism.
What I want to do," Tony said, "is follow Carl while he tracks wanted
criminals and write about what he thinks and feels, tap into his emotions

and come up with the story of a True American Lawman: Carl Webster. His picture on the cover." Tony paused. "Drawing his Colt revolver."

The editor in his office on Broadway said it didn't sound too bad, but then wanted to know, "What else you got?"

Tony said, "How about the son of a millionaire who robs banks? Jack Belmont, out to make a name for himself. His dad's Oris Belmont of NMD Gas & Oil, worth a good twenty million, into refineries, car lots, has a tank farm. He occupies an entire floor of the Exchange National Bank building here in Tulsa."

He was giving this editor hard facts, confident he could write for *True Detective*.

"Jack Belmont's a young dude. Must have a dozen suits and pairs of shoes."

"How come I've never heard of him?"

"You will. Carl Webster's after him."

"If his daddy's rich, why's the kid rob banks?"

"That's what the story's about. Why did his old man cut him off? What was he up to? Outside of blowing up one of his dad's oil storage tanks. This guy's gonna pull something big before he's through."

"How do you get to him?"

"I told you, I follow Carl Webster."

There was a pause on the line before the editor in New York said, "You know who's the big news now, Pretty Boy Floyd."

Bingo.

Tony said in the same quiet voice he'd been using, "How would you like a profile of his girlfriend, Louly Brown? I understand she's hot stuff."

"Yeah? You know her?"

"I'm meeting her at the Mayo Hotel this coming week," Tony said, "for an interview."

There was another pause on the line.

"Which one you want to do first?"

"In a way," Tony said, "they're all related. When Louly Brown shot one of the guys in Pretty Boy's gang, guess who was there?" Tony paused a moment before saying, "Carl Webster."

n 1918, when Louly Brown was six years old, her dad, a Tulsa stockyard hand, joined the U.S. Marines and was killed at Bois de Belleau during the Great War. Her mom, Sylvia, sniffling as she held the letter from his lieutenant, told Louly it was a woods over in France.

In 1920 Sylvia married a hardshell Baptist by the name of Ed Hagenlocker and they went to live on his cotton farm near Sallisaw, below Tulsa on the south edge of the Cookson Hills. By the time Louly was twelve, Sylvia had two sons by Mr. Hagenlocker and the man had Louly out in the fields picking cotton. He was the only person in the world who called her by her Christian name, Louise. She hated picking cotton but Sylvia wouldn't say anything to Mr. Hagenlocker. Louly always thought of him that way, as Mr. Hagenlocker, and her mom as Sylvia, someone she never felt close to again. Mr. Hagenlocker believed that when you were old enough to do a day's work, you worked. It meant Louly was finished with school by the sixth grade.

In 1924, the summer Louly was twelve, they attended her cousin Ruby's wedding in Sallisaw. Ruby was seventeen, the boy she married, Charley Floyd, twenty. Ruby was dark but pretty, showing some Cherokee blood on her mama's side. Ruby had nothing to say to Louly at the wedding, but Charley called her kiddo and would lay his hand on her head and muss her bobbed hair that was reddish from her mom. He told her she had the biggest brown eyes he had ever seen on a little girl.

Just the next year she began reading about Charles Arthur Floyd in the paper: how he and two others went up to St. Louis and robbed the Kroger Food payroll office of $11,500. They were caught in Sallisaw driving around in a brand-new Studebaker they'd bought in Fort Smith, Arkansas. The Kroger Food paymaster identified Charley saying, "That's him, the pretty boy with apple cheeks." Gradually the newspapers began referring to Charley Floyd as "Pretty Boy."

Louly remembered him from the wedding as cute, but kind of scary the way he grinned at you—not being sure what he was thinking. She bet he hated being called Pretty Boy. Looking at his picture she cut out of the paper Louly felt herself getting a crush on this famous outlaw.

In 1929, while he was still at Jeff City, the Missouri State Penitentiary, Ruby divorced him for neglect and married a man from Kansas. Louly thought it was terrible, Ruby betraying Charley like that.

"Ruby don't see him ever again going straight," Sylvia said. "She needs a husband the same as I did to ease the burdens of life, have a father for her little boy Dempsey." Named for the world's heavyweight boxing champ.

Now that Charley was divorced Louly wanted to write and sympathize but didn't know which of his names to use. She had heard his friends called him Choc, after his fondness for Choctaw beer, his favorite beverage when he was in his teens and roamed Oklahoma and Kansas with harvest crews.

Louly opened her letter "Dear Charley," and said she thought it was a shame Ruby divorcing him while he was still in prison, not having the nerve to wait till he was out. What she most wanted to know, "Do you remember me from your wedding?" She stuck in with the letter a picture of herself in a bathing suit, standing sideways and smiling over her shoulder at the camera. This way her full-size sixteen-year-old breasts were seen in profile.

Charley wrote back saying sure he remembered her, "the little girl with the big brown eyes." Saying, "I'm getting out in March and going to Kansas City to see what's doing. I have given your address to an inmate here by the name of Joe Young who we call Booger, being funny. He is from Okmulgee but has to do another year or so in this garbage can and would like to have a pen pal as pretty as you are."

Nuts. But then Joe Young wrote her a letter with a picture of himself showing him as a fairly good-looking boy with big ears and blondish hair. He said he kept her bathing-suit picture on the wall next to his rack so he'd look at it before going to sleep and dream of her all night.

Once they were exchanging letters she told him how much she hated picking cotton, dragging that duck sack along the rows all day in the heat and dust, her hands raw from pulling the bolls off the stalks, gloves after while not doing a bit of good. Joe said in his letter, "What are you a nigger slave? You don't like picking cotton leave there and run away. It is what I done."

Pretty soon he said in a letter, "I am getting my release sometime next summer. Why don't you plan on meeting me so we can get together." Louly said she was dying to visit Kansas City and St. Louis, wondering if she would ever see Charley Floyd again. She asked Joe why he was in prison and he wrote back to say, "Honey, I am a bank robber, same as Choc."

It seemed like every week there'd be a story about Charley robbing another bank and his picture in the paper. It was exciting just trying to keep track of him, Louly getting chills and thrills knowing everybody in the world was reading about this famous outlaw who liked her brown eyes and had mussed her hair when she was a kid.

Joe Young wrote to say, "I am getting my release the end of August. I will let you know soon where to meet me."

Louly had been working winters at Harkrider's grocery store in Sallisaw for six dollars a week. She had to give five of it to her stepfather, Mr. Hagenlocker, the man never once thanking her—leaving a dollar to put in her running-away kitty. Working at the store from fall through winter, most of six months, she hadn't saved a whole lot but she knew she was leaving. She might have timid-soul Sylvia's looks, the reddish hair, but had the nerve and get-up-and-go of her daddy, killed in action charging a German machine gun nest in that woods in France.

Late in October, who walked in the grocery store but Joe Young. Louly knew him even wearing a suit, and he knew her, grinning as he came up to the counter, his shirt wide open at the neck. He said, "Well, I'm out."

She said, "You been out two months, haven't you?"

He said, "I been robbing banks. Me and Choc."

She thought she had to go to the bathroom, the urge coming over her in her groin and then gone, Louly took a few moments to compose herself and act like the mention of Choc didn't mean anything special, Joe Young's grin in her face, giving her the feeling he was dumb as dirt. Some other convict must've wrote his letters for him. She said in a casual way, "Oh, is Charley here with you?"

"He's around," Joe Young said, acting shifty, like he was being watched. "Come on, we gotta go."

"I'm not ready just yet," Louly said. "I don't have my running-away money with me."

"How much you save?"

"Thirty-eight dollars.

"Jesus, working here two years?"

"I told you, Mr. Hagenlocker takes almost all my wages."

"You want, I'll crack his head for him."

"I wouldn't mind. The thing is, I'm not leaving without my money."

Joe Young looked at the door as he put his hand in his pocket saying, "Little girl, I'm paying your way. You won't need the thirty-eight dollars."

Little girl—she stood a good two inches taller than Joe Young, even in his run-down cowboy boots. She was shaking her head now. "Mr. Hagenlocker bought a Model A Roadster with my money, paying it off twenty a month."

"You want to steal his car?"

"It's mine, ain't it, if he's using my money?"

Louly had made up her mind and Joe Young was anxious to get out of here. She had pay coming, so they'd meet November 2 at the Georgian Hotel in Henryetta, around noon.

The day before she was to leave Louly told Sylvia she was sick. Instead of going to work she got her things ready and used the curling iron on her hair. The next day, while Sylvia was hanging wash, the two boys at school, and Mr. Hagenlocker was out on his tractor, Louly rolled the Ford Roadster out of the shed and drove into Sallisaw to get a pack of Lucky Strikes for the trip. She loved to smoke and had been doing it with boys but never had to buy the cigarets. When boys wanted to take her in the woods she'd ask, "You have Luckies? A whole pack?" It didn't cross her mind she was doing it for fifteen cents.

The druggist's son, one of her boyfriends, gave her a pack free of charge and asked where she was yesterday, acting sly, saying, "You're always talking about Pretty Boy Floyd, I wonder if he stopped by your house."

They liked to kid her about Pretty Boy. Louly, not paying much attention, said, "I'll let you know when he does." Then saw the boy about to spring something on her.

"The reason I ask, he was here in town yesterday, Pretty Boy was."

She said, "Oh?" careful now. The boy took his time and it was hard to keep herself from shaking him.

"Yeah, his family came down from Akins, his mama, two of his sisters, some others, so they could watch him rob the bank. He had a tommy gun, but didn't shoot anybody. Come out of the bank with two thousand five hundred and thirty-one dollars, him and two others. Gave some of the money to his people and they say to anybody he thought hadn't et in a while, everybody grinning at him."

This was the second time now he had been close by: first when his daddy was killed only seven miles away and now right here in Sallisaw, all kinds of people seeing him, damn it, but her. Just yesterday . . .

She had to wonder if she *had* been here would he of recognized her, and bet he would've.

She said to her boyfriend in the drugstore, "Charley ever hears you called him Pretty Boy, he'll come in for a pack of Luckies, what he always smokes, and shoot you through the heart."

The Georgian was the biggest hotel Louly had ever seen. Coming up on it in the Model A she was thinking these bank robbers knew how to live high on the hog. She pulled in front and a colored man in a green uniform coat with gold buttons and a peaked cap came around to open her door—and saw Joe Young on the sidewalk waving the doorman away, saying as he got in the car, "Jesus Christ, you stole it, didn't you? Jesus, how old are you, going around stealing cars?"

Louly said, "How old you have to be?"

He told her to keep straight ahead.

She said, "You aren't staying at the hotel?"

"I'm at a tourist court."

"Charley there?"

"He's around someplace."

"Well, he was in Sallisaw yesterday," Louly sounding mad now, "if that's what you call *around*," seeing by Joe Young's expression she was telling him something he didn't know. "I thought you were in his gang."

"He's got an old boy name of Birdwell with him. I hook up with Choc when I feel like it."

She was almost positive Joe Young was lying to her.

"Am I gonna see Charley or not?"

"He'll be back, don't worry your head about it." He said, "We got this car, I won't have to steal one." Joe Young was in a good mood now. "What we need Choc for?" Grinning at her close by in the car. "We got each other."

It told her what to expect.

Once they got to the tourist court and were in No. 7, like a little one-room frame house that needed paint, Joe Young took off his coat and she saw the Colt automatic with a pearl grip stuck in his pants. He laid it on the dresser by a full quart of whiskey and two glasses and poured them each a drink, his bigger than hers. She stood watching till he told her to take off her coat and when she did told her to take off her dress. Now she was in her white brassiere and underpants. Joe Young looked her over before handing the smaller drink to her and clinking glasses.

"To our future."

Louly said, "Doing what?" Seeing the fun in his eyes.

He put his glass on the dresser, brought two .38 revolvers from the drawer and offered her one. She took it, big and heavy in her hand and said, "Yeah . . . ?"

"You know how to steal a car, and I admire that. But I bet you never held up a place with a gun."

"That's what we're gonna do?"

"Start with a filling station and work you up to a bank." He said, "I bet you never been to bed with a grown man, either."

Louly felt like telling him she was bigger than he was, taller, anyway, but didn't. This was a new experience, different than with boys her age in the woods, and she wanted to see what it was like.

Well, he grunted a lot and was rough, breathed hard through his nose and smelled of Lucky Tiger hair tonic, but it wasn't that much different than with boys. She got to liking it before he was finished and patted his back with her rough, cotton-picking fingers till he began to breathe easy again. Once he rolled off her she got her douche bag out of Mr. Hagenlocker's grip she'd taken and went in the bathroom, Joe Young's voice following her with, "Whoooeee . . ." Then saying, "You know what you are now, little girl? You're what's called a gun moll."

Joe Young slept a while, woke up still snockered and wanted to get something to eat. So they went to Purity, Joe said was the best place in Henryetta.

Louly said at the table, "Charley Floyd came in here one time and everybody stayed in their house."

"How you know that?"

"I know everything about him was ever written, some things only told."

"Who was it named him Pretty Boy?"

"I found out it wasn't that paymaster in St. Louis, it was a woman named Beulah Ash. She ran the boardinghouse in Kansas City where Charley stayed."

Joe Young picked up his coffee he'd poured a shot into. He said, "You're gonna start reading about me, chile."

It reminded her she didn't know how old Joe Young was and took this opportunity to ask him.

"I'm thirty next month, born on Christmas Day, same as Baby Jesus."

Louly laughed out loud. She couldn't help it, seeing Joe Young lying in a feed trough with Baby Jesus, the three Wise Men looking at him funny. She asked Joe how many times he'd had his picture in the paper.

"When I got sent to Jeff City they was all kinds of pictures of me. Some I'm handcuffed."

She watched him sit back as the waitress came with their supper and he gave her a pat on the butt when she turned from the table. The waitress said, "Fresh," and acted surprised in a cute way. Louly was ready to tell how Charley Floyd had his picture in the Sallisaw paper fifty-one times in the past year, once for each of the fifty-one banks robbed in Oklahoma, all of them claiming Charley as the one who robbed them. But she knew it couldn't be true, so didn't mention it.

They finished their supper, breaded pork chops, and Joe Young told her to pay the bill—a buck-sixty for everything including rhubarb pie for dessert—out of her running-away money. They got back to the tourist court and he screwed her again on her full stomach, breathing through his nose, and she saw how this being a gun moll wasn't all a bed of roses.

In the morning they set out east on Highway 40 for the Cookson Hills, Joe Young driving the Model A with his elbow out the window, Louly holding her coat close to her, the collar up against the wind, Joe Young talking a lot, saying they'd go on up to Muskogee and hold up a filling station along the way. Show her how it was done.

Heading out of Henryetta she said, "There's one."

He said, "Too many cars."

Thirty miles later leaving Checotah, turning north toward Muskogee, Louly looked back and said, "What's wrong with that Texaco station?"

"Something about it I don't like," Joe Young said. "You have to have a feel for this work."

Louly said, "You pick it." She had the .38 he gave her in a black and pink bag Sylvia had crocheted for her.

They came up on Summit and crept through town, both of them looking, Louly waiting for him to choose a place to rob. She was getting excited. They came to the other end of town and Joe Young said, "There's our place. We can fill up, get a cup of coffee."

Louly said, "Hold it up?"

"Look it over."

"It's sure a dump."

Two gas pumps in front of a rickety place, paint peeling, a sign that said EATS and told that soup was a dime and a hamburger five cents.

They went in while a bent-over old man filled their tank, Joe Young bringing his whiskey bottle with him, almost drained now, and put it on the counter. The woman behind it was frail, flat-chested and appeared worn out, brushing strands of hair from her face. She placed cups in front of them and Joe Young poured what was left of the whiskey into his.

Louly did not want to rob this woman.

The woman saying, "I think she's dry," meaning his bottle.

Joe Young was concentrating on dripping the last drops into his cup. He said, "Can you help me out?"

Now the woman was pouring their coffee. "You want shine? Or I can give you Canadian whiskey for three dollars."

"Gimme a couple," Joe Young said, drawing his Colt to lay it on the counter, "and what's in the till."

Louly did not want to rob this woman. She was thinking you didn't *have* to rob a person just 'cause the person had money, did you?

The woman said, "Goddamn you, Mister."

Joe Young picked up his gun and went around to open the cash register. Taking out bills he said to the woman, "Where you keep the whiskey money?"

She said, "In there," despair in her voice.

He said, "Fourteen dollars?" holding it up, and turned to Louly. "Put your gun on her so she don't move. The geezer come in, put it on him, too." Joe Young went through a doorway to what looked like a kitchen.

The woman said to Louly, pointing the gun from the crocheted bag at her now, "How come you're with that trash? You seem like a girl from a nice family, have a pretty bag . . . There something wrong with you? My Lord, you can't do better'n him?"

Louly said, "You know who's a good friend of mine? Charley Floyd, if you know who I mean. He married my cousin Ruby." The woman shook her head and Louly said, "Pretty Boy Floyd," and wanted to bite her tongue.

Now the woman seemed to smile, showing black lines between the teeth she had. "He come in here one time. I fixed him breakfast and he paid me two dollars for it. You ever hear of that? I charge twenty-five cents for two eggs, four strips of bacon, toast and all you want of coffee, and he give me two dollars."

They got the fourteen from the till and fifty-seven dollars in whiskey money from the kitchen, Joe Young talking again heading for Muskogee, telling Louly it was something told him to go in there. How was this place doing business, two big gas stations only a few blocks away? So he'd brought the bottle in, see what it would get him. "You hear what she said? 'Goddamn you,' but called me 'Mister.'"

"Charley had breakfast in there one time," Louly said, "and paid her two dollars for it."

"Showing off," Joe Young said.

He decided they'd stay in Muskogee instead of crossing the Arkansas River and heading south.

Louly said, "Yeah, we must've come a good fifty miles today."

Joe Young told her not to get smart with him. "I'm gonna put you in a tourist cabin and see some boys I know. Find out where Choc's at."

She didn't believe him, but what was the sense of arguing?

It was early evening now, the sun almost gone.

The man who knocked on the door—she could see him through the glass part—was tall and slim in a dark suit, a young guy dressed up wearing a panama hat. She believed he was the police, but had no reason, standing here looking at him, not to open the door.

He said, "Miss," touched the brim of his panama and showed her his I.D. and a star in a circle in a wallet he held open, "I'm Deputy U.S. Marshal Carl Webster. Who am I speaking to, please?"

She said, "I'm Louly Brown?"

He smiled straight teeth at her and said, "You're a cousin of Pretty Boy Floyd's wife Ruby, aren't you?"

Like getting ice-cold water thrown in her face she was so surprised. "How'd you know that?"

"We been talking to everybody he knows. You recall the last time you saw him?"

"At their wedding, eight years ago."

"No time since? How about the other day in Sallisaw?"

"I never saw him. But listen, him and Ruby are divorced."

The marshal, Carl Webster, shook his head. "He went up to Coffeyville and got her back. But aren't you missing a motor car, a Model A Roadster?"

She had not heard a *word* about Charley and Ruby being back to-gether. Louly said, "The car isn't missing, a friend of mine's using it."

He said, "The car's in your name?" and recited the Oklahoma li-cense number.

"I paid for it out of my wages. It just happens to be in my stepfa-ther's name, Mr. Ed Hagenlocker."

"I guess there's some kind of misunderstanding," Carl Webster said. "Mr. Hagenlocker claims it was stolen off his property in Sequoyah County. Who's your friend borrowed it?"

She did hesitate before saying Joe Young.

"When's Joe coming back?"

"Later on. 'Cept he'll stay with his friends he gets too drunk."

Carl Webster said, "I wouldn't mind talking to him," and gave Louly a business card from his pocket with a star on it and letters she could feel. "Ask Joe to give me a call later on, or sometime tomorrow if he doesn't come home. Y'all just driving around?"

"Seeing the sights."

Every time he caught her looking at him he'd start to smile. Carl Webster. She could feel his name under her thumb. She liked the way he shook her hand and thanked her, and the way he touched his hat, so polite for a U.S. marshal.

Joe Young returned about 9 A.M. making awful faces working his mouth, trying to get a taste out of it. He came in the room and took a good pull on the whiskey bottle, then another, sucked in his breath and let it out and seemed better. He said, "I don't believe what we got into with those chickens last night."

"Wait," Louly said. She told him about the marshal stopping by, and Joe Young became jittery and couldn't stand still, saying, "I ain't going back. I done ten years and swore to Jesus I ain't ever going back." Now he was looking out the window.

Louly was curious about what Joe and his buddies did to the chickens, but knew they had to get out of here. She tried to tell him they had to leave, *right now.*

He was still drunk or starting over, saying now, "They come after me they's gonna be a shoot-out. I'm taking some of the scudders with me." Maybe not even knowing he was playing Jimmy Cagney now.

Louly said, "You only stole seventy-one dollars."

"I done other things in the State of Oklahoma," Joe Young said. "They take me alive I'm facing fifteen to life. I swear I ain't going back."

What was going *on* here? They're driving around looking for Charley Floyd—the next thing this dumbbell wants to shoot it out with the law and here she was in this room with him.

"They don't want *me*," Louly said. Knowing she couldn't talk to him, the state he was in. She had to get out of here, open the door and run. She got her crocheted bag from the dresser, started for the door and was stopped by the bullhorn.

The electrified voice loud, saying, "JOE YOUNG, COME OUT WITH YOUR HANDS IN THE AIR."

What Joe Young did—he held his Colt straight out in front of him and started firing through the glass pane in the door. Drunk. People outside returned fire, blew out the window, gouged the door with gunfire, Louly dropping to the floor with her bag, until she heard a voice on the bullhorn call out, "HOLD YOUR FIRE."

Louly looked up to see Joe Young standing by the bed with a gun in each hand now, the Colt and a .38. She said, "Joe, you have to give yourself up. They're gonna kill both of us you keep shooting." He reminded her again of James Cagney acting mad, in the movie where he squashes the grapefruit in the girl's face.

Joe Young didn't even look at her. He yelled out, "Come and get me!" and started shooting again, both guns at the same time. He stopped long enough to say to Louly, "I die, I'm gonna die game."

Louly's hand went in the crocheted bag and came out with the .38 he'd given her to help him rob places. From the floor, up on her elbows, she aimed the revolver at Joe Young, cocked it and *bam*, shot him through the chest.

Louly stepped away from the door and the marshal, Carl Webster, came in holding a revolver. She saw lawmen standing out in the road, some with rifles. Carl Webster was looking at Joe Young curled up on the floor. He holstered his revolver, took the .38 from Louly and sniffed the barrel and stared at her without saying anything before going to one knee to see if Joe Young had a pulse. He got up saying, "The Oklahoma Bankers Association wants people like Joe dead, and that's what he is. They're gonna give you a five-hundred dollar reward for killing your friend."

"He wasn't a friend."

"He was yesterday. Make up your mind."

"He stole the car and made me go with him."

"Against your will," Carl Webster said. "Stay with that you won't go to jail."

"It's true, Carl," Louly said, showing him her big brown eyes with soul in them. "Really."

The headline in the Tulsa *World,* over a small photo of Louise Brown, said SALLISAW GIRL SHOOTS ABUDUCTOR.

According to Louise, she had to stop Joe Young or be killed in the exchange of gunfire. She also said her name was Louly, not Louise. The marshal on the scene said it was a courageous act, the girl shooting her abductor. "We considered Joe Young a mad-dog felon with nothing to lose." The marshal said that Joe Young was suspected of being a member of Pretty Boy Floyd's gang. He also mentioned that Louly Brown was related to Floyd's wife and acquainted with the desperado.

The headline in the Tulsa paper, over a larger photo of Louly, said GIRL SHOOTS PRETTY BOY FLOYD GANG MEMBER. The story told that Louly Brown was a friend of Pretty Boy's and had been abducted by the former gang member who, according to Louly, "was jealous of Pretty Boy and kidnapped me to get back at him."

By the time the story had appeared everywhere from Fort Smith, Arkansas, to Toledo, Ohio, the most popular headline was GIRLFRIEND OF PRETTY BOY GUNS DOWN MAD-DOG FELON.

The marshal, Carl Webster, came to Sallisaw on business and stopped in Harkrider's for a pack of cigarets and a sack of Beechnut scrap. He was surprised to see Louly.

"You're still working here?"

"No, Carl, I'm shopping for my mom. I got my reward money and I'll be leaving here pretty soon. Mr. Hagenlocker hasn't said a word to me since I got home. He's afraid I might shoot him."

"Where you going?"

"This writer for *True Detective* wants me to come to Tulsa. They're willing to put me up at the Mayo Hotel and pay a hundred dollars for my story. Reporters from Kansas City and St. Louis, Missouri, have already been to the house."

"You're sure getting a lot of mileage out of knowing Pretty Boy, aren't you?"

"They start out asking about my shooting that dumbbell Joe Young, but what they really want to know, if I'm Charley's girlfriend. I say, 'Where in the world did you get that idea?' "

"You don't deny it."

"I say, 'Believe what you want, since I can't change your mind.' All I'm doing is having some fun with them."

"And becoming famous," Carl said. "Maybe it can get you something you've thought of doing."

"Like what, become a chorus girl? Yeah, I'll get a job in *George White's Scandals.*" Louly picked up her sack of groceries.

Carl took it from her and they walked out of the store to her Ford roadster parked on the street, Carl saying, "I wouldn't be surprised you can do just about anything you want. You still have my card?"

"I keep it in my Bible," Louly said.

Carl, holding the sack of groceries, smiled at this farm girl who'd shot a wanted fugitive and entertained herself talking to newspaper reporters. The photos of her didn't show her hair's blaze of color, or the easy way she could look up at you with those brown eyes. Or the way she said to him now, "I like your hat."

Carl couldn't help smiling. He said, "Give me a call when you get to Tulsa, I'll buy you an ice cream soda."

6

The reason Tony Antonelli was on hand to write what he was thinking of calling "The Bloody Bald Mountain War," he had returned to Krebs on his own to cover a labor strike.

The mine operators announced they were cutting wages by 25 percent, and the miners of Local 2327 walked out of Osage No. 5. Their demand: the company continue to pay them a flat six dollars and ten cents a day. Tony had grown up with most of the Italian miners and wanted to hear their side of the disagreement. They told him they were standing for a bare-minimum living wage, nothing less. It was bad enough, they said, spending ten hours in the hole with those stinking mules. They said the animals stunk so bad of putrid gas, you could blow yourself to hell striking a spark with your pick. Tony wasn't sure if this was true but wrote it anyway. It was good stuff, the attitude of the miners.

The company brought in strikebreakers along with a man by the name of Nestor Lott, at one time a special agent for the Justice Department in Georgia, going after moonshiners defying Prohibition by the unlawful manufacture and sale of alcohol. The Krebs chief of police, a man named Fausto Bassi, told Tony that Nestor Lott was known to have gunned down more moonshiners than he arrested, and that the man's judgment had a "hair-trigger."

Nestor Lott wore two .45 automatics, military issue, one holstered on each hip and snugged to his legs with leather thongs. Tony wrote in his notebook: "He is a man of small stature, no more than five-three, who stares with a look of intensity in his cold gray eyes that holds one's attention. When he smiles, which is seldom, one is never certain if it is to express pleasure, or even goodwill, for the smile never shows in his eyes of steel."

Nestor Lott got rid of the company strikebreakers saying they were drunks and derelicts with no personal stake in the situation, and recruited members of the local Ku Klux Klan for the job. He told them, "You know these dagos are all Socialists, enemies of our American way. We run 'em out now or they'll be after your jobs, your farms, and they'll lure your Christian women as Eyetalians know how to do."

The next move of Nestor and his Klansmen, they put on their white robes and pointed hoods and drove out in their cars to a ridge overlooking the Osage No. 5 shaft and the strikers standing by the fence in front of the mine works with their signs. Nestor strung his shooters— each one armed with a rifle—along the high ground, all those white sheets flapping in the wind not much more than a hundred yards from the strikers squinting up at them. Next, he sent a Klansman to drive down there with a message, an ultimatum, fixed to the radiator of his car. It said in big letters:

YOU HAVE 5 MINUTES TO LEAVE BEFORE WE OPEN FIRE

The miners never thought of leaving. They yelled at the bedsheets up on the ridge for the entire five minutes calling them dirty names, dirty laundry, and ran for their lives when the Klansmen fired a volley at them and kept firing and laughing and swearing, killing three and wounding seven before the strikers could bust through the fence to reach the cover of company structures.

The mine operators had a fit at how it would look, knowing the United Mine Workers would now slander the company in newspapers across the country. They paid the hospital bills of the wounded, gave the families of the ones killed a check for five hundred dollars, told the little two-gun weasel to go back to Georgia, and set up arbitration meetings with the union.

But Nestor Lott hung around, warmed up now, restless, feeling confident about the Klan behind him. What caught his eye was the flow of prohibited wine, beer and liquor all over this county—the Oklahoma state prison sitting there at McAlester, only a few miles from Krebs. Nestor said to Tony Antonelli, taking notes in the café where Nestor was having his noon dinner, "You know the women sell that Choc beer out the back of wagons? In tubs of ice? I'm talking about Eyetalian women making money getting people drunk."

Tony felt heat on his face, the boob not realizing he was speaking to an Italian, or not caring. He closed his notebook and said to Nestor sure, he knew of women who brewed Choc. "They make it from barley, hops, throw in some tobacco and a few fishberries, but it hardly amounts to much alcohol. Miners drink it as a tonic for health reasons, water around mining camps being of poor quality, some of it even poisonous."

It didn't move Nestor. He said, "I know of bunco joints where you gamble your money away, no chance in hell of winning. Where you can get whores who'll give you their disease, and liquor that'll turn you blind. They bring it up from places like Old Mexico."

Tony said, "I never heard of any Italians in Krebs running hard liquor."

"But the chief of police's Eyetalian," Nestor said. "Man name of Bassi, speaks with an accent I guarantee ain't American. What's he do-ing about all the liquor violations?" Nestor waited for an answer, his blunt stare bearing on Tony with suspicion. Later on Tony would open his notebook and try to describe the look, the accusing stare, everyone against this squirt upholding a law no one cared about.

Finally he spoke.

"You want to write a good story?"

Tony waited.

Nestor said, "You know that big roadhouse out by Bald Mountain? The other side of McAlester?"

Tony said, "Jack Belmont's place."

"That's the one," Nestor said. "I'm gonna ride in and hit it with my Christian Avengers. Burn it to the ground."

Tony said, "You think the police'll let you?"

Nestor said, "Boy, I don't need their permission."

The first thing Tony thought of doing, sitting behind the wheel in his car, about to turn on the ignition, was drive out to Belmont's roadhouse and tell him what was afoot. He knew for a fact there wasn't anything harmful about the whiskey. He wasn't sure about the girls, but they appeared healthy and fun-loving. A cutie out there named Elodie had caught his eye. Yeah, what he should do, let Belmont know the two-gun weasel was coming on a raid.

But then something he'd been thinking about lately popped in his mind. People in the wilds studying animal behavior, how they'd watch a pride of lions, even give each one a name, and feel sorry for the runt cub, Jimmy, that never got any tit and they'd want to save its life, bring the runt into camp and give it nourishment. But they couldn't 'cause they'd be intruding on nature with their own behavior. They had to watch the daddy lion come along and eat Jimmy. Wasn't it the same thing here? These people living by their own rules of behavior?

In no time Jack Belmont's plight had become part of the metaphor Tony was working on, scribbling in his notebook, trying to draw a literary parallel between animal behavior and human behavior, as it played out in the wilds of eastern Oklahoma.

What occupied Jack Belmont's mind these days, outside of making money and becoming a famous outlaw, was Norm Dilworth's wife, Heidi.

Heidi Winston from Seminole.

Where Norm had taken her out of a whorehouse to the shack by the Kiefer rail yard. Where she was when he and Norm went to prison. Where she stayed doing washing for railroad hands till she got a job as a chambermaid—she said—at the St. James Hotel in Sapulpa. It turned out she was telling the truth, 'cause it was what she was doing when they came out of prison to rob banks with the Emmett Long gang. Jack and Norm would swing back to stay at the St. James till Emmett called about another job. It drove Jack crazy knowing she was in bed with Norm in the next room. He'd listen, holding an empty water glass to the wall, his ear pressed against it, and he'd hear their voices, sometimes her moans when they were doing it.

Heidi still kept giving him the eye. Or she'd bend over in front of him in a low-cut dress to pick out an olive from the dish on the coffee table and put it in her mouth looking at him and kind of suck on it. The time came the gang split up after a robbery and Jack got back to the hotel before Norm. He took Heidi by the arm into his room. Didn't say a word to her getting out of his pants, Heidi pulling her dress over her head, neither one speaking while he humped her on the bed as hard and fervently as he could to show how he felt about her. After, Heidi said, "I was beginning to wonder about you."

———

In some ways Jack Belmont was growing up. He could review his failures and sometimes admit the ones that didn't work were his own fault. Like blackmailing Oris. It was a good idea but done on the spur of the moment before working it out. The same with kidnapping Nancy Polis. He'd jumped the gun on that one, not realizing she might know who he was. Or then, not believing for a minute his own dad would have sent him to prison, Jesus, for blowing up that empty storage tank. It sure made a cloud.

What did he learn about robbing banks from Emmett Long? Go in and scare the shit out of everybody and walk out with the money. How else would you do it? Emmett Long showed he was too old for the outlaw life, letting that tricky marshal set him up and shoot him. Carl Webster. No, the only thing he learned from Emmett Long was if you wanted another man's wife, you'd likely have to shoot him to get her.

So what should he do about Norm Dilworth?

For a dumb guy Norm was smart in a countrified kind of way, hooking them up with bootleggers who put them in the speakeasy business in Krebs.

He didn't want to shoot Norm when he wasn't looking. He didn't want to call him out, either, Norm a dead shot with rifle or revolver. He'd already killed two cops chasing them out of Coalgate that time. Leaned out and drilled them through the windshield of the police car. The only person Jack had shot was the colored boy running from the mob during the race riot, when Jack was fifteen. It told him he ought to shoot somebody now that he was grown, get a feel for it.

He'd been thinking of having some boys snatch Nancy Polis from her boardinghouse, send Oris a ransom note for a hundred thousand or he'd never see her again, and hope his dad still loved her. Jack was also thinking of holding up the Exchange National Bank in Tulsa, where

Oris was now on the board. Jack saw a meeting interrupted, the secretary running in to tell them Mr. Belmont's son had just robbed the bank downstairs.

It was an image in his mind Jack liked to play with.

But if you were a famous outlaw you'd have state and federal law after you, the Carl Websters wanting to shoot you down, and you'd have to have a place where you could lie low. That's why the speakeasy business coming along as a sideline was a good idea, even if it was Norm's.

It got them the café in Krebs they turned into a speak, and later on the feed store off the highway, out of business, they bought and fixed up, added rooms out the back and upstairs with fifteen hundred of bank loot Heidi had saved out of Norm's cut. Now they had a roadhouse not far from a north-south highway that ran up through eastern Oklahoma.

Heidi said she'd always wanted to be a high-class madam. She got hold of three girls who worked in Seminole and one off the street in Krebs who'd run away from home and was too scared to go back and face her daddy. Heidi put her arm around the quivering girl and told her, "Honey, take my word, you have nothing to worry about. You're sitting on what every man I ever knew wants a piece of."

It meant Heidi would stay at the roadhouse with the girls, and Jack most of the time, while Norm ran the speak in Krebs. It was the kind of town Norm liked, full of miners coming out of the hole thirsty, but the streets not clogged with traffic stuck in mud like oil boom towns.

The roadhouse had cars lined up in front all night, but was fairly quiet during the day, giving Jack all the time he wanted with Heidi. It was a sweet deal.

Only he wished she wouldn't talk so much lying in bed naked. Always speaking as a madam about business. And always had the radio playing.

Right now Rudy Vallee and his Connecticut Yankees doing "You're Driving Me Crazy." What Heidi was doing to Jack. Wanting to raise the girls' price from three to four dollars. Set it at more than half of a miner's daily wage, they wouldn't get so many of them in here.

"They're the business," Jack said.

Heidi told him there were whores in Krebs'd screw you for four bits. "Let 'em get laid in town and come out here to drink and play monte. You know what it's like to screw a coal miner, even after he's washed up? You get filthy dirty. You ever look at the laundry in the morning, the sheets? Coal miners are dirtier'n oil workers any day, and I'm talking about all kinds, roughnecks, drillers, tool dressers, tankies, tankies are the worst. Shooters, all they do is talk. Ask you how many mistakes you're allowed shooting nitro. The answer's none. The shooter's talking away while these other guys off the patch are waiting in the front room with their hard-ons."

"The girls complain about coal miners?"

"They won't dare say a word. They're clearing a buck and a half every time a guy drops his pants. What I'm telling you is how I feel about it."

Jack had got up as she was talking and put on his pants. Now he sat on the side of the bed with his shoes and socks, his back to Heidi.

"I can't imagine you working in a house."

"Stables are cleaner," she said.

Lying behind him full-length naked, tan arms and white white breasts. Nicer ones than he'd seen on any Tulsa whore. He'd bet Nancy Polis had nice ones. He saw old Oris slipping a hand into Nancy's dress.

"Why'd you stay there?"

"I'd try to run—Eugene'd have his guys he called his dogs out looking for me. I'd be dragged back, he'd put a leather glove on over his big mitt and beat my behind till it was raw. I told you, Norm saved my life.

He said the only way he could come in that house again was with a gun. He told Eugene, 'You come after us I'll shoot you dead.' This was down in Seminole. We come up to Keifer, that house you were at, and it wasn't long before Eugene showed up, him and two others with guns. They busted in while Norm and I were in bed asleep."

Jack turned enough to look at her lying naked.

"Yeah . . . ?"

"Eugene had the drop on Norm. But we always kept this gun under the covers when we went to bed. Norm shot Eugene and about set the bed on fire."

"Shot him dead?"

"It come out his back and broke a window in the front room. I got the rifle and fired at the two running away but only hit one of 'em."

"What'd you do with the bodies?"

"Laid 'em across the railroad tracks."

"Norm never mentioned that to me."

"He isn't one to pat himself on the back."

"He never once mentioned ever shooting anybody."

Jack turned his head to look at her again, Heidi digging at her navel with a fingernail. She said, "That's Norm," without looking over.

"He was a good customer of yours?"

"Norm? He came two times. I got beat in between. Norm saw my raw heinie and the next time he came with the gun."

"You got married right away?"

"He asked me—what am I gonna say?"

Jack put his socks on and then his shoes, but didn't tie the laces or get up. He said, "What do we do about him?"

Heidi turned her head on the pillow to look at Jack, her finger still fooling with her navel.

"Aren't you getting what you want?"

"I don't like you being with him."

"He's my husband."

"That's what I mean."

She said, "You want us to get married?"

Jack bent down to tie his shoes. Ruth Etting was singing now on the radio, "Ten Cents a Dance."

"Let's see how it works out," Jack said.

"How what works out?"

"You and me. See how we get along."

"Lemme ask you again," Heidi said. "Aren't you getting what you want?"

Nestor Lott said, "In the movin' pitcher you see this fella name of Ben Cameron watching these white boys putting on bedsheets, dressing up like ghosts to scare some nigger kids. It gives Ben an idea and your great organization is born that day."

Here was Nestor addressing his Klansmen inside a rickety Pentacostal church on the outskirts of Krebs. Telling them about *The Birth of a Nation,* calling it one of the greatest moving pictures of all time, first appearing eighteen years ago, before Al Jolsen and talkies, and you could see it right now at the picture show in town.

"You want to know the truth about Reconstruction after the Civil War? What it was like? You want to see niggers terrorizing white families? Shoving white people off the sidewalk? Niggers in the state legislature with their bare feet up on their desks? Well, back then the Klan was all we had to fight nigger rule and Reconstruction. Do you know if they found white robes in your closet you could get shot? The Klan rode then to put the niggers back in their place. This time it's the Eyetalians making trouble, breaking the law, and this Eyetalian chief of police they got lets 'em get away with it." Nestor stopped. He frowned at his audience, something perplexing him. He said, "How come the worst troublemakers are all dark-complected? You notice that?" Yes, they did, the audience nodding. "I went to see this police chief by the name of"—Nestor dug a piece of notepaper from his coat pocket, folded it open and looked at it—"Fausto Bassi, I think it says here. I was gonna ask him what kind of American name was Fausto Bassi, but I didn't. I asked him if he knew who I was. And you know what he said to me?"

Bob McMahon had two marshals in his office, Carl Webster and Lester Crowe, who was in his late forties now, both sitting across the desk from their boss. Lester Crowe was the marshal who'd come out to the Webster place with McMahon, that time Carl shot the man stealing his cows some years ago.

"This fella walks in the police chief's office with two .45s hanging on him, a Justice badge pinned on his lapel. He says to Fausto Bassi, 'You know who I am?' Fausto's okay, he's smart but a little too easygoing, has a belly on him. He says, 'Yes, you're Nestor Lott. We have you down for a triple homicide and seven attempted, over at Osage Mining. Why don't you sit down while we wait for the judge to sign the warrants?' Just his woman clerk's in the office at the time. She says Nestor and this local fella with him pull their guns, Nestor both of his, and lock the chief and her in a jail cell, and they drive off. This was yesterday afternoon."

Lester Crowe said, "If the chief knows who he is, knows he's wanted and the man's standing there in his office—"

McMahon cut him off saying, "I guess he didn't think Nestor'd pull on him."

"I'd of arrested him he's walking in the door," Lester said. Lester was smoking a cigaret, tapping the ash in the cuff of his pants. He had told Carl one time it kept out the moths.

"I called Justice," McMahon said, "after the mine shooting to check on Nestor. I find out they're thinking of changing their name from the United States Bureau of Investigation to the Federal Bureau of Investigation, or, the FBI."

Lester said, "It should be the FB *of* I."

"It's their bureau," McMahon said, "they can call it what they want. That lint picker J. Edgar Hoover's still running it."

"I've seen him," Lester said. "He's a slick article but acts like he's got some old-woman in him."

"They called back this morning to say Nestor Lott's no longer an agent. They had trouble with him in Georgia, shooting moonshiners he didn't have to, and fired him. All you boys have to do is arrest him for impersonating a federal officer. But now I'm thinking once you get him, hand him over to the county prosecutor. I think shooting the miners will be enough to get him electrocuted. You won't have to fuss with him over wearing the badge."

Lester said, "He's hiding someplace?"

"He's raiding places that sell liquor," McMahon said. "Nestor and about fifty of his spooks, these Klansmen he calls his Christian Avengers. All Fausto and the cops can do is watch."

Lester said, "Well, if selling booze is against the law—"

"For Christ sake," McMahon said, "I want you to arrest the man and hand him over to the county. Can you do that without arguing about it?"

"I just want it clear in my mind," Lester said, "who's who." As they got up he said to Carl, "You can drive this trip. Put a Thompson in the trunk, case Nestor wants to make something of it."

Carl was aware of Bob McMahon watching them. He didn't say anything now and neither did Carl. Carl never had much to do with Lester Crowe but listen to him talk.

Bob says he don't want me arguing with him. Was I arguing? I said if this man Nestor Lott is closing down speakeasies he's upholding the law, isn't he? Whether he's impersonating a federal officer or not. Am I right on that? You're damn tootin'."

Carl was falling asleep driving the two-door Chevrolet the hundred miles of farmland and hills thick with redbud trees, from Tulsa down to Krebs, listening to Lester talk.

"We're suppose to arrest this guy for pinning a badge on his chest while he's doing what his job was before the operators fired him and he had the coal miners shot? Bob seems to think he'll burn for it. Oh, is that right? How about leaving it to a court of law?"

Carl was wondering if he'd see Louly Brown again. If he'd be back in Tulsa while she was there for her interview.

"There's nothing simple about a marshal's job," Lester said. "Apprehend wanted fugitives. It sounds simple. But what's a fugitive? A person wanted by the law who flees or escapes. Has Nestor Lott run away? No, he's down there making raids on people breaking the law."

Carl was looking at Louly Brown in his mind, her red hair, thinking she wouldn't be too young for him if she was twenty. But she might still be in her teens. He had seen her date of birth but couldn't remember it now. He believed it was 1912.

Lester was telling Carl about Lake Okeechobee now, in Florida, where he was from originally, this giant lake thirty miles long and only six feet deep, like a huge saucer, alligators in it, and some of the finest bass fishing in the whole country.

"The hurricane of twenty-eight, a hunnert and fifty mile an hour wind blew the lake over the muck dike and killed eighteen hunnert and thirty-eight folks."

He said he was thinking of going back there.

Carl was still thinking of Louly Brown.

They came to Krebs and met with the chief of police in his office. The first thing Lester wanted to know, why in hell hadn't Fausto picked up Nestor and thrown him in jail.

"Because he has more men than I do," Fausto said. "All those bogey-men in bedsheets who enjoy shooting their guns."

Lester wanted to know what in hell the county sheriff was doing about the situation. "Some convicts ran away from a road gang," Fausto said, "and the sheriff is out with his dogs. His favorite thing."

Lester decided what they'd do. He'd stay in town with the Thomp-son, wait for Nestor to hit a speakeasy still open, here or some other coal town to the east. Carl'd go out to the roadhouse the chief told them about. Lester said, "Fella runs it use to be in the Emmett Long gang."

Carl didn't say anything.

7

The night before the raid on the roadhouse Nestor told his Avengers at the rickety church, "I want us to come at them out of the sun, first light shining hard on the window glass as we roll up on the place. They don't hear us, they're dead to the world from boozin' all night. They open their eyes to squint out the window, they don't even see us till we're spread across the front of the place. Twelve cars or more with .30-30s, a case of Austin Powder, caps, fuses, as I announce to them with the bullhorn, 'Come out with your hands in the air or get blown to hell. Bring your whores out into the light of day.' You set your torches afire and advance on the house."

These people loved their torches. They said you bet, that's how to do it, run the scalawags out of the county.

The next morning it was still dark when Nestor got to the church with his canteen of coffee laced with brandy, something he'd picked up in France during the war. It started him thinking of that time sixteen years ago, moving out of the village of Bousheres to take the woods, and how he had to keep his men moving in the howl of German artillery splintering trees, pounding out shell holes to bury them under mounds of earth. His officers had said the French command were idiots, we'd never make it to the woods. Except the Frogs were running this side of the war and if they said take the woods, even if you might get your legs blown off or your voice burned out by mustard gas, you took your men to the woods. Nestor had stood in the open waving his big revolver, the Webley he'd taken off a dead British officer some time before, waved it screaming at his men to come on, keep moving, threatening to shoot anybody pretending to be hit or trying to hide. He did, too, shot three of them looking right at him, and the rest ran across the field, most to get mowed down by machine-gun fire. Nestor lost more men that summer than any platoon sergeant in the Seventh Infantry and was given a medal for valor.

He wore it this morning, his Distinguished Service Cross, pinned to the breast pocket of his suitcoat, below the bureau shield on his lapel, waiting from dawn till going on eight o'clock before all his Avengers had straggled in. The late ones saying well, shit, they had their chores, didn't they? Or their wife was sick or their dog got run over. Nestor finally had twelve cars here counting his De Soto, a couple of men in some, no more than four in the others, thirty-four Avengers all told.

Except now the sky was overcast, no way to come riding out of the sun. Shit. But as long as they were here, armed and ready, Nestor said, "Hell, let's get her done."

Carl Webster arrived the night before.

He walked in the roadhouse and up to Jack Belmont at the bar, only a few miners down the shiny length drinking.

"You having a slow night?"

It turned Jack around and he had to look toward the door to see who else was coming in. He recognized Carl Webster in his panama, couldn't be anyone else.

"You raiding the place by yourself?"

"I'm not the one does that," Carl said.

He let the ex-convict son of a multimillionaire stare at him not knowing what was going on. Like the girls at the table in kimonos and playsuits were staring with raised eyebrows, waiting. Carl recognized a couple of them from a house in Seminole and took time to touch the brim of his hat to them.

Jack Belmont was squinting now, trying to focus on what this marshal was doing here.

"Don't tell me—you came to try to arrest me."

"I wouldn't mind," Carl said, "but I haven't seen your name on a warrant since Emmett Long passed on. You aren't a big enough name with the Marshals Service."

That caused Jack Belmont to have to think of something. He said, "Then you must've come in for a drink."

"I don't mind," Carl said.

He watched Jack Belmont motion to the bartender who brought a couple of shot glasses over and filled them up. Carl raised his and took a sip, gave Jack a nod and finished the shot. He said, "I don't raid stills or liquor joints, but you know a fella's been doing it around here. I imagine it's why you don't have too many customers this evening. Nobody wants to get shot over a glass of whiskey."

Jack said, "You're talking about Nestor Lott."

"That's the one. He comes by, I'll be here to put him in jail." He saw Jack Belmont frowning now. "For pretending he's a government agent," Carl said. "You aren't allowed to do that, even if you think it's for the national welfare. Stop men from getting drunk and beating up on their wives."

Jack said, "You want another?"

"I don't mind. He's got those Klan dimwits running around shooting people."

"You think he's coming here?"

"Sooner or later, seeing as you're in violation of the Volstead Act."

The bartender filled their glasses and Carl drank his.

Jack said, "You come here by yourself—you think you can stop him?"

"You're gonna help me," Carl said.

Jack watched this marshal in his dark suit and nifty panama roam the place looking out windows. Over at the table with the girls now, talking to them, acting like he knew Violet and Elodie. Jesus, he even knew Heidi, Heidi running up to him with a big grin. Now they were hugging each other like they were sweethearts. This marshal must've spent some time in Seminole at the whorehouse. Else he'd arrested them for prostitution, got to know them that way. But would they be glad to see him?

Carl Webster was not like any officer of the law Jack had ever met—with their official way of speaking, never smiling at anything you said was funny.

Now he was at the bar with Norm Dilworth having another drink, talking like they were pals. Talking about Emmett Long or prison most likely, the marshal knowing what Norm had been doing with his life. Jack stepped up to the bar to join them.

They were talking about guns.

Norm coming right out to tell him he had his own Winchester, his favorite gun, a couple of revolvers, .38s, and a double-barrel scatter gun. Now he was saying Jack was the one had the guns.

Carl turned to him. "Is that right?"

Jack hesitated, a government cop asking him something like that.

But then Norm said, "Jack brought a few hunting rifles to pass around and a Thompson submachine gun he bought off a guard at the prison. Case some gang tries to take over the business. Come down from Kansas City or Chicago. I wish I'd had it when Nestor Lott raided my speak. He come in shooting, killed my bartender standing with his hands in the air. One of the miners yelled at him, said something in Italian, and he got shot too, for no reason. A whole crowd of KKKers come in wearing their bedsheets and got busy busting the place up, smashing bottles . . . But you know they took a few with 'em."

Carl said, "He didn't put you in jail?"

"I slipped out while they were busy."

Carl kept facing Norm. "How many men you have here?"

It irritated Jack. He said, "We got enough."

But now Norm was telling him two bartenders, two bouncers, a couple of colored boys, one of 'em cooks. "I never asked did they know how to shoot, the two being colored. The maids don't come till morning. With us three that's seven I know of can use a gun. And Heidi, that makes eight. I know my wife can shoot, I saw her."

"No kidding," Carl said, "you two are married?" Carl grinning at the hayseed. "You got a smart girl there's had a hard life."

Jesus Christ, now his grin irritated Jack. Talking about a whore like she was some sweet girl lived down the road. He said to Carl, "You must know Heidi pretty well."

"We've talked a couple of times."

Jack said, "After you screwed her?"

Carl stared at him without a trace of what he was thinking on his face. He said, "You can be a mean bugger, huh? Nobody pays attention to you."

"I'm talking about when she worked in a cat house," Jack said, "in Seminole." He turned to Norm saying, "I don't mean since you got married. You understand that, don't you?" Norm seemed to nod his head and Jack felt he was okay, being an honest Injun and said, "I mean, after all, she was a whore at that time, wasn't she?"

Carl said, "Norm, does he run this place?"

Jack looked at Norm.

Norm saying, "He acts like it. What I think he does mostly is sniff around Heidi. If he's what she wants, I don't need her no more. But she hasn't said nothing."

"That's not my business," Carl said. "You tell him what Nestor's like?"

"I sure did."

Jesus Christ—talking about him, Jack standing only a couple of feet away.

"What'd he say?"

"Said don't worry about it."

"Means he can handle Nestor?"

"Beats me."

Jack looking from Carl to Norm and back again.

Carl saying, "Why doesn't he want me to help him?"

"He's a spoiled kid," Norm said, "thinks he's smart. But hasn't had an idea yet for making money that's worked. I'm the one said let's get in the whiskey business."

"What do you stay with him for? Find an oil patch'll hire you and get a regular job. You know how this life ends."

"Dead or in the clink," Norm said. "I been thinking about drawing my cut, take Heidi out of here before she gets in trouble."

Jack's eyes moved from Norm as he mentioned Heidi to Carl.

Carl saying, "Where's the Thompson? You ever fire it?"

Norm shook his head.

"Get it, I'll show you how it works."

Norm said, "You want a drink first?"

Carl said, "I don't mind."

They both turned to the bar.

Jack got into it saying, "Listen, I did tell Norm don't worry about us getting raided."

Carl Webster looked around, his elbow on the bar.

"I thought I'd pay a fine," Jack said, "and we'd be back in business, the way I heard it works. You say we can defend ourselves, that's different. Let's get out the guns."

"We'll take care of it," Carl said. He turned to the bar and picked up his whiskey.

Jack waited. He wanted to yell at them to look at him, goddamn it. It was like when his mom and dad used to argue about what to do with him and he's standing there listening, looking from one to the other. His mom saying he was a spoiled brat, the same as Norm Dilworth did. What took Jack by surprise, Norm thinking he was fooling around with Heidi. He never believed Norm was wary or smart enough to notice anything going on. Then Norm saying there hadn't been an idea of his yet that worked, and was thinking of pulling out, taking his cut and leaving.

All right, this Nestor, pretending to be a government agent, he'd come on a raid or he wouldn't. He came, it would be all right to shoot him. Good. That didn't seem to be a problem. But Norm Dilworth leaving, taking Heidi with him, was something Jack would have to get busy on.

Nestor, still at the church this morning but ready to go, had pictured his twelve cars of Avengers spread across the front of the roadhouse, facing it, but changed his plan.

These whiskey people were criminals and would be armed. It was too late now to sneak up on them. They start firing they'd shoot holes in the radiators and the cars would sit there after, useless till they were repaired.

The way to do it, come down the road from the highway and pull up one behind the other on the shoulder. There'd be the ditch to cross and then the parking lot, about 150 feet of hardpack to the roadhouse, open ground, shouldn't be more than a few cars parked there this morning. He'd use the bullhorn, give the whiskey people time to come out. They didn't, he'd send his Avengers to advance across the open yard in their robes, holding up their torches.

Nestor had watched these men fire their rifles and picked out the ones who'd shot and killed three of the striking coal miners: the Wycliff brothers, aggressive young punks, and a fella name of Ed Hagenlocker Jr. that everybody called Son, born of some tramp his daddy had been seeing at the time. Son liked to brag his old man was now married to a woman name of Sylvia who was the widowed mother of Pretty Boy Floyd's girlfriend, Louly Brown. "A cute girl," Son Hagenlocker said. "I can see why Pretty Boy'd want to get on top of her."

Nestor issued these three Springfield army rifles from his personal store and would keep these boys close to him, the Wycliff brothers and Son, all dead shots, on the road behind the cars. He'd send the thirty Avengers toward the roadhouse in three waves, spread out, walking toward the front entrance with their torches.

They'd likely get shot at and some would go down. Well, in any action you had to expect taking casualties. At the Somme in 1916, during the Great War, the British Expeditionary Force lost 58,000 men in one day. Second battle of the Marne, 12,000 American boys were killed during the assault. Hell, from July to November the British counted 310,000 casualties trying to take Passchendaele during the Ypres offensive, and the town wasn't even that important. It's what happened in war, men got killed.

———

Tony Antonelli was pretty sure there'd be shooting, mortal wounds suffered, and he'd get to call it "The Bloody Bald Mountain War." He could open the story with:

"It began with an imposter named Nestor Lott, a cold-blooded killer who wore a .45 automatic on each hip, a man who had no regard for human life. Nestor Lott had been dismissed by the Department of Justice as a special agent, but chose to continue his mission, not simply to close speakeasies but to destroy—"

No, first he'd have to tell about Nestor being hired by the coal operators to break the strike. How he got the Klan to help him. How they shot and killed three Italian miners, wounded seven others—

Or save the strike stuff, put it in further down in the story and concentrate on the raid in the opening with Nestor Lott the key figure, responsible for the shoot-out that ensued.

He could even call it that, "Shoot-out at Bald Mountain."

That would be perfect, if the roadhouse was called the Bald Mountain something or other, club, resort. On the title page a photo of the roadhouse with the sign prominently displayed. Where, when the gun smoke cleared, saw—put in the number of men lying dead. Tony had been out there a couple of times and met Jack Belmont and the girls—one in particular, Elodie, catching his eye—but *damn* if he could remember if there was a sign in front.

Tony got there before Nestor and the Klansmen arrived. Earlier, he'd been told something was going on at the Pentacostal church on the edge of town, went out there and saw them getting ready and had a chance to speak to a Klansman named Ed Hagenlocker Jr., who told him what was going on and didn't mind Tony writing his name in the notebook. He had talked to Ed Jr. once in Krebs—where everybody called him Son—Son telling where he was from and about his dad being married to Louly Brown's mother. This time Son told him they'd either blow up the roadhouse or set their torches to it, burn the liquor place to the ground.

Right after this Tony drove out to Bald Mountain that was all dark trees and not bald anywhere that he could see, rising behind the roadhouse. He pulled up in front and said, "Nuts." There wasn't a sign on it that said Bald Mountain or any name at all. No cars here either, and he realized his Ford Coupé could be in the middle of the action, end up with bullet holes in it. Tony drove around back to see six cars parked in the yard in a row facing the back of the place, Tony assuming they belonged to Belmont and people who worked for him and didn't want their cars shot up. Tony left his car and walked around to the front. So far he hadn't seen a soul or any sign of life.

Not until he walked in the barroom, empty in dull morning light, and one of the bouncers appeared out of the back of the room and went behind the bar. Tony watched him reach underneath and come up with a revolver in each hand he laid on the bar. Now he set up a bottle of whiskey and a glass and poured a generous double shot. The bouncer's name was Walter. Not Wally, Walter. He saw Tony standing in the middle of the room and said, "We're closed."

It was in Tony's mind to say, *You better be,* but kept quiet. If they didn't know Nestor was coming and he said anything about it, he'd be intruding on the natural passage of events; he'd be putting himself in the story and have to explain why he tipped them off, these people selling liquor illegally. He didn't think *True Detective* would go for it.

Tony had asked Walter one time how he became a bouncer. Walter said he'd worked in oil fields and liked to get into fistfights. He was a big boy in his thirties, two hundred pounds or more on a Charles Atlas kind of build. Had a neck on him like a tree trunk and never smiled, nothing Walter thought was ever funny.

Now a man about fifty was coming down from upstairs putting on his suitcoat, his necktie hanging loose. Down the staircase Belmont must've picked up at an estate sale, once in the home of some guy who went out his office window in '29. Tony could check, find out where they got the stairway. Or write it assuming that could easily have been the situation, lot of it had been going on. Tony watched the guy go to the bar and pick up the whiskey waiting for him. He could be a lawyer or somebody in the oil business. Tony wondered if the man had been with Elodie. The times he was here before he'd seen her sitting in that plush area toward the back of the room, an arrangement of uphol-stered pieces, chairs and settees done in red damask to show off the whores. Elodie could be this man's favorite, spent the night with her while his wife thought he was in Tulsa. It got Tony wondering about Elodie, if she'd be all right when Nestor came on his raid—and my God, there she was.

Coming down the stairs in her pink kimono, her dark hair pinned up. The man at the bar raised his glass and she stepped over to give him a peck on the cheek. But now she was coming this way, the sweet girl, with a worried look on her face, Tony wishing more than anything in the world she wasn't a whore.

She offered her hands and he took them saying, "Where's everybody?"

"Busy," Elodie said. "You shouldn't be here."

He wanted to tell her, *You shouldn't either*. He wanted to ask her to leave right now, run away with him and quit being a whore. But what he said was, "I saw them. Nestor and the Klan are on their way."

Jack Belmont was sitting on the side of the bed with Violet, his hand on her bare knee with her white shorts hiked up, his Winchester on the windowsill across the room, pointing out, a revolver on the floor over there.

Carl Webster appeared in the bedroom doorway.

"I don't see you're paying much attention."

"I'll hear their cars, won't I?"

"What if they leave 'em down the road?"

"I'm just getting a cigaret."

Violet put one between her lips, struck a kitchen match to light the cigaret and handed it to Jack. Violet had dark shiny hair and was maybe the best looking of the girls, Carl might say a beauty; he believed she had some Creek in her. Violet reminded him of a thin Narcissa Raincrow, his dad's housekeeper he slept with every night, only Violet was better looking. Carl now favored redheads with pure white skin and brown eyes; though he'd have to admit he liked Crystal Davidson's blonde hair, the way it was marcelled. Crystal was a few years older than Carl, while Louly Brown was a good five years younger but seemed grown up, the little girl with the cute smile who'd shot a wanted fugitive.

He said to Jack Belmont, "You don't fire less I tell you."

Carl walked a few strides along the upstairs hall to the next bedroom where Norm Dilworth was crouched at the front window with the Thompson, a 1921 model with a buttstock attached and a drum that held a hundred rounds of .45s. Norm had a pair of binoculars on the floor next to him. Heidi was stretched out on the bed, her head raised on pillows. She saw Carl and said, "Norm, Carl's here." That's all. She was quiet this morning, like Norm'd had a talk with her last night. Heidi had on a playsuit with bell-bottoms that looked Mexican to Carl. A .38 lay on the quilt next to her thigh.

Carl said to Norm, "You fire for range?"

"I lay it on the sill and get down behind it, these two nails holding it? It's set on the road."

"They could drive in."

"I raise up, keep the barrel on the sill."

It wasn't a minute later they heard a girl's voice yelling something, sounding like it was coming from the stairs.

The voice brought Heidi upright on the bed. "Lord, that's Elodie. Something's wrong."

Now they heard her in the hall and Carl stepped out of the bedroom to see Elodie coming toward him wide-eyed saying, *"Tony saw them— they're on their way."*

Carl stopped her, resting his hand on her shoulder.

"Who's Tony?"

"The writer," Elodie said, sounding out of breath.

"I don't think I know him," Carl said. But there he was coming along the hall in a hurry, an eager young guy in a suit, a full head of combed hair. Carl said, "Who're you with, one of the newspapers?"

Now he looked surprised saying, "I write feature stories for *True Detective.*"

"No kidding," Carl said. "That's a good magazine."

"You read it?"

"When I get a chance."

They heard Norm in the room yell out, "Carl, they're here!" And yelled Carl's name again while Carl stood in the hall with Tony Antonelli.

He said, "You the one gonna interview Louly Brown in Tulsa, at the Mayo Hotel?"

Tony said, "How'd you know that?"

"I'll tell you right now," Carl said, "she isn't Charley Floyd's girl-friend or ever was. So don't ask her."

———

Tony followed the marshal into the bedroom, Carl Webster in person, here, to meet Nestor Lott and his Klansmen. Tony couldn't believe it. He'd try to stay close to him.

They could see the cars coming in from the highway, about a quarter of a mile to the road and turning into it, one behind the other coming past the woods that stood at the north end of the property. Now they were slowing to a stop, closing up almost bumper to bumper across the front of the yard, Norm saying, "The lead car's Nestor's, the De Soto. There he is getting out. See him?"

Carl said, "He's a little fella, huh?"

Tony said, "This is the first time you've seen him?"

Heidi, standing over Norm, was in the way. Carl Webster moved her aside and said, "Go tell Jack not to fire till I tell him. I want to see how Nestor wants to work it."

Heidi left in a hurry, not saying a word, and now Norm asked, "What's that he's holding?"

"A bullhorn," Carl said.

Tony got out his notebook and started writing, describing Nestor standing in the road behind his dark blue De Soto four-door sedan. Now two more with army rifles joining him. Now a third one, also with a Springfield coming out of the car and Tony said, "I know that one, he's called Son. He says his dad's married to the mother of Pretty Boy Floyd's girlfriend, Louly Brown?" Tony stopped as Carl turned to look at him, but then said, "I can't help what he says, can I?"

"He doesn't know what he's talking about," Carl said. "Write that in your notebook."

Tony wrote: "The marshal doesn't raise his voice but has an amazing presence (command?) and you want to believe what he says, even though he's still young. Wearing a navy blue two-piece suit, pressed. Maybe a sixth sense telling him this would be a memorable day. Impossible to tell where he carries his gun, a Colt .38 with a six-inch barrel. No hat this morning, the well-publicized panama he was wearing when he shot Emmett Long."

Carl picked up Norm's binoculars and studied the row of cars. "The ones sitting in there are wearing their robes, but not the three with Nestor. They're his shooters. Keep both your eyes on them. Nestor's wearing his old shield and a military decoration. It means this squirt was in the Great War, been in battle."

They heard a static sound from the bullhorn Nestor raised to his face.

Carl said, "Norm, put your sights on the last car." It's rear end was no more than ten feet from the edge of the woods. "That's where you'll start. Nestor's gonna give us five minutes to come out with our hands up or he'll . . . do whatever he feels like. As soon as he starts to talk rake those cars left to right across the tires, your finger stuck on the trigger. Get to his and stop. Let's see what they do."

Norm rested his front sight on the right rear tire of the last car.

Nestor said, "I'm giving you people five minutes—"

And Norm raked that line of coupés and sedans, the Thompson chattering from one end to the other, Carl watching through the glasses, Tony hunching his shoulders at the racket filling the room.

"You rose up on the two middle cars," Carl said. "I think you might've hit the ones inside."

"It got away from me," Norm said.

"Yeah, I can see blood on their robes. They're getting out the other side." Reporting it in a natural tone of voice while Tony made notes, seeing Klansmen piling out of the cars on the off-side to crouch behind them.

Now firing was coming from the next room, Jack Belmont snapping off shots. Carl lowered the glasses to look at Heidi.

"Go tell him I said to quit shooting."

Heidi ran to the other front bedroom to see Jack and Violet at the window, Jack firing at the cars. Heidi pushed Violet aside.

"The marshal says to quit shooting."

Jack said, "He did, huh?" levered the Winchester and fired another round before turning to look at Heidi.

She said, "He wants to see what they're gonna do next."

"They're armed," Jack said. "Ask him what he thinks they're gonna do."

Nestor was standing, looking over the De Soto's hood toward the roadhouse. Now he turned to the Klansmen hugging the ground behind their cars, all those white bedsheets that looked like piles of wash dumped in the road, a few pointed tops with eyeholes rising now to look through their car windows at the roadhouse. The Wycliff brothers and Son looked up at Nestor showing himself, hands on his hips, hat down on his eyes, looked at each other and got to their feet.

Nestor said to the Klansmen, "What's wrong with you? Come on, get up. They weren't trying to hit anybody, they're shooting at the tires."

A Klansmman said, "They's some here got shot."

"'Cause these people don't know how to fire a Thompson submachine gun. You got to hold her down," Nestor said. "I'm telling you they weren't trying to hit anybody, those boys got shot by accident. Come on, get out your torches and light 'em up. Cock your pistols and stick 'em in your pants, in front like I told you. I want to see you all advance on that position like nothing's gonna stop you. They see fire coming at 'em they'll panic, throw up their hands and run. I guarantee."

orm said, "Carl? They're lighting torches. See 'em? Coming out from between the cars, across the ditch—"

"Lay it down in front of 'em," Carl said. "They'll stop and think about it." He watched them forming a line, ten across with their torches, holding them high. Carl thinking, Like the nitwit is saying, here, shoot me in the chest.

Norm, on his knees, raised the stock of the Thompson, getting the front sight on the middle of the yard.

Now another row of Klansmen was coming from between the cars with their torches, forming behind the first row.

Counting the ones still hiding back of the cars, Carl decided there were about thirty of them. He said to Norm, "Lay it down."

Norm fired left to right and with the clatter they watched the dirt kicked up about ten feet in front of the leading row, stopping them in their tracks, confused, pulling revolvers, turning into one another with their torches blazing, turning to Nestor behind his car.

Norm was grinning, watching them come near setting one another on fire. He said, "They don't know whether to piss or run home, do they?"

hey aren't a hundred feet away," Jack Belmont said, "and he can't hit 'em? I should've kept the Thompson." He raised the Winchester and sighted against the black cross on a Klansman's chest, telling himself, Your first one. Take a breath and hold it, start to let it out . . .

"I think Carl just wants to stop them," Heidi said. "It looks like it did. They don't know what to do. Look at 'em." She was crouched next to Jack on the floor, holding the revolver he had given her.

Jack fired and saw the Klansman knocked off his feet, the torch flying. "Got him."

He levered and fired.

"Got him."

Levered and fired.

"Another one. Shit, this is like fish in a barrel."

Levered and fired.

"How many's that?"

Levered and fired and handed the Winchester to Heidi. "You counting? Keep track while you load that for me." He took the revolver she was holding and the one on the floor by his knee and fired one and then the other at arm's length, moving his head from gun to gun, fired at the cars and the bedsheets squeezing between them. "Now they're running across the road. Look, they're out in that pasture, some cows grazing there." Jack raised the revolvers and fired at them long range until he heard the guns click empty.

Heidi said, "Jack," touching his shoulder.

"Let me have the rifle."

"I didn't load it," Heidi said. "Carl's here."

Jack turned to Carl above him looking out the open window at the Klansmen lying in the yard, none of them moving. Tony, his notebook open, was standing next to him.

Carl said, "I told you to quit shooting."

Jack said, "You did? I must not've heard you. I know I got those seven out there, maybe a couple more. I fired at some I could see through the car windows, and they took off across the pasture over there. I fired a few shots at them."

"You hit a cow," Heidi said. "See the one like it's limping? Look, quick, now it's lying down. I think you killed it."

"I have to admit," Jack said, "firing at those bedsheets was like a shooting gallery, but I stopped them, didn't I? Heidi says she lost count." He looked up again at Carl Webster. "How many is it you've shot in your life? Just the four I've heard of?"

Carl, staring out the window, didn't answer him, Nestor on his mind.

Now Tony looked at the line of cars, steam rising out of a couple of their radiators, and made a note of it.

Carl said, "Where's Nestor?"

Jack looked out the window.

"Running, I imagine."

Carl said, "The ones in the pasture are all wearing robes."

"Then he's still behind the cars."

Tony got ready to speak as Carl said, "And the three boys with him? They didn't run. And if they're not lying out in the yard, where are they?"

It was quiet outside and in the room that smelled of gunpowder. Tony made a note of it and said, "I caught a glimpse of Nestor and those three—the ones with army rifles?—sneaking along behind the cars while Jack was shooting. They got to that last car and, I'm pretty sure they ducked into the trees."

Again it was quiet until Carl said, "So they're still around. Good."

8

They followed the marshal downstairs, Norm with the Thompson under his arm, Jack behind him, a revolver in each hand, Jack thinking how easy it would be to raise one of the .38s and shoot Norm in the back of the head, stick the barrel in that thatch of dark hair. Stumble against him as he fired and say oh my God, it was an accident. Jack felt good and said to Heidi over his shoulder, "I want it known I didn't shoot any cow."

She was carrying his Winchester and said, "I saw you, you did it on purpose."

"It must've stepped in a hole, why it fell down."

He felt like talking, proud of himself shooting those dumbbells coming with their torches. Wasn't anything to it. Lever and fire and watch them get knocked off their feet. He'd have to wait for the right time to get Norm, now wanting Norm looking at him when he did it. He wouldn't mind getting the drop on Nestor Lott and plug him, too.

Carl had the two bouncers with revolvers and pick handles at the front windows downstairs, on either side of the entrance, guys Norm had hired: Walter the fistfighter and the other one they called Boo, who'd been in a storage tank fire and was lucky to get out alive. From his left profile Boo could be taken for William Boyd, the movie star. He turned his head and Carl saw his right ear had been burnt off, the skin on his face red and shiny. One eye was gone and he wore smoked glasses day and night to hide his disfigurement.

Carl had the feeling he knew him. Not since he was in the fire, before that, up to a year ago. And had the feeling Boo was watching him, biding his time. He asked Norm what Boo's name was.

Norm said, "Billy Bragg. I hired him, he was selling whiskey his brother made, up in the Cookson Hills."

Carl was nodding. "I knew the brother, Peyton Bragg."

"You arrest him one time?"

"I shot him."

The two Negroes watched the back of the place from the kitchen, Franklin Madison and his grown son James, by an Indian woman. Carl had spoken to Franklin last night, learned the man had served on a frontier station out west and in Cuba in '98, the same war Virgil had fought in. Franklin had been married to a Chiricahua Apache woman, the daughter of a reservation jumper who'd been shipped to Oklahoma with Geronimo and that crowd. It gave them more things they had in common to talk about. Carl telling Franklin his grandmother was Northern Cheyenne, giving him some Indian blood. Franklin telling about the fight at Las Guásimas in Cuba where the Tenth saved Teddy Roosevelt's Rough Riders after he'd marched them into a jackpot. Carl had listened to him last night and got rifles for Franklin and James.

Outbuildings stood along the back of the property, what looked like a pump house, a tractor shed, a chicken house, then a thicket full of scrub standing behind the structures that became dense with redbud as the hill rose to Bald Mountain. Then, in the middle of the lot, the line of seven cars parked facing the house.

Carl said to Franklin, "You ever get a look at this Nestor Lott?"

Franklin said no, but he'd heard the man was evil, had those coal miners shot.

"He could sneak up behind the cars out there." They stood a good sixty feet from the back of the house. "I'll bet anything," Carl said, "Nestor won't want to go home till he's settled this."

"He's still here," Franklin said, "you won't have to track him."

Carl judged Franklin's age as close to seventy, a mostly bald black man with a sprinkle of white stubble over his jaw. They stood on either side of the kitchen window looking out at the yard, sunlight had given the cars a shine, but the sky closed in and now rain was coming down.

Franklin said, "What about the dead people in front? I know they ain't going nowhere, but was it all right to shoot 'em like that?"

"I have to phone Tulsa," Carl said, "ask my boss about it. I came here with another marshal, but I don't know where he is, or what he's doing."

Franklin said, "What if the sheriff come along?"

"Then the county'll look into it. The coroner will say those fools out there died of gunshot wounds, making it official. Then the county prosecutor will want to know who shot them, maybe have Jack Belmont brought up on manslaughter. That's if the Klansmen want to testify. But if they shouldn't be here in the first place, maybe they won't say anything. If the judge is in the Klan, that's something else."

"Will you appear?"

"If they charge Belmont."

"What if they don't?"

"Then I'll take him to Tulsa," Carl said, "and get him charged with *some*thing."

Carl glanced at the *True Detective* writer standing in the kitchen doorway. Tony waiting until Carl finished before saying, "You won't be able to make your call, they cut the telephone line. I tried it a minute ago."

Carl said, "So he's close by."

"You sound like it pleases you," Franklin said. He called out, "James?" And told his son to come in here.

Carl watched Franklin talking to him, James nodding, Franklin giving him an old converted Navy Colt from out of a kitchen drawer, winking at Carl. Now James took off his shirt. He walked through the bar to slip out the front in the cold rain.

"Gonna see if he can locate Nestor," Franklin said.

"He can do it," Carl said, "without getting shot?"

"James knows tricks from his mama's people," Franklin said. "How to stand almost in plain sight and you don't see him."

Nestor had picked Son to work around through the woods to where the telephone wire came out from the house. "Shimmy up the pole with a knife in your teeth, boy, and cut the wire, so they can't call anybody for help."

Son came back to the tractor shed with his arms skinned but had done the job.

Nestor looked out of the shed now to see the rain coming down hard to wash the cars parked back there and turn the yard dark. Man oh man, perfect. He could start making his move, not have to wait till night.

All three boys had been patient so far. Now they were acting restless and would voice their anger over the dead lying out front. Or they were putting it on, wanting to start shooting. Son telling him, "They's two of 'em show theirselves at that window," and raised his rifle to draw a bead. Nestor had to tell him to keep his pants on while he worked out what they'd do. How he'd set it up to take every last person in there.

One of the Wycliffs said, "Some of 'em's women."

"Whores," Nestor said.

Son was afraid somebody'd come along the road and see the bodies. Nestor said, "And keep driving, not wanting any parts of this business. Or going by they might only see the cars parked along the shoulder." But the boy was right, they had to get her done pretty soon. He said to the Wycliff brothers, "You two think you could sneak out there, see if anybody left the key in their car?"

You bet they could, and slipped out of the shed to slither through the weeds, the cars between them and the back of the house. Watching them through a space between the boards, Nestor said, "You know their Christian names?"

All Son knew they was Wycliffs. Him and the brothers had never been close, other than when they were out burning crosses or throwing rocks at the Eyetalians, over in Sans Souci Park, the Eyetalians celebrating Mt. Carmel Day, whatever that was.

Nestor said, "Those boys must've fallen off the turnip truck, but they sure can shoot."

The Wycliffs came back to the tractor shed soaking wet and grinning at Nestor. Yeah, the Ford Coupé on the end and that black car right in the middle of the row both had keys in them. Nestor, pressed to the slit between the boards, said, "I believe it's a thirty-three Packard, the new one. Has that sporty look, a spare tire on each side. You know what they say, 'Ask the man who owns one.' I bet a dollar it's Jack Belmont's, but I ain't asking him nothing."

One of the Wycliffs said, "We gonna ride off in the Packard?"

Nestor said, "Hell no, we gonna bust in the house with it."

He had all three of the boys grinning at him now.

Jack Belmont wondered what they were waiting for, standing around in the semidark, Heidi next to him reloading his guns and placing them on the bar. The other girls were upstairs, the bartenders watching over them, and seeing what they could see from the windows.

"You want to tell me what we're doing?"

Speaking to Carl at the front entrance with the two bouncers, Carl holding one of the doors open, waiting for James to appear out of the mist. He said to Jack, "It's Nestor's call."

Jack held up his pocket watch trying to catch some light from the windows. "I can't even read my goddamn watch. He don't come pretty soon, I'm leaving. We aren't doing any business, those dead fools lying in the yard. I mean it, he don't start something, I quit. Come back when the sun's out."

Carl said, "You're going to Tulsa with me. You and that two-gun midget, if I can work it."

"You gonna arrest me? For what?" Like he couldn't believe it.

"There's seven people lying dead outside."

"Jesus Christ, what're you talking about—they're gonna burn down my place I didn't stop 'em. You saw 'em, with their goddamn torches?" Sounding a bit frantic and had to calm himself down. Trying to think of a way to do Norm—counting on Nestor starting a gunfight to give him the chance—and now the goddamn marshal wanted to arrest him. Saying if he could work it. *Telling* him that. He glanced at Norm sitting on the stairs with his Winchester now across his knees. Then turned to Carl at the front door.

Carl pushing it open and Jack saw the colored boy, James, come in with his old-fashioned Colt pistol, hair lying flat on his head, his body glistening wet. Jack watched James give Carl a nod and now the two of them were walking past him, going to the kitchen.

Jack followed behind saying, "You hear what I said? They're coming after *me,* with no right to do it's why I shot 'em. You know that."

The marshal didn't comment on it.

In the kitchen James laid his pistol on the counter by the window where Franklin handed him a dish towel. James dried his face before looking up at Carl. "I see these two come in the thicket from the lot, like they been up to the house."

Franklin was shaking his head. "I'd of seen 'em."

"Now the other two come out of the shed," James said, "and they all behind it, the little fella with the pistolas on him asking the two questions. I can't hear what they saying, but the little fella, he seem pleased by what they told him."

Franklin said it again, "They came up to the house I'd of seen 'em."

"Or they were looking at the cars," Carl said, "see who might've left a key."

Jack got on that saying, "Nobody works here leaves a key in their car. You can't trust our patrons. They leave here drunk, with drunk intentions. The only one might've been the *True Detective* writer." Jack looked around. "Where is he?"

"He's upstairs," Norm said. "I 'magine talking to Elodie. He was asking me about her—can't believe that nice-looking girl's a whore. I said give her three bucks and see what she does for you." Norm stood in the doorway to the main room, turning his head to look at Heidi now, in there at the bar. Norm said to her, "How much he give you for loading his gun?" Now he turned and was looking at Jack Belmont in the kitchen.

Norm giving him a hard stare.

It told Jack his old buddy'd had enough of his fooling with Heidi and meant to do something about it. For a few seconds Jack thought of staring back at him, get it out in the open between them, but caught himself in time. Where was the advantage in doing that? No, Jack grinned like he'd thought of something and turned to Franklin at the window.

"Franklin? You hear the one, the woman of the house asks her colored girl Dinah if her husband is a good provider? Dinah says, 'Yessum, he's a good providah, all right, but I'se always scared dat niggah's gwine get caught at it.'"

Jack was still grinning, waiting for Franklin to laugh.

Franklin nodded, looking like he was trying to smile. But now his gaze moved to the window again, Franklin saying, "They at the cars," his voice raised. "Sneaked up, getting in the one in the middle, the Packard. Backing out, behind the other cars now."

Carl, with him at the window, picked up the navy Colt from the counter, telling Franklin to fire through the windows of the cars in front, and they both began firing, not knowing if they were hitting the Packard or the ones in it. They paused and could hear the car's engine being throttled up, running high, and now they saw the black shape in the clear, streaking through the mist toward the trees on the far side of the lot and the drive that curved in from the road. But now it was slowing, starting to make a wide turn through the lot, churning up mud as the black Packard swung around to head toward the front of the roadhouse.

Son, at the wheel, began to brake coming on to the bodies lying in the empty parking lot. It turned Nestor from the windshield as the car came to a stop.

"What're you doing?" The man excited and showing it. "Roll over 'em, for Christ sake. They aren't gonna be any deader."

Son couldn't do it. He looked at the rearview mirror and told the Wycliff brothers to get out and pull the bodies out of the way, Nestor yelling at him, "Goddamn it, go on. You aren't gonna hit 'em all." Son shook his head. This time he turned to the Wycliffs in the backseat and told them to hurry up and get to it, drag 'em out of the way. The brothers felt the same as Son about running over the bodies. They hopped out of the car and started pulling them by the arms back toward the cars standing on the road.

Nestor, watching through the windshield, quieter now, said, "You're giving 'em time to get ready for us."

Carl told Jack and the bouncers, Walter and Boo, to get down behind the bar and wait till he saw what was going to happen. He expected an argument from Jack he wouldn't have time for, and when Jack asked him where he'd be, Carl didn't answer. He told Norm and Heidi to run upstairs and get the bartenders and wait up there in the hall.

"Don't show yourselves or come out to the stairs till somebody starts shooting."

Jack said to him again, "Where you gonna be?"

Carl said, "I want a word with this Nestor."

Son saw a clear fifty feet ahead of him now, plenty of room to make his turn and head directly for that big wooden front. The Wycliffs would come running behind the Packard with their rifles. Son gunned the motor, pressed down hard on the gas pedal and swerved toward the doors, Nestor yelling at him to "Bust through, bust 'em down!" and

Son drove that Packard through the entrance, banging the doors off their hinges, pieces of lumber bouncing off the hood, smashing the windshield, a fragment coming past him like a spear, but they were inside, Nestor hanging on, his jaw clenched, and Son braked and plowed into tables and chairs that put Nestor up against the dashboard, the Packard plowing furniture to wedge it against a post in the middle of the room. Son turned his head to see a man in a suit and panama hat watching him from behind the bar, the guy standing there like he was the only one in the place.

Upstairs, Tony Antonelli heard the car smash through the front doors, heard the howl of the engine and knew what was happening down below. He had to stick his shirttail back in his pants and pull up his suspenders looking at Elodie on the bed in only a pair of lace panties, God Almighty, her ninnies pointing straight at him, her expression scared to death. He said, "Stay here, I'll come back to get you," and ran out of the room and down the hall past the bartenders reaching out too late to stop him. He had to pull his arm away from Heidi grabbing on to him and saw Norm waving at him from the other side of the hall to get back.

But Tony was at the top of the stairway now looking down at the Packard and the smashed furniture, and realized, damn it, he'd left his notepad in the bedroom.

He saw Carl Webster behind the bar facing Son getting out from behind the wheel, with a rifle, and now the Wycliff brothers were coming up on the driver's side of the car, both holding rifles he believed were Springfields. Tony judging the distance between the three locals and Carl Webster less than thirty feet.

He saw Nestor Lott come out of the front passenger side and move up to face Carl from across the car's hood. This was the tableau Tony committed to his memory, looking down not quite directly at the front of the Packard, but more to Nestor's side of the car. From this angle he could see Nestor holding a .45 automatic in each hand, below the level of the hood, close to the spare tire mounted there.

Carl, behind the bar, arms hanging at his sides—Tony thinking of the way he would write it—with a relaxed demeanor, would not see that Nestor was ready to shoot. Tony thinking he should yell out, but not wanting to involve himself, hesitating . . .

And Carl Webster got his attention.

Carl saying, "Am I speaking to Nestor Lott?"

" 'Course you are," Nestor said. "Don't confuse me with these share-croppers holding rifles on you. Where's everybody? I want to know who killed my boys. And where you stole that Thompson."

"I'm Deputy United States Marshal Carl Webster," Carl said. "I'm placing you under arrest for impersonating a federal officer. Wearing that badge like you deserve it."

"You see what else I got on my chest?"

"That medal," Carl said, "don't mean a thing to me."

"You ought to be ashamed of yourself," Nestor said. "Boy, you're on the wrong side of this shenanigan, working for the whiskey people. You ought to be over here with me."

"I've told you," Carl said, "you're under arrest. My partner has the warrant."

Tony watched Carl turn his head to the three locals with their army rifles. Carl said to them, "You people can go or stay. You stay, I'll arrest you for helping this monkey break the law. Which is it gonna be?"

Son and the Wycliff brothers didn't stir, their rifles pointing at the bar, Tony would bet, waiting for Nestor to give the word. He heard Carl tell them, "Put down your guns."

The locals still didn't move, covering the marshal with their Spring-fields. Tony would remember the marshal standing with his arms at his sides, *his demeanor relaxed as he looked at sudden death staring him in the face.* Now Nestor was saying, "Call your people out. They upstairs? I want to see what we have here." Tony would write: *No one moved. All waiting for Nestor's deadly signal, firing the first shot.*

But now Carl said to Nestor, "Let me see your hands. Lay 'em on the hood there."

For a few moments the room was quiet, Tony looking down at the four men by the car, Carl facing them, Tony pretty sure Carl knew about Nestor and his two guns and that Nestor's game was to bring on a gunfight, but only on his terms. Now Nestor was speaking.

"Marshal, you have it ass-backwards. It's your hands I want to see. Bring out your gun and lay it there on the bar."

Tony turned his gaze on Carl Webster.

Carl saying, "I want to be clear about this so you understand. If I have to pull my weapon I'll shoot to kill."

Amazing—the same words, according to Crystal Davidson, Carl had said to Emmett Long before he shot him. Tony sure of it—he could hear Crystal telling it again in that suite at the Georgian hotel in Henryetta, Tony and the roomful of newsmen writing it down. *If I have to pull my weapon . . .*

"Show me you understand," Carl said to Nestor, "by laying your hands on the hood."

Tony, above the scene, saw it about to happen.

Nestor thumbing back the hammers on his .45s, one and then the other, starting to bring them up, Tony staring at the .45s clearing the Packard's hood . . .

And saw Carl extending his Colt .38 straight out over the bar—had it already drawn in that split second of time—and shot Nestor, *bam,* filling the room with that hard sound, and shot Son, *bam,* and saw Jack Belmont behind the bar now, and the bouncers Walter and Boo bringing up their revolvers, and it stopped the Wycliff brothers, surprised the hell out of them—heads popping up from behind the bar—and *bam,* Carl shot the first one as more gunfire filled the room, coming from either side of Tony at the top of the stairs, but he made himself keep looking at the scene, at Jack Belmont holding a Winchester and looking up this way like he was checking on Heidi, concerned about her as the second Wycliff fired the rifle wedged against his side and Tony saw bottles on the shelf behind Carl shatter and mess up the mirror, saw Carl extend his Colt and shoot him, *bam,* as this second Wycliff was throwing the bolt of his rifle to put a round in the breech. Now the one-eyed bouncer was firing, shooting the Wycliff boy again before he went down. Tony saw Carl turn to Nestor, even though he was already dead, Tony knowing it because Carl knew it, or he'd have shot him again. It got Tony thinking of Carl's words, *If I have to pull my weapon I'll shoot to kill.*

But how'd he pull it so fast? How did he get it out from under his coat in that split second? Carl was reloading his gun, taking bullets from the side pocket of his coat. He walked around the end of the bar and went over to the other side of the Packard to take a look at Nestor.

Tony came down to stand next to him to see Nestor dead and tell Carl Webster something.

"When he asked you to bring out your gun"—Tony hesitated saying it—"you told him the same thing you told Emmett Long. Word for word."

Carl said, "I did?"

"Crystal Davidson told us, that time at the hotel."

"You remembered it?"

"I wrote it down. Everybody in the room did. Now you said the same thing and proved it, shooting three more."

"Four," Carl said.

Tony paused before saying, "You're right."

"Any of 'em shot by these bozos," Carl said, "were already dead."

Tony looked up at the tin ceiling. "My ears are still ringing." He looked down to see Carl give Nestor's gut a nudge with the toe of his shined black boot.

Carl turned to the stairs then as Heidi called out, "Jack? . . . Where's Jack?" and told them, "Norm's been shot. I think he's dead."

9

The first thing Bob McMahon told Carl, seated across the desk, he was getting time off while they investigated the roadhouse shootings. Carl would make his statement and they'd see how it compared to what witnesses said, all the ones on the scene. Carl said, "You aren't taking my word?"

"Your account," McMahon said, "you shot all four once they were in the place, Nestor Lott and the three boys with him."

Carl nodded saying, "I was trying out a new Colt thirty-eight special on a forty-five-caliber frame."

"That's a heavy weapon."

"Less kick to it. You hit where you point it."

"The bouncers"—McMahon looked at pages of reports on his desk—"Walter and that one-eyed guy, Boo Bragg, they claim they shot two of them."

"They want the credit," Carl said, "they can have it, but Nestor and his boys were already dead or dying. Talk to the *True Detective* writer. He saw the whole show."

"He was here this morning," McMahon said, "Anthony Antonelli. He said you told Nestor Lott if you pulled your weapon you'd shoot to kill. You remember saying that to him?"

"If I had to pull it," Carl said.

"You remember saying it to Emmett Long? That time it was his girl-friend told us, Crystal Davidson?"

"After I told him he was under arrest. It was the same thing here, they could put their weapons down, but if they intended to use them I'd have to shoot."

"Anthony says he's never seen a gun appear so fast."

"You ask him how many gunfights he's seen?"

"What he's saying, he didn't see you draw. He looked over, your gun's out and you're firing."

"What part of that bothers him?"

"He wants to know if you were holding it in your hand," McMahon said, "below the counter."

"I gave 'em a chance to put down their guns," Carl said, staring back at his boss. "They didn't do it."

"Were you holding your weapon or not?"

"I was holding it."

"The Tulsa paper said you drew and fired."

"They asked me if I shot all four," Carl said. "I told 'em yes, I did. They didn't ask if my gun was already in my hand."

"They like the idea of a marshal with a quick draw," McMahon said, and looked down at his papers. "Anthony wants Belmont arrested for stealing his car."

"I know. I told him he shouldn't of left the key in it. I was sure the Packard was Jack's but he never said it was."

McMahon was staring at him again. "I notice you always refer to Belmont by his first name. Like you know each other pretty well."

"I know him," Carl said. "Set me loose I'll find him for you."

"Where you think he is?"

"The first place I'd look is Kansas City."

McMahon said after a few moments, "Maybe."

"He'd fit right in."

"You know for a fact he killed those Klansmen?"

"As fast as he could. Norm Dilworth shot the two in their car. The Thompson got away from him."

"And you believe Belmont shot and killed Dilworth."

"I know he did, so he could have Norm's wife," Carl said. "Check the round they took out of Norm. Was it from a Winchester or a Springfield oh-three?"

"It went through him and through the house," McMahon said. "It's outside in that thicket. And I doubt anyone who was there, the bouncers, the bartenders, will admit seeing Belmont shoot him."

"They don't work for him now," Carl said.

"But they don't have a reason to name him. Even if we find those guys, I don't see they'll do us any good. And this Heidi Winston, you think she ran off with him?"

"I guess so. Unless he twisted her arm."

"I doubt she minds him being the son of oil money."

They were both quiet for several moments.

Carl said, "You remember Peyton Bragg, a couple years ago? Cooked whiskey and robbed banks? That half-ugly, one-eyed bouncer's his kid brother."

"Does he know who you are?"

"I believe so, but he hasn't said anything."

"We have a warrant out on him?"

Carl said, "The Volstead. We can get about anybody on that one."

They were quiet again, both of them with their thoughts for about a minute this time.

McMahon said, "I don't see how you let Belmont get away."

"I made a mistake," Carl said. "He's acting like he had a good time shooting those people, nothing to it. I told him I was taking him in."

"For irritating you?"

"I wasn't sure if there'd be a charge against him."

"For shooting people coming to burn his house down?"

"Yeah."

"So you wanted to hand him over to a prosecutor," McMahon said, "but you let him slip away. At the time Dilworth was shot, what were you doing?"

"Nobody knew about it till Heidi called out he'd been hit."

He paused and McMahon said, "Yeah . . . ?"

"She said she thought he was dead."

McMahon waited.

"I'd gone around to the other side of the Packard to look at Nestor lying there. I saw the medal for bravery he'd pinned on his chest, a Distinguished Service Cross from the war. My dad won a medal for bravery in Cuba."

McMahon saw him frowning now.

"But Nestor—Jesus—wasn't anything like my dad."

They sat on the porch of that big California bungalow among pecan trees in the evening, having their drinks before supper, Virgil with the pile of newspapers the Texas oil people brought whenever Carl Webster's name appeared, this time with pictures.

"You sure like that hat. You're turning into a regular jelly bean, aren't you?"

They were drinking sour mash over ice with a slice of orange and a little sugar, Virgil's favorite. " 'Twelve Slain at Roadhouse,' " Virgil said, reading a headline. You shoot four of 'em and they give you a vacation, huh? That's a pretty good deal."

Carl let his dad talk.

"The newspapers are eating this one up. Can't get enough. Some more reporters come by yesterday, and that one with *True Detective,* Anthony Antonelli? He says he's writing a story about it. Gonna call it 'Gunfight at Bald Mountain.'"

"I didn't know he was coming right away."

"Wants to do what he called cover stories about you and another one on Jack Belmont. Wants to ask you about all the bad guys you had to shoot. How many is it now, eight counting the cow thief? He says he's gonna ask you if you told each one the same thing, if you pulled your weapon you'd shoot to kill."

"I'm stuck with that," Carl said.

"It's what happens you become a famous show-off. You have to keep track of what you said. You get a name for shooting outlaws, one'll come along, try and shoot you to make his own name. Something this Jack Belmont could have in mind. Anthony says he wants to ask Jack why he robs banks and sells bootleg liquor when his dad's richer'n sin. I told him the boy either wants to embarrass his daddy or show him up. How many people has Jack shot, the seven at the roadhouse?"

"One before that, when he was fifteen."

"Same as you."

They let it hang.

"His dad's Oris Belmont," Carl said.

"I know who he is. But what can he offer his boy? Work up there in the office with him? Get to look out the window at Tulsa? Or he can clean out storage tanks if he wants. I said to Anthony, take me and Carl, we have the same situation here. I'm fairly rich and Carl don't make much more'n a few thousand a year, but we don't compete with each other."

"No, I listen to you tell me your opinion of things," Carl said.

"I advise you. I give you the opportunity to become a famous pe-can planter, eek out a living hitting trees with a fishing pole. I tell you, stay out of the oil business. Right now it's down around four bits a barrel 'cause there's too much of it. That East Texas field come in and I'm making less than four cents a barrel." He reminded Carl the governor of Oklahoma, Alfalfa Bill Murray, had put every producing well in the state under martial law, armed guards on over three thousand wells until the price went up to a dollar a barrel. "It could take a while, but it'll come back. You know why? There's so many people own cars now, and there more every day."

Carl said, "You're not broke?"

"Honey, I been making royalties since the Glenn Pool come in," Virgil said. "Like I told Anthony, I'm fairly rich. What I didn't tell him, I keep out a good hundred thousand in cash at all times—"

"Where?"

"In the house. It's enough to live like a third-rate king for a good twenty years. The rest, I got a few filling stations and cafés with a business partner. People have to buy gas to run their cars and they have to eat."

"You keep a hundred thousand dollars in the house?"

"And a few guns. Don't worry about it," Virgil said. He sipped his whiskey and said, "You're not here, the reporters start asking me questions. They follow me out to the orchard wanting to know what I do with all my money. See, they'd noticed the wells pumping. First they ask me what I think about my only son on the trail of fugitive outlaws and bank robbers. I said, after the crash of '29 I didn't think there was any money left in the banks to rob. They want to know if I went bust. I told them we ever get Repeal I'm opening a few saloons somewhere. Not here, we're dry as a bone on account of we was Indian Territory not too long ago. That and the Baptists, this state'll vote dry forever. I told them hell no I ain't broke, I got investments. They said you can still go broke. I said not how I'm set up, I'd still live the life of a second-rate king. I thought about it since, five thousand a year for twenty years, and changed it to a third-rate king."

"You told them," Carl said, "you had cash put away?"

"Never did, but that's what they kept asking, if I'd hide away money. I told 'em it was none of their business. They're the nosiest people I ever met."

Carl said, "What'd you say to make 'em think you'd put away cash? If you're gonna live like a second-rate king—"

"Third-rate."

"It means you have money to do it with."

"I never said a word about my money."

"You told them you had guns in the house and you were a crack shot?"

"They're asking me later on about being with Huntington's Marines in the Spanish War. That's all."

"You tell them you won a medal for bravery?"

"For getting shot by a sniper." Virgil took a good sip of his drink and said, "This writer, Anthony Antonelli? Said you told him you'd be home."

"I was in Henryetta yesterday."

"You still crave that gun moll?"

"Some oil man's been seeing her, thinks he's daring. Crystal and I had supper, talked about different things. I like her, but it don't mean I want to marry her. You know she lived with Emmett Long after he killed her husband. It's the same with Heidi Winston, the girl that ran off with Jack Belmont."

"You can talk to those people?"

"I can ask questions. What's it like being with a man's wanted dead or alive? I ask Crystal if she was scared all the time. She says, 'Well, sure.' But she sounded surprised, like it was something she hadn't thought about. Being scared was so natural to her. Heidi's different, she was a whore and I think she likes the excitement for a change. At the roadhouse she's kidding Jack about shooting a cow, saying he did it on purpose. Right below them out the window are seven dead guys he shot lying in the yard."

Virgil said, "There's no way to understand people like that."

Carl told him Nestor Lott had a Distinguished Service Cross pinned to his coat he must've won during the war.

"When you shot him?"

"I almost hit the medal."

"I imagine you were more dead center," Virgil said. "It sounds like he wanted everybody to know he'd been a hero at one time. If it was his medal."

"I'm pretty sure it was. The man had no feelings," Carl said, "but when the time came to stand up, he did."

Virgil said, "You run into some strange birds, don't you?"

Narcissa Raincrow appeared from the kitchen holding her drink, whiskey and Coca-Cola, to tell them supper was ready.

T hey sat at the round table in a back corner of the kitchen, windows on two sides, pecan trees everywhere you looked out there.

Narcissa served them steak and eggs and potatoes, all of it fried, a bowl of leftover white beans with salt pork, a loaf of bread she'd baked and a dish that looked like sauerkraut with tomato sauce on it. Narcissa sat down at the table and listened to them talk about Franklin Roosevelt winning the presidential election, happy that he'd skunked that constipated Herbert Hoover.

"Will Rogers says the Democrats have gone in," Virgil told them, "with all kinds of promises to regulate the stock exchange, help out the farmers, support veterans' pensions, and they'll come out with all kinds of alibis. Will Rogers says we don't vote for a candidate, we vote against the other one."

"Says he never met a man he didn't like," Carl said. "You believe that?"

"No, I don't," Virgil said, "but it sounds good. You know when he was in vaudeville doing rope tricks and talking, he'd twirl two ropes at the same time, the idea to set one loop on the horse and the other one over the rider. Will Rogers had a list of things he'd made up to say if he missed. Like, 'If I don't loop one on soon, I'll have to give out rain checks.' Or he'd say, 'This is easier to do on a blind horse, he don't see the rope coming.' He'd get so many laughs making excuses he'd muff a rope trick on purpose so he could say something funny about it."

Carl said, "You're sure full of Will Rogers lore, aren't you?"

"He's a movie star, he appears on the stage, he writes a newspaper column full of misspelled words—he's our greatest American, the funniest man I ever heard speak."

"And he's part Indian," Narcissa said.

"He's nine-thirty-fourths Cherokee," Virgil said, "a quarter Indian if you fudge it. Will Rogers'd say, 'We didn't come over on the *Mayflower*, we met it.'" Hunched over his supper plate Virgil said to Carl, "You remind me of him sometimes. I don't know why but you do."

Carl said, "I can think of all kinds of people I don't like, so that ain't it."

"You're both kind to animals," Virgil said. "You're modest in your way, or know how to put it on. Remember seeing him in the Ziegfeld Follies that time? You were just a kid then."

Only a few days after Carl had shot the cow thief out of his saddle.

He nodded to his dad, remembering chorus girls with long white legs tap-dancing around the stage and Will Rogers coming out in black chaps and a hundred feet of rope coiled in his hand, his range hat cocked to one side, hair hanging on his forehead. Carl remembered the cow thief's name was Wally Tarwater.

Virgil was saying, "She keeps shoving this sauerkraut at me claiming it's good for you."

"It is," Narcissa said. "Ellen Rose Dickey in her radio talk says it's the perfect health food. I sent away to Clyde, Ohio, for fifty recipes. I put ground-up pecans in it. I put onions in it and made a tomato sauce to put on it. He pushes it away."

"It smells," Virgil said.

"You smell and you don't know it," Narcissa said, " 'cause you have B.O. I buy Lifebuoy soap at the store. He don't wash under his arms with it every day like I tell him. No, once a week he takes his bath. I tell him to wash his mouth with Listerine. He don't have time reading his papers. I tell him Listerine kills two hundred million germs in only fifteen seconds. He still don't have time. I try to get him to eat Fleischmann's yeast every day, three cakes, so he can be regular sitting on the toilet. I hear him groaning in there trying to make poo-poo. No, he says he don't need Fleischmann's yeast. You see how he's losing his hair? I try to get him to use this tonic they call Hair-Medic. He won't do it. I tell him the famous Harry Richman likes to use it. I tell him Ruth Etting the singer uses it. She says it does wonders for her scalp. Virgil says he don't need it. Virgil reads about Ideal Manhood in my *Physical Culture* magazine, that old guy Bernarr Macfadden showing you how to exercise? Virgil don't get out of his chair. I send for the free book of Charles Atlas, how Dynamic Tension gives you everlasting health and strength. He won't read it. I get him Earle Liederman's book that tells how to strengthen your inner organs. I send to Newark,

New Jersey—maybe he'll like Lionel Strongfort's book, how to energize your body. Virgil don't even open it. He says, 'Strongfort, you kidding me? The guy made up that name.' "

Virgil said, "Tell him how you bought a tube of Ipana on account of my pink toothbrush."

Narcissa was shaking her head, worn out, through with him.

"I use Ipana now," Virgil said. "I get a new toothbrush and she stays white." He chewed on a piece of steak he'd dipped in his egg yolk and said to Carl, "Did you know thirty thousand people a year are killed in car wrecks? They must be out on the road trying to run into each other." He said, "I just read that," and looked at Narcissa. "What was it in, *Liberty*?"

"I believe *Liberty*," she said. "Or it was in *Psychology*, the one that's called *Life in the Modern World*?"

10

The first time Crystal saw Carl's apartment she had come to Tulsa on a shopping trip. He showed her around the two-bedroom place, where he'd been living since joining the marshals, saying he paid thirty a month for it furnished, including heat and light, a new kitchen, the sleeping porch in back . . . Crystal said, "Not bad." He told her he was due to repaint the walls and lay new carpeting, but hadn't done anything but hang those pictures in the living room. He waited for Crystal to wander over to the wall of framed photographs, some of them enlarged.

"That's my dad in uniform, when he was a seagoing marine." He waited until she was close enough to touch the photo before saying, "He was on the *Maine.*"

By this time he'd said the same thing to all the different girls who'd been here during the past few years: "He was on the *Maine.*" And every one of them knew what happened in Havana Harbor in 1898 and listened to him describe how Virgil was blown off the ship when it exploded and into a Spanish prison.

"You told me about your dad," Crystal said. "One of those afternoons you stopped by."

"When you were still in the farmhouse?"

"It wasn't long after you shot Emmett. You told me about all these people, your family, your life when you were a little kid." She turned enough to look at him. "I had the feeling you wanted me to see you as a regular guy, not a dumb cop or someone, all you do is shoot people." Crystal turned to the wall of photos again saying, "I've never seen these, but I bet I can pick out your people from what you told me about them." Crystal nodded to a photo. "This is your mother. I believe her name is Grace?"

"Graciaplena," Carl said, "Full of Grace. But that's my grandmother, not my mother. She's part Northern Cheyenne."

"My mistake," Crystal said. "If she's part Indian then you are, too." She looked at him again with a faint smile. "I would never of suspected."

"The first time I met Emmett, at the drugstore, he said it made me a breed. That's me in the cowboy outfit when I was four. My dad bought it for me. He wanted to be a cowboy when he was a kid. Fifteen years old he bought a horse for five dollars, thought he'd ride off and find work on a spread. But his stepdad, a preacher with the Church of the Most Holy Word, sold the horse from under him and kept the money. He joined the marines instead, still only fifteen, and his mom ran off to Lame Deer, Montana, to live with her people. She's still there, but I've never met her. Or my mother, she died having me. That's Grace in the white dress the day they got married in Havana. That's her dad with her, Carlos, the one I was named for. I met him one time my dad took me to Cuba. Those are some of my dad's oil wells. There's the two of us on a derrick platform when I was a kid. He likes to pose."

"That's where you get it," Crystal said.

"But he's no oil man. Even with the checks coming in he keeps working his pecan trees."

"He must've spoiled you when you were a kid."

"Virgil always bought me good horses. I worked stock from the time I was about twelve and could ride like a man, right up till I joined the marshals. That enlarged shot of the house? That's my dad and Narcissa and me on the front porch the day we moved in. We used to live down on the county road, where you turn into the property. Narcissa's his housekeeper."

Crystal said, "I bet she's more than that."

"Yeah, well, they're close, been together twenty-six years now. Narcissa takes good care of him. He reads newspapers and she reads magazines and they tell each other things. I drive down to Okmulgee weekends I get the chance. My dad and I sit on the porch and talk."

"Couple of pards, huh?"

"He likes to hear what I'm up to."

"When you could be living on the homestead?"

"Yeah, picking nuts. But he's always let me have my head."

"He must wonder though."

"What I like about being a marshal? He thinks I'm a show-off, out to make a name for myself."

She said, "You are, aren't you?"

Carl grinned at her and Crystal came over to take him by the arm toward his bedroom, Crystal saying, "Can we make it a quickie so I can get out of here, please, and go shopping? How about if I just pull up my skirt and take my panties off?"

"You're wearing panties?"

"Honey, I told you, I'm going to Vandever's, see what's new. And try not to muss up my hair for a change, okay?"

This morning he got home from his dad's place and took a shower standing in the tub, shaved and combed his hair, wetting the comb to get a straight part and rubbed bay rum on his face. He'd wear the vest that was part of his dark suit. It was cold out, too cold for the panama.

He'd wear his brown felt, get used to it over the next couple of winter months, the hat taking on a good shape and he liked the feel of it, pinching the front of the crown to drop it on his head and knowing it looked good, a slight curve to the brim. He didn't care for overcoats. When he was in the country he'd wear a cowboy coat, a fleece-lined over his suit. In towns, in and out of cars, a raincoat was enough. He picked out a burgundy necktie to go with his blue shirt and the dark blue suit and slipped on his shoulder holster. Wearing his revolver on his hip was a little more comfortable, but the big Colt on the .45 frame was easier to pull from under his left arm and he could pull it sitting down. He spun the cylinder to check the loads and slipped the revolver, its front sight filed down, into the holster he softened every couple of weeks with saddle soap. He put a fresh pack of Luckies in his coat pocket and a book of matches, but left the Beechnut scrap on the bureau—what he chewed sometimes when he was in the country or at his dad's place; his dad loved that Beechnut scrap. He slipped a pair of handcuffs into a pocket of the raincoat—he didn't like the hard metal feel of the cuffs on the back of his belt. Spare rounds were always in his suitcoat pocket. What else? His wallet, change, a pack of gum, the keys to the Pontiac Eight sedan they were letting him use. Nine minutes later he pulled up in front of the Mayo Hotel. In the lobby he glanced at himself in a mirror, lifted his hat and eased it down a bit closer on his eyes, the brown hat working, Deputy Marshal Carl Webster looking good.

11

Carl knocked on the door of 815. It opened and Tony Antonelli was standing there looking at him. Carl said, "I understand you want to talk to me."

"Yeah, but not now. I'm about to interview Louly Brown."

"You haven't started yet?" Carl said. "Lemme just say hi to her." He could tell the *True Detective* writer didn't want him to come in, but had to step aside as Carl moved past him to look around at a sitting room. Now Tony motioned to a door.

"She's in the bedroom."

"You got her a whole suite of rooms?"

"Two rooms and bath, fifteen dollars."

"There's good money in writing, huh?"

"It's on an expense account." Tony raised his hand and said, "Wait a minute, I'll check on her." He walked to the bedroom door, rapped with one knuckle twice and said, "Louly?"

Carl could hear her voice but not the words, Tony saying, "Yeah?" Saying, "That's a shame." And finally, "Of course I'll wait." He turned to Carl. "She says she's got a darn pimple and is trying to hide it."

"What is she," Carl said, "a movie star? Tell her I'm here waiting to see her."

"She's quite self-conscious," Tony said, "bashful, all this attention more than she can handle."

Carl turned around and sat down in a big, comfortable chair at the end of the sofa. He looked up to see Tony coming over, Tony saying, "If we have a few minutes, I'd like to hear about the shootings you were in, ones I only read about in the paper. I had to dig back in the clip morgue at the Tulsa *World* to get the one called 'Gunfight at Close Quarters' and the other one, 'Marshal Shoots Machine-Gun Killer from Four Hundred Yards.' "

Carl said, "Those were the only two. The one was like most situations like that and the other wasn't a gunfight."

"I was in Kansas City on and off last year trying to get the lowdown on Boss Pendergast and his cronies. Good luck to any journalist who wants to try." Tony went on talking as he sat down at the end of the sofa, on the edge of the cushion and got out his notebook. "I'd like to hear about the one where you used a rifle."

"You mention Kansas City," Carl said, "I'm thinking of going there."

Tony said, "Well . . . it's the biggest city in area in the entire U.S., known as the Paris of the Plains. And it's wide open. K.C. has all the betting, booze, and babes anyone could want. I mean people who go in for that kind of stuff."

Carl said, "Have you seen Elodie?"

It straightened Tony. "Not since the other day."

"She's over at the courthouse talking to marshals. I told her, 'You go back to Seminole I'll put you in jail.' "

"I haven't seen her," Tony said. "She's at the courthouse, uh?"

Carl said, "You want to talk about Elodie or hear about a shoot-out?" See how professional this *True Detective* writer was.

It took him only two seconds to get back on the job saying "Yes, absolutely. I want to hear about shooting the machine-gun killer. You were actually four hundred yards away?"

Carl said, "The other one's a better story."

He watched Tony get up from the sofa and smooth out the front of his pants saying, "Can you hold it a minute? I want to check on Louly, see how she's doing."

Carl watched him go to the bedroom door and put his ear close as he knocked and said, "Louly? Are you gonna be long? I have to go to the bathroom." Carl watched him fidget at the door, heard him say "What?" a couple of times, having trouble hearing her.

"You're paying for it," Carl said. "Go on in."

"I can hear the water running," Tony said, walking toward the door to the hall now, telling Carl, "I'll be right back," and left the suite.

The door closed and Carl pulled himself out of the chair, crossed to the bedroom and walked in saying, "Louly, where you hiding?"

She was in the bathroom. He saw her, the door open, stepping out of the tub full of foamy bubbles, the redhead naked and looking right at him as she reached for a bath towel, in a hurry to get it, but then more relaxed holding it in front of her.

Carl had the feeling she was deciding in these moments how to act with him, like a good little girl, mortified that he'd seen her naked. Or as Tony described her as being self-conscious, bashful. Oh, was that right? But not too bashful to shoot Joe Young that time at the tourist court, the day after Carl first laid eyes on her. He watched her turn around to dry her back.

Louly saying, "Are you still watching me?"

"I can't help it."

She dropped the towel, giving him a clear shot of her pert little fanny, and reached to take her green bathrobe from a hook on the wall.

She kept her back to him slipping into the robe, showing some modesty, since he'd already seen that patch of red fuzz against her pure white skin. It looked like Louly was going to be herself with him.

She came out of the bathroom saying, "Where's Tony?"

"He had to pee."

"I never met a writer who was so polite and considerate." She sat at the vanity and began brushing out her hair. "And I never had a bubble bath, so I bought some, see what it's like. It's okay, has a nice smell, but all you do is sit in it."

"You miss a lot," Carl said, "living on a cotton farm." He stepped closer to see her in the vanity mirror, head lowered, her fierce strokes brushing her hair pulling her robe open.

She stopped brushing and looked up at him.

"I'm getting tired of these interviews. I've had to make up stories so they stay interested. I told one guy, a reporter, well, I did happen to run into Charley Floyd by accident one time, when he was living in Fort Smith. The guy interviewing me says, 'By accident, huh. Sure.' I said, 'If you don't believe me why should I talk to you?' he says, 'What were you doing over in Arkansas if it wasn't to see him?' Then I had to think of something right then."

"That you don't want him to believe either," Carl said.

"Yeah, and it gets confusing. I heard in Sallisaw Charley *was* there, in Fort Smith with Ruby and their little boy, Dempsey, and I did think of driving over to see Ruby. But they moved again and nobody knows where." Louly brushed out a few more strokes, stopped and looked up at him again. "You know what I decided to do? Go to Kansas City. They say it's some town, all kinds of jazzy places to see, and now I can afford to do it."

"There's a lot to see in Tulsa," Carl said.

She caught him looking into her robe and pulled the front of it together saying, "You know I have that five hundred they gave me for shooting Joe Young. I want to spend it in Kansas City, not some oil town."

"You want to see Tulsa and save your money," Carl said, "you could stay at my place."

She held the brush above her head.

"Stay with you?"

Carl watched the robe come partway open, but this time, looking at him in the mirror, she didn't touch it.

"I've got a two-bedroom apartment with a new kitchen, a comfortable living room and a big Atwater Kent up next to the couch. A maid comes in once a week, cleans and does the laundry. Stay, I'll show you around town."

"Don't you work?"

"I'm taking time off to relax."

She stroked her hair twice, stopped and said, "What would people say, I was to move in with you? Like my mother, she finds out?"

"Don't tell her."

"How about your neighbors?"

"They don't care."

Louly said, "I hardly even know you."

"I'm offering you a room," Carl said. "You don't want to see the town, the hot spots, go dancing, it's up to you. You can sit on the couch and listen to the radio."

Louly said, "You'd take me dancing?"

Tony pulled the key out of the lock, closed the door and turned to see Carl Webster coming out of the bedroom.

"She's getting dressed," Carl said.

Tony stood there. "You talked to her?"

"She's thinking of staying in Tulsa a few days."

"Well, she can't stay here."

Tony said it right away.

"She can tonight, can't she, if she wants?"

"We only have the suite till six."

"They gave you a rate," Carl said. "You didn't pay any fifteen dollars, did you, Tony? You lied to me."

He was sure the marshal was kidding. Though not absolutely sure. Tony walked to the couch saying, "If that's what I told you, yeah, that's the full rate. I had it on my mind, 'cause if we go past six we have to pay it."

Carl said, "Where's Louly gonna sleep, in her car?"

"We arranged with the hotel, they're giving her a deluxe room for two dollars."

"You bring the little girl to Tulsa and you make *her* pay?"

"I'm gonna take care of it," Tony said.

"You work for a cheap outfit," Carl said. "But don't worry about paying her way, I'm fixing her up. Sit down, I'll tell you about the one, 'Gunfight at Close Quarters.'"

He was doing it again, putting him on the spot, manipulating him. The same thing he did with Elodie, brought her up and then cut him off from finding anything about her. Or he liked to hear himself talk about himself.

"No," Tony said, "the one I'd like you to tell me is 'Marshal Shoots Machine-Gun Killer from Four Hundred Yards.'"

"That's what happened," Carl said. "That's the whole story right there."

"The only time you used a rifle."

"The only time I've had to."

"I know it started with a bank robbery in Sallisaw. But why there? What was the guy's name, Peyton Bragg? I'd like to hear the details."

"They're hard to remember."

It was quiet in the room before Tony said, "Why don't you want to tell me about it?"

"I'll tell you," Carl said. "See how much I can remember."

You know that ugly one-eyed bouncer wears smoked glasses? They call Boo?"

"He turned his head," Tony said, "he was a good-looking guy."

"But his ugly side's what you remember," Carl said. "His given name's Billy Bragg, the kid brother of Peyton Bragg, the machine-gun killer shot at some distance."

"Right," Tony said, "Peyton Bragg," and wrote it down.

"Peyton worked stills. He'd set his mash, run it through the cooker to drip into jars his brother Billy would deliver to customers. Then Peyton'd go out and rob a bank. The time the law finally got on him he robbed the Sallisaw State Bank. You know why he chose it?"

Tony said, "Sallisaw's close to the Cookson Hills?"

"See, you know why. But that's only one reason. The main one, Pretty Boy Floyd had robbed the same bank—in his hometown, you understand—and only got twenty-five hundred thirty-one dollars and seventy-three cents. Peyton said watch, he'd rob it the same way Choc had, with a machine gun, and ride out of Sallisaw with a teller on the running board and way more cash than twenty-five hundred and thirty-one dollars."

"Where'd you get this, what Peyton said?"

"From the kid he had driving for him."

"What was his name?"

"I don't recall, but the one that went in the bank with Peyton was Hickey Grooms, armed and dangerous, Arkansas banks had five hundred dollars on him. See, Peyton was sore 'cause Charley Floyd was getting credit for banks Peyton had robbed. In fact at that time, witnesses were putting Choc at almost every bank robbery in Oklahoma. So Peyton's intent was to show him up."

Tony said, "They say Pretty Boy was supposed to have robbed fifty-one banks in less than a year."

"You know that isn't true," Carl said. "Peyton and his partner are in the bank, Peyton waving his machine gun to get everybody's cooperation. Now they're in the vault loading sacks with cash . . . while the kid driver's sitting in the car revving the engine, wants to make sure it won't quit on him. He keeps watching the bank and doesn't see the police car drive past."

"But they see him," Tony said, "acting suspicious."

"So you know what's gonna happen," Carl said. "By the time the kid driver notices people looking toward him as they hurry past the bank, and finally turns his head to see police on the street he starts blowing his horn."

"What kind of car?"

"An Oakland. Brand-new eight the kid swiped off a lot in Muskogee. Peyton comes running out of the bank, gets to the car, the police yelling at him to stop, put up his hands, and he rakes the Thompson at them, shooting up parked cars, storefronts . . . His partner comes out with the bank sacks as Peyton's firing and the police shoot down Hickey Grooms he's barely out of the bank. Peyton's in the car now looking at his partner lying dead on the sidewalk, about ten thousand dollars of cotton money in the sacks."

"You learned this after, how much they took?"

"That's right, but the kid driver said in his statement Peyton knew about how much they had and looked like he was gonna try to get the sacks. The police and others were shooting at the car now, so the kid said he punched the gas pedal, 'held her down' and they got out of there."

Tony said, "You mentioned Peyton fired the Thompson."

"He killed one of the officers and a couple of people standing there. Once they're out of town it was a chase through the hills, no paved roads up there, we're following tire tracks and dust most of the time. The Sequoyah sheriff set up a roadblock near Brushy. Peyton busted through and killed a deputy. By the time they got up toward Bunch, the Adair County sheriff with us now—"

"Wait," Tony said. "What were you doing in Sallisaw?"

"Inquiring after Charley Floyd. I went there to talk to his wife's relatives. A cousin named Louise had written to him in prison."

"You mean Louly?"

"I didn't know her then. She wasn't there anyway. Her stepdaddy, Mr. Hagenlocker, said she'd stolen his car. I drove back to Sallisaw, the bank'd been robbed."

"So you joined the chase."

"I believe I was telling you, we got up toward Bunch, there was the Oakland off the side of the road, its rear end sticking out of the growth, the kid driver waiting there, putting his hands up as we approached him. He said Peyton had him pull off the road to hide the car, but when he did it got hung up in the undergrowth, why the ass end was showing like that. The kid said a car happened to come out of a road almost across the way, where there was a filling station had gone out of business. Peyton ran out and stopped the car—the kid said a woman driving—and rode off in it."

Tony said, "What make of car?"

"A 1930 Essex two-door, green, one the Adair County sheriff said belonged to Venicia Munson, an old-maid schoolteacher from Bunch."

"So you went to see her."

Carl wanted to say he'd get to it, all right? But kept his peace, wanting to tell this part the way he remembered it.

How he spoke to the sheriff from Adair County about Venicia Munson, the sheriff, an old boy, reminding him of his dad, the chew in his jaw, direct when he spoke but in no hurry. He said, "I've known Venicia since she was a little girl, more'n thirty years, but have no idea what she thinks. They say she almost ran off with an oil patch roughneck one time when she was a kid, but her old man put a stop to it. I never heard of her seeing anybody else. She don't talk 'less you talk to her first. She don't fix her hair or doll up any." The sheriff said, "No, I take that back. I saw rouge on her face the other day at the post office she was mailing a letter. She wouldn't be too bad she fixed herself up. Except she's I mean skinny, hardly any sign of breasts on her to speak of."

"Who you think she writes to?"

"I been wondering about that."

"You think she knows Peyton?"

"She could."

"They both like to hide out."

"I know what you're saying. Your hunches any good?"

"Sometimes."

They found the house at the end of a mile of ruts in a straight dirt road, through land swept bare by wind and drought, the house old, left over, Venicia Munson the last of her family to live here.

The green Essex stood close to the house.

Carl told how she came out on the porch as their four cars crept into the yard: two from sheriff departments, Sequoyah and Adair, one sedan holding the Sallisaw posse with their shotguns and rifles, and Carl's Pontiac, the kid driver riding with him.

"Look at her," Carl said to the kid driver, "and tell me if she was in the Essex."

"I never saw her good."

"It's the same car, isn't it?"

"It sure looks like it."

"Tell me," Carl said, "if Peyton stopped that car or the car stopped for him?"

The kid said, "What's the difference?"

"Did he threaten her with the machine gun?"

"He wasn't holding it then."

"He left it in your car?"

"I think he forgot it."

"He have a gun in his hand?"

"I didn't see one."

"Do you recognize her?"

"I told you, I didn't see her good."

Carl, with the Adair County sheriff, got out and approached the woman on the porch, touching their hat brims. Carl gave his name, told her he was a deputy U.S. marshal, and said, "How're you today?"

Venicia didn't say, she stood waiting, hugging herself with skinny arms, red circles of rouge on her drawn cheeks.

"Tell me," Carl said, "if you stopped your car to pick up a man on the road, not more'n a couple hours ago?"

She shook her head.

The sheriff said, "Venicia, this is Peyton Bragg we're talking about. A witness saw you pick him up in your car."

She said, "Whoever thinks he saw me's mistaken."

The sheriff said, "There's only a couple Essexes in this county I know of and this is the green one."

Carl saw the way she looked right at the man in his worn-out wool suit and tie, the plug in his jaw. Now she shrugged her shoulders.

Carl said, "You mind if we go in your house and look around?"

She said, "Why? You think Peyton Bragg's in there?"

"You know Peyton?"

"What difference would it make?" Venicia said. "You aren't going in my house."

The sheriff said he was sorry but they had to. "Peyton killed three people, one of 'em a police officer, robbing the Sallisaw bank, and shot a Sequoyah deputy at a roadblock." He turned and motioned to the others to come on, they were going in.

Now Carl told the *True Detective* writer how they searched the house, the upstairs, the storm cellar, poked through wardrobes full of family clothing . . . It was Carl who looked in the stand by the front door, wondering why there were so many umbrellas in it, and found the Winchester .30-30 among the black folds of cloth. It had a scope sight mounted on it and was loaded. Carl held it up to Venicia Munson.

She said, "It's mine. All right?"

Carl put the rifle in his car and came back to see everybody outside now looking off at the land, all of it dead to treelines in the distance, the closest maybe a quarter mile away.

Carl said to the woman, "Miss Munson, if you see Peyton before we do, tell him to give himself up while he's still alive."

She didn't say anything, but it got him strange looks from the others. The posse from Sallisaw walked back to their car talking about what he'd said to her. The Sequoyah deputies took their time, turning to look at the woman and comment among themselves.

Carl said to the Adair sheriff, "She and Peyton know each other. Before he robbed the bank he made plans to hide out at Venicia's." The sheriff frowned at him, working the chew in his jaw, and Carl said, "Peyton didn't stop her car on the road. She was there to pick him up."

"This is your hunch?"

"I got it from the kid driver. Only nobody told him about it."

The sheriff looked out at the nearest treeline and tugged his hat brim down against the late sun.

Carl said, "He'll be back tonight."

All Bunch had was a filling station, a sawmill that cut rough lumber, a frame church and a general store with the post office one of the counters, mail slots behind it on the wall.

Carl told this to Tony in the Mayo Hotel suite.

"We sent the kid driver back to Sallisaw with the posse, five of 'em packed in the car. They had to promise to keep their hands off him since he was just a dumb kid. We had the two Sequoyah deputies, and two from Adair County the sheriff got hold of. He's the one I was talking to, Wesley Sellers, if you want to write his name in your notebook. He's coming over to Okmulgee sometime, talk to my dad about the Spanish war and we'll shoot at crows eating pecans. Wesley brought us to his house and his wife fixed us egg and onion sandwiches and opened a can of deviled ham for whoever wanted to spread some on bread, while we decided how to lay for Peyton. One good thing, we knew he'd left his machine gun in the car."

"But he'd be armed," Tony said.

"We didn't have any doubt of that. We decided I'd be the one to go in the house, the last resort if Peyton got past the others spread around outside."

"You'd talk to her?"

"If I could think of something to say."

"How did you feel, face-to-face with the woman, knowing you or the sheriff's people were gonna kill her sweetheart?"

"Did I sympathize with her?"

"Feel sorry for her—this old maid with a bank robber for a boyfriend."

"She wasn't anybody to me," Carl said. "Soon as it was dark I drove up to the house, as if I'm visiting. I see her car turned around, the Essex, its rear end toward the house, ready to shoot straight down the road. I thought if the key's in it I'd yank it out. But I hear Venicia's voice—she's on the porch in the dark—ask me what I want. I have to get her in the house, so the others can walk up the road and take their positions without her seeing them."

"She'd know you weren't alone," Tony said.

"Most likely," Carl said, "but you never know. I told her I wanted to talk to her. She asked if I'd brought her rifle back, said I had no right to take it—the Winchester with the scope. It was still in my car, but I didn't tell her that. I said why didn't we go in the house and sit down. She said all right, I suppose curious, wanting to hear what I had to say, and took me through the living room to the kitchen and turned on the light over the table."

"She knows you're not gonna ask what you do around there for fun. I bet she broke down," Tony said, "pleaded with you to spare his life, only the second boyfriend she'd had in her thirty-odd years."

"No, but she surprised me," Carl said.

She asked him if he wanted a drink.

Carl said no thanks, and watched her open a cupboard to bring out a fruit jar of moonshine and two glasses and put them on the table. She said, "In case you change your mind," and poured herself two inches of the whiskey that looked no more potent than creek water. She wore a wool housecoat, green, like her car, that came to the floor and looked too big for her, the sleeves too long. She wore rouge, circles of it on her cheeks, and lipstick tonight, bright red in the light hanging above them. Venicia sat down with her back to the sink and cupboards and Carl took the chair to her left, to be facing the back door. He didn't like sitting in the light.

"You're a schoolteacher, uh?"

"And I drink wildcat whiskey," Venicia said. "What do you make of that?"

"There's no taste to it—it must give you what you're looking for. Peyton brings it?"

"When he remembers."

"What do you do, you run out and he's not around?"

"Honey, you're in the Hills. I can go a mile in any direction and pick up what I need for social occasions. You understand, I only drink when I have company." She raised her glass to him and took a sip, a good one, then touched the sleeve of her housecoat to her mouth. "What I'm always running out of are cigarets."

Carl took out his pack of Lucky Strike, popped a couple of cigarets to stand up and held the pack to her. Venicia took a cigaret and lit it from a book of matches she brought out of her housecoat. It said BE MOUTH-HAPPY on the cover, SMOKE SPUDS. Carl slid the pack across the table to her, its green wrapper close to matching her robe.

"If you're trying to get me to talk about Peyton, keep it up. But I doubt I can tell you anything you don't know. I will say one thing. Peyton gets to the house and sees you through the window, he'll shoot you dead." She raised her face to blow smoke that swirled in the light.

Carl said, "What grade do you teach?"

"All of them."

Carl said, "Peyton's already killed four people today."

"Yeah? You think I don't know what he is?" Venicia got up and came back from the sink with a tin ashtray. "You'll get him or you won't. You do, I'll have to go up the road for my whiskey." She drew on the cigaret again and said, "How many people have you killed?"

It was in his mind that he hadn't killed any *people* and said, "They were wanted criminals, fugitives."

"Aren't they people?"

"You say 'people,' I think of innocent people, not mad-dog ex-convicts and murderers."

"How many of those have you killed?"

Carl hesitated. "Just three."

Only three by that time, he told Tony. Wally Tarwater, the one stealing his cows; Emmett Long, in the farmhouse near Checotah; and David Lee Swick coming out of the bank in Turley with a woman hostage, the one Carl had approached from across the street telling Swick to let the woman go and drop his gun, and when Swick fired, Carl pulled and shot him through the head at fifteen feet, the reason the Tulsa paper called it "Gunfight at Close Quarters."

Venicia was saying, "You shoot Peyton you'll be even with him, won't you? He did shoot a man in Tahlequah one time, fighting over some whore, but only winged him. The man survived Peyton's wrath."

She sipped her drink and smoked her cigaret and asked Carl, "Are you nervous?"

He said, "I'm all right. Are you?"

She said, "To tell you the truth, I'm scared to death."

"It's what happens," Carl said, "you get mixed up with a man like Peyton."

"You're the one scares me," Venicia said, "not Peyton. You know why? 'Cause you'd rather shoot him than try to bring him in."

"It's up to Peyton," Carl said. "What'd I say to you a while ago? You see him, tell him to give himself up if he wants to stay alive."

"Where am I gonna see him before you do? I hope to God he doesn't come, 'cause you'll shoot him down like a dog."

Carl was shaking his head telling her, "Uh-unh, we shoot when there's no other way to stop the fugitive."

"That's your excuse," Venicia said, "why you became a marshal and get to carry a gun. You like to shoot people. I think you get a kick out of it."

He didn't tell Tony what Venicia said—it wasn't a detail of shooting the machine-gun killer.

Carl kept it to himself, because that whole time they were tracking Peyton Bragg, it was in his mind that when they caught up with him and there was a gunfight, he'd have a chance of making Peyton No. 4.

He did, he saw Peyton as a number.

But was that bad, wanting to put a desperado out of business? It was what marshals did and he was proud to be one—even though his old dad thought he was crazy trading high risk for low pay. The only thing he'd ever felt after was relief that it was over and he was still alive. That time in Turley he was shaking after. The woman hostage fainted she was so scared and he thought he had shot her.

First relief, then later on he'd feel proud of what he did, the way pilots in the war, Eddie Rickenbacker, had German crosses painted on the side of his Spad, under the cockpit, proud of his kills. Rickenbacker had twenty-six. That German, though, the Red Baron, was the ace of aces with over eighty kills. They went up and looked for enemy planes to shoot down. Marshals went out to take wanted felons dead or alive. What was the difference?

He had made balsa models of the war planes when he was a kid. The German Fokker with three wings he painted a bright red.

Carl said when they heard the gunfire Venicia was lighting a cigaret. He jumped up but remembered the match burning her fingers—if Tony wanted details—and saw her drop it on the table. He told how the shooting was coming from the front and by the time he got to the porch the Essex was driving away from the house, the key in the car or else Peyton had it. Carl said he ran to the Pontiac and reached in to get the Winchester, the deputies and Wesley Sellers around front now firing at the Essex running away from them. Carl said he saw the red taillights come up big in the scope sight, aimed a little bit above the left one, the deputies yelling at him to shoot, and fired, levered the rifle to fire again, but the Essex had veered off the road, crop furrows slowing the car down till it rolled to a stop.

"The round caught Peyton in the back of the head," Carl said.

Tony, writing in his notebook, said, "Number four for you, uh?"

Carl didn't respond to that. He said, "A deputy paced off the distance to where the car went off the road and said it was four hundred yards, give or take."

"Did you consider it a lucky shot?"

"I hit what I aimed at."

"But at that distance—"

"It was more like three hundred yards."

"You see Venicia Munson again?"

"When I went back for my car."

"Was she crying?"

"I couldn't tell."

"She say anything to you?"

"Asked could she have her rifle back."

"You give it to her?"

Carl shook his head. "It was evidence."

Tony went to the bedroom door to check on Louly again. She told him she'd be out in two minutes. Coming back to the sofa Tony looked at his watch.

"She's been in there almost two hours. What do you think she's doing?"

"Looking at herself in the mirror," Carl said. "It's what girls do."

"There's something I want to ask you," Tony said, "about the gun-fight at the roadhouse." He sat down again and flipped back a few pages in his notebook. "Everything happened so fast."

"You want to know," Carl said, "who shot the Wycliff boy, me or that one-eyed bouncer. I'll tell you, I think by the time Boo got around to shooting him rigor had already set in."

Tony grinned. "I know, I saw you shoot him first, and I'll swear to it in court. What I'm not sure of, you told Nestor if you had to draw your gun—you know, you'd shoot to kill."

"What bothers you?" Carl said. "You think I had my gun in my hand?"

"That's what I want to know."

"Why's it matter to you?"

"I'm writing the story, I want to be able to describe what happened."

"If I had it in my hand—when did I pull it?"

"I'm not positive you were holding the gun."

"But if I was," Carl said, "if I already had my Colt out, would I have been lying to Nestor about pulling it?"

Tony was shaking his head. "It's got nothing to do with telling the truth or not. They bust in with the car, you know any second they're gonna start shooting."

"But was I lying to him?"

"No—as I said, it wasn't about lying or telling the truth. I guess it's what you say in that kind of situation."

"You were up on the stairs, had a good view. Tell me what you saw happen."

"Nestor raised his guns and you shot him."

"What's wrong with leaving it at that? Just telling what you saw?"

Carl left a few minutes later saying he was going to stop by the Belmont estate, see if he could have a word with the dad, Oris. "But listen, you want to ask the little girl about Charley Floyd, go ahead. I'll be anxious to hear what she says."

12

I f your boy robbed banks, broke the law selling alcohol and shot different ones with every intention of killing them, would you protect him? Hide him? Carl believed most parents would lean toward making excuses for their boy and try to help him, but wasn't sure about the Belmonts, especially Jack's mother.

Carl called Oris Belmont's office to make an appointment to see him, but was told he was in Houston, Texas, this week. Carl had already checked on Mr. Belmont's personal life and wondered if he might be at the Mayo Hotel with his girlfriend. Carl decided no, not all week, a man who'd been a wildcatter and now ran a number of businesses. Or he could be home for some reason.

That's where Carl went, to their mansion among all the mansions in Maple Ridge, that rich area south of downtown Tulsa. He parked his Pontiac on the street and went up to the door. The six giant columns holding up the portico, as big as they were, didn't impress Carl; there were twenty-two columns across the front of the federal courthouse he entered almost every day of his life. He was about to ring the bell, but then decided to have a look around first, in the open about it, here in pursuit of a fleeing felon—Eddie Rickenbacker looking for Fokkers to shoot down, though he'd rather have the score of the German ace, Manfred von Richthofen, who'd press the buttons to fire his machine guns and another Spad would go down smoking, or a Sopwith Camel, the German the same age as Carl when the Canadian got lucky and shot him down. Walking past the side of the house he thought about the model planes he'd made and painted and was allowed to hang from the ceiling of the living room because Virgil liked to look at them.

He came to the back of the property and saw the swimming pool covered for the winter. He turned to the house—there was Mrs. Belmont on the patio standing with her back to him at a window, washing it with a sponge, a dish towel over her shoulder. The husband worth twenty million dollars and the wife did the windows?

She turned and Carl saw he startled her. He used a quiet tone of voice stepping up on the patio, touching his hat brim and telling who he was and showing his star. She didn't say a word. He asked if Mr. Belmont was home and it got her to shake her head. He said, "I'd like to talk to you if it's all right and you have the time." He paused and said, "About your son," just as a colored woman in a white uniform with a heavy coat sweater over it came along a walk between the patio and the swimming pool—pushing Emma in a wheelchair, strapped in, the girl's head hanging in the collar of a fur coat. Carl knew about Emma, how she'd gone in the pool without her water wings and almost drowned, her brain shut off for fifteen minutes before she was revived. The colored woman called to Mrs. Belmont:

"You washing windows again? Where you want me to put her?"

"Right there," Doris Belmont said and turned to Carl. "I'll talk to you." She hesitated and said, "Let's go inside."

Doris took him through the house to the front hall and up a staircase that had to be six feet wide to a semicircular sitting room that appeared lived-in and Carl believed was her dayroom where she spent her time by herself with this heavy, upholstered furniture; a decanter of sherry sat on a silver tray with stem glasses, the tray on a round table in the middle of the room. The windows looked out the back to the swimming pool and the lone figure, this woman's daughter head-down in the fur coat in late-afternoon sunlight.

Carl tried the edge of a deep chair and then sat back as Doris Belmont sank into the middle of the davenport and wiggled her fanny into the cushion.

She said, "You think Jack's here, hiding out?"

"It depends how you feel about him?"

"You see that girl out there? She can't walk or speak 'cause he let her drown, watched her drown, and we went and brought her back."

"You saw him do it?"

"I *know* he did it—God have mercy."

Carl looked out at the girl, Emma, about twenty now, her face hidden in the fur coat. He turned back to Doris.

Waiting for him, Doris saying, "I'll tell you something," then paused and sounded like she'd changed her mind saying, "I'm tired. I am *so* tired. You know why? There isn't nothing to do. I have two maids and the woman who takes care of Emma. This is her time off now, having a smoke with her coffee. You happen to have any cigarets?"

Carl got out his Luckies. He went over to her and struck a match to light hers and then his own, Doris saying, "Pour us a glass of sherry while you're standing there. Else I'll get you whiskey if you rather."

Carl said no, sherry was fine, saying, "We have some at Christmastime." If Virgil remembered to tell his Texas oil buddies to bring a couple of bottles. He said to Doris Belmont, "You were gonna tell me something, and then realized how tired you are. Though you look like you're in good health."

For a stick of a woman with pale, sunken cheeks.

"But you don't have anything to do," Carl said, "except wash windows?"

"I was cleaning off something a bird left."

"Instead of getting one of the maids? I guess you've worked all your life, haven't you? I imagine you were raised on a farm?"

"We moved in this house," Doris said, "I got turned upside down. I mean it. Nothing a-tall's the same as any place I have lived. I'd go back to Eaton, Indiana, tomorrow and all that ever amounted to was hard times."

"What's Mr. Belmont say about it?"

"About what? My not liking it here?"

"Or having Jack on your mind—what he did."

"What the boy's done all his life, whatever he wants. You know why he tried to kill Emma? 'Cause Oris named his first gushers for the child, Emma Number One and Emma Number Two, and never named a well for Jack." Doris took a sip of sherry and puffed on her cigaret. She said, "You know what I do mostly? Make sure that decanter always looks about half full. It's cooking sherry, but serves my need."

Carl said, "You must talk to Mr. Belmont."

"You mean about Jack? Whatever I say Oris agrees in a soft voice patting my hand, then thinks of something to tell me, like he says they're talking about changing the name of the bank. Oris has a guilty conscience, but I'm not sure if it's for sending Jack to prison or 'cause he's still seeing this old girlfriend of his. One time Oris showed hisself, he said, 'Jack's so bad you want to hit him, only now it's too late, and when I should've been hitting him I was looking for oil.'"

Carl, trying to think of something to keep her busy, said, "You cook?"

"We have one I'm finally getting use to, a colored man from New Iberia, Lou'siana. Oris brought him from down there he was looking at oil property. We have all these people, the maids, the cook, the one takes care of Emma, all living here in this house. My mother comes to visit . . ." Doris shook her head, tired.

"You say Mr. Belmont agrees with you," Carl said.

"On account of his guilty conscience. I say, 'If Jack should come home, you won't let him in, will you? Or let him talk to you?' "

"What's Mr. Belmont say?"

"Says a course not."

"Jack hasn't been here?"

Doris said, "You know what I have under this cushion? A thirty-two caliber pistol." She wiggled her fanny to show Carl where it was. "He comes up those stairs and walks in here to kiss me on the cheek? I'm gonna shoot him and watch him bleed on the carpet."

"You tell Mr. Belmont that?"

"I told him he tries to stop me I'll shoot him, too."

In five days Louly had seen Carl Webster twice, both times when he came home to freshen up and change his clothes. They hadn't even spent the night together yet.

"Oh, you're gonna take me dancing? See the sights of Tulsa?" Using her best sarcastic tone of voice. "You know who's appearing at Cain's Ballroom all this week? The Light Crust Doughboys featuring Bob Wills. The ad in the paper calls them the hottest hillbilly swing band you'd ever want to hear. Every night the ballroom's crowded with two-steppers."

Carl told her from the bathroom, "Honey, I'm on the hottest investigation of my career, working surveillance, watching for a certain fugitive."

"You told me you were taking time off."

"I been called in special on this one."

The second time he came home she said, "All I do is talk to you through the bathroom door. What're you doing's so special?"

Carl said he couldn't tell her.

"Well, all I been doing every night is listening to *Amos 'n' Andy*, George Burns and Gracie Allen, Ed Wynn, or Walter Winchell talking to Mr. and Mrs. America and all the ships at sea, and you don't tell me nothing."

She gave him that the second time he was home and Carl said, "Okay, we're closing in on your boyfriend, Charley Floyd."

The words stunned Louly.

"He's here?"

"Living on East Young Street with Ruby and the boy, according to the police informant, one of the neighbors. And a guy with them the police think is George Birdwell, Choc's partner."

"All the time since they left Fort Smith," Louly said, "he's been in *Tulsa*?"

"The past month. The informant says Ruby shops at the grocery store on credit, tells them she'll settle when her husband gets paid at work. Meaning, when he robs a bank."

Louly said, "What is *wrong* with me? This is the third time I'm only a few miles from Charley Floyd and I don't know it."

"You've been lucky," Carl said.

"Where's East Young?"

"I'll tell you tomorrow."

"You're gonna get him tonight?"

"Dawn, the dawn patrol swoops in."

"You're not taking part?"

"I get to watch."

"So you won't have a chance to shoot him?"

Carl paused. "Why'd you say that?"

Louly said, "I don't know," in her own head. "What about Ruby and the boy?"

"They'll be allowed to walk out."

"I can't even drive past the house?"

"They won't let you on the street. You'll have to wait and read about it in the paper."

The headline on the front page of the *World* read: OFFICERS FOILED BY "PRETTY BOY" IN GAS-BOMB RAID.

The story said that when the police tossed the tear gas bomb through the front window, Floyd and Birdwell went out the back and drove away.

There was more to the story, how the police moved into the dark house and rooted around once they found it empty. There was an editorial saying the police had blundered. Another one quoted the secretary of the Oklahoma Bankers Association saying, "Floyd must be killed before he is captured."

Louly Brown, who had gone as far as the sixth grade, said, "Why capture him if he's already dead?" It surprised her that she noticed this, written by the secretary of the Bankers Association, instead of feeling heartbroken about Choc. Maybe because she was tired of thinking of him as a good guy once you got to know him. Tired of sticking up for him. She listened to *Amos 'n' Andy* and went to bed and lay there in the dark thinking of what she'd say in the note, if she felt the same in the morning.

She did. She wrote the note on Mayo Hotel stationery she'd brought with her and left it on the kitchen table with the newspaper. The note said:

Dear Carl,

I have given up on the two men I thought I admired most in the world—you and Charley Floyd. I can't wait any longer to go dancing with you and see the sights as you are always busy. The same is true of Charley Floyd. (Boy is he busy!) I have stopped letting people believe I am his girlfriend. There is no way to keep up with you two boys. I am going to Kansas City since you have not even called since Choc got away. Am leaving this morning. I will stop at a gas station and get a map.

Love & kisses,
Louly

P.S. I am thinking of changing my name to Kitty and starting a new life.

13

A few days after Jack Belmont and Heidi rented a furnished bungalow on Edgevale—*Modern, 6 rooms with sleeping porch*—an Italian-looking guy in his fifties wearing glasses, a fitted Chesterfield coat and snappy gray fedora, rang the bell and identified himself saying, "Good afternoon, I'm Teddy Ritz, welcome to Kansas City. Where might you folks be from?"

Heidi thought it was funny a guy his age calling himself Teddy and chewing gum. She said, "We might be from the North Pole, Teddy. What business is it of yours?"

Jack had noticed the second dude standing by the La Salle—a young guy, Teddy's driver or bodyguard—and could see that Teddy was somebody who didn't care for smart talk from a girl. Teddy Ritz stopped chewing his gum and stared at Heidi through his rimless glasses. He said, "Sweetheart, I'm vice president of the Democratic Club and head of all the precinct captains in Jackson County. In other words, my position is right under the Boss." He said again, "Welcome to Kansas City."

This time Heidi kept quiet and let Jack say, "It's a pleasure to meet you, Mr. Ritz," shaking the man's hand and telling him they were both Democrats from Tulsa, just nosing around, seeing what Kansas City was like.

Teddy asked if they had their utilities hooked up or any problems with the rental. Jack said everything was fine except they were still waiting for a phone. Teddy said, "Let me take care of that for you." He said, "And I'll get you registered to vote you let me have your names." He wrote them down in a black leather book, glancing up at Jack as he heard the name Belmont.

Heidi, by the window, had noticed the young dude outside. She asked Teddy, "Would your friend like to come in where it's warm? I can make you gentlemen a cup of French-drip coffee."

"Lou's use to waiting for me," Teddy said. "It's what he does."

"I see a resemblance," Heidi said. "I thought he might be your son."

Teddy stared at her again. "You think I look like a wop? He's my bodyguard, Lou Tessa."

Jack smiled at him. "You know she wasn't trying to be offensive in any way."

"I was kidding," Teddy said, and left.

"He'll be back," Jack said, watching the La Salle drive off, "as soon as he looks me up."

"He tells you who he is," Heidi said, "I thought you were gonna kiss his butt."

"We're driving here, I told you about Tom Pendergast? You don't listen, do you? Boss Tom, he runs the machine that runs Kansas City. I told you the town's wide open? Twenty-four hours a day you can do anything you want? Drink, gamble, spend all day in a whorehouse? There's a hundred and fifty of 'em in this town. Pendergast gets a cut from the rackets, his 'lug' they call it, and uses it to pay off the cops. He owns the police and gets the judges and politicians he wants on the bench and into office."

"How's he do that?"

"Teddy says he'll get us a phone? Like that, does favors for people.

By tomorrow we'll have a phone and I'll vote for anybody they want. Doesn't matter if it's a close race, they have thousands of names to use as voters, a lot of ghosts who'd died and gone to hell."

"Have you ever voted?"

"Not yet."

"How do you know all this stuff?"

"Honey, I did time. Convicts like to talk, show off they know things and I listened. You're on the dodge and need a place to hide out, you come to Kansas City. Why do you think it's called 'The Playground of Criminals'? You're safe as long as you vote the right ticket and you don't kidnap some judge's wife. You get the nod from the Pendergast machine you're free to have a good time. You're downtown, you feel like having a drink but don't know where the nearest speak is? You ask a cop."

"Come on—really?"

"Honey, there's no limit to this town. Why do you think all the conventioneers, the Shriners, come here and go crazy? Why do you think we're here?"

Heidi took her time now. "They allow you to rob banks?"

"That's something we'll have to find out pretty soon," Jack said. "We're getting low."

"What'll you do, ask permission? Teddy, can I knock over one of your banks?"

"We pick one out of town. Pull it off—how do they know it's us?"

The bell rang. Heidi looked out the window going to the door and saw the La Salle at the curb. It was the bodyguard at the door. He winked at her, said, "How you today?" with an accent and walked past her to the kitchen.

"Can I help you?"

"Jack is here?"

"Not right now."

He walked past her in his black overcoat, a stick pin in his tie, going the other way now, down the hall to look in the bedrooms, the bath and the screened porch and came back saying, "You right. I don't see him." He stepped to the door, still open, and waved for his boss to come in. Now he turned to her with pleasure in his eyes. "I'm Lou Tessa," the accent there. He was shaved and smelled good, but would show a beard no matter how many times he shaved and she wondered if you could feel it.

He said, "You get your phone?"

"The next day."

"What if I give you a call?"

She liked dark guys and raised the back of her hand to brush her fingers along his jaw. His skin felt smooth.

"When?"

He said, "Sometime," and stepped aside for Teddy Ritz, telling him, "They got the phone."

Heidi said, "Jack sure appreciates your help. He said we'd be waiting forever without it."

Teddy glanced at Lou Tessa and the bodyguard walked out closing the door.

"His old man's Oris Belmont," Teddy said, "and Jack can't get service when he wants it?"

"He's sort of bashful," Heidi said. "But the big problem, he and his daddy don't get along too well."

Teddy said, "On account of Bashful Jack robbing banks or selling whiskey?"

Heidi laughed out loud. "Well, you sure learned about us in a hurry."

"About Jack. Nobody knows of any Heidi Belmont. You two aren't married, are you?"

"We talk about it once in a while. No, I'm still Heidi Winston."

"You have any kind of talent? You strip?"

She could tell him she was an experienced madam, as young as she was, but held off about that or screwing commercially, believing, from the way his eyes kept falling into the scoop neck of her peasant blouse, she could do a lot better than minding whores.

"I can work as a hostess in some high-class joint," Heidi said, "keep the gentlemen coming back."

"Yeah? How you do that?"

"I know how to treat a gentleman."

"Show 'em your goodies?"

"In a tasteful way. I bend over the table, he's hoping my titties fall in his crawfish bisque."

Teddy was breathing Juicy Fruit on her, smiling now.

"I see that could happen."

"I'm looking for a high-class place that suits my personality, not one that caters to a bunch of louts. You happen to know of any?"

"I sure do, sweetheart. I know one's just the ticket."

"What's the name of it?"

"Teddy's," Teddy said. "Eighteenth and Central."

A few days later in the afternoon, Jack and Heidi were driving through town in the *True Detective* writer's Ford Roadster on their way to North Kansas City, a different town but right across the Missouri River. Jack wanted to show her a bank he had in mind. They'd been driving Tony's Ford since stealing it in their escape from the road house.

Heidi was now working at Teddy's from 10 P.M. to the next morning as a cocktail waitress. They had a host instead of a hostess, an Italian named Johnny, a nice guy; he'd step out the back to smoke reefer and let you have a puff. Heidi had said to Jack after her first night, "You know what we wear?"

"Some kind of revealing costume?"

"I'll give you a hint. What's the name of the club?"

"You wear a teddy?"

"That's all, rose or peach."

"Yeah? Where do you keep your tips?"

"In my garter. They give me silver—it doesn't happen much—I hold it in my hand, give the big spender a look and drop the change on the table. This place, they know how to tip. There's a group of rich old geezers, six of them, they come in wearing their tuxes after some kind of affair or the symphony? Their limos drop them off, take the wives home and come back to wait. They have Cuban cigars and cognac, always in one of the private rooms."

"That's all they want?"

"It's *how* they want it," Heidi said. "Johnny calls me into the private room, easy chairs around a cocktail table. He tells them, 'Gentlemen, we have a special treat for you tonight, Heidi. She's come all the way from Switzerland to wait on you.' He's already told me their favorite thing is to be served by a bare-naked girl wearing just black silk stockings and high heels."

"Yeah . . . ?"

"I curtsey."

"Yeah . . . ?"

"I unsnap the crotch, fling the teddy aside, then go around pouring cognac and lighting cigars."

"They cop feels?"

"They talk business and tell jokes."

"While they're staring at your cooze."

"I'm telling you, these old guys are honest-to-God gentlemen. I'm serving them, they hunch over for a light, my puss is practically in their face, but they're casual about it. Once in a while I got a pat on the fanny. That's all. They have a couple of snifters, smoke their cigars and go home. *But,* each one gave me a peck on the cheek and at least a five-buck tip."

"You made thirty dollars?"

"Forty, the time I did it. They said they want me whenever they come in."

Jack said, "I have to get a look at this Teddy's."

"It's a mansion," Heidi said, "he bought off an estate. It's huge, all dark-wood paneling, bar, dining rooms on the first floor, private rooms upstairs, a ballroom on the third floor—"

"What kind of music?"

"A white band nobody listens to. They finish and the younger crowd runs upstairs to hear the colored guys who come in to jam. That's what they call it. Guys with names like Count, Big Daddy, Speedy . . . Hot Lips—"

Jack said, "I don't know about that nigger music."

"They start on a tune like 'Lady Be Good' and each one comes in on a sax or trumpet playing jazz, but whatever they feel like, making it up, and they still all end up together on the tune. Without any music in front of them."

"That's what I don't understand," Jack said.

"You're not suppose to understand it," Heidi said, "you feel it and tap your foot and move your body. There's a colored girl name Julia Lee? She sings a song, 'Won't you come over to my house, nobody's home but me,' and you know from how she sings it what she wants. There's another one sings 'T-Town Blues.' She's going back to Tulsa, to Greenwood where she used to live."

"Niggerville," Jack said. "We burnt Greenwood down must've been ten years ago. They sort of built it up again."

"It's real bluesy," Heidi said. "And there's a girl from Oklahoma working at Teddy's started the same time I did. Cute little redhead from Sallisaw. You ever been there?"

Jack said no, but believed Pretty Boy Floyd use to live there, or near it.

Crossing the bridge to North Kansas City Jack said, "I've read everything written about Pretty Boy and haven't learned one new trick about robbing banks. Or from working with Emmett Long that time. I told you coming here there's only one way to do it. Walk in, show 'em your gun and ask for the money."

They were coming along Armour Avenue now in the heart of downtown. Jack said, "There it is, the National Bank and Trust, next to the Kroger grocery store." He had to turn the corner at Swift Avenue to find a place to park.

"Last week," Jack said, "they sent a girl works at the bank, Dortha Jolly, to the post office—see the flag, right over there? They sent Dortha to pick up a registered package with fourteen thousand dollars in it. You either go to the Federal Reserve to pick up money you need or they mail it to your post office. If they used an armored truck the bank has to pay for it. So these cheap fuggers sent Dortha, a stenographer, to pick up the package with a city marshal as her armed guard. They come from the post office, turn the corner and now they're approaching the bank. They see a shotgun sticking out of a car window parked in front of Kroger's and Dortha is told to drop the package. She drops it and runs into the grocery store.

The city marshal goes for his gun and is shot a couple of times but makes it, he isn't killed. A constable across the street sees what's going on and opens fire. There's a gun battle that shoots up some of the stores along Armour Avenue, one of them a beauty parlor, and the bandit car drives off heading north. Three police cars get after it, but have to stop at a filling station to have roofing nails, ones the bandits threw in the road, pulled out of their tires. Does that sound like the Keystone Cops or what?"

"They get away?"

"So far."

"When was this?"

"I told you, last week. It's the third time the bank's been robbed, Dortha was there for two of them."

"You don't think after being robbed three times," Heidi said, "they haven't learned something and be ready now?"

"If they're too cheap to hire an armored truck," Jack said, "they're not gonna spend money on a bank guard. Even if they do, it'll be some hayseed they pay no more'n a buck and a half a day." Jack brought a .38 revolver from his coat pocket, handed it to Heidi and told her to put it in her purse.

Heidi said, "You want to rob the bank right now?"

Jack said, "It's as good a time as any."

He had told her during the 360-mile trip from the roadhouse, they'd have to rob a bank if they planned to stay in Kansas City awhile. Heidi asked him, didn't he know he might have to leave in a hurry? Didn't he have cash ready, just in case? Jack said sure, he did, there was a thousand bucks in the Packard, hid in where the spare tires were. He said any time he planned something ahead, like kidnapping his dad's girlfriend? It never worked out. He said but he was lucky, so don't worry about it.

Now, sitting in that same Ford Roadster on Swift Avenue in North Kansas City talking about robbing a bank, Heidi said, "Do we have to?"

Jack said, "I've told you why."

"But I'm making money now."

"Enough to get by on isn't what I call making money."

"I never robbed a bank before."

"But you shot a man and laid him across the railroad tracks, didn't you?"

"That was different, they came to kill me and Norm."

"Different," Jack said, "'cause it took way more nerve. Honey, there's nothing to robbing a bank. Come on, let's go do 'er."

They walked around the corner, came to the bank and entered to leave a dismal sky, rain threatening, for bright chandeliers shining down on marble: four cashier windows but only one occupied by a teller, a blonde girl; a bank official at his desk toward the rear, behind the low fence, busy with papers; and a guard on the floor, a skinny old coot in a gray uniform too big for him. Jack had called that one. The guard stood with his hands behind his back, the grip of a pistol showing in the holster on his hip.

Jack, an unlit cigaret in his mouth, his hands in the pocket of his coat, was ready for him. He walked up to the guard and asked if he had a light. The old guy patted his pockets and shook his head. Jack was still ready. He said, "I only have one hand that's any good," and brought his left hand out of his coat pocket with a book of matches. He said, "Would you mind lighting me up?" The guard took the book of matches and Jack looked around at Heidi.

"Why don't you make the withdrawal?"

Heidi walked over to the blonde girl, who smiled at her and said, "Can I help you?"

Heidi set her purse on the counter in front of the window and saw the blonde girl look past her and then stare in that direction. Heidi wanted to look around but was afraid of what she might see. She brought the .38 out of her purse and pointed it at the blonde girl still looking past her and said, "You gonna wait on me or not?"

The blonde girl, seeing the gun pointing at her, said, "Oh my God—"

Heidi told her to take the cash out of the drawer and put it in the purse. Watching her do it, Heidi said, "Are you Dortha Jolly?"

The blonde girl paused, holding bills in her hands. "Somebody from school called and she went home. I think one of her kids took sick. You know Dortha?"

Heidi said no, shaking her head, and said, "Don't stop what you're doing." When she did stop Heidi said, "Is that all you have?" The blonde girl said yes, it was, and Heidi told her to move to the next window and empty the drawer there. Now she looked around to see the bank guard lying on the floor on his stomach, his head raised to watch Jack coming this way, to the window where the blonde girl was now, Jack saying to Heidi, "How we doing?"

She said, "Okay, I guess," handing him the purse. He was holding an old .44 Colt she thought of as a horse pistol he must've taken off the guard. He set both the pistol and the purse on the counter and said to the blonde girl, "Are you by any chance Dortha Jolly?"

"No, I'm not," the blonde girl said. "She sure is popular since she got her name in the paper."

"Well, you're doing fine," Jack said. "Keep up the good work," and shoved the purse toward her.

Heidi was looking at the bank official at his desk, the man staring right at them now. She said, "Jack—" and he turned from the counter and started toward the bank official, drawing his .38 from his coat.

"You press an alarm button?"

He stopped within ten feet of the man shaking his head, swearing now, he never touched it.

All Heidi wanted to do was run. She grabbed the purse from the blonde girl stuffing bills in it and started for the door yelling, "Jack, he did, I saw his hand go under the desk." Heidi scared to death while Jack stood there pointing his .38 at the official swearing honest to God he never touched the button.

Jack said, "You sure about that?"

Taking his time now to show off. It drove Heidi crazy and she said to him again, "Jack, I'm leaving," and watched him turn and come toward her in kind of a slow strut, pausing to say something to the old coot still on the floor, and finally, *finally*, they were out of the bank.

Jack picked up the pace now, grinning at her, saying, "I told you there's nothing to it. What can they do? We're holding guns on 'em."

As he said it she thought of the guard's gun, the big horse pistol still on the counter.

"What did you say to him?"

"The manager?"

"The old coot."

"I said, 'Papa, you ought to find some other work.'"

"You know what you did?" Heidi said. "You left his gun in there, by the teller's window."

It caused Jack to stop and look back toward the bank, then at Heidi before they started walking again. "I thought you picked it up." They were coming past Kroger's now. "I was busy with the manager."

"Showing him what a cool customer you are."

"You're saying it's my fault?"

"You took it off the old coot, didn't you?"

"You picked up your purse, it was right there."

"Nothing's ever your fault, is it?"

Jack stopped to look around again, kept staring to make sure and said, "Jesus Christ."

Heidi looked around and saw the old guy coming toward them on the sidewalk, trying to hurry, almost to Kroger's when he started shooting, holding that big .44 straight out in front of him as he came cocking and firing the revolver, an old Peacemaker. Heidi turned and ran.

Jack stepped behind a parked car, got out his .38 and shot the coot, stopped him inside of thirty feet.

By the time they reached the car Heidi had decided she was through with Jack Belmont, leave him or become a nervous wreck.

Something Heidi was curious about, if Teddy Ritz wasn't Italian, what was he? She asked Johnny, who ran the club, and he said, "I'm Italian, Lou Tessa's Italian, Teddy's Jewish." She told Jack and he said, "You didn't know he was a Hebe? Look at the honker on him." Jack had to let you know, if just by his tone of voice, he was smarter than you were. He'd insult you and think it was funny. Show off and scare the hell out of you. She was thinking seriously of leaving him, but wasn't sure how to do it. Tell him they were through or not tell him. He'd kept the money from the bank, close to seventeen hundred, and made her give him most of what she earned at Teddy's. If she left Kansas City she could clean him out, take all the cash he kept in the Quaker Oats box in the kitchen. But she liked her job and the way rich guys tipped and knew if she offered a little commercial screwing now and then, being selective, she could buy anything she wanted, clothes, even her own car. But if she stayed at the club she'd have to forget about taking the money; Jack would know where to find her. Even walking out on him without the money she'd be taking a chance. She was thinking that if she ever got something going with Lou Tessa, it would be a lot easier to break it off with Jack.

Four days after the bank job the La Salle pulled up in front and Teddy Ritz walked in, with Lou, to solve her problem.

It started out like a social call, Jack offering to take Teddy's hat and coat, Teddy saying no, they weren't staying long. He sat down in the morris chair, a newspaper folded in the pocket of his Chesterfield. Tessa, his bodyguard, stood by the front door wearing his long black coat, hands folded in front of him, reminding Heidi of a funeral director she saw one time. Jack offered Teddy a drink, coffee, whatever he wanted. Teddy said he wouldn't mind a cup of hot tea on a cold day. Heidi gave Lou Tessa a careful look and went out to the kitchen to turn the gas on under the kettle. She came back to the living room, Teddy was telling Jack what a bang-up job she was doing with their customers. "From the first night, Jackie, she's one of our most popular girls."

Jackie? She had never heard him called that before.

"I believe it," Jack said, "she's a little sweetie."

Teddy took out a cigar and bit off the tip.

"So what've you been up to?"

"Not much, this'n that."

Teddy lit the cigar and blew a smoke ring, not a perfect one but it was okay. Watching the ring he said, "Which was the bank in North K.C.?"

Jack was watching the smoke ring, too, dissolving now, and took a moment to say, "Excuse me?"

"The one you knocked over the other day. Was the bank *this* or was it *that*?" Teddy looked at Heidi. "Pretending he don't know what I'm talking about."

Heidi nodded saying, "Mmmmm." She quit glancing at Tessa to pay closer attention.

Teddy leaned to one side to bring the newspaper from his pocket folded to an inside page, and dropped it on the coffee table. Heidi saw a headline that said BANK & TRUST ROBBED OF $5000!

Jack said, "Wait a minute. You think I robbed that bank?"

Teddy said, "You and little sweetie."

The teakettle started to whistle.

Heidi rose from her chair.

Teddy held up his hand to hold her there. "Twice in the bank she called you by name. When she told you the manager pressed the alarm button, and when she said she was leaving." He looked at Heidi. "The manager said you couldn't wait to get out of there. Go on, make the tea. I won't tell Jack any more till you get back."

She started for the kitchen hearing Jack say, "That's why you think it's me? A woman calling to some guy named Jack?" And Teddy saying, "You hear what I told her? We wait till she comes back." Now she stopped in the kitchen doorway hearing, "Sweetheart, what kind of tea is it? Where's it from?"

"It's Lipton's," Heidi said. "I don't think it's from anywhere."

Teddy winked at her and she went in the kitchen telling herself she'd be okay. Jack was the one in the fire.

Jack finally came clean: all right, he and Heidi had robbed the bank, but he thought it was okay since it was out of the city limits. Teddy said, "You think Tom's influence ends at the river?" Jack said he should've known better—sounding like a kid who got caught stealing a candy bar from the dime store. Heidi loved it that he couldn't get smart and put on that tone with Teddy Ritz, sitting there puffing on his cigar. He'd dip the tip into his tea and slide his lips around it before taking a puff, his shadowy cheeks drawing in before blowing out a cloud.

He said, "Jackie, I'm gonna forget about the bank job, you're new here. But you created a problem we have to take care of."

Jack squinted at him. "What problem?"

"The first thing you do is put the five in a bank."

"I didn't get five."

"And cut a check for half of it, twenty-five hundred."

Jack had to hold on to the arms of his chair. "I'm telling you we never got any five grand. They always do that, give the papers a higher figure than was taken."

Teddy held up his hand.

"You cut a check for twenty-five hundred made out to the Democratic Club—no cash that can be traced. That's what it'll cost to keep the police and the sheriff's department over there looking the other way. You killed a seventy-eight-year-old bank guard who spent fifty years in law enforcement and was loved and respected by the community. His people get a remembrance."

"That's a shame," Heidi said. "Jack even told the old guy he should find a different job."

Teddy looked at Jack. "Day after tomorrow around noon? I come by for the check made out to the Democratic Club of Jackson County. After that I watch you get in your car and leave Kansas City and I never see your face again. Sweetie stays here."

Heidi wanted to ask him, Keep my job? Hoping to God that's what he meant.

But Jack said, "Or what?"

Teddy frowned at him. "What're you talking about, 'Or what?' "

"I don't give you the check, you shoot my sweetie?"

Teddy started to smile. He leaned forward in the chair and looked around at Tessa standing by the door. "You hear what he said?"

Tessa nodded showing a faint smile. "I heard him."

Teddy said to Jack, "Shoot *her*—Lou shoots you, you dummy."

14

Carl, carrying his grip, walked in the Reno Club on Twelfth as the band was leaving the stand: colored guys looking sharp in their gray, double-breasted suits, the piano player, a woman wearing a red silk headband, closing the cover over the keys. Carl said to the bartender, "I'll try that Ten High with a touch of water," and asked if the band was through for the night. It was only half past twelve.

"'Nother band's coming on." The man placed Carl's drink on the bar. "The Count, Lester, Buck Clayton, whoever wants to sit in."

Carl said, "They any good?"

The bartender had turned away and a colored guy sitting at the bar, a scar under his left eye, a space between his front teeth, was looking at Carl holding his grip. He said, "Just come to town, huh? You one of those crazy Shriners?"

Carl said, "No, I'm a crazy U.S. marshal. I'm looking for somebody I know ain't here. Everybody in this joint's darker than she is."

Carl sat down wearing the hat he was breaking in and his raincoat. This tough-looking guy next to him had turned and placed his elbows on the bar in front of his bottle of Falstaff. Carl drank the top part of his highball and got out his Luckies. The guy next to him already had a cigaret going.

"I came in to the Union Station," Carl said. "That's the biggest place I've ever been in, like a cathedral only bigger. They got a Harvey's, a bookshop, a waiting room just for women . . . What I don't understand, the ceiling in the lobby must be a hundred feet high. What good's all that space?"

The guy next to him, leaning on his arms, said, "You never heard of Count Basie?"

Carl paused before saying no, he hadn't. "But I think I've seen you someplace."

The guy shook his head looking tired. He said, "Man, don't pull that shit on me. I never been arrested in my life."

"You ever been to Tulsa?"

"A few times."

"You play piano," Carl said. "Where'd I see you, at Cain's Ballroom?"

A painful look passed over the guy's face. "Man, I don't do that hillbilly shit. I played at La Joann's with the Gray Brothers."

"That's where I saw you," Carl said, "yeah, La Joann's. You were playing piano . . . Your name's McShane?"

"Jay McShann. You saw me play, huh? But you never heard of Count Basie?"

"I might've, I don't recall the name," Carl said. "I got interested in the music and bought some records. Andy Kirk—"

"And his Clouds of Joy."

"Chauncey Downs and his Rinky Dinks."

"Has a tuba in his band."

"George Lee and his sister."

"Julia. They the ones just left the stand."

"Yeah? I didn't know it was them."

"You want to meet 'em? I'll introduce you."

"Yeah, I wouldn't mind."

"Shake the Count's hand too. He's coming when he gets here."

"You play with him?"

"No, uh-unh, the man owns the piano, any piano he sits down at. I'm on later at a club with cats from around town. We piss on the stage, man, sit down and wail till the sun comes out. You never heard anything like this at La Joann's."

"I heard Louis Armstrong in Oklahoma City when I was there and bought one of his records. I took it home, my dad only listened to it once. He said that was enough."

"You live with your daddy?"

"I'm in Tulsa, he's in Okmulgee. I go down there sometimes for the weekend."

"Man, I was born in Muskogee, left there as soon as I had a pair of long pants." This piano player named McShann stared at Carl before saying, "You know, there's something about *you* looks familiar. Like you had your picture in the paper?"

"A few times."

"You shot somebody famous, didn't you? I'm thinking it was a bank robber."

"Well, I shot Emmett Long—"

"That's the one, some years ago. I remember reading you knew him from before."

"When I was fifteen, still living at home. I stopped at the drugstore to get an ice cream cone and Emmett Long came in for a pack of cigarets."

"You knew him by sight?"

"I recognized him from wanted dodgers. He's there and a tribal cop I knew happened to walk in, a Creek named Junior Harjo and Emmett shot him twice, for no reason." Carl paused and said, "Before Junior came in I was eating the ice cream cone . . . Emmett asked me was it peach. He wanted a taste, so I handed him the cone and he held it out in front of him as it was starting to drip. He took a bite . . . I looked at him, there was ice cream on his mustache."

McShann started to grin. "That stuck in your head, didn't it? Stole your ice cream cone and the next time you saw him you shot him dead."

"He was a wanted felon," Carl said, "The reason I tracked him down."

"I understand," McShann said, "but it's a better story you popped him for taking your ice cream cone." He looked straight at Carl Webster and said, "You sure you didn't?"

McShann told how he never took lessons but started playing in church, then with the Gray Brothers, played in Tulsa with them, in Nebraska, in Iowa, came to Kansas City and started playing for a dollar and a quarter a night; then after hours would drop around to other clubs. He said Julia Lee was the best piano player around for making money 'cause she knew the tunes everybody liked and asked you to play. So he learned these tunes—never mind if you liked them or not, you had to make money to live—and pretty soon he was working in the better clubs making two dollars and fifty cents for the evening and another five or six bucks from the kitty they put in front of the stand.

They each had a couple of drinks while they were talking about music and clubs.

Carl saying, "It sounds like you've played in all the clubs around town."

McShann said, "Most of 'em. I get old I'll play whorehouse piano."

Carl said, "I'm thinking this girl I'm looking for, she could be attracted to the excitement—I mean the clubs, not the whorehouses—and could be working in one of the joints. You happen to know of a redhead with pure white skin named Louly?"

Carl heard the name out loud as he said it and knew he had it wrong. But McShann was already telling him, "No, but I know a redhead with pure white skin name of Kitty."

The name she wrote on the note Carl had in his pocket.

She'd say to the gentlemen at the table, "Well, *hi*," sounding pleased to see them, "I'm Kitty. What can I serve you fellas?" Every once in a while she'd forget and say, "Well, *hi*, I'm Louly," and they wouldn't know the difference, more interested in seeing what they could see through her peach teddy. Just once a gentleman said, "I thought your name was Kitty," and she had to make up a story: how she was trying out her middle name, Kitty, 'cause she liked it better but wasn't used to it yet. After that happened, she'd remind herself who she was before going to the table.

It was the reporter from the *Kansas City Star*—the one who came to her home in Sallisaw *before* she went to Tulsa for the *True Detective* interview and then wasted her time waiting for Carl Webster to take her dancing—that reporter who told her if she ever went to Kansas City, get a job at Fred Harvey's in the Union Station. He said those girls made good tips for not having to take their clothes off. He said if she got a job at a club she might have to work bare naked. Louly said, "Oh . . . ?" The reporter said his favorite was Teddy's, once a millionaire's home at Eighteenth and Central.

He said, "But don't go near the place if you're Baptist."

When she applied for a job, Johnny the manager said, "You're a cutie, but our customers come first. They want to mess around with you, while they're in the club, like have a feel? You let 'em. Outside the club, they want to take you to a hotel when you're through work? That's up to you."

Young rich guys who'd come in late, horny and half smashed and want to get to it, were kind of a problem. They'd grab her in a back hall, a private room, even in Johnny's office, work a knee between her thighs and breathe hard trying to get her to leave with them.

"Parker, please, I don't work I'll get fired."

"Arthur, I'm so tired I could sleep standing up."

"Chip, I hate to say it, but I fell off the roof today."

She kept them coming back. They all had money, a couple were good-looking enough to be in the movies, and every one of them was married.

"Chandler, what will your wife say, you come home with my scent all over you?" It wasn't easy but worth it. These guys knew how to tip. Kitty's real problem was with Teddy Ritz.

She had scrimped to hold on to the $500 check the Oklahoma Bankers Association gave her for shooting Joe Young. Most of the $100 check from *True Detective* went for gas coming here and renting an apartment on West Thirty-first near the Lutheran Hospital. She had gone to the club to apply for a job and spoke to the manager. Johnny looked her over and said she'd hear pretty quick.

The next day Teddy Ritz himself stopped by with a dark-haired young guy, really handsome but dark, and with little cut scars on his face like you see on fighters. She had just moved in and was unpacking, a suitcase and a few boxes. Teddy prowled around opening doors, chewing his gum. He came out of the bathroom saying, "I like to know how hygenic my girls are," and to the young guy, "You ever sleep in a Murphy bed?" The young guy said, "What's that?" with some kind of accent. When Teddy was finished looking around, sat down and said to Kitty, "Okay, what do you do?"

"I kept books at a department store."

"You're lying. Doesn't matter—I wouldn't have a good-looking red-head working a comptometer. You strip?"

"I wouldn't know how."

The young good-looking guy with all that curly dark hair said with his accent, "You don't know how to take your clothes off?"

She saw Teddy Ritz give the young guy a serious look, cold, and the young guy shrugged.

Teddy was sitting on a chair half-turned from the junk desk that came with the furnished apartment. He brought his arm back to lay it on the desk, not looking, and pushed her rental agreement and check from the Bankers Association off the desk. Teddy looked down at the floor, then bent down and picked up the envelope the check was in, leaving the rental agreement.

He said, "What's this?"

"A reward they gave me?"

"For what?"

Teddy looked like the kind would get a kick out of her answer, so she told him. "Shooting a bank robber."

He stared at her for a few minutes.

"You're telling me you're in a bank while the guy's robbing it?" He saw her shaking her head, but knew everything and said, "What were you doing with a gun, in a bank?" Now he seemed confused, frowning. "You were with the guy you shot?"

Louly said, "You want to hear what happened?"

She began telling him how this convict Joe Young stole her stepfather's car and was holding her against her will in a tourist cabin when the police came looking for him and she was trapped in the cabin with a wanted man. Got that far and saw Teddy wasn't listening. He had the check out of the envelope and was glancing at the letter from the Bankers Association, thanking her for her courageous act. Teddy looked up.

"What were you going to do with this?"

"I thought I'd put it in the bank."

"Sweetheart, banks are shaky. Let me take care of it for you. Some guy'll come along and sell you something."

Louly made a face and said, "Gee, I don't know," like she had anything to say about it.

Teddy slipped the check inside his Chesterfield saying, "Don't tell me you don't trust your own boss."

She had a feeling the young guy, if he had been a fighter, might say something in a kidding way—if it would work with his accent—She's a big girl, can take care of her own money. But he didn't. He shrugged.

This evening, Kitty was serving sidecars to three young hotshots at a table in the bar, bringing them each two cocktails at a time so they wouldn't die of thirst between drinks, Kitty with a smile frozen to her face.

She was waiting for Teddy. When he came in she'd make herself walk up to him and ask for her $500, because her mom had to have an operation and they didn't have the money, account of their cotton crop had failed this past summer, as so many did, dried to kernels and blew away. She had to see that her mom had her operation.

And Teddy'll say, You're lying.

She looked toward the foyer—her story ready, though not anxious to try it on this gangster—and there was Carl Webster.

It *was*, it was Carl in his raincoat hanging open and his hat that had to sit just right, Carl holding a worn leather grip and standing with a piano player she recognized, both of them looking her way and grinning. Now the piano player was taking the grip from Carl and heading for the coat check and Carl was coming this way and Kitty felt her frozen smile thaw and heard her own voice in her mind say, *My God, look at him.* She wanted to run into his arms and tell him she was sorry for taking a powder on him, leaving Tulsa the way she did, and thought of that blues song the colored girl sang about going *back* to Tulsa. He was coming through the bar with only kind of a smile but his eyes not leaving hers.

One of the hotshots was saying, "Kitty Cat, pay attention. What do I have here?" Another one said, "What's wrong with her?" The first one said, "Take this, Kitty Cat, and fill it with nuts and bring us more side-cars, if you're not busy."

She felt Carl's arms come around her and she slid her bare arms inside his open raincoat, getting in there tight against him and feeling his gun between them, his suitcoat open, too. They were eye to eye grinning and now they were kissing and he was *good,* Kitty loving his smell of bay rum and whiskey but hearing a hotshot trying to ruin it, the hotshot saying, "Kitty Cat, the hell you doing with this bird?"

They stopped kissing but kept their hands on each other. Carl said, "That's what they call you, Kitty Cat?"

"These fellas are the only ones."

Carl was looking at them past her red hair straightened with an iron and brushed as hard as she could stroke it. Carl said to them, "Fellas, don't call her Kitty Cat no more. She doesn't like it."

She said close to him, "It's all right, they're just drunk."

"You want to be called Kitty Cat? Like you're their pet?"

She hadn't thought of it like that, but said, "Well, I'd rather not," knowing she didn't have to work here or be Kitty, or have to work anywhere or have to stay in Kansas City; knowing it because he had come to get her and she wasn't alone now.

The hotshots lounging at the table were after Carl now in their lazy way, wanting to know who the hell he was and what he thought he was doing, saying things like, "Who the fug you think you are?"

Carl moved Louly aside, took the dish one of them was holding and handed it to her. "They want some nuts." She looked confused holding the dish. Carl said, "Why don't you get 'em some?" She started toward the bar as he turned to the table.

Carl said, "I'm sorry if I disturbed you," and leaned over to get closer to them, placing his hands flat on the table, his raincoat and suitcoat hanging open. "But don't call her Kitty Cat again, okay?" Carl's tone quiet. "You do, I'll throw you girls out on the street." There was a silence as he kept looking at their upturned faces, young guys about Carl's age, giving them time to see his holstered revolver and make a judgment about him and say something to him if they had the nerve. Their time ran out and he turned to Kitty bringing the dish of peanuts.

She said, "I bet I just lost my job."

"What do you need it for?" Carl said, scooping up a handful of nuts. "You got *me*."

They went to the servants' quarters in back to what looked like a dressing room for showgirls: a mess of makeup at a row of vanities, clothes thrown on chairs, dozens of pairs of teddies hanging from an overhead pipe, a pile of torn ones in a trash basket and on the floor around it. Carl noticed the bathroom door closed while Louly put on her street clothes, Louly telling him she couldn't wait to get out of here.

"They're so confident the way they treat you. Especially the real rich ones, copping a feel whenever they want." But Teddy had her reward money, damn it, and she didn't want to leave without it.

"What's he doing with it?"

"I don't have any idea."

"We'll go see him and get it."

Carl walked toward the dozens of teddies hanging across the room wall to wall.

"I've got a story I made up," Louly said. "I tell him my mom needs money for an operation."

"It's yours—why you have to make up a story?"

"You don't know him."

Carl parted the wall of teddies to look at the rest of the room. "I read up on him in Marshals Service reports on Kansas City. Teddy supervises Jackson County precinct captains." Carl stepped through the underwear toward a window that looked out on part of the backyard, a garden illuminated by a spotlight mounted on the house. "Teddy's got four hundred men under him, some of 'em ex-convicts. His bodyguard did time in Oklahoma. Luigi Tessa."

He walked back to the curtain of teddies and parted them as Louly said, "Luigi? That's his name?"

"He's called Lou. From that coal mine district."

"Was he a prizefighter?"

"Yeah, but he wasn't any good. He went to work for the Black Hand some boys started up again, selling protection to Italian stores and restaurants. The owners are told, leave a thousand or so a month at the Choctaw Brick Company's abandoned works or some night your place of business goes up in flames. Tessa was caught and convicted of arson and did six years at Atoka, that's a prison farm. He came out—now they'd tell the owner of the business, pay up or some night when you aren't looking you get shot. This time they came after Tessa with a couple of homicide warrants."

"If they know he's here," Louly said, "why don't they come get him?"

"You're in Kansas City. They can't get a judge to sign the extradition order."

They heard the toilet flush.

Both looked at the bathroom door as it opened, swinging in. From where she stood Louly had a direct view inside. She said, "I didn't know anyone was in there. You entertain the old guys?"

Carl, standing to the side, heard a girl say, "You know what wears you out? Acting like you're having a good time."

"Smiling," Louly said, "till your face aches."

"Yeah, but I made sixty bucks. Not bad, uh? Now I go upstairs and work the ballroom."

She came out in her black stockings and heels, the crotch of her teddy hanging open, unsnapped.

Carl said, "Heidi?" stepping out of the wall of underwear. "Sounds like you're doing okay."

It wasn't the same as at the roadhouse, Carl appearing and Heidi throwing herself at him, old friends. This time she said, "Oh, shit. How in the world did you find us?"

"You know her?" Louly said, and to Heidi, "He came looking for *me*, not you." Serious about it.

"Are you kidding?" Heidi said. "He's looking for Jack, wants to take him back to Oklahoma."

"I swear," Carl said to Louly, "you're the reason I'm here." He turned to Heidi, noticing her crotch hanging open, "But if Jack's around, I wouldn't mind saying hello to him. Where y'all staying?"

Heidi stood with her legs apart, hands on her hips. "You think I'd tell you?"

"I swear I don't have a warrant," Carl said.

"You can shoot him. How'd you know to come here?"

"That piano player, McShann, told me a girl named Kitty worked here. Go up and ask him."

She stared at Carl like she might be thinking about it. Now she slipped her hands down her hips, turned around to snap herself up, squirmed to adjust the fit and turned back to Carl. "You could take him back to Oklahoma if you wanted, couldn't you? With or without a warrant."

"Now you want me to arrest him?"

"How about for taking that reporter's car?"

"I could."

"Why don't you?"

"He's in some trouble, huh?"

"Teddy says Jack owes him twenty-five hundred and has to pay it by tomorrow. Jack doesn't owe him, and wouldn't pay him if he had it."

"Why doesn't he run?"

"The car won't start."

"Boost another one."

"Teddy says if he leaves the house he's dead. Carl, all you have to do is walk in and make out like you're arresting him, taking him back to Oklahoma."

"If he's charged with anything he'll likely do time."

"That's better'n getting shot and dumped in the river."

"They don't mess around here, do they?"

"They're mean and evil," Heidi said. "Tell me you'll arrest him— please?"

"Tell me the truth," Carl said, "is this to save him or take him off your hands?"

Heidi said, "Would it matter?" And said, "Elodie's working here and Jack's making eyes at her."

"She quit selling it?"

"'Cause of the *True Detective* writer. She wrote to him and is waiting to hear if he loves her."

"You think they've done it yet?"

"I doubt it."

"Write down your address."

Heidi took her purse to a vanity and crouched over it. Kitty came over to stand by Carl.

"You sure know all the whores, don't you?"

He said, "Be nice."

Heidi came over now to hand him a piece of notepaper folded. She said, "Make it before noon, okay?" She opened the door to leave, stopped short and said, "Lou—"

Lou Tessa, wearing a tuxedo, came in looking at Carl. He turned to Heidi standing in the doorway and said, "You waiting for the streetcar?"

Heidi rolled her eyes at Carl and walked out, and Louly said to him, "We were just talking about you."

Tessa said, "Yes?"

"Carl told me all about you."

Carl got out his I.D. and star, wishing Louly hadn't said that. Who he was. He offered his hand.

Tessa said, "I know who you are," not taking his hand, and Carl got ready for whatever was coming. Tessa said to Kitty, "Teddy wants to see you," then turned to Carl with, "You too, sport."

Carl could see this as a movie set, the office of a guy who ran a night-club, all white and chrome, potted palms, photos of celebrities and Tom Pendergast on the wall, a pale desk with round corners where Teddy Ritz sat waiting.

His manager, Johnny, came past them to stand at the side of the desk and light a cigaret. He said to Carl, "I'll tell you this once. You get frisky, Lou will knock your head off."

Carl wondered if he meant Lou Tessa would use his fists and looked around. No, Lou Tessa in his tux was holding a baseball bat.

Teddy said, "What's going on?" to Louly, ignoring Carl and sounding surprised. "You want to get fired?"

She was looking at celebrity photos, at Will Rogers on the wall, Amelia Earhart and that flyer with the eye patch, Wiley Post. She turned to Teddy. "I've already quit."

Teddy frowned. "What're you talking about?"

"She means she's leaving," Carl said, "after you return her check. Or keep it and give her cash."

"Before I talk to you," Teddy said, "I want you to remove your weapon. Hand it to Johnny."

Carl paused, wondering about delivering his line. But it wouldn't make sense, it wasn't that kind of situation. He wondered if he could get by saying, *The only time I pull it . . .*

But Teddy was saying, "These guests of mine you insult to their face told me you came in with a gun. I want to see what you pack."

Teddy looked at Lou Tessa, and Carl was aware of the guy moving up on his right with the bat cocked, Carl thinking to use it as a threat—pull your gun or get your head knocked off—but he was swinging through with it, slamming the Louisville Slugger across Carl's midsection hard enough to pound the air out of him and double him over gasping, stumbling into Johnny who caught him, reached into his coat and pulled his gun from its holster and handed it across the desk to Teddy. Carl went to his knees and Johnny's hand slipped into his suit again to come out with the I.D. wallet and slide it across the desk to Teddy, Carl hanging on to the desk with his elbows, Louly trying to get to him but Johnny holding her away from him.

Teddy said, "Deputy United States marshal," and raised his eyes from the I.D., Carl almost close enough to touch. He said, "Boy, you don't have to get on your knees to me. I have a number of friends are marshals, good boys, too." He released the Colt's cylinder and dumped out the bullets, saying, "Tell me what you're doing here. Come all the way from Tulsa to help out your sweetheart?" He shoved the wallet and empty revolver across the desk at Carl, who opened his hands to catch them. Teddy said, "Lou, help the marshal up. He's got a tummyache."

Carl felt Tessa's hands under his arms lifting him. He pushed his thighs against the desk while he picked up his gun and wallet. He said to Tessa, "I bet you learned to hit like that on a prison farm."

"Hurts, don't it?"

"Hurts like hell. Can I see the bat?"

Tessa cocked it. "Where you want it? Is a Pepper Martin thirty-four inch."

"I played high school ball," Carl said. "I liked a thirty-five-inch brown bat with white tape on it. I'd choke up a couple of inches."

Teddy said, *"Hey,"* to get Carl's attention. "You believe Kitty Cat shot a bank robber and this association gave her a check for five hundred dollars?"

"I was there," Carl said, "when she shot him, a fugitive felon. I don't think he was worth five hundred, but that's what they gave her. Do I believe you took the check from her? Yes I do, 'cause she told me you did and I wouldn't put it past you."

Teddy said, "Can you walk okay?"

"I'm pretty sure."

"Then you better walk out," Teddy said. "I see you here again, Lou'll fix it you ride in a wheelchair the rest of your life."

Louly held him by the arm. She asked a few times if he was all right, if he wanted to go to the hospital. There was one close to where she lived. Carl said no, he'd make it. He said it was like getting thrown off a bull and landing on your stomach. Other than that they didn't speak until they came to Louly's Ford, the one she stole from Mr. Hagenlocker, parked on Twelfth Street.

Getting him in the car she said, "I don't suppose you want to go dancing."

"When we get home," Carl said. "I mean Tulsa."

She turned on to Central heading south, Carl's hands flat on the seat on both sides of him, trying to hold himself off the bumps in the road.

"I had something I wanted to say to Teddy, but Lou Tessa was dying to swing at me again, go for the fence this time."

"What did you want to tell him?"

"To keep five hundred bucks on him, so the next time we saw him he could give it to you."

Louly turned from headlights and what traffic there was to look at Carl. "I'm there with you?"

"The way I see it, yeah. Tomorrow at Heidi and Jack's. Why I got their address."

15

Jack Belmont was the only man Heidi had ever known who put on a bathrobe when he got up in the morning. She thought he might've picked it up from the movies; guys who were well-off put on bathrobes over their pajamas even if they got up to answer the phone. Jack was still sleeping when she came home at half past seven and had to keep shaking him before he opened his eyes, cranky as hell.

She said, "Jack, you want to get shot lying down or standing up? Teddy's coming for his check today. But guess what. Help is on the way."

He sat in the kitchen now in his robe drinking French-drip coffee she'd had to learn patience to make, adding just a speck of water at a time and heating the milk without letting it boil over. When Heidi sat down with him and first mentioned Carl Webster coming, Jack wanted to know how Carl found out he was here.

"He came looking for that redhead, not you. But he's willing to put you under arrest and take you back to Oklahoma."

"In chains?" Jack said.

"To keep Teddy from shooting you."

"So Carl can do it?"

It went on like that, Jack not caring to put himself in the hands of this marshal who liked to shoot offenders. He said to Heidi, "How much money have you got?"

"A hundred and sixty, tip money you never found."

"I still have what the bank gave us, just about seventeen hundred."

"What about my tip money you took?"

"I spent it," Jack said. "But I'm thinking, if we offer Teddy—what's a hundred and sixty and seventeen hundred . . . twenty-three hundred? I bet he'll settle for it, it's close."

"It's only eighteen hundred and sixty, you dope. He'll take it," Heidi said, "you bet he will, and then he'll shoot you. He swiped five hundred off that little redhead, Kitty? And kept it."

"Five bills—with all the money he's got?"

"It's his nature. If there's money Teddy can get hold of he'll take it. He don't have to need it, it's why he's a crook. Carl came from Tulsa to help Kitty get her money back and Teddy had him beat up. With a baseball bat."

"Then how's he gonna help me?"

"Kitty says he's all right, just sore. She called this morning to find out when Teddy's coming. I told her he said noon. But then I said he might come earlier to surprise you, thinking you might take off on him. She mentioned that's what Carl said he'd do, not trusting you to wait around."

"But I'm supposed to trust him."

"Honey, he's all you have."

"How do I know he'll come?"

"He's still set on getting Kitty her money."

They sat in the Ford Roadster on Edgevale, on the same side of the street and three houses down from the bungalow they were watching. There was one car between them and the Ford Jack Belmont stole

from the *True Detective* writer but now wouldn't run. According to
Heidi.

"If it's true," Carl said.

"Why would she lie about it?" Louly sat behind the wheel wearing a
cloche down on her eyes, beige, to go with her camel coat.

"I can't think of a reason," Carl said. "I already told the marshals office here to let Antonelli know where to pick it up."

"How will they find him?"

"Call the magazine long-distance."

She turned her gaze from the house to look at Carl. "What are the
chances Teddy having five hundred dollars on him?"

He could sit and stare at her dark brown eyes all day.

"Better than fifty-fifty."

"Don't I wish."

The edge of the cloche came straight across her eyes and gave her a
smart look, not some country girl from Sallisaw but still a girl, Jesus,
that perfect mouth pouting at him.

"I think Teddy gets payoffs wherever he goes," Carl said. "He's out
driving around—why not make some stops?"

"Will he be alone?"

"Not if he's out collecting. I hope Tessa's along, with his Pepper
Martin bat."

Louly said, "You scare me sometimes."

"Did I scare you last night?"

Now she was grinning at him, not at all self-conscious. "It was the
best time I've ever had in bed—my God, in my life."

"I was afraid at first," Carl said, "you'd never done it before."

"I have, but just once."

"Well, you sure catch on quick."

"And you were in awful pain."

"It wasn't that bad, or you took my mind off it. I woke up this morning I was stiff—I mean my entire body was stiff and sore." He said, "You know what I'm dying to do right now?"

Louly said, "Why don't you?"

He slipped his arm around her. She sprang at him and they were kissing, meaning it, and didn't let go till she bumped his hat from the way he'd set it and he had to take it off knowing he looked dumb. Louly said, "Carl, you're the best kisser I've ever kissed. You don't ever get too wet and sloppy, just enough."

"We take Jack with us," Carl said, "we won't have much time for ourselves."

"Have you decided where we sit?"

"You drive, he's in back."

"What about going to the bathroom?"

Carl said, "What about it?" and saw the La Salle glide up the street past them.

They watched Teddy Ritz in his black chesterfield come out of the passenger side of the sedan, parked behind the *True Detective* writer's Ford. Lou Tessa came out of the driver's side in his long black overcoat and hustled to join Teddy on the front steps. They saw Heidi open the door. The two entered and the door closed. Louly looked at Carl.

Carl said, "Let's give Jack a few minutes with them."

Louly said, "That's mean."

"When was it Teddy swiped the check?"

"Four days ago."

"Where'd he put it?"

"In the inside pocket of his overcoat."

"The one he's wearing?"

"Yeah, with the velvet collar."

"What do you know about Tessa?"

"He might be the best-looking guy I've ever seen."

"That's all you know?"

"He gives you the eye, acting like Casanova, but doesn't do anything. He told Heidi he'd call her but never did."

"Sets you up and then plays hard to get?"

"I don't know," Louly said, "he's strange."

"You ready?"

They walked up the street to the bungalow and the door opened before Carl could touch the bell, Heidi waiting for them but acting surprised—"Well, hi, you two"—asking what they were doing in the neighborhood. Louly saying Carl had a surprise for Jack and Heidi saying, "Really?"

Teddy watched deadpan from the morris chair, Tessa a few steps away from him. Jack was to the left, toward the kitchen. Carl was eye to eye with Teddy staring at him before turning to Jack, deciding to do him first. He didn't care if Teddy believed this show or not.

He said, "John Belmont, I'm placing you under arrest for multiple felony allegations pending. I'm taking you back to Oklahoma to face these charges. Turn around."

Jack said, "What charges you talking about?"

Carl brought a pair of handcuffs from the pocket of his raincoat hanging open. "One's parked out in front."

"The Ford? What's his name, Tony, said I could borrow it. That writer."

"What about the seven guys in bedsheets?"

"I was protecting my life. Jesus, yours, too."

Carl thought Jack was doing okay in front of Teddy, Teddy looking from one to the other, but now Carl wanted to get it done and stepped up to Jack, took him by the arm and snapped a cuff on his wrist. This stirred Teddy.

He said, "Hold it there. I don't know if this is a show you're putting on—"

"Watch," Carl said, "I'm taking him in."

"Well, before you get him trussed up, me and Jack are doing some business here."

"You can write to him," Carl said, "care of the Oklahoma State Penitentiary." He brought Jack's other arm in front of him and cuffed his wrists together, the way he'd ride the 350 miles south and realize the fun was over. He said to Jack, "You weren't gonna pay him, were you?"

"I told him the other day I didn't have it."

"He must've thought you'd go out and steal it."

"He said this wop'd shoot me I didn't pay him."

"You mean Luigi?" Carl looked at Tessa staring at them. He said to Jack, "How were you gonna handle it?"

"I was about to go in the kitchen," Jack said. "I got a gun in the bread box. I'd lock these guys in a closet if I didn't have to shoot 'em, and me and Heidi'd drive down to Old Mexico in Teddy's La Salle."

Heidi said, "*Mexico?*" The idea not sounding much fun to her.

Teddy was hanging on every word, his hands gripping the arms of his chair, pushing himself up now. Carl didn't know what he had in mind, but stepped over to push him down again and stand over him. He saw Tessa's hand go inside his overcoat.

Carl said, "Luigi, you want to get involved in this?"

Tessa didn't answer or move. It was like his hand was caught inside his coat.

Carl shook his head from side to side, slow about it, and looked over at Louly and Heidi, the two of them smoking, Heidi holding a glass ashtray.

"Show you how dumb these two are, Teddy thinks this ex-convict, who blew off seven guys like he was in a shooting gallery, is too scared not to pay him, even if he doesn't owe it. And Jack thinks Teddy would let him out of his sight, go in the kitchen and get his gun out of the bread box." He said to Heidi, "That's where he keeps it?"

"One of 'em," Heidi said. "He keeps his money in a Quaker Oats box."

"You know where he got it," Teddy said, "across the river. He held up the National Bank over there."

"I believe it," Carl said, "but can't see him giving you any of it. You told him you'd have him shot if he didn't? If I was Jack I'd get hold of that Pepper Martin bat—I bet a dollar's out in the La Salle—and use it on Teddy, after I worked over Luigi with it."

See what they thought of that.

Tessa held his pose, hand in his coat, giving Carl his deadpan stare. Teddy's look said he was listening to Carl talk, no more than that.

"But I'm not Jack," Carl said, "or a sucker-puncher like Luigi." He looked at Louly and Heidi. "This jelly bean's wanted in Oklahoma on a pair of homicide warrants, one in Krebs, one in Hartshorne. He killed a man in each town. Each owned a restaurant. Each was shot in the back. But he works for Teddy Ritz, so the courts here won't send him back."

Carl's hand went to Teddy's shoulder and he leaned in close to him saying, "Where's Kitty's check?" as his hand slid over the velvet lapel to dip into Teddy's chesterfield. "In here?" and came out holding an envelope, Carl sure it was the one the way Louly screamed and came to get it. She took out the check, but then hesitated and looked at Teddy.

"Where's the letter that was with it?"

Teddy looked up at her. "What're you trying to pull?"

"From the Bankers Association."

"It isn't even your check." Teddy getting in a huff now. "It's made out to somebody else."

"He threw away the letter," Louly said, "didn't even read it."

Carl laid his hand on Teddy's shoulder again. This time he gave it a pat saying, "That's her name, Louise Brown. She only uses Kitty for serving drinks in her underwear."

He stepped away from Teddy in the morris chair to stand facing Tessa.

"What're you holding on to in there?"

Carl felt he'd have to say something this time.

He did, he said, with his accent, "Keep shooting off your mouth you find out."

Carl shook his head. "You won't pull unless I turn my back on you," and stared in Tessa's face giving him time, his moment, the way he gave the sidecar drinkers time, the hotshots having fun with Kitty Cat. What you did, you called. And what they did next let you know who they were. He turned to Louly to see her brown eyes wide open beneath the hat brim, Louly ready to scream.

But she didn't, and this business was over.

Heidi was staying. She could make more wearing only a pair of black silk stockings than she could screwing commercially. She went in the kitchen to make her boss a cup of tea, and while the water was on to boil, she took Jack's money out of the Quaker Oats box and wedged it behind the twenty-five-pound block of ice in the icebox.

Louly came in to say good-bye and Heidi said, "Who are you now, Kitty or Louly?"

"Carl likes Louly, so I guess that's who I am." She said, "I know he's kind of a show-off—"

"Kind of?"

"The way he talked to Lou, kept egging him on. I was scared to death."

"Got him down and wouldn't let him up," Heidi said.

"But Carl's a nice guy, really."

"He's also a federal marshal and wants you to know it. Tell him to keep Jack away from me, all right? I don't want to have to talk to him. He's cute but he's crazy. I mean there's something wrong with his head. His mama didn't nurse him long enough or something. I don't want to tell him I'll wait for him when I know I won't." She nodded at the bread box. "Take that thirty-two's in there. You're driving to Oklahoma with a crazy man."

Louly said, "Which one?"

In the front room Teddy, on his feet now, told Lou Tessa to go get in the car and wait for him. He said to Carl, "There's something I have to ask you. You're packing that Colt you had last evening, right?"

Carl said, "You could've had your boy find out."

"Tell me you're packing," Teddy said. "Clear my mind."

"I'm packing."

"You want a job? You can have Lou's."

Jack said, "I'll take it," jumping at the offer.

"What do you pay a man," Carl said, "goes around with his hand stuck in his coat?"

"I'll pay anything you want."

"Just so you know," Jack said, "he ever spoke to me like he did to

Lou Tessa, in front of everybody like that? The first remark out of his mouth, I'd of pulled and killed him where he stood."

Teddy looked at Carl and Carl said, "Jack's never faced an armed man looking him in the eye."

Jack said, "How do you know?"

Carl took a moment to say, "You want us to meet sometime, don't you?"

Jack said, "Don't you?"

They brought Jack out to Louly's car and put him in the backseat with her things. Jack said, "What about my clothes? I got shirts, I got a brand-new suit hanging in the bedroom closet." Carl didn't answer him. Jack said, "You gonna take these cuffs off?" Carl told him not yet. Jack said, "Well, when are you?"

This time Carl walked away. Louly, sitting behind the wheel, watched him go up to the driver's side of the La Salle and rap on the window. It seemed like Tessa hesitated before rolling it down. Carl said something to him that only took a moment. He came back to Louly's car and got in.

"What'd you say to him?"

"I told him he ought to find a different line of work."

Jack said from the backseat, "I told a fella that once. Seventy-eight years old with a Frontier-model Peacemaker in his holster."

"The bank guard you shot?" Carl said.

Jack caught himself. "I'm not saying another word." But he did, he said, "Why don't we get out of here?"

Louly got the car going and turned south at the corner.

"We're going back the way I came."

"Any way you want," Carl said, "me and Jack are along for the ride."

He turned enough to look at him. "I recalled Teddy saying you robbed a bank across the river. You're facing more charges'n I thought."

It brought Jack forward to grab on to the front seat.

"You told Heidi you don't have a warrant. All you're doing, you're pulling me out from under Teddy, keep him from shooting me. Isn't that right?"

"No, I told her you'd likely go to prison on one charge or another. She said prison was better than getting shot and thrown in the river. I know that's a matter of opinion, so I didn't argue with her. I didn't care if she told you or not."

Carl watched Jack staring at him from barely two feet away.

"You thought I'd turn you loose?"

"It's what she told me."

"Then what? I blindfold my eyes, count to a hundred and say here I come ready or not?"

Jack said, "Buddy, if I go back to prison," making it sound like he was taking an oath, "I'm gonna bust out shortly and come looking for you."

"'Cause I said you'd likely do time and Heidi didn't tell you?"

"She knows how I see prison. She'd of given me the choice of taking a chance with Teddy or being locked up."

"I can't help it if she didn't tell it straight."

"I remember saying to her, 'I'm suppose to trust him?' I let you trick me." Jack eased back in the seat. "It's my own fault, but I'm gonna get you for it. Only you don't know when."

"Jesus Christ," Carl said, "grow up, will you?"

"I promise," Jack said, "I'm gonna plug you as soon as you're in my sights. You know why? So I won't have to hear that horseshit about you shooting to kill if you have to draw your weapon. Any time you shoot some poor fella and get your picture in the paper, there it is, 'If I have to draw my weapon—' Or do you say if you have to pull your weapon?

I know you say it the same way every time. The hell are you pulling it for you don't shoot to kill? What're you packing a gun for? Saying that never made sense to me. But it gives you an excuse, huh? There's a dead man lying there—somebody says, 'It's too bad he's dead, but it's his own fault. He made Carl pull his weapon. Yeah, otherwise Carl wouldn't hurt a flea. He's a swell guy. Loves peach ice cream cones."

Louly glanced at Carl to see him looking straight ahead.

Now Jack raised his hands in front of his face.

"I suppose, now that I've said my piece, you're leaving the cuffs on."

"All the way to Tulsa," Carl said. "Keep talking, I'll cuff you from behind and gag you."

16

The sky hung as a shroud over the Bald Mountain Club, gray and unforgiving, a day that dawned with an indifferent beginning, but would end in violent deaths for twelve victims of the massacre.' "

Bob McMahon looked up from the magazine.

"That's how he opens it."

Across the desk Carl said, "What's he call it?"

" 'Massacre at Bald Mountain.' "

Carl said, "I wonder how many you have to have killed for it to be a massacre." He was thinking of last summer: five lawmen and the escaped convict they were returning to Leavenworth gunned down outside the Union Station, and they called it the Kansas City Massacre. The shooters opened with Thompsons and disappeared.

"I think Tony liked the sound of *massacre* and *mountain* together," Bob McMahon said. He kept his copy of *True Detective* in front of him with one finger marking a page. "The boy knows how to write a good story. Eight pages with pictures, most of them from the past. One of Jack Belmont, on trial for destruction of property. One of Nestor Lott in uniform, during the war."

"Is he wearing his medal?"

"Tony calls him 'the diminutive two-gun avenger, dedicated to killing violators of the liquor law.' You know there's more information in this story than I've been able to gather from all the sources we've used? Tony Antonelli, bless his heart, has all the facts, the correct names, who they are, backgrounds . . . He's wearing his medal lying dead."

Carl said, "But he calls the roadhouse the Bald Mountain Club. I think Tony made it up. There's no name like that outside or anywhere inside the place."

"He said that's what Jack Belmont called it."

"It's the first I've heard."

"Another place in the story he calls Nestor 'the former Bureau of Investigation agent turned renegade.' You want to hear how Tony describes your shooting Nestor?"

"I'll read it sometime."

"He says you tell Nestor if you have to draw you'll shoot to kill."

"Bob, I was there."

"Remember my asking you if you had your gun out? And finally got you to say you did? Tony said he asked you the same thing and you danced around it. You asked Tony if he thought you'd be lying to Nestor saying 'if I have to draw' when your gun's in your hand."

"I was having fun with him."

"You want to know what he wrote?" McMahon flipped the magazine open with his finger inside, seemed about to read, but then looked up at Carl.

"How come none of the good guys got shot?"

"There weren't any good guys."

"Norm Dilworth?"

"He was getting better."

"You still believe Belmont killed him."

"I know he did."

"I didn't tell you," McMahon said, "Lester Crowe's quit the marshals."

"That's a shame," Carl said.

"He didn't think we were treating Nestor right."

"You gonna read what Tony wrote?"

McMahon looked down at the magazine and read, " 'Nestor Lott brought up both of his chrome-plated .45s at the same time to clear the car's hood and Marshal Carl Webster,' " McMahon looked up again, his eyes on Carl, " 'with lightning responses, shot him through the chest.' There's one more word at the end of the sentence," McMahon said, " '*Bam.*' "

"He wrote '*Bam*'?" Carl grinning now.

" '*Bam.*' "

"I told him to write what he saw. He had the best seat in the house." Carl felt good, everything working for him. "Bob, I gotta get going, I'm seeing Oris Belmont at two."

"What about?"

"Jack called him wanting a lawyer for his appeal and his dad hung up on him. I think the old man should help him out."

"Hire a good lawyer to get him off," McMahon said. "Why, so you can shoot him?"

Carl smiled without wanting to, knowing Bob was kidding. "You don't believe that, do you?"

"No, but it could happen," McMahon said. "I'm putting you on court duty for a while."

"Why, what'd I do?"

"You went to Kansas City on your own."

"To look for Belmont. We talked about it."

"We agreed he could be there. That's all the talking we did. You're lucky you brought him back."

"He swears he's gonna bust out of prison and shoot me."

"How is it," McMahon said, "you go after an offender, it seems to become a personal matter?"

Carl wasn't sure what he meant.

"Starting with Emmett Long, you were sure out to get him."

It was funny how every time Carl pictured Emmett it was with the ice cream on his mustache. And yet Carl saw him as an outlaw as tough as they come, his first big test.

"Just certain ones," Carl said.

"How about Nestor? You have a personal feeling there?"

"Nestor—Nestor was spooky. He was so serious about being stupid."

Carl remembered his dad saying, "You work high up in that bank building you get to look out at Tulsa." Another time he said, "Strike it rich, you get to put up a building with your name on it and buy a house in Maple Ridge."

Oris didn't have his own building but sat high up at his desk with aerial views to either side of him, his hands on the leather arms of his chair. Carl recognized him from pictures in the paper, though he no longer had his bushy mustache; that time was gone.

Oris said, "I don't care for you knowing about Jack calling me. That's a personal matter." Now he crossed his arms and held on to one elbow but didn't look comfortable.

Carl told him a deputy at the county jail was standing there and overhead Jack make his call, say he needed a lawyer. That's all was said before Jack hung up the phone.

Oris said, "You brought him to jail, didn't you? You weren't satisfied with his sentence?"

"It wasn't a fair trial," Carl said.

"What do you care?"

"Jack's lawyer was a young Italian guy from Krebs appointed by the court and approved by the judge, somebody he knew he could handle.

The lawyer's first mistake was trying to get the judge taken off the case."

"Recused," Oris said.

"That's the word. On account of the judge is a known supporter of the Klan and the seven guys Jack shot were all Klansmen. The judge told the lawyer if he kept after him he'd be held in contempt and thrown in jail."

Oris wanted to know what the defense was.

Carl said the fact that Nestor Lott had no authority in the matter and the Klansmen had no business coming at the roadhouse with guns and torches. The prosecutor got his witnesses to say they saw the defendant kill their friends in cold blood, seven men with families, their only intention to help uphold the law of the land. "The prosecutor," Carl said, "described the case as based on an unusual circumstance, the ones on the offensive becoming the victims. But that's why he's charged with manslaughter and not first-degree murder."

"And got twenty years," Oris said.

"I guess the most the judge could give him."

"Where's he serving it?"

"McAlester."

"Where he was before."

Carl almost said, *Where you sent him,* but held off and thought of what Mr. Belmont said a minute ago, *What do you care?*

"I read in the paper you come out of this a hero. You shot Nestor Lott and three others, boys. How is it you weren't brought up?"

"The way the court presented it, I was there to close down the roadhouse. Nestor Lott attacked a federal officer by mistake. I was a prosecution witness, but they never called me to testify. They saw it might give Jack's lawyer a position to argue self-defense. The trial took a day and a half, the jury made up its mind this morning in about an hour.

The way they saw it, Jack's a bank robber, wasn't he? Hell, send him to prison."

Oris said, "Why don't you like the idea?"

"I'm being picky. I think he should be in prison, but not for this one. The marshals office in Kansas City'll take him right now. They want him for shooting a seventy-eight-year-old man, a bank guard, in a robbery up there."

"The man die?"

"Yes, he did. Jack can shoot. He'll serve time here or get off on appeal, I could be the one takes him to Kansas City, and I'll do it, like I brought him back from there."

Oris put his hands on the arms of his chair to shift his position, settling in.

"I've read about you." Nodding his head up and down. "You shot Emmett Long a few years ago. I saw him one time in Sapulpa. He seemed like an egotistical man. You shot Peyton Bragg, didn't you? From four hundred yards. In the dark. I should've known you right away, you're the millionaire marshal."

"That's my dad has the money."

"I know him, too, Virgil Webster. We wanted him on the board of this bank we have down in Okmulgee and he turned us down. He seemed friendly though."

"He does okay growing pecans and reading the paper," Carl said. "Neither of us is up on business, though I ran a cow outfit till I came of age and became a marshal."

Oris pulled out his pocket watch, looked at it and asked Carl if he'd eaten yet. Carl shook his head. Oris flicked on the office intercom and leaned toward it to say, "Audrey? Call Nelson's and see if they have any chicken-fried steaks left. They do, have 'em put two aside and we'll be over. With potatoes and green beans." He said to Carl, "Sometimes by three they run out."

Nelson's Buffeteria was Carl's favorite restaurant in Tulsa. He said, "Do people here eat anywhere else?"

Audrey came back on to say they were all set.

Oris said to Carl, "Why should I help him?"

Carl said, "He's your boy," and saw Oris shaking his head.

"Not anymore."

"I spoke to Mrs. Belmont," Carl said. "I know she has no sympathy for him. What I wondered, if you knew what a bum deal that trial was and had some time to think about it. Or talk to a good defense lawyer and get his opinion."

"I'll see about it," Oris said. "I want to know what your game is. Why you want him out."

"I don't want him out. But I can't see Jack in prison doing twenty years, and he can't either. He says he's gonna bust out, he said shortly, and he might be able to do it. McAlester hasn't been the toughest joint to bust out of."

"He told you he plans to escape?"

"In Kansas City and on the way back in the car, he talked all the way here."

"What about?"

"Himself. He's having a good time packing a gun and being a wanted desperado, but he thinks he deserves to be more famous. His goal in life is to be Public Enemy Number One. I told him shooting the Klansmen should help, get him known all over the country. But he'd have to escape from McAlester to make Public Enemy Number One. John Dillinger has that spot locked up. Dillinger's robbed banks in Indiana, Ohio, Wisconsin, Idaho, Illinois. He's escaped from jail twice, and got away from that resort in Wisconsin, Little Bohemia, when federal agents had it surrounded. Dillinger appears to have a first-class outfit. Those fellas know what they're doing."

Oris said, "What about Clyde Barrow and Bonnie Parker?"

"What do they rob," Carl said, "grocery stores? They're bush league. They spend all their time shooting law officers and trying to get around roadblocks. You want another one to put up there with Dillinger? Take our own Oklahoma boy, Charley Floyd. I told Jack if he's made up his mind to be a bad guy, read up on Pretty Boy. I said in the car, talk to Louly here, she's a first cousin of Charley's wife, Ruby, and knows him. She says he's kind and considerate to his family, gives money to people who don't have any. You could say he comes the closest of any bank robber to acting like a human being."

Oris was scowling now. "You encourage him to continue being a criminal?"

"I didn't waste time trying to *dis*courage him. He's made up his mind what he wants. Louly told him he was good-looking enough to have girls swooning over him, but what good is it if he's hiding out all the time?"

Oris looked lost. "You're saying it's too late to turn him around."

"Way too late," Carl said. "Jack busts out of prison he could become our most famous desperado. For a while anyway."

There was a joke they told about church pews. "You know why church pews are so uncomfortable?"

"No, why?"

"They're made by convicts."

It's what they had Jack Belmont doing for seven months in the Oklahoma State Prison at McAlester, messing up his hands making church pews. He said to the captain, "I belong in an office. I never even *sat* in a pew in my life."

Jack knew about the captain, Fausto Bassi, fired from his job as Krebs' chief of police for letting Nestor Lott stick him in his own jail cell. But then stepped into this corrections job because of his experience with offenders.

"So you shoot seven members of the Ku Klux Klan," Fausto said with his accent.

"As fast as I could," Jack said, and it got Fausto to smile.

They sat in his office where Jack had first met Carl Webster, looking out through bars at the rotunda, the birdcage as big as a church between the cell houses, four floors of prison bars painted white, where they heard the sound of beating wings.

"Pigeons find their way in," Fausto said, "but can't remember how to go out. Like inmates, uh?" He said, "They making me a deputy warden pretty soon. They need one and don't have anybody else. I'll see if I can give you a job in the office. You know how to use a typewriter?"

"Is it hard?"

Fausto, with his big stomach, smiled again. "All you have to do is learn, uh? You know you shouldn't be here. The judge and the prosecutor made up their mind they going to put you away. You hear from your father?"

Jack said, "No, why?"

"He's hiring a lawyer to appeal your case. Cecil Guyton. You know that name?"

Jack said no.

"You never heard the name Cecil Guyton?"

"I don't know, maybe."

"He was prosecutor in Tulsa County a few years, quit and became a famous defense lawyer, like Clarence Darrow. You know him, don't you?"

"Clarence Darrow," Jack said, "the Monkey Trial."

"They both take the same kind of cases, ones that attract a crowd."

"I'm the monkey this time?" Jack said. "Where will the trial take place?"

"I think here in the district court, unless he wants to change the venue. But Cecil Guyton's on a case right now. It could be a month before he can take you on."

"What's he charge?"

"Ask your father."

"He usually wins?"

"Almost always. You walk or have your sentence reduced. This one, he should have no trouble. But there is a condition Guyton always insists on. He won't come to the prison."

"What do you mean?"

"To talk to you, tell you what to say. He has to have permission from the prison for you to go to him. He takes a suite at the Aldridge to see you there. If it can't be arranged to let you out he won't take your case."

"You might be afraid I'll wander off?"

"Why would you if he's setting you free? Or you're given a year or so, with credit for time served, instead of twenty years? Still, I think your daddy will have to put up a bond."

"Well, if he's hired this guy . . . Why won't Guyton visit the prison?"

"He says it's unsanitary. Cecil Guyton is careful of his health. We will let him have his way because, first, we know you were railroaded and, second, it gives us a chance to look intelligent and right this wrong. Also, we don't like the judge who sentenced you."

"You're saying I'm as good as free."

"In Oklahoma," Fausto said. "They holding a detainer on you in Kansas."

"I'm arrested right away?"

"It could happen."

"Walk out of the courtroom . . . ?"

"And there's a marshal there to pick you up," Fausto said. "Or they take you back to prison to wait for the marshal. What's the hurry?"

Jack talked to inmates who'd been here a while about escape attempts. Most seemed to take place when convicts were used on work crews outside the prison. On a signal they'd make a run for it in different directions and a couple would get shot by the guards and a couple would get away, for a time. There were convicts who had guns smuggled in and slipped away in delivery trucks and the prison mail truck. Two inmates working in the women's cell house scaled down the outside of the building and drove away in the assistant matron's motorcar. Two others tunneled out of the tubercular ward of the prison hospital, hiding the dirt in the basement.

Jack's favorite: a convict inside only eighteen months of a thirty-year stretch got permission to see a member of the parole board at the county offices in town. The convict talked his guard into stopping for a soda in the drugstore. Once they were inside he ran out the back, around the corner, jumped in a taxi, and got all the way to Muskogee, seventy miles.

Jack would be taken to town pretty soon to meet with the famous lawyer at the Aldridge Hotel. He'd have to look at his chances of going a hundred miles, all the way to Tulsa.

And not get shot by the police once he got there. Like the convict who went to Muskogee.

17

Court duty gave Carl time to think. The first thing he wondered about was why any marshal liked working as a bailiff; and most seemed to. They gave different reasons like, "You get to see justice carried out." Carl actually heard that said. Or, "You don't get shot at." That could happen though. A woman standing in the back of the courtroom walks up to the defendant sitting at the table with his lawyer and puts one in the back of his head. Then she panics and shoots at the marshal—he's in his stance, his revolver extended—she misses and people right there grab her. If they'd waited another second the marshal would've shot her. Or somebody comes in to assassinate the judge and starts firing and there's a shootout. But the assassin barely knows how to shoot and he sprays the courtroom, the ceiling, till the marshal shoots him down.

Carl stood by the door on the side of the courtroom away from the jury. It led to where they kept the defendant and either took the cuffs off or left them on before bringing him in. There were more bank robbers this year than before, most of them tough young guys, but even some family men out of work, respectable-looking men. Trials that should take ten minutes and went on all day, the defense lawyers not having any idea where they were going.

During these first months no one he had arrested appeared before the court. Most of them, though, were familiar from their case files or Carl had seen them on wanted sheets.

The one he saw in the audience that surprised him was Venicia Munson, Peyton Bragg's girlfriend from Bunch. That scene at her house, the night they waited for Peyton to make his move, had been more than a year ago.

Carl's reasoning had her here on behalf of a bootlegger pal who'd been arrested, caught in what was still a dry state even though Prohibition had been repealed. Here you could buy 3.2 beer and that was it.

He saw her looking at him standing by his door. He looked back at her and smiled, but she didn't. They met in the hall at the end of the session. Carl reached to touch the hat he wasn't wearing.

"Miss Munson, it's nice to see you again."

He thought she looked pretty good, like some girl with style had shown her how to put on makeup and cock that little pillbox down on one eye. Carl would say she looked almost saucy in her hat and coat.

He said, "You have business with the court?" Making it sound like a pleasant experience.

"I have business with you," Venicia said. "I've come for my rifle, a Winchester with a scope sight you took from my house."

He remembered aiming at that Essex in the dark, the taillights . . . "I never returned it, did I?"

She said, "Would I be here?" Her mouth a slit of red saying it, the memory of his shooting her boyfriend, Peyton, still in her eyes.

"You understand," Carl said, "the rifle had to be described in the coroner's report and a Bertillon exam made, showing I had fired the rifle. I got it back and was gonna bring it to you the next time I was out around Bunch . . . Or give it someone going that way—"

"You still have it?"

"Yes, I do. It's at my apartment, on South Cheyenne."

"Why don't I pick it up?" Venicia said. "It's only been fourteen months since you took it."

Carl said, "Listen, I'm really sorry. I forgot all about it."

She said, "If you're going home now I'll follow you and be out of your hair."

They walked out of the courthouse together, Carl making conversation.

Louly would say to him, "Do you love me, Carl? Do you really love me?"

He'd say, "I'm nuts about you, baby."

She'd say, "Can't you ever be serious."

He'd say, "Tell my dad I'm nuts about you, a man whose heart is in his nuts, and see what he says."

She'd punch him on the arm and give him a push. Louly was nuts about Carl, too.

She'd say, "Aren't we gonna get married?"

"I don't know if I could put myself all the way into my job if I was married and had kids."

She knew he was serious, not making up an excuse, and would say, "Don't put yourself all the *way* into your job but almost." He'd grin and take her by the arms and kiss her.

This evening she waited looking out the front window, thinking she *was* still awfully young.

He'd come home and have a beer while he changed from his suit to a wool shirt and cowboy coat and they'd drive down to Okmulgee and spend the weekend with Virgil and Narcissa, their third visit since Kansas City. This one special, Virgil was turning sixty tomorrow. Louly told Carl he looked it, too. Carl said his dad knew how to live; he watched the world go by but only paid attention to certain parts.

The birthday present was a Krag-Jorgensen five-shot magazine rifle Carl had bought off a gun collector in Bixby, the same model Virgil had carried around Cuba, nine pounds of .30-caliber army rifle.

Louly was anxious to get going after sitting around the apartment all day. It was about time she got a job—not like the one in Kansas City—maybe as a saleslady at Vandever's. Wait on rich Tulsa women and get to talk like them. A few times a week she went to the picture show.

She liked that slow way Virgil had of talking to Carl about criminal offenders, the oil business, movie stars, Will Rogers—whatever subject they got on they could wring it dry.

She liked Narcissa, too. While she fixed supper Louly would listen to her talk about the human body and how you had to respect it. "You can't believe," Narcissa said, "how that old man don't take care of himself but is so full of vigor in bed."

Like his boy. At this moment arriving home. From the window Louly watched Carl getting out of the Pontiac.

But now he was waiting on the sidewalk, facing the way he had come. Checking his hat. Lighting a cigaret.

Now a green car pulled in behind the Pontiac. Louly watched a woman who looked at least forty get out of the car. She wore a pillbox trying to look saucy, her mouth bright with Tangee. Now the two were coming up the front steps, Carl getting his key out. Louly left the window and went to the kitchen.

The front door opened and Louly came out of the kitchen raising her eyebrows to show surprise and then smiling while she dried her hands on a dish towel. Carl said, "Louly, this is Miss Munson from Bunch. She's come to pick up a rifle I have belongs to her." Carl went out to the closet in the spare bedroom, leaving Louly with this woman from Bunch. Louly remembered a road sign one time that said BUNCH, but couldn't recall where she was going.

She smiled at Miss Munson and said, "Are you and Carl old friends?"

"No," Venicia said. "Carl Webster shot my boyfriend one time with my Winchester and kept it fourteen months."

Louly took that into her head and said, "Oh . . ." and, "Is that right?" Because it didn't seem to matter what she said. Now she remembered where she saw the road sign, BUNCH, one end of it pointed, on the way to Stilwell to pick up seeds or something, for Mr. Hagenlocker.

It was later on it occurred to Louly for the first time she could run into friends and relatives of people Carl had shot or sent to prison. The way he was adding to his score it seemed likely. She believed they'd look at her a certain way . . .

What Venicia did when she left the apartment with her Winchester, she got in her car, her green Essex, drove to the next cross street, turned left and went all the way around the block, returning to South Cheyenne and pulled in to the curb at the corner. Venicia parked close enough to Carl's street that she could see the apartment building and remembered the name of it cut into the concrete block above the entrance, THE CYNTHIA COURT.

Now she waited, checking her watch.

She waited forty minutes for them to come out with one suitcase and get in the Pontiac, Carl Webster and cute little Louly, his little homemaker who wasn't his wife.

Walking out of the courthouse Carl sounded embarrassed about holding on to the Winchester so long and started talking to be talking, telling her he and Louly were driving down to Okmulgee for the weekend, tomorrow his dad's birthday, turning sixty, and they were stopping in Bixby to pick up a present he'd bought from an ad in the paper. He didn't say what it was and Venicia didn't ask, not wanting to seem interested in his life. She learned his dad had a thousand acres of pecan trees in the Deep Fork bottom west of town, but didn't ask anything about the property. She barely spoke coming out of the courthouse and going to their cars. She'd follow them without getting too close and ask directions to the nut farm once she got to Okmulgee. Forty miles, figure on three hours round-trip. Hurry back to Tulsa to tell Billy.

She never thought of him as Boo.

Louly said to Virgil, all of them sitting around the table in his kitchen, "Your boy says he's nuts about me."

Virgil was putting chili sauce on his meat loaf, popping the bottom of the bottle with the palm of his hand. He paused to look at Louly.

"I don't blame him. I'd be after you, too, if Narcissa didn't look like Dolores Del Rio. And I'll bet you Dolores Del don't even know how to cook. But if he's nuts about you and doesn't marry you, it'll be the biggest mistake of his life. But the way he'll tell it, after it's too late, it was the *only* mistake of his life. Once you hear him say that, you begin to realize what his problem is."

Louly held her fork raised with grits on it and a touch of meat loaf gravy. She said, "Well, I do have something to say about it. I'm years younger'n he is, I don't have to rush into anything. Carl could be fifty years old before he gets around to asking me."

"By then," Virgil said, "you'll have been married to oil men a couple of times and you're doing okay. You don't need to get married to anybody."

Carl was paying attention. He said to Louly, "You want to get married?"

"You mean to you, or do I want to be married?"

"Be married."

"Not especially."

"Then why do you keep bringing it up?"

"I want to hear you ask me. Not set a date, but I want to know we will sometime."

"Are you thinking like in a year?"

"Make it two years."

"Yeah . . . ?"

"Make it whatever you want."

"You keep living at my place?"

"Carl, it's called living together. Does your dad approve of that?"

"He's been doing it for twenty-five years. Says it's okay in his case."

"'Cause I'm Creek," Narcissa said.

"We're common-law by now," Virgil said. "I die, she'll be the richest Indian woman in the county."

Carl said, "Aren't you leaving me anything?"

"We'll see how long you survive," his dad said, "before I put you on the list. But if what this girl says is true, you're nuts about her, I think you ought to get married. See, then if you don't make it—"

"Somebody shoots me in the back?"

"See, I know when you're kidding, 'cause you never boast on yourself. That might be the only way, shot from behind, and it could happen. I was gonna say, if you don't make it, I'll scratch your name off and leave it to your heir, or heirs, you have these little redheaded nippers running around."

Louly said, "I hadn't thought about becoming a widow."

Narcissa said, "No, you think he's wonderful. If he's like his daddy then he's also lucky and that can carry him."

Louly said, "Yeah, but Mr. Webster doesn't do the same thing as Carl. He doesn't have people shooting at him."

Carl said, "When did anybody take a shot at me?"

Louly said, "You know what I mean."

"You know Virgil's lucky," Narcissa said. "He let people discover oil on his property, didn't he?"

They followed the county road that lay west out of Okmulgee, Venicia wanting to show Billy Bragg the private road that turned into the nut farm. An old single-story house with broken windows and missing shingles stood there empty. Billy looked at it through his dark glasses and didn't say anything. Venicia told him she left her car out here last night across the road, and ruined her high heels walking through the pecan orchard. Finally she came to where his dad was living now, in a huge house with a porch clear across the front. A garage stood to one side and Carl Webster's car was parked in front of it, his Pontiac.

Venicia said they could take a place over in the cover of trees, not more than fifty, sixty yards from the car, and when Carl came out to go someplace, he'd be almost life-size through the scope sight.

"How long," Billy said, "we have to stand out there in the pe-can trees freezing our asses off? How do we know he'll come out?"

"I'm saying this is one place you could do it. I'll show you another one, you won't have to wait long."

In the car, following the next dirt road left, coming to oil derricks that Carl hadn't mentioned, only the pecans, and finally coming to a road that crossed the bottom of the property, she turned in and came to a stop. Venicia pointed across a winter pasture starting to sprout, up a low grade to a light showing through pecan trees.

"That's the house."

She couldn't look at Billy when she spoke to him. All the way coming here from Tulsa the burnt side of his face and little nub of an ear were toward her in the car. They got in an argument when he said this was a lot of trouble for a hundred bucks. She said to him, looking straight ahead at the road, "You're avenging the murder of your *brother*. Doesn't that mean anything to you?" He said at the time it happened, yeah, he went looking for Carl, set on shooting him for nothing. But it wasn't till about a year later he ran into him. "At the roadhouse I told you about? But there was always a crowd of people around and they all thought he was a swell fella. Then we had that gunfight with the Klan." She offered him the C-note knowing she'd also have to let him screw her. Last night at the dingy hotel in Tulsa they had a bottle and she saw it was going to happen, so okay. What she did, she kept her eyes shut tight so she wouldn't have to look at him and twisted her head around, stretching her neck as far as she could, like Billy's loving was making her go crazy.

Looking toward the house now, she said, "Last night I crept up the side of the pasture toward that same light you see now, with my high heels off and cut my feet up. I got close enough to see the table through the kitchen window? Set for supper."

Billy said, "They were right there?"

"His girlfriend and some Indian woman."

"But you knew they'd be in to have supper?"

"When it was ready."

"And you had your rifle?"

"In the car, but I didn't have bullets till this morning."

"Jesus Christ, you could've done it right then."

"What I need," Venicia said, "is somebody knows how to shoot. Somebody that can hit him with the same gun he killed Peyton with.

Don't you understand that? I'd give you anything you want if you could hit him in the back of the head at four hundred yards."

"And if you were good-looking," Billy said, "we could set up house-keeping."

"Damn," Venicia said, "I'm missing out again. But we don't always get what we want, do we? You rather walk up to the window and shoot him eating his eggs, go ahead and do it. I'll settle for that."

Louly drove to Deering's drugstore in town for cigarets and today's paper. She got back to see Carl and his dad standing on the porch in their wool shirts, hands in their pockets. "We waited breakfast," Carl said. "I hope you're hungry."

She was, but it wasn't on her mind. Louly said, "The woman who came yesterday for her rifle, Miss Munson? I saw her car in town."

Carl paused to glance at his dad. "Remember Venicia Munson?" and said to Louly, "You sure it was hers?"

"How many times," Louly said, "you see a green Essex coupé two days in a row, red spoke wheels, and it isn't the same one?"

"Hudson makes it," Virgil said. "You don't see too many of them, either."

Carl said, "But you didn't see Venicia?"

Louly said no. "I was in that creeping Saturday morning crowd on Main, families in horse and wagons in town to buy stuff. I saw the car parked on my left, facing me, by the hardware store. A guy was sitting in the passenger seat but no Venicia. I went on to Deering's and introduced myself, talked to Mr. Deering for a while. I came back by way of Main and the car was gone."

"The guy in the car," Carl said, "what'd he look like?"

"I couldn't tell. He was wearing dark glasses."

Carl looked out at the pecan trees and said, "Let's go in the house."

They went inside and Carl kept going, up the stairs.

Louly called to him, "What're you getting?"

He said, "My gun," without stopping.

"He'll take a look out the upstairs windows," Virgil said.

Louly was starting to catch on.

"Miss Munson told me yesterday, when she came to get her Winchester? Carl had shot her boyfriend with it. Who was that?"

"Peyton Bragg," Virgil said, opening his gun cabinet. "Peyton robbed the bank in Sallisaw—you remember that?"

"I wasn't there at the time."

"He planned to hide out at Venicia's, near Bunch. Only Carl got in the way. Peyton's the only man Carl shot with a rifle," Virgil said— bringing a Remington twelve-gauge out of the cabinet—"since he was fifteen and shot a cow thief in that back pasture. Took a long shot and hit him square. Carl said after he should've stepped down from his horse, he didn't mean to kill him."

"Carl was fif*teen*?"

She tried to picture him but couldn't.

"The man was stealing his cows."

She felt in the middle of something she didn't know anything about. "Who's the one with the dark glasses?"

"Boo Bragg, Peyton's kid brother. Boo was in an oil tank fire that burnt half his face off. You don't want to look at it."

"He's out for revenge," Louly said.

"Or Venicia has him along." Virgil brought a Winchester out of the cabinet. "This is the one Carl used to put the cow thief out of business. Fella name of Tarwater. I saw him lying dead waiting for the undertaker. Nice-looking young fella. I have both shootings in a scrapbook, his and Peyton's, you want to see 'em. News accounts describe Carl as must be one of the world's deadliest shots. He knows he was lucky to hit Peyton."

He was coming down the stairs now with his revolver.

"I've told him," Virgil said, "that kind of publicity can get some rascal sneaking up on him."

Louly watched him shove the revolver into his waist and take the Winchester from his dad. He seemed different now, concentrating on loading the rifle while his dad slipped shotgun shells into the Remington.

She said, "Does this happen much?"

Carl looked up. "What?"

"Somebody wanting to pay you back?"

"Uh-unh, but I had a feeling about this one. You saw me hand the rifle to Venicia? I said, 'You aren't gonna shoot me with this, are you?' I was kidding. But you notice she didn't say anything."

"She just stared at you," Louly said.

"The poor woman has nothing in her life to smile about."

Carl seemed himself again, like a big kid, grinning, an idea coming to him.

"Why don't we give my dad his present? Isn't this a perfect time?"

"What is it?" Virgil said, sounding anxious now, sixty years old today.

"You're gonna love it," Carl said. "What you always wanted."

"But it's out in the car," Louly said.

"Take me half a minute," Carl said.

They had come up through the trees along one side of the pasture and now Venicia was crouched behind a pile of firewood, not thirty feet from the back of the house. Through the window she could see the table set, the Indian woman busy at the stove. Venicia turned and motioned to Billy, then hunched her shoulders at the noise he made moving through the leaves. He sunk down next to her and raised up enough to look past the woodpile.

"They haven't sat down yet?"

"Another few minutes, the cook's just put the bacon on."

"They sure get up late."

"It's his daddy's birthday, they slept in."

"Soon as he shows his face in the kitchen," Billy said, "I'm on step up to the window and bust him." He had taken the scope sight off the Winchester and left it in the car. Now he pulled a Browning automatic from under his sheepskin coat saying, "This close, I don't know which to use."

Venicia was retying her crepe-sole Keds good and tight, getting ready, thinking she might have to run for the car. The longer she was with Billy Bragg, the less confidence she had in him. He was jumpy and trying not to show it. When they were still down at the bottom of the pasture he'd said, "What if he has his gun on the table?"

She said, "Having his breakfast?"

Billy said, "You don't know anything about him?"

Things like that gave Venicia pause.

Carl came in with the birthday present, stayed long enough to see his dad's eyes light up and went out again with the shotgun, saying he'd keep close to the house, since this was where they had to come. He'd work his way around back.

Louly looked worried, saying to Virgil, "But he hasn't any idea where they are. They could be way off in the trees and shoot at him."

"The way I got shot at Guantánamo," Virgil said, looking over the five-shot Krag-Jorgensen, raising it to his shoulder to sight down the barrel. "I went up a hill to flush a sniper, but not paying attention, thinking of something else, and the don sent me home with a bullet through my side. Carl, he keeps his mind on what he's doing, he's always wide awake. This Krag's a good rifle, the army carried it all through the Spanish-American War, as it was called. But I was with Huntington's Marines, clearing that Guantánamo area for a coaling station and we were issued Lee rifles. Carl must've forgot that for some reason. Hey, but don't tell him. This Krag's a honey, I'll hang it on the mantel."

Louly was anxious. She said, "Shouldn't we keep a watch out the front?"

"You're right, let's get to a window."

They're in the house," Billy said. "Where else'd they be? If they're home."

They hadn't looked to see if Carl's car was still there.

Venicia said, "They're waiting on that woman to call them. The bacon's done, she's laying it out."

Billy said, "It looks good, don't it? We should've ate when we got to Okmulgee. I told you, didn't I?"

"She's putting the grits in a bowl."

"I like to crumble my bacon in it when I have grits," Billy said.

"I imagine they're just in the next room," Venicia said. "She wouldn't of started breakfast if they weren't all downstairs near ready to eat. Would she?"

Billy said, "She fry any eggs?"

"I think she's waiting on the eggs, see how they want them fixed. The toaster's on the table. Jelly. What else? Lea and Perrins."

Billy, watching Narcissa, got up on his knees behind the woodpile. "She's bringing the coffeepot over . . . filling the cups." He said, "I'm going in. Be standing there when he walks in."

Venicia said, "Give me the rifle." She took it from him and cocked it and said, "Ready? I'll count to three."

Carl was in the trees forty feet behind them and to one side. He wanted to work closer before telling them to drop the guns. But now they were moving toward the house and Carl went after them. He saw them enter through the back door—leaving it open—and were out of his sight until he reached the door and looked inside.

He saw Venicia holding the front sight of the Winchester under Narcissa's chin, Narcissa holding her face raised as she tried to do what Venicia wanted, call to the next room, "Come and sit down now. It's all ready."

Both of them, Billy and Venicia, faced the door to the sitting room. Carl stepped inside the kitchen. Next to the table now he was about twelve feet from them. Billy was looking around that side of the room. He was turning his shoulders until Carl could see his sunglasses for a moment at an angle, and Billy turned back to see Louly, Louly first, and then Virgil coming into the kitchen.

They looked right at him like they were wondering what he was doing there.

Venicia was saying to Virgil, her voice loud, "Where's Carl? Get him in here or I'll shoot this girl."

What Carl did, he racked the pump on the shotgun back and forth, that ratchety sound telling the two they were about to get a load of double-ought buckshot.

But so would Louly and Virgil, right behind them.

Carl did think of giving them his warning: drop the guns or he'd shoot to kill. But they were out of place here pointing guns and Carl could tell they knew it, Venicia pathetic-looking with her red circles of rouge and Boo Bragg looking at Carl through his blue smoked glasses, glancing for help at Venicia. Virgil knew it, too. Virgil's gaze with a sad look going from Carl to Venicia right next to him and then making his move, Virgil taking hold of the Winchester to wrest it from her as Carl went for Billy, swatted the pistol out of his hand with the barrel of the Remington, then gave him a backhanded swat across the side of his damaged face that might've hurt like hell but wasn't as bad as getting shot. Carl took the poor dazed man by the arm, without his gun or his glasses, pulled out a chair from the table and sat him down. Virgil brought Venicia over, Louly watching, Narcissa saying, "I have to feed them, too?"

It amazed Louly watching Carl set cups of coffee in front of these two, offer cigarets and hold a match to them. She watched Carl pick up Boo's dark glasses from the floor and hand them to him. Maybe not as an act of kindness, but so they wouldn't have to look at his empty, burnt-out eye socket.

Virgil said this was police business. He'd call Bud Maddox, get him over here.

"No, it's settled," Carl said. "Venicia knows she made a mistake. Talked herself and Boo into a deal that could've left them lying on the floor. For what? 'Cause Peyton was so good to her? Brought her whiskey when he remembered?"

Louly felt the need to speak up.

"Carl, the woman was going to kill you."

Carl said, "She got it in her head I became a marshal so I'd get to carry a gun." He looked at Venicia. "You said in your house that night, I got a kick out of shooting people. Remember that?"

Venicia kept looking at him, staring, but didn't answer.

Carl said, "I didn't shoot you, did I? Or Boo? Why don't you go on back to Bunch and behave yourself?"

18

During the past seven months, while Jack Belmont was making church pews waiting to see the famous lawyer he'd never heard of, Fausto Bassi had been promoted from guard captain to deputy warden of Oklahoma State Prison.

"This Cecil Guyton," Jack said, "what kind of case is he on takes this long?" They were in Fausto's office talking about Jack's appeal, the sound of wings beating in the rotunda.

"Guyton has been deciding who to defend next," Fausto said. "At first he thought George Kelly."

"George *Kelly?*"

"George Machine-Gun Kelly," Fausto said, "arrested for kidnapping a millionaire oilman in Oklahoma City. But Cecil found out Machine-Gun Kelly is a phony. His wife, Kathryn, met him he was a bootlegger for the rich people. She bought him his first machine gun and made up the story he is a mad-dog killer. Cecil Guyton talked to Kelly for five minutes, saw who he was and walked out on the case. He don't want to be surprised in court. So then," Fausto said, "Cecil Guyton looks at a choice, wait for John Dillinger or Lester Gillis."

"John Dillinger hasn't been arrested?"

"Lester Gillis hasn't either. But you know J. Edgar will find them pretty soon. Or they be shot coming out of a bank."

"Who's Lester Gillis?"

"Known better as Baby Face Nelson. This one *is* a mad-dog killer. He's shot two bank guards, a guy he got in an argument with on the street—Lester ran into the guy's car—and shot three FBI agents, one of them when Lester was hiding out at Little Bohemia. But since these two are roaming the countryside, Cecil Guyton has decided to take a rest, go to Hot Springs for the baths and maybe get laid, uh? Now he's ready to defend the famous Jack Belmont, with permission to meet you at the Aldridge, the newest hotel in town. He's taking a suite on the top floor."

"How many times I get to meet with him?"

"Once, anyway. And I'll be as close as a Siamese twin, so don't get any ideas."

"If this hotshot lawyer's setting me free, what kind of ideas would I have? I'm thinking I'll need something to wear besides these striped pajamas."

"You get a new pair of overalls."

"You could get my suit out of the inmate storage room. I can wear it to the hearing."

"You get a pair of overalls," Fausto said.

"I thought we were friends."

"Where did you get that idea?"

This time at the prison Jack had complained about a Creek Indian being in the same cell with him. But then when he found out the Creek had worked for Carl Webster's dad harvesting pecans he shut up. The Creek told Jack that when he got out in a few years he was going to rob Virgil's house, break in while Virgil was working in his orchard and clean him out. He said the man had a pile of money he kept in there. The Creek said he heard the man telling newspaper reporters who came to talk to Carl but was never there, the banks could close, it wouldn't bother him none. He had a rich oil lease and there was always money coming in.

Jack asked him how he knew he kept the money in the house.

The Creek said, "If he don't keep it in a bank, where else does he hide it but someplace close to where he's at?" The Creek heard the man tell the newspaper reporters he was as rich as some kind of king. He heard the reporters ask him what he thought of his son going after bank robbers. And the man saying he was surprised there was any money in the banks to rob.

It sounded good if it was true. Jack asked the Creek, "Yeah, but how much does he have?"

The Creek said, "If you a millionaire oilman, how much would you put someplace so you never be poor as long as you live?" It was what he told the reporters. They're out resting from shaking trees and the reporters squatted down in the weeds to ask him questions. "He said he had some guns, too, so he wasn't afraid of being robbed."

"Has guns, uh?"

"He was in that war in Cuba."

They brought Jack to town in a Chevrolet Suburban Carryall, a gray one with OKLAHOMA STATE PRISON stenciled on the doors. It was like a panel truck with windows and two rear seats. Fausto sat in front with the guard driving, Jack in the far backseat away from the door. Fausto might not be his friend but had given Jack an old suitcoat out of inmate storage to wear with his overalls.

It hit Jack between the eyes, as soon as they reached the center of town, he was dressed like most of the working men milling along Choctaw Avenue. Hundreds of them.

Some in a procession of cars creeping along past every parking place taken on both sides of the street, men in the parade holding American flags out the car windows.

"What's going on?"

"Coal miners putting on the dog," Fausto said. "The United Mine Workers showing off. They holding meetings at the fairgrounds, talking about if they want to strike."

Jack watched a streetcar stop at the corner of Choctaw and Second Avenue, in front of them, and a mob of coal miners rush the narrow front door, shoving and fighting one another to get aboard, the motorman dinging his bell, wanted to get started.

Jack said, "How'd you like to be a coal miner?"

Fausto said, "A man chooses what he does."

"And you didn't want to be one?"

"These miners, a lot of Italians like me, they get drunk and demonstrate, walk picket lines with 'unfair' signs, 'We want more money.' Don't they know times are bad, the owners aren't making what they should?"

Jack would bet his dad sounded just like that.

"They get arrested for unlawful assembly and are taken up to the prison to be housed."

"You mean locked in a goddamn cell."

"You choose what you do," Fausto said. "Guys who don't want to cause trouble go home, take the interurban. That trolley line goes to Krebs, Alderson, goes all the way to Hartshorne, sixteen miles."

Jack said, "Ain't the modern world something?" He liked the fact that most of these miners going home were dressed the way he was, the old suitcoat over the overalls they wore to town. But they all had on a cap or a hat, something he was missing.

They crossed Choctaw while miners were still climbing into the streetcar. Jack turned to look out the back window of the Carryall until they were up the street, turning into the back entrance of the hotel.

Fausto wore a brown hat with a black band he must've had for years, the pinched front of the crown showing signs of a hole wearing through. His suit was black, starting to shine. No vest. His holster was strapped under his left arm.

The guard driver had stayed with the Carryall.

Fausto pushed the button for the freight elevator—they're standing in the back hall—and Jack said, "Don't you want to see the lobby? Come on, this is a brand-new hotel. Let's see what they got?" He touched Fausto's arm and that was all it took.

Now they stood looking at the furniture, the oriental carpets, palm trees, three cuspidors along the front desk, the cigar counter busy.

"I know he's gonna be smoking," Jack said. "I could join him if I had a pack of cigarets." He held out his hand, grinning at Fausto.

It didn't work. Fausto, the son of a bitch, said, "You want to smoke, bum one off Guyton."

They rode up in an elevator with Jack standing close behind the little-girl operator in her uniform, her brown hair giving off the best scent he'd smelled in seven months. He pulled his right hand from his overalls pocket and placed it on the right cheek of the girl's behind. She stiffened, but then looked up over her shoulder at him and smiled. He leaned closer and whispered something into her hair.

Fausto saw it. He pulled Jack away from her and yelled in the girl's startled face, "What'd he say to you?"

She looked at Jack wide-eyed, like she needed permission to answer. But then must've felt it was okay and looked at Fausto.

"He said he was falling in love with me."

Jack waited for Fausto to say something, but he didn't.

They came to the eleventh floor. Getting off, Jack winked at the girl and she smiled back. He believed he had given her something to remember and tell about for the rest of her life. *How this good-looking guy put his hand on her fanny and said he was in love with her, and you know who it was, honest to God . . . ?*

Cecil Guyton's colored man, in a waiter's coat and black bow tie, opened the door to the penthouse suite and brought them into the moderne sitting room, Jack struck by the sight of white furniture, a peach shade of paint, strange shapes of colors framed on the wall, a tea trolley offering whiskey and seltzer water. The retainer said, "Mr. Guyton, here your guests," and stood by.

Cecil Guyton kept his seat, a drink on the table next to him. Jack thought the man would have weight to him, but reminded Jack of a fox, that pointy face and little pencil mustache. He wore braces, a blue collarless shirt but a white silk scarf draped around his neck. The first thing he said, "If you're the infamous Jack Belmont you must resemble your mother, you sure don't look like your daddy. I've played cards with Oris in the basement of the Mayo Hotel a few times. He wins 'cause he's so goddamn serious. He's playing cards, by God he's gonna pay attention to what he's doing. Barely speaks. He's the most serious man I ever met. I won't criticize him for it, though, it's made him a rich man. Or you wouldn't be here, would you?" Cecil Guyton paused and said, "I wonder if that's truer than I meant. You want a drink?"

"He's not allowed," Fausto said.

The lawyer turned to him. "You're Fausto Bassi, assistant to the warden? I'm Cecil Guyton, all this boy's got. I wasn't told of any rules of procedure."

"Sir, prison inmates aren't allowed alcohol."

"Are you kidding me? They get stone drunk every chance they have. One of the reasons I won't visit your prison is the smell of home brew cooking. That tomato puree they turn into booze at your joint is the most nauseating smell in the world. I get a whiff of it I gag."

"I can't drink it," Jack said.

"Another place has a terrible smell is a coal camp. They bring up those mules pull the cars? They fart a gas can kill you you step too close. Craig Valley has twenty-eight miners suing them out at their Messina dig. The owners want me to talk nasty to these people, get them irritated enough to be held in contempt of court. It's something I'm good at, getting people irritated. But I'm not going out there, not with that stink hanging over the place and they don't want to come to the hotel."

He turned to Fausto.

"I treat my clients like they're guests in my home. What we discuss is naturally confidential, so I can't have any observers, can I? No one listening in on what Mr. Belmont tells me. Fausto, that means you gonna have to leave."

Fausto said, "But I'm suppose to always have him in my sight."

"Fausto, you're giving me a difficult time here. Your prison and the appellate court have approved my client meeting me here and they understand how it works. You want those judges pissing in their robes, keep giving me your rules."

Fausto said, "Where am I suppose to go?"

"Anywhere you want. You like to stay close, use the bedroom down the hall you don't see any clothes in. Lie on the bed and take a nap. You want something to eat, a drink, call Alexander, he'll get it for you."

Jack said, "He your slave?"

"I bet you were always a bad kid," Cecil said to him. "I heard you tried to blackmail your dad one time. Still, he's paying a lot of money to get you off 'cause he's stuck with you being his son." Cecil said to his man, "Alexander, take care of the warden, would you, please? Show him a room." And said to Fausto, "Go with Alexander," like he was talking to a child. The two left the sitting room, going off down the hall, and Cecil said to Jack, "You imagine that man telling fifteen hundred convicts to behave themselves? Fix yourself a drink and sit down. I want to ask you about witnesses, who liked you, who didn't and where they are."

Jack walked past Cecil Guyton's chair to the windows that faced west, late afternoon sun still showing over there. He looked south an angle and could see a streetcar passing from sight on Choctaw Avenue, behind the hotel. Now he moved to the tea trolley and poured himself a whiskey, neat.

"The whores liked me," Jack said, "the bouncers. Get hold of Heidi Winston in Kansas City, she'll say anything you want." Jack sat down on the sofa. He watched Cecil Guyton pick up a notebook and turn a couple of pages.

"What would the marshal have to say, Carlos Webster?"

"That's his name, Carlos? I didn't know he was a greaser."

"I understand he goes by Carl."

"He said I'd likely do time on one charge or another."

"I spoke to the Tulsa marshal in charge. He said it was Carl Webster's opinion you got a bad deal. Said he thought with the right lawyer you'd get off on appeal."

Jack said, "That ain't what he told me. He wants me locked behind bars."

"Has it in for you, huh?"

"Nothing he'd like better. I told him, soon as I got out I'd shoot him on sight."

"Let's hold up on that one," Cecil told him, "till I clear you of your shooting spree. It says here you shot seven men in less than half a minute."

"If it took that. They're coming at us with torches."

"You must've been scared to death."

"I was too busy shooting 'em down."

"No, you were scared of being burned to death, a horrible way to die. I'm gonna have to get those girls and the bouncers in court to tell how frightening it was." He got out a cigaret and lit it.

Jack said, "Can you spare one of those?"

Cecil threw him the pack of Old Gold, almost full, and a book of matches and told him to keep them.

So far this meeting was working out.

Cecil said, "How are these girls, pretty fair looking?"

"For whores," Jack said.

They smoked their cigarets. After a few moments Cecil touched his stomach and said, "Uh-oh. I believe I still have a touch of the trots. Spaghetti and meatballs I had last night in Krebs. Supposed to be the best Italian restaurant in town. Sit still," Cecil said, getting up. "I'll be back in a few minutes," and hustled off down the hall with a magazine and his shoulders hunched.

Jack waited till he heard the bathroom door close. Now he went down the hall to where Fausto was waiting in the second bedroom, the door open. Fausto, stretched out on the double bed, started to get up.

"You through already?"

"We just started. Cecil got the shits from the Italian supper he had." Jack watched Fausto's head sink back into the pillows he'd piled one on top the other. His coat hung from a chair, his hat on the seat, holster hanging from one of the arms, his gun, a .45 auto in plain sight on the night table.

Fausto saw Jack looking at it.

"You touch that you going back. Understand?"

Jack moved up on the right side of the bed toward the night table, his gaze holding on Fausto looking up at him, Fausto saying, "Stay away from the gun."

The man didn't know he was making it easy. Jack could see how Nestor Lott had no trouble putting Fausto in a jail cell. This wop one-time chief of police was about to become a one-time deputy warden—in the half minute it took Jack to pick up the .45 from the night table and bring the barrel down hard on Fausto's forehead—maybe too hard—blood pouring out of the wound, the man's eyes going cockeyed staring at him. Jack pulled the sheet free to wipe off the gun barrel. He found twelve dollars and change in Fausto's pockets, picked up the hat from the chair and put it on, tight but okay. He heard the toilet flush behind him as he reached the front hall and Alexander appeared from somewhere.

Alexander saying, "You decide to leave, huh?"

Jack showed him the .45. "You care?"

"It don't mean nothing to me, I haven't seen you. But the man gets off the toilet, you know what he's gonna do. You cheating him out of a big fee."

Jack got going. Down the hall, down the stairs, eleven floors and across the lobby, out the front and down Second Avenue to another crowd of miners pushing and shoving to get on the eastbound streetcar. Jack used his elbows, seeing it as life or death to bore through the miners, got them swearing at him but made it aboard, dropped Fausto's change in the till and pushed his way past miners hanging from leather straps till he heard a voice call from close by, "Jack Belmont?"

It was the *True Detective* writer, Tony Antonelli, looking up at him from one of the wooden seats.

The first thing Jack said to him, "Boy, I'm sicker'n a dog. I guess I can't take that stink out at the mine works."

Tony started to get up saying, "Here—"

Jack said, "Stay there," and pulled the miner out of the seat next to Tony, pulled him up by the front of his overalls to say in his near-toothless face, "Thanks for the seat, partner. I don't sit down I'll fall down, I'm sicker'n a dog." He sat down next to Tony, got out an Old Gold and lit it. Tony was staring at the frail, stooped miner turning his head now to cough, the sound, like it was ripping his chest open. Jack said, "Black lung," and said right away, "Listen, I want to thank you for letting me and Heidi use your car."

Tony looked at him but didn't speak, in his wonder letting Jack talk.

"What we did after leaving Bald Mountain, we went up to Kansas City. I dropped Heidi off, she wanted to stay a while and I came back. See, what happened, somebody stole your car, so I had to take the train." Jack drew on his Old Gold and tried to blow a smoke ring.

It gave Tony time to get ready and tell him, "I got my car back. A marshal called and I went to Kansas City to get it."

"They catch the guy stole it?"

"No, but the car was okay," Tony said, going along—why not? "It wouldn't start till I fooled with the motor, dried the spark plugs."

"I was gonna pay you," Jack said, "if they didn't find it. I came back, I got a job on an oil lease cleaning storage tanks."

"I thought that's what you were doing when the tank caught fire that time and you were trapped."

"Facing a fiery death. Yeah, I was doing the same thing before and they put me on it again, since I had the experience."

Tony said, "What's the matter with me. Seven months ago you were convicted of manslaughter and got twenty years. The last I heard you were in McAlester."

"I'm out on bond awaiting my appeal. My dad, bless his heart, got me a smart lawyer, Cecil Guyton."

"He got you the best. You back with your dad?"

"We'll see how it goes. Everybody says I got a bum deal in that trial."

"You did. But you *know* you still belong in jail. I can't believe my luck," Tony said, his shoulders bouncing with the streetcar, "running into you like this. I need to get your side of the trial. I'm doing a feature on it as soon as I cover this UMW business, the meetings they're having. Doing it for the Tulsa *World*. I'm interviewing these fellas who live out here and work some of the mines." He said, "Jack, if you don't mind my asking, where the hell are you going?"

"I'm at Messina, that Craig Valley works out by Hartshorne? But they're in court now, so I'm looking around. I think it's that stink out there affected my stomach. Those old mules passing gas."

"You really are sick?"

"Since I tried coal mining. I may have to go back working for my dad."

"I'm trying to understand," Tony said, "how you managed to do all these things since the roadhouse. You went right to K.C. but you didn't stay."

"I saw some of the sights."

"Robbed a bank?"

"Where'd you hear that?"

"It was in every paper I picked up."

"You still have any of 'em?"

"I clipped the stories, then covered it for *True Detective* while I was up there getting my car. I can't believe you're out walking around."

"I told you, I'm out on bond."

"Isn't there a detainer on you?"

"Don't ask me what the marshals are up to."

They rode along, Jack smoking his cigaret. He said, "I stayed at the Aldridge while I was talking to Guyton."

"Where'd you stay in Kansas City?"

"Me and Heidi rented a house."

"I thought you came right back."

"I told you, I saw the sights."

Tony hesitated before saying, "You didn't by any chance run into Elodie, did you?"

"Yeah, she was looking fine."

"I didn't see her when I picked up the car," Tony said. "I meant to. She dropped me a note saying why didn't we get together, but . . . I don't know."

"I recall you were interested in Elodie we're all at the roadhouse that time. You ever pop her in the rear? Heidi says she liked it as a change of pace. But she doesn't do commercial screwing anymore—what Heidi calls it—she's a cocktail waitress. I told Heidi that was a shame."

They rode without speaking for a while, the car swaying, clanging as it came to crossroads, Jack shoving at miners hanging on to overhead straps as they bumped against him.

Tony said, "You think I should see her, uh? I go back to Kansas City?"

Jack said, "Who, Elodie? You're missing something you don't."

They got off the streetcar at the east end of Hartshorne, only a couple of blocks from the roominghouse where Tony was staying and kept his car. He told Jack he'd been riding the rails two days talking to miners. Jack said he'd only come back to pick up his things at the Chinese laundry—the reason he was wearing work clothes. He hoped the Chinks hadn't ruined his good shirts.

Nothing he said made sense to Tony.

Like he'd spent the afternoon at the Aldridge with Cecil Guyton and Cecil wanted him to pick up his things and come back.

"But if you want to ask me about the bum deal I got in court . . . I was talking about the trial with Cecil. He says he'll parade in the witnesses, they'll tell of their fear of being burned alive and I'll walk out of the courtroom."

"But what about the bank in Kansas City?"

"North Kansas City. Cecil says 'Did you know there isn't one witness to the bank guard getting shot?' I said, 'And do you know why? The witnesses got paid off by a man doesn't want me to sit in the electric chair. He wants to stick my feet in a pail of cement, let it harden and drop me in the Missouri River. That's how they do things.'"

Tony said, "You know who this guy is?"

"He's right under Boss Pendergast—you want a good story about politics up there. This guy says I owe him twenty-five hundred bucks. I say I don't and I'm not gonna pay him. What's he gonna do about it, come to Oklahoma for me?"

They reached the roominghouse and there was Tony's Ford parked in front, a kid in knickers wiping it off with a rag. Tony called him by some nickname, flipped him a quarter and the kid thanked him and ran off to spend it.

"What Cecil Guyton does," Jack said, "he pours a good drink before he starts asking questions. You got anything?"

Tony said, "I wasn't planning on having a party."

"A bottle, Cecil says, keeps the talk flowing. I know a bootlegger lives here used to supply me when I had the roadhouse. Let me use your car, I'll go pick up my laundry and a bottle while you look at the paper. How's that sound?"

"I don't know," Tony said. "This car's already been stolen once."

"Don't worry," Jack said, "I stop at the Chinks' I'll be sure to lock it up."

19

Bob McMahon was telling Carl they weren't doing too bad lately. "Outside of Jack Belmont," Carl said. "He was a good boy his daddy'd give him all the money he wants."

"Cheer you up," McMahon said, looking at a report on his desk, "Clyde Barrow and Bonnie Parker met their end yesterday."

"It's about time," Carl said.

"Near Gibsland, Louisiana. It says at a roadblock, but it sounds more like an ambush. Somebody who knew where they'd be told on them and the Texas Ranger heading the posse said they fired a hundred and eighty-seven shots to stop the car."

"That's all?"

"Bonnie was eating a sandwich. The most they ever got in a robbery was fifteen hundred. John Dillinger called 'em a couple of punks."

"What's the most he ever took, Dillinger?"

"Seventy-four thousand," McMahon said off the top of his head, "from a bank in Greencastle, Indiana, last year. He said Bonnie and Clyde were giving bank robbing a bad name."

"I'm sure glad they're done," Carl said.

"Next thing is get this Jack Belmont out of our hair. The guy is driving me nuts. His daddy's got all that money, why doesn't Jack be a good boy and enjoy it? Twice now he's run off with the *True Detective* writer's car. Says he's gonna pick up his laundry. Why didn't Tony go with him?"

"Jack's a talker," Carl said. "He'd of thought of a reason to go alone, pick up a bottle? And Tony's polite, he would've said don't steal the car, okay?"

"You know how he got out? He's in town to see a lawyer on his appeal."

"Cecil Guyton," Carl said. "I read about it."

"He called me up, Cecil did. He seemed confident he'd get Belmont off and must've told him. Why would he try to escape?"

"He didn't try, he did. And almost killed that warden. He told me he'd bust out so he could shoot me on sight. Another reason might be, avoid that detainer in Kansas. But he claims he'd never be convicted. Nobody saw him shoot the old man."

"He robbed the bank, didn't he?"

"I don't know," Carl said. "That Kansas City's different than anyplace else I've ever been. If Teddy Ritz wants to punish Jack himself, like shoot him, then even the bank people never saw him."

"Well, Jack Belmont hasn't been seen anywhere since he left Hartshorne."

"He said he and Heidi were going down to Old Mexico in Teddy's La Salle, but now he'll put shooting me ahead of his vacation."

"And if he's serious, he'll have to come here, won't he?"

"He's good for his word," Carl said. "I can think of places I'd rather be than standing in that courtroom."

Bob McMahon didn't say anything but kept staring at Carl.

Carl said, "What're you doing? You see me as a goat on a tether, waiting for the lion?"

"It's an idea," McMahon said.

"He isn't that dumb."

"But you thought it might tempt him."

"Bob, he isn't gonna walk into a federal courtroom, even for me."

"All right, you're off court duty," McMahon said. "Go find him."

"I'm gonna talk to Anthony Antonelli afterwhile. We're gonna meet at the Mayo."

"No court this afternoon?"

"We're adjourned till tomorrow."

"Who's up?"

"Some poor boys should be home making whiskey."

McMahon went into his pile of reports. "You ever see a picture of Dillinger's girlfriend?"

Carl said, "Billie Frechette? You bet," and grinned.

Carl walked behind most of the twenty-two columns dressing the front of the federal courthouse, looking out at a different part of the street at each open area but not pausing.

Jack said he'd be out shortly and he wasn't kidding. He was the most confident guy Carl had ever met. Or had the biggest mouth. Or was the dumbest. He had to be dumb to walk away from his dad, and it was this state he found himself in that made him mean and ugly. He'd failed at blackmail and kidnapping—those didn't count—'cause he was set on being an outlaw. He liked to shoot guns and he was fast. He'd have to get a car. He couldn't hang on to Tony's for long. And a place to stay.

Think of him in Tulsa with a place. Maybe with some prostitute he's known for a while. Since he was a kid and she likes him and who his dad is and sees a future in Jack. He uses her car. She's been popular with rich oilmen, has some money, can finance him. Thinks he's cute . . .

He crossed the street and walked to the Mayo Hotel on the near corner of Fifth and Cheyenne. The uniformed doorman gave him a salute, said, "How you doing, Mr. Webster?" and stepped over to pull open one of the doors. He let go as Carl walked into the opening and the glass in the twin door next to him shattered with the report of a pistol shot and another punched into the copper door frame and a third shattered the door swinging closed behind him, high-caliber sounds from the street, from the car he had seen double-parked across from the hotel, the shots rapid-fire, semiauto. Carl hit the marble floor inside, rolled and came up holding his Colt, pushed back through the shattered glass to see the double-parked car leaving the scene like it was stripping its gears, a black Ford Coupé, too quick for Carl to get the number, but a black Ford like half the people in Tulsa drove.

Carl, sitting in the lobby with Tulsa detectives and reporters from the *World,* told them how Jack Belmont, seven months ago in Kansas City, swore he was going to shoot Carl on sight. Swore he would bust out of prison to do it. And wasn't kidding, was he?

No, he couldn't tell it was Belmont in the car and wasn't able to get the license number. The doorman didn't get it either. And fortunately none of the stray shots hit anyone sitting in the lobby. The police had dug two bullets out of chairs and found the one in the dirt of a plant pot it had shattered.

"I'm sure it's Jack Belmont," Carl told the reporters. "Only fired three times and lost his nerve. Couldn't finish the job. How about if I give you my phone number? Put it in the write-up so Belmont can call me. I'll tell him where to meet so he can try again."

The reporters loved it, the sheer bravado of this cocky young marshal, who had so far shot and killed eight offenders, daring a fugitive to meet him and shoot it out. Bob McMahon wouldn't love it, but Carl believed he knew what he was doing. Beginning to work a scheme.

Once the police and reporters left, Carl sat with Tony Antonelli, Carl's back to one of the columns that rose past the second-floor balcony that rimmed the lobby full of red-patterned chairs and green ones and the red orientals that covered the marble floor.

"Jack tells you he's gonna shoot you," Tony said, "he isn't fooling. But isn't every lawman in Oklahoma out looking for him? Why hasn't he been picked up? I didn't think he'd get too far out of Hartshorne. As soon as they found the deputy warden bludgeoned, they sent out an all-points, didn't they? Thank God the man's gonna make it. They say Jack almost fractured his skull. A few minutes later we're riding on a streetcar together. He said he was feeling ill. I imagine so."

Carl was patient, smoking a Lucky as he waited for Tony. Finally he said, "Your car was found in Vian."

"In better shape than the first time he stole it."

"Did he happen to mention Vian for any reason? Or when you were looking up his background, doing your story on him—"

"I haven't started writing it yet. That's what he and I were gonna talk about, his early life."

"So Vian doesn't mean anything to you."

"Some of those Cookson Hills bandits were from around there. When he was in McAlester he might've met one or two."

Carl nodded. "That's something I could look up. Jack stole another car in Vian, one like yours—"

"Same model," Tony said, "and drove through to Stilwell. I wondered if he'd stopped off in the Hills, it was always a favorite place for fugitives to hide out, but they had that roundup a couple months ago, deputies and national guardsmen, hundreds of 'em driving through there like it was a tiger hunt. Let's see, from Stilwell he went to Muskogee, stole a car—another Ford and a half-dozen license plates. Steal a

Ford, all you have to do is stick a coin in the ignition. And after Muskogee it looked like he was coming here."

"But only got as far as Sapulpa," Carl said, "and the trail ends. He ever mention Sapulpa?"

"He talked about working on an oil patch, cleaning out storage tanks, what he was doing when he set one afire and his dad sent him to prison. But I'm sure he didn't work there again. The next thing, he says he was digging coal out by Hartshorne, but I checked. For the past seven months he was at McAlester waiting for his appeal."

Carl said, "You ever been to Sapulpa?"

"I've been through. They finally paved all the streets."

"You know who lives there? His daddy's girlfriend, Nancy Polis."

"Well, she and Jack can't be friends, can they? But his dad's wells are around there—he could know some people he can get to hide him. It's close to Tulsa, and we know he was right here not an hour ago."

"But he didn't know I was coming to the hotel," Carl said.

"No, he couldn't of known that."

"He must've followed me in the car across Cheyenne."

Tony, nodding, said, "Too many people on the street to get a clean shot at you. He believes you're heading for the hotel and pulls up across the street."

"That's how I see it," Carl said. "Only it wasn't Jack Belmont in the car."

It stopped Tony, got him frowning at Carl.

"But he told you he was gonna shoot you."

"That's the point," Carl said. "He tells you that, you know he means it. I don't see him firing three shots and running off. He's got the drop on me, what's he afraid of? I see him coming in to make sure. Jack Belmont wouldn't of left with bullets in his gun."

"But you told the reporters you're sure it was Jack."

"So the guy did the shooting'll know I didn't see him. And if Jack reads the paper he'll know I insulted him—said he didn't have the nerve to do it right—and he's got competition. I'll bet you a dollar he calls me."

"You know who it was shot at you?"

"I'll make a phone call and find out for sure, but I think it was a guy from Kansas City, Luigi Tessa."

Tony started to smile. "You mean Lou Tessa from Krebs?"

"You know him?"

"*True Detective* wants me to do a piece on him. 'The Black Hand Rides Again' spreading terror and death. They think Lou Tessa's a natural to sell magazines. They've been wanting a Black Hand piece ever since I started with them."

"You want to meet him?" Carl said. "I'll see what I can do."

Teddy Ritz said, "I couldn't imagine why you're calling."

"You sent Luigi to Tulsa?"

"What happened to him?"

"Did you send him?"

"It was his idea. Does you, he gets his job back."

"You fired him?"

"Of course I fired him. What happened?"

"He took three shots at my back and left in a hurry."

"Lou wants so bad to be a torpedo."

"I told him before we left he'd never make it."

"I told him the same thing. What can you do?"

"Call him and fire him again."

"Next time he might get lucky."

"Okay, give him my address, 706 South Cheyenne."

"You want him to come see you?"

"I don't want to keep looking behind me."

"You know he's from Oklahoma?"

"With two homicide detainers on him."

"So, he's done it. Give him a chance."

"He laid for both. Neither one saw him."

"Once a punk, uh? What about Belmont?"

"He's around someplace."

"I read about his escape, on a streetcar."

"Why don't you put Luigi on him?"

"He'd fuck it up."

"You said he might get lucky."

"How's he find him?"

"Have you talked to Luigi?"

"He called, said he almost got you."

"Yeah?"

"He said it won't be long."

"Where's he staying?"

"I tell you, I'm giving him up."

"What's wrong with that?"

"It wouldn't be fair."

Carl said, "It wouldn't be *fair*?"

"It'd be the same as finking on him."

"Then give him my address."

"I don't know—"

"He could get it. What's the difference?"

"I didn't write it down."

"It's 706 South Cheyenne, second floor."

"You think he'll knock on the door?"

"I think he'd wait for me to come out."

"You gonna pop him?"

"You mean is that what I want to do?"

"What is it you say? 'If I have to draw my gun—I will shoot to kill,' uh? I like that," Teddy said.

Carl said, "Tell him where I live. And tell him there's a magazine writer wants to talk to him."

Louly was in the kitchen making them each a Tom Collins, Carl's without the cherry he always picked out and set in an ashtray, and she'd have to take it out before they were flicking ashes on it making a mess. Carl came in and she asked if he'd got through to Teddy.

"Yeah, but he said Luig came on his own. He said he fired him, but if Luig was able to do me, Teddy would consider taking him back. I asked where he was staying. Teddy said it wouldn't be fair to tell me. You imagine him saying that?"

"It wouldn't," Louly said, with a cute foam mustache on her upper lip.

"When's Teddy ever fair? He walked off with your Bankers Association check."

"He can't send the guy to shoot you and then tell you where he's staying."

"He said he didn't send the guy."

"Well, you know he did. Why would Lou come on his own?"

"Make up for not pulling on me. So I said okay, give him my address and I gave it to Teddy."

"You're telling the guy who wants to shoot you," Louly said, "where you live?"

"He won't come to the door. He'll wait outside for me to come out, in the morning. That's how he should do it. If I wanted *him,* I'd go upstairs and take him out handcuffed."

"You come out in the morning," Louly said, "and you know he's waiting for you, what do you do?"

"I'll think of something. In the meantime, from now until this happens, you have to stay at the Mayo. I worked it with that assistant manager for events—"

"Winona?"

"Is that her name? I told her it's Justice Department business and got a special rate. Housing a federal witness."

"I'm not going," Louly said. She had her hands on her hips, to Carl, a bad sign. She said, "You're not here half the time you're supposed to be, and now you're pulling this. You're here and you make me leave."

"You liked it the last time, didn't you?"

"I had a suite."

"Is that what you want, a living room you won't need?"

"And a girl to do my hair."

"I'll see what I can do."

"And I get to stay in the suite at night and not in some dinky room."

"You know who I saw in the lobby, I was talking to Antonelli? Amelia Earhart."

Louly had another Tom Collins, Carl switched to bourbon and they were on the sofa fooling around, not sure yet if they were going all the way and then they'd eat, or hold up and eat first, since Louly had a chicken in the oven. The phone rang. Louly said, "It looks like we eat and do it tonight at the regular time."

Carl went in the kitchen to get the phone.

Jack Belmont said, "Hey, Carlos, this guy shoots at you going in the hotel and runs and you think it's *me*? Tries to shoot you in the *back*? I told you, I'm bustin' you on sight, but it won't be from behind. I have to I'll call your name. You know who this guy sounds like?"

"It was."

"Lou Tessa?"

"I called Teddy to check. He said Luigi came on his own."

"Yeah, after you showed him up. But he's still a punk, huh? I'm not surprised he shot at you and ran."

"I said to Teddy, why don't you put him on Belmont? He said he'd never find you."

"You won't either," Jack said. "You can't even start to guess where I am."

Carl said, "Sapulpa?" and listened to a silence.

"I stayed there at one time, when I was with Emmett Long? Stayed at the St. James Hotel, where Heidi was working at the time cleaning rooms. Me and Norm Dilworth. I'd hump her when Norm wasn't looking. I don't need her right now, but that girl's still my favorite hump."

Carl said, "You still want to shoot me?"

"Hell, yeah. I made a vow."

"You want my address?"

"I know where you live, Carlos, over on Cheyenne. Anthony told me. He says he hasn't been to your apartment, but visited your daddy's place near Okmulgee, his nut farm. Tony says he likes your dad, he's interesting to talk to. He says you start to tell him something and change the subject in the middle of it."

Carl said, "I do?"

"Tony said you and Lou-Lou go down there to visit your old dad. I might look in on you there at the nut farm. Get 'er done like a couple of cowpokes. I been thinking, I want to be facing you from not too far."

"You want to meet somewhere?"

"Has to be a surprise."

"I can come wherever you're hiding," Carl said.

"Boy, if you knew. I've acquired more respect in the past few days . . . I'm gonna stop right there before I give it away. You gonna take care of Lou Tessa?"

"I hope so."

"Well, you get me next. Be seeing you."

Jack hung up the phone.

Carl turned to Louly looking at the chicken in the oven.

"You know who that was?"

"Your buddy Jack. I could tell."

"He's dying to let me know where he's hiding, 'cause I'd never believe him."

"He's at home," Louly said, "with mommy and daddy. Right here in Tulsa."

"I thought of that," Carl said. "But his mom told me she'd shoot him if he ever showed up. And he might sense that she would."

"You believe it?"

"She showed me her thirty-two. Then Jack started to say, 'I've acquired more respect in the past few days . . .' and stopped. He said, 'Before I give it away.'"

"More respect for what," Louly said, "a person? A place? A way of living? A kind of work?"

"I asked him was he in Sapulpa," Carl said, "and it caught him by surprise. That's where his dad's girlfriend has her boardinghouse."

"Does Jack know her?"

"I heard one time he tried to kidnap her."

20

He was almost to her house and still hadn't made up his mind how to play it.

Not exactly beaten but hat in hand? "Miss Polis, you remember me? I'm Oris Belmont's son, Jack." And hope she sensed a change in him, his tone so different it touched her heart, gave her a tender feeling she couldn't help.

Except that time he had kidnapped her and realized she knew who he was, *she* was the one said, "You want to be a real crook, go rob a bank."

Remind her of it.

"Nancy, remember what you told me in Norm Dilworth's house that time? The one near Kiefer by the railroad tracks?" Then with kind of a grin, "Well, I took your advice."

Or tell her the truth.

"Nancy, I've always thought of you as a woman dying to get in bed naked with a man just about anytime, and I'd try to imagine you with Oris if I wasn't the one myself jumping on your bones, getting in there between your legs." And then, " 'Cause I have this passionate affection for you I'd hate to have to shoot you."

Something like that, but toned down.

He had left the car parked behind the St. James Hotel and walked the three blocks to the big, two-story frame house painted white, kept up, flower beds around it, young redbud trees along the street.

Nancy Polis opened the door as he came up the walk, stood there in a cotton shift with thin straps, the skirt halfway to the anklets she wore and heels with bows that looked like tap shoes. But look at her—standing with her hip cocked, her hand high on the edge of the door.

"You come to kidnap me again," Nancy said, "you're out of luck. I haven't seen your daddy in close on a year."

But Oris had given her a farewell speech and enough money to live on for the rest of her life, a hundred thousand dollars. She told Jack not to get any ideas, the money was in the Exchange National Bank, which Oris swore would never close but might change its name. And if for any reason she ran out, Oris said to let him know.

Jack hadn't got around yet to thinking of robbing her. No, but it put him in mind of that Creek at McAlester, his cell mate, telling him about Virgil Webster putting away money to last so many years, a lot of money if he was to keep up running his nut farm, sounding like at least as much as Nancy had, a hundred thousand, Jesus Christ, but cash. Inside his house.

That was one thing to think about. See how he could work out popping Carlos and picking up Virgil's extra cash at the same time. A trip to Okmulgee for a twofer. The other more immediate thing was Miss Polis. She certainly had a nice plump figure. You'd never call her fat. The only word for her figure was plump. You wanted to dive on it.

She was way more relaxed than when he first met her as a Harvey Girl in that uniform. He walked in the house, looked at her pumps with the bows and said, "What're you fixing to do, some tap dancing?"

She said, "If I feel like it," looking him in the eye. It was the same as telling him they'd be in bed by the time the sun set.

She had whiskey, Choc beer, and a sign she put on a tree out front that said NO VACANCY. Nancy had five rooms upstairs counting her own and eight beds for boarders, but no one staying here this week; so she put up the sign and told her colored girl, Geneva, who cleaned and did some of the cooking for ten bucks a week, she'd let her know when to come back to work. Got rid of her so they'd have the house to themselves.

Jack told Nancy some of what he'd been up to since the last time they had seen each other: mostly about robbing banks, doing time for the storage tank fire and running a roadhouse.

Nancy ate it up, listened with a look of amazement, and said she'd love to manage a roadhouse sometime. She said working as a Harvey Girl was like she imagined serving in a high-class prison cafeteria, if there was such a thing.

Jack said, "You couldn't sell prison food if everybody's starving to death."

"Remember that lacy apron I wore," Nancy said. "They still wear it. No makeup, no jewelry, no stains allowed on the uniform. No conversing or flirting with patrons. The head waitress was like a prison guard."

"Why do you keep thinking of it like prison? I loved that chicken à la king."

"No men in dorm rooms, ever."

"You wanted to dress up and go out, didn't you? I remember you and my dad whispering."

"You'd leave and I'd hear it from the head waitress. I had to sneak out of the dorm while I was living there."

"I remember your uniform, your hair, how you fixed it."

"Hairnets were mandatory. But you know what?" Nancy starting to smile. "At times it was a thrill. If you were a Harvey Girl you were somebody. You'd get recognized on the street like a movie star. Little girls would ask for your autograph."

She took Jack out to the kitchen and poured him a beer, Jack smelling vegetable soup on simmer. She said, "Do you know what I've been doing since I first met Oris? I've been waiting. Fourteen years, since I was twenty years old I've been waiting. Alone. By myself."

"Why'd you stick with him?"

"I thought he'd leave your mom."

"He promise you he would?"

"He'd say he had to get out of that house in Maple Ridge . . . with the roller-skating rink on the third floor where Emma would beat her dolls to pieces on the wood floor."

"He tell you all that?"

"He told me everything. I should've known he'd never leave her."

"My mama's tough," Jack said. "I have a feeling if I ever showed up she'd pull a gun out of her sewing basket and drill me."

These fourteen years, she told him, she was never so lonely.

Drinking his beer and smoking a cigaret it was in his mind to tell her he was sorry for different things he had caused to happen, but thought, For what? He stubbed out his cigaret and said to Nancy, at the kitchen table with him, "That's over, what're you looking for, some action? Want to pull a job with me?" Seeing a light coming into her eyes. "Can you drive? Can you drive fast? I'll give you ten—no, I'll give you twenty percent of the take. What do you say?"

Now she was looking right at him with that sparkle in her eyes, lighting a cigaret, taking two puffs and stubbing it out.

She said, "I want to go to bed with you. Right now."

"I'm ready," Jack said. "But tell me if you like the idea of turning gun moll."

"What would I wear?"

"I think something sporty."

The next day they laid around, Nancy asking about his home life when he was a kid and Jack barely telling her anything. Then Nancy telling him about being raised on a farm, as boring as all stories about living on farms. It wasn't until late afternoon Nancy went to the grocery for coffee and a few things and came back with that day's Tulsa *World*.

Jack opened it on the kitchen table, his drink and ashtray moved aside, and saw the story headline in two lines across two columns, MARSHAL SHOT AT, PHONES WOULD-BE KILLER. There was Carl Webster's picture in both columns, the one he's holding his Colt. "And there's a picture of me in it, smaller than his, with a number under my face. But it's not too bad for a mug shot. That son of a bitch. He knew it wasn't me."

Nancy had turned from the icebox to watch him as he read the story aloud, saying "That son of a bitch," a couple times, and then going to the phone carrying the paper coming apart and telling the operator he wanted Tulsa and give her the number.

So after he talked to Carl he had to settle down again with his drinks and cigarets and tell Nancy what was going on. Tell her about "Massacre at Bald Mountain" and not just about running a roadhouse.

Nancy standing through the first part holding on to the back of a chair.

Tell her about shooting the seven spooks in their bedsheets and some of the gunfight inside—no mention of Norm Dilworth—and how he was able to slip away in Tony's car and end up in Kansas City. No mention of Heidi, either.

She thought some of it funny, most of it hair-raising and sat down at the table.

He told her how Carl tricked him into coming back to Tulsa and told how he'd shoot Carl on sight, or almost on sight, so he wouldn't have to listen to that If-I-have-to-pull-my-weapon shit.

She said, "That what?"

He didn't tell her because he didn't want to hear it again. They had it in the news story he'd just read. He moved on to meeting the famous lawyer and his escape from McAlester on a streetcar.

How he stole Tony's car for the second time, turned it in along the way and left the last one in back of the St. James.

She made them new drinks and they lit cigarets.

"On the phone he wanted to know where I was. I said, 'You can't even begin to guess.' He says, 'Sapulpa?' "

Nancy said, "Oh, my God. I'm in it now."

"All it means," Jack said, "they're following the trail of stolen cars. Now they have to check on ones stolen from here, see if it keeps going."

She said, "Does he know I live here?"

"Carl? He might, but I doubt it."

Sapulpa Police called the Marshals Service responding to the all-points on Jack Belmont: they had a Ford Coupé stolen in Muskogee that might trace back to the end of the streetcar line. The marshals located the points in between where motorcars were stolen before coming to Anthony Antonelli in Hartshorne, his coupé stolen again by Belmont. There was reason to believe he was still here.

The next day Carl Webster was showing Belmont's mug shot around the St. James without any luck. Now he sat in his Pontiac outside the hotel asking himself if Jack would've gone to see his dad's girlfriend.

Why? 'Cause he and his dad were so close?

The minute Jack wasn't looking, like taking a leak or something, she'd of run out of the house to find a cop.

In the conversation Carl had going in his head, he said, "You're sure of that, huh? But what if they were seeing each other—something Jack would think was funny—during these last few years, while his daddy was buying her things, like her '32 Chevrolet coupé.

At the roadhouse Norm Dilworth had told him Jack tried to kidnap her one time. It was when he set the storage tank on fire and brought her to Dilworth's house near Kiefer. But Nancy knew who he was, so the kidnapping wouldn't of worked.

There was too much going on at the roadhouse to look into it then. Go back to the time of the storage tank fire, Jack went to prison for it, and Nancy Polis never filed a kidnapping complaint.

What Carl could do, drop in on her now, say he was investigating the rumor of a kidnapping.

Finally, huh? It had only been seven years.

Jack was in the living room, the door open, and saw the Pontiac pull up in front. He called out, "Nancy? Where are you?"

Her voice, faint, came back, "Upstairs."

"Look out a front window."

"What is it?"

"Take a look."

He ran up the stairs two at a time, the stairs polished, slippery in his socks without shoes. Nancy was at the window of the bedroom they'd used last night, the bed unmade, a mess, looking at the Pontiac sedan parked on the street and the man in a light gray suit and panama hat starting up the walk. Not having any idea who it was, she said, "He looks like an in-surance salesman. I don't answer the door, he'll go away."

"You have to," Jack said. "It's wide open to let some air in the house. And you got that Lanny Ross record on the Vic."

"He's just selling something."

"Then you don't care if I get rid of him." Jack reached under the pillow he'd used last night and brought out Fausto Bassi's .45 automatic, telling her, "Honey, that's the marshal, Carl Webster. Can you beat it, he's come to see *me*?"

Nancy said, "You're not really going to shoot him," smiling a little, letting him know he'd had her fooled.

Jack said, "You have to talk to him while I put on my shoes. It's bad luck ever since Billy the Kid was in his socks when he was shot dead. It's a fact. He says, *'Quien es?'* Wanting to know who's come to see him in the dark."

She sounded more determined than nervous saying, "Jack, you're not going to shoot him in my house and get me involved."

It was good she was thinking instead of becoming hysterical, and what she said made sense, but it didn't move him. He laid the .45 on the pillow and sat on the side of the bed to put on his shoes. He said, "I thought you wanted to be a gun moll."

She didn't say yes or no. Jack looked around with a shoe in his hand to see her up next to the bed holding Fausto's .45.

She said, "I'll throw this through the window and scream as loud as I can and run downstairs."

The doorbell rang.

There was a silence in the bedroom until Jack said, "The first situation that tightens your butt, you don't want to be my girlfriend no more? I was with a nervous woman in a bank one time and it's no fun."

The doorbell rang again.

"It's a shame, though, 'cause you're a smart babe. You're older than I am, but I think we could've gone to town together. For a while anyway." Jack said, "Come on back when you're through."

They took off their clothes in another bedroom to get in a fresh bed.

"He wanted to know why it says there's no vacancy when there's no one here but me. I said I'm getting ready to do housecleaning and I want the house empty."

"What'd he ask you, if I'd been here?"

"I started the conversation. I said is this about Oris Belmont? Acting nervous. He said no, his son, Jack. I started to shake my head to say I never met you in my life and he's telling about the time you wanted to kidnap me. *That's* what it was about. That dumb idea you had, as if I didn't know who you were. He asked if I'd seen you since then. I said, 'You think it's likely?' "

"After you went downstairs," Jack said, "I was thinking, this wasn't the place to shoot him, where we'd have to do something with his body—even though it was a perfect setup. Come down the stairs and surprise him . . . No, first you tell him you're busy."

"I did, I said I had to get started cleaning the house."

"See, and then you say wait, you have a surprise for him and I come down. He can't believe it's me. We both draw and I beat him by a hair."

Nancy said, "If he didn't shoot you first."

They finished some serious loving and Nancy got dressed to go to the grocery to pick up something for their noon dinner. Jack told her, don't forget the paper; he'd stay here and rest awhile.

As soon as she was out of the house he was prowling around the master bedroom, where they'd spent the night. He found an old three-piece suit of his dad's in the closet with a few ties and a half-dozen white shirts in a drawer, the suit going back to the 1920s. Next he looked for money and found a little over three hundred dollars in a drawer in her secretary. He put on the suit with one of the shirts and ties and was ready by the time Nancy turned into the driveway in her Chevrolet coupé, leaving the car at the side door to unload groceries into the kitchen.

Jack walked in, Nancy was placing a sack on the table. He saw the Tulsa paper and the car keys sitting there.

She said, "You have your dad's suit on."

"You think he'll mind?"

"I'm surprised it fits you."

"It's big around the waist."

"It looks good though." She took her time now and said, "Are you getting ready to leave?"

"I thought I would."

"I was about to fix us dinner. I have some nice veal chops, tomatoes, corn on the cob . . ."

"I better get going," Jack said. "I thought I'd take your car."

"Oh, you're coming back?"

"I doubt it."

"Then how can you take my car?"

Jack unbuttoned the suitcoat. He said, "You won't need it," pulling Fausto's .45 from his waist and shot Nancy twice looking right at him.

21

Carl listened to McMahon tell him the only reason Miss Polis' col-ored girl Geneva stopped by the house this morning was to pick up her money for the past three days, since she didn't know when she was suppose to come back with this man in the house. She looked at the mug shot, the same one Carl had left the police the day before, and said that's him, the one staying with her.

Carl drove to Sapulpa again and went through the house with Geneva and two detectives, Geneva saying they already done the housecleaning in the spring. You didn't do no housecleaning in July. The detectives believed Belmont had left a pair of overalls with PROPERTY OF OSP marked inside, but didn't know what he was wearing when he drove off in Nancy's Chevy. The coroner had taken her body to the morgue. Apparent cause of death, pending a postmortem, the gunshot wounds to the chest. Sometime yesterday.

After Carl had spoken to her.

While Jack was still in the house.

But if he was there and wanted to shoot Carl on sight, why didn't he?

McMahon brought it up and Carl thought about it driving home, picturing Nancy standing in the living room answering questions. He had paid attention to her tone and the way she spoke to him and had no reason to feel she was nervous or on guard.

While Jack was somewhere in the house.

Carl spoke to her for no more than ten to fifteen minutes, Nancy anxious to get started with her cleaning. Carl not thinking it strange, spring cleaning being done in the summer. The detectives said they had located a sizeable bank account in her name, but were still looking through her correspondence for a next of kin. They said there were letters from Oris Belmont going back at least ten years. It was all they could find out about her. One of the detectives said, "That's the oil man's boy killed her?"

They looked at the two beds Nancy and Jack had used and made comments.

"I'd say they got along pretty well."

"I know what you mean. You count the rubbers he used and threw under the bed? Three of 'em in the main bedroom."

"What you suppose got in his head to shoot her?"

It's what Carl kept wondering on the drive back to Tulsa. Why would he shoot her if they got along?

He wasn't thinking of anyone shooting at him.

The bullet came from across the street as he pulled up in front of his apartment house and cut the motor, from no more than thirty feet away. The bullet shattered the driver's-side window, that same high-caliber round that took out the hotel doors and Carl went flat across the seat, got the passenger-side door open and slid out to the sidewalk, more .45 rounds shattering his windows.

There was a pause.

Carl got to his knees and raised his head to window level and more gunfire ripped through the car from the Ford standing on the other side of South Cheyenne, the Ford Coupé that had raced away from the

Mayo. Luigi Tessa behind it. It had to be Luigi. Carl stayed low and yelled out, "Lou?" Lou this time, no Luigi. "Lou, hold your fire. Don't shoot and I won't, okay? Look, I'll put my hands on the roof of the car," Carl said, rising to his feet behind the Pontiac. "See? I'm not holding a gun. Keep me covered if you want and come over here. Okay? Listen, I know a guy wants to meet you and write a piece about the Black Hand for *True Detective* magazine. How's that sound? Make you famous."

Carl said, "I know you feel you have a bone to pick with me. But it was you shot at me, I never shot at you, not once, or ever threatened you with a weapon."

They were on the sidewalk now and it was getting dark, Tessa holding his .45 in Carl's face, neighbors looking out windows at them.

"Or hit you in the gut with a Louisville Slugger. I'm the one's been abused. I don't know what you have to complain about. You think I insulted you? It's how you took what I said. It was nothing but friendly banter. You know what banter is, Lou? Bullshit among friends. Come on, let's go on upstairs and have a drink. I'll call this writer's anxious to meet you. He'll be tickled to death, and you'll be glad to know he's another Eyetalian, Antonio Antonelli," Carl giving the name as much accent as he could. "You two can shoot the shit in your native tongue. He's even from Krebs."

Carl got hold of Tony at the Mayo.

Tony came in the apartment saying, "I had my hat on going out the door. If I hadn't decided to step back inside to answer the phone, I'd of missed one of the great opportunities of my career as a journalist, to interview an assassin of the dreaded Black Hand, and learn some of the history of your secret society and what you've been up to lately."

"In your native tongue," Carl said.

Tony repeated in Italian everything he had said. Then Tessa, Carl believed, said in Italian with a shrug, shaking his head, that assassinating someone was nothing to him, no problem.

It sounded a lot more interesting in Italian.

Carl took their drink orders, both whiskey and Coke, set out a plate of Velveeta and crackers and left them alone. He stayed in the kitchen with the *World,* would hear Tony ask a question and then Tessa sounding like he was acting out the answer that went on and on. Carl gave Tony nearly an hour before walking in the front room. He had left his suitcoat on.

"How's it going?"

Tony closed his notebook. "I believe that ought to do the job."

"I bet you got more'n you expected."

Tony raised his eyebrows. "Quite a bit more."

Tessa was looking from one to the other, his .45 on the table next to his chair with his glass and the ashtray holding cigaret butts.

"You have the feeling," Carl said, "holding the interview in Eyetalian is like keeping the whole thing off the record?"

"I was surprised," Tony said, "he told me as much as he did. Most of it was old 1900s Black Hand throat-cutting stuff, but I can use it for background."

"He bring you up-to-date?"

"The businessman doesn't pay the extortion, they don't burn the place down anymore."

"Not since Luig did time for arson. He shoots 'em now," Carl said. "That's why I'm bringing him up on two counts of first-degree felony homicide in that coal-mining county."

Tessa looking up from his chair, mouth open, confused, like wondering if he was hearing right.

"I'm gonna make a phone call," Carl said, "get him transportation to the federal lockup here, so I won't have to take him. What happens to you after that," Carl said to Tessa, "once you get to McAlester, you aren't gonna like at all. I only have one question for you," Carl said. "You gonna stick your hands out to take the cuffs, or you want to see if you can pick up that gun?"

I've got my ending," Tony said. "Lou Tessa, the Black Hand assassin's moment has come. He knows if he doesn't reach for his gun he's going to prison."

"He's going to the chair," Carl said.

"All the more reason to pick it up. But he knows the marshal standing before him is armed and will draw and shoot to kill if he does."

"I didn't tell him that."

"You didn't have to. But did you know he wouldn't make the move?"

"If he hadn't ever done it by now," Carl said, "I didn't see him reaching for it."

"Well, what he gave me is perfect, lurid as hell. You sure set him up for me."

They were still at Carl's after marshals arrived to haul Tessa off to the lockup in the federal courthouse, Tessa yelling at Carl in Italian—Tony translating—that he'd tricked him, Carl shaking his head.

He said to Tony, after, "It's strange the way these people talk about being tricked and what's fair. Teddy Ritz saying it wouldn't be fair to tell me where this boob was staying in town. I said, 'It wouldn't be *fair?*' I can shoot at 'em, but not lie to 'em."

He had told Tony about Belmont killing Nancy Polis, because it was on his mind, and said he had talked to his boss about it from her house, long-distance. Belmont killing her for no reason. Taking her car. Carl said, "Got what he wanted and shot her."

He seemed to have a different attitude about Jack Belmont now, but wouldn't talk about it. Before, Carl took him seriously but still seemed to laugh at him for wanting to be a famous public enemy. Now, Tony had the feeling, Carl had looked at Nancy lying dead in her kitchen, killed for no reason, and stopped laughing at him. Jack had become that public enemy and had to be put away.

"You have an idea where he is?"

"He's around," was all Carl said.

As soon as Tony left he phoned Bob McMahon at his home.

He told him the guy with two detainers was in custody.

"Every time you embarrass me," McMahon said, "and I hope embarrass yourself, you come out smelling like a rose."

"It's not the main reason I called," Carl said. "I'm going after Jack Belmont. You put me on something else, I'll quit the marshals."

McMahon said, "Meet me at Nelson's tomorrow morning, seven A.M." and hung up the phone.

W hy're you becoming emotional on me? I told you you're going after Jack Belmont. We're all going after Jack Belmont. Because he's a fugitive from justice. Not because you were both in that house at the same time, and you feel to blame for not knowing it. Have more egg on your face than on your plate."

They sat at a table in the Buffeteria's clatter of breakfast noise, McMahon hunched over his three two-minute eggs, straightening now to crumble a piece of bacon in his egg soup. Carl hadn't touched his breakfast.

"Am I right? We don't have to get worked up over what he's done. We'll get him because it's what we do."

"He didn't have to shoot her," Carl said.

"What you're telling me, you thought you knew him but realize now you don't. Do me a favor and think of yourself when you were still Carlos, at the drugstore the time Emmett Long shot the Creek. You're fifteen, a well-behaved young boy. As a rule you don't speak out to grown-ups unless they want to hear from you. You remember, about that time, the name of the cow thief you ran into?"

"Wally Tarwater."

"You said you admired the way he bunched the cows without wearing himself out."

"I remember he knew how to work stock."

"But you told him you'd shoot him if he tried to ride off with your cows, and you did. Shot him out of the saddle at a good two hundred yards. Remember what you told me? You said you didn't mean to kill him."

"I didn't."

"Just wanted to wing him? I thought you were doing a little strutting there. I thought, Is he that good or wants me to think he is?"

Carl kept quiet. He'd started dabbing his fork at his fried eggs and potatoes.

"I didn't mind your sounding cocky, showing off in a quiet way. You're a fifteen-year-old kid and you handled the situation. I said to myself that day, I want him when he's of age, and I gave you my card. I let you show off now, because you always come out, as I said last night, smelling like a rose. You've been a marshal seven years, a *marshal,* and you're almost as well known as that FBI showboat Melvin Purvis."

McMahon paused to sip his coffee.

"You might not've heard. Purvis got Dillinger late last night on a tip. The FBI laid for him coming out of the Biograph movie theater in Chicago. Shot him down in the alley that runs next to it."

Carl hadn't seen a paper and wanted to know everything at once. If it was Purvis who shot him. How many times he was hit. Was he dead on the scene. Was Billie Frechette with him. But what he said was, "What picture was playing?"

McMahon looked up from his runny eggs.

"Is that Carlos I hear? The kid wanting to know what the last movie was Dillinger saw? I don't know, but it'll be in all the papers."

Walking to the courthouse they talked about Belmont, Carl looking for the reason he killed Nancy Polis. McMahon said, "He couldn't trust her to keep her mouth shut. What other reason is there?"

They talked about where he might be. Carl saying, "He swore he's coming after me and I'm counting on it. But if you put a watch on my building he'll wait it out. I think it'll annoy him and he'll call me about it and complain, trying to be funny. He's a famous criminal but doesn't know how to behave like one." Carl said, "Except when he killed Nancy Polis. What I'm thinking, let him find out I'll be at my dad's place. Maybe Tony, the *True Detective* writer can get in touch with him and tell him—let it slip. He'll keep calling me at home and I won't be there. He'll call the office, he's told I'm on leave. He won't believe it, but might think I'm at the farm. I know Tony's told him about it, that I like to visit."

"He calls the office," McMahon said, "I'll have Evelyn tell him where you can be reached, like we do it all the time. Carl, let's get 'er done."

———

I t's what every farm girl dreams of," Louly said, "lie around in a de-luxe hotel and get waited on. After two days I'm thinking, Hasn't he shot that guy yet?"

Carl had just brought her home from the Mayo.

"I didn't shoot him," Carl said.

"He tried to shoot you, didn't he?"

"He's Boob McNutt, he didn't know what he was doing. But the next time I have to be gone—"

"Wait a minute—"

"I mean the next time we have to be apart. I got the same situation coming up. Guy wants to shoot me."

"I know—Jack."

"But this time I'm gonna be at the nut farm."

"So . . . ?"

"I don't want you to be with me."

She stayed calm.

"Why not?"

"I don't want you maybe getting shot on my account."

"Why? 'Cause we're pards? Who're you, Tom Mix?"

Louly turned her voice up and was herself saying, "You jerk, we're the same as married. When we're apart I miss you 'cause I love you so much. Honey, I love even to look at you when you don't know it. If we're gonna be apart all the time I may as well become a nun. I'll even turn Catholic and my stepfather Mr. Hagenlocker will see if he can get me burned at the stake. Carl, I have to be with you. That's all there is to it."

He had said he didn't want her to get shot. What was a better reason to leave her home? Now he said, "I love you with my whole heart.

That's why I don't want any chance of him shooting you." Carl added, "The way he shot Nancy Polis."

Louly said, "So that's it. Well, I'm going with you."

He had said it twice now and it hadn't changed her mind any. He was thinking it was something guys in movies always said to the babes, and that's why he said it. Except this girl had shot Joe Young in a moment when she had to. She was no shrinking violet, she stepped up.

He said, "All right, if you want."

"You knew I was going," Louly said. "I want to make a bet. If you get Jack at the nut farm we get married there, this year."

"That's what you win?"

"What *we* win. You want to get married, don't you?"

"Yeah . . . ?"

"But you have this fear that if we're married you couldn't put yourself all the way into your job and take chances. You'd hold back being a marshal. You get Jack, it would show you can do your job and not worry about me."

He wasn't sure if that made sense, but said, "What if he gets me?"

She hesitated. "You've never thought that before, have you?"

"Or he gets away. He's always getting away."

She said, "Or what if you give me a gun and I get Jack? I wouldn't mind, since the man's a poisonous snake."

"Or Virgil shoots him," Carl said, "with his new Krag?"

They were having fun kidding around. Still, neither one offered Narcissa as a shooter.

22

Carl and Louly arrived at sundown in the '33 Chevy they gave him to replace the shot-up Pontiac. Carl didn't even get inside the house before he and his dad were sitting on the porch talking about the weather: over a hundred degrees for the past twenty-five days, Virgil said, from July into August.

"A hunnert eight to a hunnert eleven in Okmulgee. It got so bad shade trees were dying in town. I haven't counted what we lost, must be a couple dozen. No discovery wells are going in anywhere less they're near water. The crew working the Deep Fork section were sucking water out of the creek and the graze was starting to look burnt, so I had 'em shut down the wells."

"You can't live on oil," Carl said.

"That's the truth."

"You told me that a long time ago. The night Dillinger went to the movies it was a hundred and two in Chicago."

"With those two women," Virgil said.

"The Lady in Red, a whorehouse madam named Anna Sage, and Polly Hamilton, his girlfriend while Billie Frechette's doing two years. They say Dillinger wouldn't let her drink 'cause she's Indian."

"I never heard that, she's Indian. So it was these two other women."

"Everybody was going to the movies during the heat wave. Get some of that 'Modern Refrigerated Washed Air' blowing on them."

"Here you see in the movie ads 'Air-Cooled for Your Comfort' with a polar bear sitting on a block of ice."

Narcissa appeared saying, "For you two polar bears," and set a tray holding a bowl of ice, a bottle of whiskey and two glasses on the table between them—once Virgil moved his newspapers.

Carl said, "You know what that last movie was Dillinger saw?"

"If it was Dillinger," Virgil said.

"You want to get into that?" Carl sounding tired. "There's some question it wasn't Dillinger. But he did have plastic surgery and that's all I know. Right now it's still John Dillinger they got."

"I won't argue with you," Virgil said, pouring their sundown drinks. "It opened Friday at the Orpheum. I've been hoping you get here before it leaves."

"I sat home all last week," Carl said, "waiting for Belmont to call and complain about the surveillance around my apartment. He has my number, but must've lost it. I doubt he takes care of his things. This afternoon he called the marshals asking for me and was told I was on my way here. They gave him your number. They don't do it as a rule, but want to get this business done."

"There gonna be marshals around here?"

"I told Bob McMahon, you want to get this over with, stay away. He said, once he knows Jack is on the property—I call and let him know—he'll set up roadblocks so he can't get out."

"So you expect Belmont to show."

"He seems stuck on living up to his word—at least with me. He says he's gonna shoot me, he has to try. Tony, the *True Detective* writer, phoned to tell me Jack's killing Nancy Polis got him on the wire service as a possible number one public enemy. Now he has to live up to it, even though he's still only a flash in the pan. Tony wants to be here if Jack shows up. Says he'll write the story and use 'Jack Belmont's Last Ride' as the headline. But Tony doesn't think he'll show, not with every law officer in Oklahoma looking for him."

Virgil said, "I don't think he will either. I was him, I'd think about lying low till I was an old man."

"He was going to Mexico in a La Salle from Kansas City, but then I brought him home and he changed his plan."

"If you think he's coming," Virgil said, "what're you doing sitting out in the open?"

"He has to get here first, then work out how he'll do it before he can shoot me."

"All by himself?"

"I don't know," Carl said. "But who'd want to help him?"

The first ones Jack thought of were his roadhouse bouncers, Boo and Walter. He didn't think he could get used to being in the same car with Boo, but Walter would make a good partner, for a while anyway, and Walter had come from Seminole, same as Heidi and the roadhouse whores. To get there Jack needed a different car, one that wasn't hot for a change.

What he did, he left Nancy's Chevy on the street in downtown Tulsa and walked all the way home, to the Belmont mansion in Maple Ridge. It took him nearly two hours. He sneaked around back to the maid's room, the one who'd taken in his overalls, and got her to the window in her nightgown buttoned to the neck. He said to her, "Margaret, mama said I could use her car, but I need the key. It's in the cupboard in the butler's pantry on the second hook. It says Cadillac V-twelve on it."

Margaret, thirty-six, never married, had turned to stone looking at him. Jack said, "But don't wake her up to tell her. Wait till she needs the car. Tell her don't worry, I'll bring it back." She got him the keys and still didn't say one word.

That same night he drove to Seminole and parked his mom's Cadillac in front of the whorehouse where Heidi and the girls used to work. Not one of them was back. Jack got to drinking with a whiskey runner he knew, a young guy from the Cookson Hills who'd made a few deliveries to the roadhouse. Jack asked did he know what'd happened to his bouncers. The whiskey runner said yeah, Boo was living up at Bunch with some woman keeping a vegetable garden these days. "Walter, hell, Walter's back in Seminole keeping the peace in a roadhouse, the one out this way across from the Philips station."

Jack said, "He worked for me and I never knew his last name. You know it?"

"Walter's a heinie," the whiskey runner said. "He doesn't have a sense of humor and doesn't like people making fun of him. I saw it written down one time, on some papers he had. It's Schitterer."

"How do you spell it?"

"*S-c-h-i*-double-*t-e-r-e-r*. But you smile saying his name, like some drunks have done? He'll break your jaw. He won't tell his full name as a rule and stays out of trouble."

Jack said, "Schitterer," and couldn't help but smile.

He recognized Walter from behind by that tree trunk of a neck growing out of his shoulders, part of his Charles Atlas build. Walter recognized Jack from the picture of him in banks and his name on the list of the 10 MOST WANTED. He brought Jack outside to ask him, "Are you crazy, showing yourself?"

It meant this fistfighter was sympathetic to Jack's plight. Or hadn't yet heard about the thousand-dollar dead-or-alive reward.

"Walter," Jack said, tempted to call him Mr. Schitterer, but not sure he could keep from grinning, "see that Cadillac V-twelve parked over there? It's mine. What I'm driving to the home of a wealthy oilman who doesn't trust banks. He keeps enough money in his house to last him all his life. I estimate a hundred thousand or more. You want some?"

"How much?"

"Forty percent."

"How you come to that?"

"We each take half, but I get ten percent more for knowing about it."

"How do we work it?"

"Watch the house. Wait for them to drive into town for some reason, for supper, and we go in."

"You say, 'Wait for them.' Who's them?"

"In case he has company, or takes his housekeeper."

"What if we can't find where it's hid?"

"Ten bucks it's in his bedroom. How about we leave tomorrow?" Jack said. "You want to, you can drive the car, that brand-new Cadillac V-twelve."

Sunday afternoon the four of them got in Virgil's car to go to the show in Okmulgee. Virgil had said he'd bought the '31 Nash because he liked the upholstery's floral design, shades of rose and green on the beige fabric; it was like driving around in your home. The reason they took Virgil's car—Narcissa in front with a big paper sack of popcorn on her lap, Carl and Louly in back—was in case Belmont knew

Carl was driving a Chevy now and was out on the road waiting for it to come along.

Going east toward Okmulgee Virgil's gaze went to the rearview mirror and fixed on it. He said, "Oh, my God, look behind us." And got the others to look around at the solid mass of dust moving across the sky from the south, a heavy yellow-brown curtain closing off the horizon. Carl said it was getting worse; he'd only seen dust storms like this out in the panhandle. Louly took his arm and Carl told her it was way over in Oklahoma City; it wasn't going to catch them. Virgil said farmers kept plowing through droughts; nothing grew, and with the ground cover plowed over there was nothing to hold the topsoil. Winds would come up off the plains and blow away farmland. He said, "Around Guthrie they're shooting cattle that're starving, dying of thirst." They didn't talk much with the dust behind them, miles and miles off but they could feel it, living on the edge of the Dust Bowl.

Carl said, going in the Orpheum, "I hope this is a funny movie."

Manhattan Melodrama.

Clark Gable is Blackie. William Powell is Jim. Myrna Loy is Eleanor. They said Myrna Loy was one of Dillinger's favorites. Muriel Evans is Tootsie, the platinum blonde, and she ain't bad. Blackie loses Eleanor to Jim, because Jim's such a swell guy. But it's okay with Blackie because he and Jim were boyhood pals and are still close friends, even though they're on opposite sides of the law, Blackie a gangster and Jim a prosecuting attorney and finally the governor. Blackie bumps off Jim's assistant, a snake who has evidence that would keep Jim from winning the governor's seat. Blackie is tried and convicted, sentenced to die in the electric chair. Jim, now the governor, could commute his sentence to life, but won't because he lives by the letter of the law. Evelyn tells Jim if Blackie hadn't plugged his assistant in the men's room at Madison Square Garden, witnessed by a blind beggar, he wouldn't of been elected governor. Jim still won't budge. Evelyn can't believe he won't help his friend. She leaves Jim, unable to continue being his wife. At the last moment Jim gives in, commutes Blackie's sentence to life. But Blackie won't accept it. If he doesn't go to the chair, Jim will have to resign his office. Blackie goes to the chair, Carl thinking during the scene, They're going to muss his slick hair with the metal skullcap, that part that looks like it was cut into his scalp. Carl only used a little water. He'd lost interest knowing what was going to happen. There was a good scene of Jim and Evelyn getting back together, out in the hall. Carl felt his eyes dew-up just a little. That Myrna Loy was all right.

On the trip home Virgil said, "You believe a guy sentenced to die would turn down getting off?"

"Uh-unh," Carl said. "Except Blackie said he'd rather fry than spend the rest of his life inside. That could be."

Virgil said, "I wanted to see more of Tootsie. I saw her in some westerns, Muriel . . . Something."

"Evans," Carl said.

They all thought the plot was okay, even if it wasn't believable, since it was a movie.

"You notice," Carl said, "how Blackie jabbed the gun as he fired it? That jabbing doesn't help any."

"I'll tell you something," Narcissa said. "That boat, the big excursion boat catching fire, the two boys become orphans and live together a while? It was Irish families on the boat in the movie. It was in 1906 and it's true, it happened in the East River of New York. But it was Germans it happened to, not Irish people. I read about it."

It wasn't six o'clock yet, the sun still beating down when they got home. Narcissa went in the house to cut up chickens. Sunday dinner was always fried chicken. Louly went in to use the bathroom. Carl stood on the porch with his dad while Virgil explained Roosevelt's Farm Mortgage Act, how it helped farmers stay out of the hands of the banks. Virgil kept up with what the New Deal was doing for farmers and Carl felt obliged to be patient and listen. Virgil was getting into the Farm Bankruptcy Act and Narcissa stepped out on the porch.

She said, "Virgil?" and waited while he finished what he was saying to Carl.

"What is it?"

"Somebody broke in the house."

Carl first thought, A hundred thousand stolen while we're at the show. He expected his dad to have a fit.

Virgil said, "They take anything?"

"They pulled stuff out of drawers. Tore pictures from the wall."

"Looking for a safe," Virgil said. "Why would they think a pe-can farmer would have a safe?"

"Outside of you being a millionaire pe-can farmer."

Louly came banging through the screen.

"Somebody wrecked the bedrooms looking for something."

Virgil said, "You know this is the first time I've been broken into since we built the house?" He turned to Carl. "How old were you?"

"Four," Carl said.

"That's twenty-four years ago, give or take. I use to tell these pe-can crew guys I'd pick up every year? You bust in my house, I won't hesitate to shoot you. The newspaper guys would ask what I do with my money and I'd notice my tree shakers listening in."

"Aren't you gonna look," Carl said, "see what was taken?"

"Right now," Virgil said.

"What about that money you kept in the house? You told me one time a hundred thousand dollars."

"This past winter I put it in the Okmulgee bank. Oris Belmont, one of the owners, asked if I'd be on the board. I ever tell you that?"

"Oris did," Carl said.

"He seemed like a guy knew what he was doing," Virgil said. "I thought hell, let him hold it. The bank's close enough I ever need it in a hurry."

They went inside to look around. The first thing they noticed, the shotgun was missing from the gun cabinet.

Louly said to Carl, "You think it was Jack?"

"I wouldn't be surprised. Twenty-four years the house is never broken into, till Jack Belmont comes along."

"If it *was* Jack," Louly said, "you think it's funny his dad's holding Virgil's money?"

23

That Sunday morning Walter saw this works as the place to make their camp: the pumps shut down, nobody around the derricks. They pulled casings and drilling tools out of a good-size shed and put the Cadillac inside early that morning. Later on they crept through the pecan groves and found a good place to lie hidden and watch the house.

Jack's idea was to slip up on Carl—say while he was on the porch with his dad—coming around from the side of the house. Surprise him with, "If I have to pull my weapon I'll shoot to kill." See how he liked it. Pull the .45 and shoot him. Then put the gun on the dad and tell him to bring out the money or he gets one in the head. "Then we don't have to spend time looking for it," Carl said to Walter. "The old man hands it to us and we get out of here."

"You want to shoot that marshal," Walter said, "do it some other time. I was only in a shoot-out once in my life and I pissed my pants. I saw that marshal knock off four armed men in less than five seconds. You know the best time to shoot him?"

He waited, making Jack ask, "When?"

"When he's in bed sleeping. There was an outlaw this posse was so afraid of, that's what they did, waited for him to go to sleep and shot him through the window. You ever hear of that?"

Finally in the afternoon they watched Virgil bring his Nash around to where the others were coming out on the porch and down the steps, Carl and Louly and another woman.

"There he is," Walter said. "What're you waiting on?"

"How'm I gonna hit him from here with a forty-five?"

"Whyn't you bring a rifle?"

"'Cause I want to use this."

"Move in closer."

He could sneak up to the edge of the grove, the one facing the house, he'd still be fifty or sixty yards from the car. It would take a lucky shot to hit Carl with a pistol. Jack had talked himself into using his .45, so he could recite Carl's famous line.

They watched the party drive off in that Nash done up in floral upholstery. Jack recognized the car; he'd stolen that model for a job and felt like a fairy driving around in it.

They were on their feet now, Walter with his arms crossed, hands resting on his biceps that were like footballs stuffed in his sleeves.

"We going in?"

"I told you how we're doing it. Shoot Carl and put the gun on the dad."

"Then he tells the police who you are."

"You want, I'll shoot the dad too."

"And the girlfriend and that other woman?"

"We don't know where they went," Jack said, "or when they'll be home. We don't want to be in the house and get surprised."

"Jesus Christ," Walter said, "we got a good two hours. You saw Carl reach in the paper sack the woman had? He got himself some popcorn and she slapped his hand? Sunday afternoon, they went to the show. Let's quit fuckin' around and get to it."

They broke a pane in the kitchen door to enter the house; crept through rooms till they knew for certain some old granny hadn't been left behind, no radio playing, and they went to work. They looked everywhere you could hide a sizeable amount of cash and places where you couldn't, attic to root cellar and in the kitchen, Jack saying he'd kept loot in a Quaker Oats box.

In a desk drawer in the living room they came across $480 rolled up in a rubber band and some silver.

Walter said, "This Creek that told you about the money—"

"My cell mate," Jack said. "He worked here and heard about it. Said he's coming back soon as he gets out."

"Said they'd be thousands of dollars?"

"How much would a millionaire put away?"

"I don't know. Four hundred and eighty dollars? I don't know who's dumber," Walter said, "me or you. My excuse—a man drives up in a Cadillac V-twelve you think he's got a pretty fair idea he knows what he's talking about. Who do you listen to? Some Creek drinks that hooch they make outta tomatoes. God *damn* but it smells."

"Let's think of places we might've missed," Jack said. "Like under the house."

"There isn't no under-the-house under there," Walter said. "I'm going back to the camp, I'm hungry."

They brought a bottle of whiskey with them, a case of Falstaff beer Walter put on his shoulder, the Remington shotgun from the gun cabinet—Walter liked it—and a chicken he said he'd cook on a spit. It came to Jack too late he should've taken that Winchester. He didn't think the shotgun would do him any good.

What came to annoy Jack was watching Walter cook the chicken like they were camping out. He'd made a fire, got it going good with extra kindling to throw on, pushed a three-foot stick through the chicken and sat down on the ground to hold it over the fire.

And kept holding it, his arm extended, rigid, locked in that position. After about ten minutes or so, Jack watched him switch the stick to his left hand and waited for Walter to flex his right arm, work the stiffness out. No, he laid the arm in his lap to rest, staring into the fire.

Jack had taken a gulp of whiskey when they got back, a couple ounces worth, and took another good one now, Jack sitting on the case of beer somewhat behind Walter but more to his left. When Walter wanted a beer Jack would have to get up and hand him one. They had forgot to bring a bottle opener from the house, so Walter had to pry the cap off with his teeth, hook the bottle in the side of his bite and yank up on it. Usually it took a few tries.

Walter had his hat off now. Jack stared at his head that reminded him of a block of wood: Walter at his campfire turning the chicken every few minutes from one side to the other, the bird taking on color. Thanksgiving, Jack's dad had always called the turkey "the bird."

Jack said, "There's no money put away in that house."

Walter said to the chicken, "You just realize that?"

"I should be waiting for that Creek when he gets his release—"

"Yeah . . . ?"

"And hit him in the mouth with a hammer."

"The claw side," Walter said to the chicken.

Jack took another swig of whiskey. He was disappointed, sure, but there was still the shooting of Carlos Webster to think about. Do that first. Wait for the chance to walk up and pop him.

Then get his mom's car washed and take it back.

No, take it to Old Mexico and sell it to some rich chilipicker. And then rob him. What he'd plan to do with Teddy's La Salle.

Come back to Tulsa and hold up the Exchange National Bank. It had a different name now he couldn't think of.

Get some guys first. The Jack Belmont gang.

Walter?

Walter was a camper. And a chef, but he didn't need Walter. The chicken was about done, done enough. Give it a few more minutes.

Jack brought his .45 automatic out of his waist from against the small of his back. Walter looked over. Jack pulled out his shirttail and began wiping the gun, concentrating on it, busy, Walter watching him.

If he shot Walter in the head from here, Walter and the chicken could both fall in the campfire. How would he save the chicken? Jack got up and moved to the other side of the fire to face Walter, Walter watching him sit down and continue wiping down the gun. Shot from here Walter would fall back, punched by the .45 slug, taking the chicken with him or dropping it in the fire. Walter had finished off four bottles of Falstaff while he cooked the bird, spitting some blood after opening the last bottle.

He said, "What're you cleaning the gun for? You gonna go shoot him, wait till after we eat. It's done if you like it pink inside."

Jack said, "Can I ask you a personal question?"

"How personal?"

"Do you mind being a big Schitter?" Jack grinned. "I mean a big Schitter-*er*?" and laughed out loud at the dumb look on Walter's face. Jack brought the .45 out of his shirttail and shot Walter in the middle of his forehead, lunged for the chicken but missed, Walter's iron grip on the stick taking it with him as he fell flat on his back, the bird landing on his legs.

Jack used Walter's teeth as a beer opener and broke off a couple of molars before he got the cap off. He took the bottle of beer, the chicken, the Remington and at the last second what the hell the bottle of whiskey, back through the pecan groves to the spot with the view of the house.

By the time the Nash returned with the moviegoers Jack had finished his meal, had a swig of bourbon and smoked a couple of cigarets. He'd bet $480 they saw *Manhattan Melodrama,* noticing it on the Orpheum marquee this morning, he and Walter coming through town. Now the good part:

Watching Louly and the other woman go in the house while Carl and his old man stayed on the porch talking. Damn, he wished now he'd brought a rifle. Or taken the Winchester in the gun cabinet. The woman came out in a hurry, but wasn't anxious to interrupt Carl's dad. Finally gets his attention, tells him they'd been robbed. Now Louly comes out and they're all talking, but no one's too excited. No, what'd they lose, a case of beer, a chicken . . . Now they were all going inside.

He wondered if he should've tried the shotgun? But if it was too far to do any good they'd know where he was and he'd be out of business—unless it drew Carl into the trees.

Not an hour later a car came up the drive to the porch, a Ford, one he recognized. He ought to, he'd stolen it twice.

They were inside straightening up. Carl told about the break-in while they were at the show, Louly sounding sure it was Jack. "He came looking for Carl and took a case of beer, a shotgun and a chicken."

Tony said, "How do you know it was Jack?"

"He called the marshals," Carl said, "to locate me and they told him I was here."

"How did *they* know it was Jack?"

"Evelyn told everybody that called where I was and recorded it. They all identified themselves but Jack. I listened and recognized his voice."

"So he'll try to sneak up on you," Tony said, "and you're not supposed to know he's here. What if he has a gang with him?"

"They only took one chicken out of the icebox," Carl said, "Narcissa hadn't cut up yet. But can you see Jack cooking it, like he's camping out?"

Tony looked off through the open doorway toward the pecan grove, the one closest to the house, beyond the cleared area where the drive came in, his car standing with its front end at the porch.

He said, "I better move my car."

Carl said, "Take the key out this time."

Tony left his Ford around by the garage. He came back to the porch, most of it in deep shade. He saw Carl at a window and heard Virgil coming in the front room saying, "The son of a bitch—I hadn't noticed—took a bottle of bourbon."

Carl said, "I hope he drinks it before he starts something."

Tony came inside. He said to Virgil, "You haven't done your harvest yet, have you?"

"We have one it'll be going on Christmas, and that's if it rains. We had drought, spring through summer, as bad as I've seen."

"But Jack could be hiding in there, waiting for a shot?"

"In there with the squirrels and the crows, all of 'em eating pe-cans dried up and dropped from the trees. That grove facing the house, you can see is denser than the rest? Those are old babies, the first ones I planted. See, then I learned these trees need sunshine and space for it.

I started out I must've planted forty, fifty trees to the acre instead of twenty to thirty. That's how come those trees across the drive you can't even see through 'em, and they're sort of in rows. I have to get Preston Raincrow in there, clear out the brush, but I have to wait for him to get over his heat prostration. I said to him, I never heard of a Cherokee getting heat prostration. Preston's Narcissa's daddy. Some of my groves have as few as ten trees the acre. They're up eighty to a hunnert feet and aren't as ugly as these here, all gnarly."

"No," Tony said, "he wouldn't have any trouble hiding in there."

"He'd still need a rifle," Virgil said.

"How far to the trees?"

"Fifty-three yards," Virgil said, "a hunnert and fifty-nine feet. You'd be doing good to hit the house with a pistol."

"How come you're so sure of the distance?"

"I was thinking of putting in a horseshoe court one time."

"Louly said he swiped a shotgun?"

"By the time the buckshot reaches the porch," Virgil said, "I see it splatter on the steps. A shot might sting you, but it won't hurt much."

Tony looked at Carl.

"Could you hit him from here, he's standing at the edge of the trees?"

"I'll hit him four out of five times," Carl said, "if my dad lets me use his thirty-eight still has a front sight on it. It's like mine, on a forty-five frame. But I can't say where I'll hit him. I'd have to move in closer."

"While he's shooting at you?" Tony said. "That's the most courageous thing a man can do, walking into withering gunfire to take out his opponent."

Virgil said, "Where'd you read that?"

"I wrote it," Tony said, and looked at Carl again. "Where would you want to hit him?"

"You have your notebook on you?"

"Don't worry, I'll remember."

"One in the arm or shoulder," Carl said, "so he'll drop his weapon, and one in the leg to put him down."

"Why're you so careful?"

"I don't want to kill him," Carl said.

24

Virgil was upstairs with a pair of binoculars and his Krag rifle. Carl and Louly were in the front room by a window. Louly kept touching him, moving her hand over his back. She asked him what he was going to do. Walk through the groves, try to track him?

"I don't want to look like I'm doing anything. I'm not supposed to know he's here."

"But since you do—"

"I find out he's got a rifle with him I'm not leaving the house."

"What about while it's still light I take a ride around the property? Back where that woman and Boo were. Look around the oil wells, since they're down. I'd use your car, see if I can scare him up."

"That's what Virgil wants to do. I said go ahead."

"You think he'll let me go with him? While you stay home?"

"Ask him. He gives you any of that 'you're just a girl' tell him what you did to Joe Young. Ask him for my pistol. I trade with him. Or take the Winchester if you want, and some extra loads to put in your purse."

She gave him a punch in the back, then a pat and said, "What if I shoot him?"

"I'm so tired of this guy. I can't wait to see it end."

"But what if *I* shoot him?"

"We get married any time you want."

"Next month, and we go to New Orleans on our honeymoon."

"What do we need a honeymoon for? We're already doing it. But listen now. You get a bead on Jack, hold your fire. You might hit him in the wrong place and finish him."

"What's wrong with him dying of gunshot?"

Carl said, "Jack deserves the chair."

He told me that," Virgil said. "I told him, 'Oh, I see him throwing down on me I'm not gonna shoot him?' Carl didn't say a word. I don't think he cares that much."

"He's tired of chasing after him," Louly said. "Tired of Jack's dirty ways. I said, 'What do you expect? He's dying to be a famous criminal.' All I hope is Carl doesn't try to talk to him."

Louly was driving the Chevrolet sedan Carl had got from the marshals. Virgil wouldn't take his car, not if there was a chance of getting blood on the upholstery. Virgil pointed the way, around the property to his oil patch and the derrick that rose near the creek. It was going on eight, but still sunny. They got out of the car, Louly with the .38 revolver, Virgil with the Winchester carbine he was used to.

Louly had said to Virgil before they left, "Why doesn't Carl use the carbine?" Virgil said, "'Cause he's Deputy U.S. Marshal Carl Webster, and he'll tell you a .38 Colt is enough gun for him."

They saw what had been the cookfire, the ashes still warm, and stood where they were looking around, until they saw Walter, part of him showing in the weeds. Virgil said, "You know him?" Louly looked at him again, at the round black bullet hole, his eyes looking back at her, and shook her head.

Virgil pulled open the door of the shed and they were staring at the yellow front end of the Cadillac pointing out of gloom to catch the light. "He's still here," Virgil said.

Louly was looking inside the car now. She said, "We have to keep him here," and turned to Virgil raising the hood.

"That's what I'm doing."

"Then what? You want to look for him?"

Virgil was disconnecting all those spark plugs. He said, "Yeah, let's see if we can flush him."

Jack was looking for a way to use the shotgun. Lying on his belly he had a clear view of the porch, with enough brush on the low end of his line of sight he could drop his head and they'd never know he was here.

Like seeing Louly and Carl's daddy come out of the house, the old man saying something to her and going back in. Neither one looking this way. She ran toward the garage in a pair of overalls too big for her and brought the Chevy around front that must belong to Carlos. Then the old man comes out to the car with his woman. Jack thought they were both getting in, but the woman went back in the house. Had come out to tell Louly don't forget the chicken. Jack rolled to his side to take a leak and there was a squirrel sitting up watching him from a few steps away. He said to it, "You ever see a snake like this here?" He let go with a stream and the squirrel was gone. He buttoned his fly and reached for the bottle of bourbon and took a swig to relax him, give him ideas.

All right, they get back, Carlos comes out to help with the groceries. He paused. But is the store open on Sunday? No, they buy the chicken off a farm, and corn and tomatoes. Carlos comes out . . . You have to get closer, with the shotgun. Carlos is helping now, has something in his hands, and you rise up and run straight at him, get to the open—

He heard their car, back already but still off a ways.

Now he heard it getting louder, the motor running high like the car was laboring up a steep grade. But there wasn't any grade back there and the sound kept getting closer. The sound telling Jack they knew he was here and were hauling ass through the pecan trees straight at him.

Virgil spotted Jack first.

He'd told Louly they'd take a shortcut to the house, straight through the groves. She said, fine, but where's the house? Virgil pointed and she nosed the car into the grove nearest the wells, the trees spaced for sunlight here and easy to get through. The trouble was, the ground had once grown crops and the Chevy began bumping and banging over old furrows hidden beneath a cover of weeds and wild growth, almost getting stuck in places, Louly hanging on to the steering wheel and gunning the motor to force their way through. Virgil kept pointing, "That way." Getting cranky. "I told you straight ahead."

"I gotta get around the trees, don't I?" Sounding just as cranky.

He said, "We're gonna tear up the underside of this vehicle."

And she said, "The government's got plenty of 'em. Carl's last one had the windows shot out."

Virgil surprised her saying, *"I see him."* Shouting it.

"Where?"

"Straight ahead in that old growth. See him? The boob has on a white shirt and pants. Going to the club when he's through here. He's looking back now. He *has* to hear us if he don't see us." Virgil brought up his Winchester and laid the barrel on the windowsill.

"I don't see him," Louly said.

"Straight ahead, for Christ sake, not a hunnert feet." Virgil excited.

So was Louly, her voice raised telling him, "I got your goddamn pe-can trees in the way." She cleared the ones in front of them and mashed the accelerator the moment she felt level ground under the wheels, swerved around trees and there he was in his white clothes, a housepainter in the dense part of the grove. He was putting the shot-gun on them. Louly, set on riding him down, saw him aim and fire and a cloud of steam came pouring out of the radiator. She couldn't see him now but kept her foot hard on the gas and heard a report as buck-shot punched a hole the size of a bowling ball through the windshield dead center and ripped into the rear seat. She jammed on the brakes and they were out of the car rolling through leaves and over pecans, Jack still firing, shooting up the empty car. Virgil yelled, "He's got to reload," and began firing and levering his Winchester, snapping shots at Belmont moving away from them in the trees. Louly hadn't fired yet. She ran after him hoping for the right moment.

The way Tony saw it happen:

Moments before they heard the gunfire, he and Carl in the front room, he said, "But what if they do see him?"

Carl said, "My dad was a Fighting Leatherneck."

"Louly wasn't."

"You think she'd run?"

"No," Tony said, "that's what bothers me."

They heard the first two blasts from a shotgun out in the grove and Carl was on the porch. They heard three more of those hard bangs fol-lowed by the Winchester firing and Carl was crossing the open area and Tony was on the porch writing in his notebook, *159 feet to the trees,* and under it, *Claims he hits target 4 of 5 times from this range.*

Tony looked across the open ground to see a glimpse of white, Jack coming through the trees? It was, it was Jack trying to reload the shotgun on the run, concentrating, his head lowered. He came out of the trees two, three strides, and looked up.

And there was Carl Webster standing in the middle of the open ground, Colt revolver held arm's length at his right leg. Tony noted, *Eighty feet between them?* He saw the shell Jack wanted to shove into the breech of the shotgun slip from his fingers. He did not bend down to retrieve it. He stared at Deputy Marshal Carl Webster, the hot kid of the Marshals Service, a recognized and respected U.S. lawman, and said, "Tell you the truth, I thought this was one of my better plans."

And the marshal replied, "You *told* me you were coming, didn't you?"

Jack looked defeated, his head hanging, when suddenly—Tony would write—he threw the shotgun to his shoulder. Webster, in a firing stance, brought up his revolver to arm's length and *bam*, shot the Remington out of Jack's hands at the split second he fired. The impact of the bullet jerked Belmont half around and he grabbed his right shoulder, tried to get back into the cover of trees, and Carl shot him in the left thigh this time, high up.

Where he said he would, Tony wrote in his notebook, *the shoulder and the leg.*

But it didn't put him down. This stone-cold killer had the will to reach out and catch hold of the trunk of a pecan tree to keep himself from falling.

Just then Louly appeared.

Tony watched her come out of the trees—*Not more than 30 feet from Jack.* He made a note to include that in the piece he'd write, the distance between them. Louly looked exhausted, but kept her calm gaze on Belmont as Carl asked after his dad. Louly said he'd be along any minute, he was picking chiggers out of his socks.

She watched Jack reach around to his back—pressed against the tree to keep him on his feet—then planted his good leg and leaned away from the tree enough to slip his hand in there. He settled back again and said to Carl, "Well, Carlos, we have time to talk before you get me a doctor. Share our opinions of Oklahoma as we find it."

"Right there," Carl said, "that's all you're ever going to say to me." He raised his Colt. "Open your mouth again, I'll lay this iron across it."

Louly said to Carl, "You have to take him somewhere, I'm going with you."

Carl was looking at Louly as he said, "I'm only taking him to Tulsa."

Louly turned to Jack in time to see his hand come out from behind him holding his .45. She brought up Carl's gun with the front sight filed off and shot Jack Belmont in the chest, shot him three times, wanting to make sure.

The sound hung there, Carl staring at Louly and Louly staring back at Carl. Now they were both looking at Jack Belmont lying dead, neither one saying a word.

Their silence can be explained, Tony noted. After while he'd talk to them both.

But the piece, "The Death of Jack Belmont" would need dramatic effects, a certain tone and a strong sense of place. Maybe call it "Death on an Oklahoma Oil Lease." That wasn't bad.